Iris G[...] [...]
four g[...] [...]
hu[...]and in Swansea in a house [o]verlooking
[...] [...]e loves. She has written o[ve]r fifteen b[ooks]
T[...] [...] novels, and has recently been awarded
th[...] [...] English at the University of Cardiff. This is
[...] third novel in her *Firebird* sequence, and
[Da]ughters of Rebecca, the fourth novel in the series,
is [n]ow available from Bantam Press.

SWEET ROSIE

Iris Gower

CORGI BOOKS

SWEET ROSIE
A CORGI BOOK : 0 552 14449 5

Originally published in Great Britain by Bantam Press,
a division of Transworld Publishers

PRINTING HISTORY
Bantam Press edition published 1999
Corgi edition published 2000

3 5 7 9 10 8 6 4 2

Copyright © Iris Gower 1999

Set in 11/12pt Plantin by Falcon Oast Graphic Art

Corgi Books are published by Transworld Publishers,
61–63 Uxbridge Road, London W5 5SA,

Addresses for companies within The Random House Group Limited
can be found at: www.randomhouse.co.uk/offices.htm

The Random House Group Limited supports The Forest Stewardship
Council (FSC®), the leading international forest certification organisation.
Our books carrying the FSC label are printed on FSC® certified paper.
FSC is the only forest certification scheme endorsed by the leading
environmental organisations, including Greenpeace. Our
paper procurement policy can be found at
www.randomhouse.co.uk/environment

MIX
Paper from
responsible sources
FSC® C018072

Printed and bound in Great Britain by Clays Ltd, St Ives PLC

To my dear friends Rhys and Les

CHAPTER ONE

The summer sun rose high above the sprawling streets of the town, frosting the surrounding waters of the bay with glittering foam. On the sloping banks of the river, the pottery buildings buzzed with activity. Apprentices whistled as they stacked the saggars, still warm from the kilns, in neat rows against the walls. It was 17 August and Llinos Mainwaring had been in labour for the best part of two days.

'Will it be long now?' Llinos's voice was thin with pain, her brow was beaded with sweat and her face flushed from her exertions. The midwife stood near the bed, her narrow arms folded, and looked down at the woman, pitying her. This child had better be healthy for it was the last one madam would bear.

'Not too long now, Mrs Mainwaring.' The midwife glanced at the doctor; he was seated close to the large window, reading the paper. He was not concerned about his patient; he would be paid whether the child was safely delivered or not.

Mrs Mainwaring had been a model patient and

she enjoyed all the priviledges money could buy: good clean sheets, no layers of paper to save the bed from staining, not for Mrs Mainwaring. If sheets were ruined they could be replaced. A pile of fluffy pillows supported her head and the counterpane was rich old-gold satin. But the woman was suffering and it was time the doctor did the job he was being paid for.

'Dr Rogers, could you come over here, please?' The midwife spoke meaningfully and, with a sigh, the doctor shook out the newspaper and reluctantly closed it.

'Very well, Mrs Cottle, if you can't manage alone, I suppose I will have to assist.' He came to the foot of the bed and the midwife spoke quietly to him. 'I'll have to turn the baby's head; by the look of it the child is pushing against the pubic bone.'

'I see the problem, what do you want me to do?' Dr Rogers asked.

'Be ready in case she floods on delivery,' the midwife said tersely. She turned to the patient. 'Just a little help needed here, Mrs Mainwaring, and then the baby will be born; be brave now, this may hurt a bit.'

Llinos wanted to nod her head but she was too tired. She seemed to be lapsing into a haze of pain and weariness. She no longer cared if she lived or died. She had tried so hard to give birth and to no avail. Had she felt this sick when her son had been delivered? But then Lloyd was an amenable child, he had been born wanting to please. She felt a flicker of strength, she must fight to live; if she gave up now she would leave her son to grow up motherless.

Pain swamped her; she growled low in her throat. She felt the midwife's hands helping her as she strained with every vestige of her remaining strength. The world seemed to stand still; a silence fell upon the room. Llinos was in despair, convinced she would die in the attempt to give birth to her child. And then, at last, the baby slipped silently into the world.

Llinos fell back against the pillows; her face was wet, sweat ran like tears down her cheeks. She was exhausted but her child had been born at last. Already the pain was receding and Llinos was able to draw breath without the pain tearing at her like claws. She closed her eyes, waiting for the sharp cry of her child. It did not come.

'It's a girl,' Mrs Cottle said quietly. 'Oh Lordy.' She turned the child and cleared her mouth, slapping her back briskly. The child lay inert, her face pale, too pale. An ominous silence filled the room. Llinos lifted her head in time to see the midwife shake her head.

'The labour was too long, Mrs Mainwaring. I'm so sorry.' The midwife laid the child on Llinos's breast. Llinos looked down at the small face, the eyes closed, long lashes resting against alabaster cheeks. 'My little girl,' she whispered. 'My poor little girl.'

Tears ran down her face. A sense of disbelief came over her. Her baby could not be dead. She looked at the small still face again. All her efforts had been in vain. Her baby was stillborn.

Mrs Cottle busied herself, moving the baby into the crib and tenderly covering the tiny form with a sheet.

'Terrible it is seeing a little 'un stillborn. I feel the loss of each one of my little pets.' She sniffed as the doctor stood uselessly by the crib, not knowing what to say or do.

'You go on home, sir,' she said. 'Nothing you can do here, not now.'

She washed Llinos with warm water, her hands gentle, comforting. 'At least you've come through your ordeal without losing too much life blood.' She forced a smile. 'You'll soon be up and about again.' She glanced over her shoulder at the doctor who had not moved. Mrs Cottle made a wry face and returned to her task.

Llinos felt as if she would never have the strength to rise from the bed. The ache, low in her belly, was nothing to the ache in her heart. She had failed to give Joe the gift he had wanted for five long years. A daughter.

When Llinos was clean and neat in a bed covered in fresh sheets, her husband was allowed into the room. He sat beside her and took her hand, kissing her fingers one by one. Llinos tried to smile bravely but she did not feel brave.

'My poor Llinos,' he said. Even with sadness etched into his face, he was still so handsome, the sunlight bronzing his fine-boned cheeks. His eyes, startlingly blue, looked down at her, seeing into her soul, and Llinos felt fresh tears start in her eyes. Mrs Cottle coughed to hide her emotion. 'I think we should all have a cup of tea.' She spoke briskly. The doctor, galvanized into action, moved to the door.

'Not for me, I'd better get back, I have other patients to see.'

As he left the room, Mrs Cottle grimaced at his

departing back. 'Doctors! Not one of them worth a half-penny dab.'

Mrs Cottle followed the doctor to the door and Llinos heard her calling for some tea. Mrs Cottle was a good woman, careful and kind, but even her skills had failed to save the baby.

'Rosie is bringing a tray for us,' Mrs Cottle said with satisfaction. 'I'm gasping for a cuppa, mind.' She spoke cheerfully, as if to dispel the air of sadness in the room.

Rosie was new to the job and she bustled into the room with her eyes downcast. She was a shy girl, unlike her mother Pearl who worked in the paint shop.

'Put the tray down by there, love,' Mrs Cottle said. 'I'll do the honours.' Rosie bobbed and curtsied and risked a look at the bed.

'How are you doin', Mrs Mainwaring?'

Llinos made an effort to lift her head. 'I'm all right, Rosie, thank you.'

'But you had a bad time, I can tell. My mam just births easy, like shelling peas.' Rosie smiled; she was a sweet girl, smaller than her mother and finer boned. She had curly hair and a peachy skin that enhanced her blue eyes.

'All right then, girl,' Mrs Cottle said briskly, 'enough chattin'. Be off with you now. Mrs Mainwaring needs a bit of peace after all that work.' She looked at Llinos. 'I'll take my tea down to the kitchen.'

She hesitated near the door. 'Shall I send one of the maids for the vicar?' She glanced quickly at Joe. 'But perhaps you don't want no vicar, sir, you being foreign-like.'

Llinos shook her head. 'My husband will see to it.' Would the people of Swansea never stop thinking of Joe as a stranger? Llinos was glad when she was alone with him. She glanced across to the silent crib and Joe followed her gaze. Tears brimmed in her eyes and she wiped them away. She watched Joe cross the room and lift the sheet away from the face of his daughter.

He carried her to the window, holding the tiny motionless body above his head. He was chanting some words, a prayer, Llinos thought, to the Great Spirit and the monotonous sound of his voice brought her some sort of comfort. She knew Joe's beliefs were strong, they sprung from the American Indian culture into which he had been born. After a moment, he kissed his daughter's face and returned her to the crib.

'I haven't cried, not in all the long hours of my labour,' Llinos said, her voice little more than a whisper. 'Now I can't stop crying.'

'You've had a bad time,' Joe said, pushing back her tangled hair. 'I prayed to the spirits to help you, my little firebird, but this was woman's work and something you had to do alone.'

He bent and kissed her mouth. Llinos felt his lips, warm, loving, and her heart contracted. She put her arms around his neck and held him close.

'There will be no more children.' The words were a sigh and Llinos fell back against the pillows exhausted by her efforts.

'I know,' Joe said and he did. Her husband was wise beyond imagining. Joe seemed to know most things about her without being told. 'But we have a wonderful son, you must never forget that.' He paused. 'Are you strong enough to see him? Lloyd's been asking for you.'

Llinos's heart lifted as she thought of her son; she felt an overwhelming sense of love and gratitude that Lloyd was a strong healthy boy. She had so much to thank God for. 'Of course I'm strong enough,' she said.

The boy came into the room slowly, he was not used to seeing his mamma in bed. He stood beside her, head bowed.

'Come on, Lloyd, give me a kiss.' Llinos drew him nearer, holding him and kissing him and he wriggled away. He was growing up, the plumpness of babyhood was leaving his face.

'You grow more like your grandad every day, Lloyd,' she said softly. 'You could be the spit out of his mouth.' She was glad she had named him after her father. She and Joe had debated long and hard about the name of their first-born; they had considered many names but, even from the first, the boy had the stamp of Llinos's family and so he had become Lloyd Mainwaring.

'Grandad was a soldier,' Lloyd said proudly. 'Will I be a soldier too, Mamma?'

'I hope not!' Llinos looked down at her son; he was tall for his age and held himself well. He learned his lessons quickly and was blessed with a good memory. But then he had been given a good start, a secure home life had seen to that.

Llinos thought briefly of her own young days, unhappy days with a stepfather who abused and insulted those he claimed to love.

Lloyd walked towards the crib. Llinos opened

13

her mouth to protest but Joe held up his hand warningly.

'Is the baby asleep? She's very small, isn't she? Will she grow big enough to play in the trees with me?'

Joe touched his son's shoulder. 'She's gone to her long sleep. You know what that means, don't you, son?'

Lloyd nodded. 'She has died and gone to heaven.' Over her son's head, Llinos met Joe's eyes. She was grateful to him for breaking the news gently.

'I didn't want her to die, I wanted to play with her, to show her the wind in the trees and the grasshoppers in the hedge.' His eyes filled with tears. 'I want Granny Charlotte. Can she come and see us, Father?'

'What does your mother think about that?' Joe looked at her and Llinos nodded. 'You can fetch her in a minute,' she said, her voice small. It would be just as well to let everyone know at the outset there would be no new baby in the house. 'But give me a kiss first.'

Joe sat beside Llinos and took her hand in his. 'This is so hard for you, I know that, my love, but together we'll come through it.'

Llinos sighed. 'It's hard on all of us. I know Charlotte's looked forward to the baby so much.'

'She still has Lloyd.' Lloyd was Charlotte's two eyes; she loved the boy as if he was the child she had never borne. Charlotte was Joe's sister, older than he was by many years. She insisted on being called 'Granny' by her brother's son. It gave her a sense of belonging, she said.

'Go on,' Joe urged as his son hesitated in the doorway, 'fetch your Granny Charlotte, if it will comfort you.' He forced a smile. 'We shall let her see how well your mother is looking, shall we?' It was a lie; Llinos was looking pale and worn. There were tears on her lashes and lines of strain etched around her mouth. Joe touched her cheek.

'I know you're exhausted but you'll always look beautiful to me.'

Charlotte entered the room peering from beneath her mourning veil. She continued to wear her widow's weeds even though she had lost her husband some years ago.

Lloyd tugged Charlotte's hand. 'Come and see her, Granny. Our baby has gone to the long sleep. She'll be in heaven with grandpa and Uncle Samuel. They'll take care of her.'

Joe took his sister's arm and shook his head. Charlotte understood at once. Her face paled, she put her hand to her lips to stifle a cry. Then she looked down at Lloyd and took a deep breath before turning towards the crib.

'She is so beautiful!' Charlotte touched the delicate hands with the tips of her fingers. 'What name are we going to give her to take her on her journey?' Charlotte drew Lloyd close to her side. 'Do you think your mamma will let me call the baby Letitia? It's a name I like very much.'

Llinos felt weariness seep through her. 'Yes, we'll call her after your sister, Charlotte. It's a lovely idea.' She closed her eyes. She was so tired. She felt the late sun on her face and with the hum of voices, hushed now as a background, she slept.

* * *

'She had a bad time, then, Watt.' Maura pinned up her long red hair, twisting it into a bun at the nape of her neck. In her grey gown and with her chatelaine of keys hanging from her belt, she was once more the efficient housekeeper. 'Still, she must be well over it all by now, lying abed for weeks is a privilege given to the rich.'

Maura's lips tightened. 'I was up and about only days after my baby was born.'

Maura had lost her child when she was at her most vulnerable and alone, carrying the stigma of a deserted wife.

'Still an' all it's sad for Llinos to lose her daughter after waiting so long. But she's got her boy and to be sure Llinos Mainwaring is a woman with more than her share of God's gifts.'

Watt lay across the bed, wondering if the stern-looking woman standing before the mirror was the same one he had just bedded. Maura was older than he by a few years and she was an enigma, a woman of depths, depths he had not yet plumbed which was probably the reason he remained loyal to her.

He loved Maura and, though he could never make her his wife, he would always love her. It was strange to think that Maura was still married to a man who lived far across the sea in America. She seemed to pick up on his thoughts.

'It doesn't matter a jot about Binnie Dundee.' She glanced at him. 'You've been more of a husband to me than ever he was. Now get up and get dressed, you shameless man or you'll tempt me back into bed again.'

'If only,' he said, feeling aroused at the warmth

in her eyes. 'I can never get enough of you, Maura, my love.' They were fortunate that they could be together so often. Eynon Morton-Edwards was a good employer and a kind man. He turned a blind eye to their illicit affair. He welcomed Watt into his home as though he was an equal.

In return Maura had been good to Eynon. When his wife had died it was Maura he had chosen to care for his daughter. When the child was older it was Maura who selected the best tutor for the girl. She did all this as well as seeing to the smooth running of the Morton-Edwards's household.

'Get up, you lazy idle wretch!' Maura leaned over and poked Watt's chest. 'Come along now, we've both got work to do, we're not privileged like the idle rich, remember!'

Reluctantly Watt slid from the bed. He stood for a moment at the window, staring out at the long garden and the river beyond. 'You are pretty privileged if you ask me,' he said. 'Look at this room, fine bed, rich drapes, good paintings on the wall. You are valued in your job here, which is more than I feel in mine at the moment.'

'Ah well, I'm older and wiser than you, lad.' She pushed him playfully in the back. 'And, remember, Eynon is far wealthier than Llinos Mainwaring even though she married a rich foreigner.'

Watt was aware of her watching him as he dressed. He smiled at her as she stood neat and ready for duty, impatiently waiting for him.

'You never did like Llinos, did you?'

'Sure, I don't care one way or another about the woman,' Maura said icily. 'She seems happy enough with the Indian fella but it's not the sort of life for a lady, is it?'

'I thought you didn't care one way or another about her?' There was a touch of asperity to Watt's tone that was not lost on Maura.

'Go on, defend her!' Maura's colour was high. 'You're like a little lap dog around her. I just don't understand you.'

'I'm not a lap dog,' Watt said. 'I'm grateful to Llinos, she gave me a home when I was alone. I love her like a sister.'

Maura's shoulders were stiff. 'Are you sure about that?'

Watt relaxed suddenly. 'You're jealous!' he said. 'You are actually jealous of my affection for Llinos Mainwaring.' Laughingly, he swept her into his arms and threw her on the bed. 'You silly goose!' He leaned close to her, his fingers twined in her red hair. 'I love Llinos like a sister, I love you like an eager lover should love the woman of his dreams.' He kissed her and though she wriggled a little, her mouth was warm against his. Finally, she pushed him away.

'Sure an' now I'll have to comb my hair again!' She pretended to be angry but the glint in her eyes told him she was mollified.

'Right then, I'll be off back to Pottery House.' Watt allowed his arm to linger around Maura's shoulders. 'Will I see you tonight?'

'You'd better!' She touched his face lightly and her features were softened with love. Watt's heart beat faster; she made him feel ten feet tall. He was loved and that was the most precious gift any woman could give a man.

18

The kilns above the pottery wall shimmered with heat and Watt, approaching uphill towards Pottery Row, watched, without really seeing it, the cloud of mist rising from the ovens. As he drew nearer, the sharp smell of turpentine and lead oxide brought a wave of nostalgic memories. Watt had worked at the pottery as a child; he had come from the workhouse and his first job had been collecting the shards of pottery, cleaning up the yard and acting as a dogsbody for all the other workers.

Watt smiled; now he was manager, handling imports of china clay, ordering the raw material for the work. He had the power to hire and fire. He was a fair man and so long as folk gave their best, that was enough for him.

As Watt neared the house, Joe emerged holding his son by the hand. Joe was a handsome man; he stood tall and powerful, his long black hair framing a strong-boned face. But today there was an air of sadness about him; a drooping of the shoulders that was uncharacteristic of the man. Joe usually dealt with life's blows with fortitude and courage.

'How is Llinos feeling today, Joe?'

'She's much stronger now. Go talk to her, Watt, I'm sure she won't rest until she begins to take charge of the pottery affairs again.'

Watt entered the house, the sun shone across the hallway in a slant of warmth. The hall and stairs were richly carpeted now, unlike the old days when threadbare rugs were the only luxury Llinos could afford. The curving banister shone with polishing and Watt sighed in contentment. Pottery

House was his home and though it was not as palatial as the home of Eynon Morton-Edwards, it suited him just fine.

Llinos was sitting near the window of her bedroom; the sun was sending shards of light across her face and Watt's gut contracted, she had a pureness of features that brought an ache to his heart. Her face lit up when she saw him.

'Watt, I'm glad you're back. Come and tell me about the pottery, how are the new patterns coming along?'

He stood at her side, staring down at her. 'You are still very pale,' he said. 'It's not long since you lost the baby. You'd better concentrate on getting well again and leave the potting to me.'

Llinos rested her hand on his arm. 'Isn't it time you were getting married and having a brood of children of your own?' she asked quietly. He met her gaze; he hid nothing from Llinos.

'You know life is not that simple for me.'

'I know. But you are like the brother I never had. I care about you, Watt, I can't bear to see you wasting your life on a woman who can never really be yours.'

He moved away. 'Llinos, you're overstepping the mark, what I do in my private life is my own business.' His gaze softened as she lowered her head. 'Look, I can't help how I feel, can I? I'm in love with Maura and none of us can choose who we fall in love with, can we?'

She nodded, accepting his point, she herself had married a man most people, including her father, had considered unsuitable.

'I only want what's best for you, Watt.'

'Well try to accept that Maura is best for me, she is the only woman I'll ever love. I didn't know what love was before she and I . . .' His voice trailed into silence, he was thinking of Lily, his first love, Lily the talented painter; Lily, the girl who had betrayed him, betrayed them all.

The silence stretched on and, in the way that women have of knowing a man's thoughts, Llinos touched his hand. 'You are right. We must forget the past, put all of the bad things that have happened out of our minds. That's something Joe doesn't seem able to do. Is he acting strangely, Watt?'

'He's acting like a worried husband! He adores you and so do I.' They smiled at each other. They had shared a great many bad times which was why Watt could never leave Pottery House and seek a more lucrative post somewhere else.

'I'd better let you rest.' He moved to the door. 'We can talk later if you feel up to it.'

She looked up at him. 'I'll be up to it! I need to get back into the swing of things, it's pointless sitting brooding all day. It's time I got back into harness.'

As Watt left the sunlit room, he sighed. Like Llinos he had had his share of problems but he was a happy man now, all thoughts of the past were well and truly behind him.

Lily Wesley walked through the soft grass of the gardens that surrounded Portland House. The riot of roses ran over the arbour arch, drooping petals, ready to fall as though tired of their full-blown heaviness.

21

She sat on the garden seat and looked back at the house. It was not a large house, just a cottage really. Its name implied a much grander establishment but Lily loved the place; she had been secure there these past three years.

She had married a good man, a man so old she thought he would be past all the urges that seemed to rule men. She had been mistaken. Tom Wesley had been a vigorous man despite his years. But she had endured and now he was dead. And she was the new owner. She smiled to herself: she was a woman of property, as good as Llinos Mainwaring any day. Better, because she had married a respectable Englishman and Llinos had married a savage.

Briefly, Lily thought of Saul Marks, the man who had taken her virginity. She had thought she had loved him, thought he was going to take her to the heights of society, but she had been wrong. Still that had been an unhappy time of her life; now she was the Widow Wesley, respected in the small community of Lougher. She felt happy and secure living in her own cottage that faced the might of the great estuary where wild ponies grazed on mossy banks, sometimes up to their thin flanks in water.

She rubbed her arms; the sun was dropping away beyond the horizon, the evening was growing chill. It was time she went indoors and lit the lamps. Reluctantly, she turned her back on the garden, so peaceful, so quiet.

The cottage was well planned. The large sitting room opened out into a dining room and, at the other side of the passageway, there was a small study. Beyond was a large airy kitchen. Above stairs, there were three bedrooms, all of a good size. So much room for one woman.

Lily wandered into the study; it was there that her husband had kept all his business papers. Tom was a methodical man and so it had been no surprise when Lily had learned that there were no outstanding bills to pay. She felt alone, lonely for the first time in her life. There seemed no direction, no purpose any more. Looking after Tom had been her work, something she was good at. A girl came in to clean every day and Lily, with a little effort, had learned to be a modest cook.

Thinking of cooking made her realize she was hungry. There was some cold ham in the larder and a few slightly over-ripe tomatoes. The bread was freshly baked that morning and Lily sat down to what would have been a feast in the days when she had worked at the pottery as a painter.

Seated at the table alone, she realized she actually missed Tom. He had been a big man, a genial man. He had been happy, asking little of her except that she cook his food and warm his bed when required. That was something she had come to accept; though she never enjoyed the intimacies of the bedchamber.

She was clearing away the dishes, folding up the big damask tablecloth, when there was a knock on the door. She hesitated, wondering who could be calling on her at this time of the evening. She tidied her hair and pressed down the creases in her black dress and walked along the coolness of the passage.

'Yes?' She stood a little inside the front door

23

looking at the man who waited on the step. She could not help noticing there was a large bag at his side and his clothes were dusty as if he had been travelling.

'Good evening.' He lifted his hat. 'I'm sorry to call so late and without warning but the journey has taken much longer than I had anticipated.'

He spoke nicely, with a cultured English accent, and Lily looked at him, wondering what he could possibly want with her.

'Can I help you, are you lost?' she asked hesitantly. He was clearly an educated gentleman and Lily had never overcome her sense of respect, amounting almost to awe, of anyone with learning.

'I think you can. I'm James Wesley, Tom's nephew.' He moved past her into the passage and put down his bag. He dusted his hat and hung it on the hallstand before slipping out of his coat. 'I expect he's told you all about me. I'm afraid I have been something of a thorn in his side.'

'What are you doing?' There was something like panic in Lily's voice. 'This is my house and I can't have you staying here. It just would not do, you must see that.'

He walked through into the sitting room and dropped into the big chair that had been Tom's.

'Sorry, little lady, this is my home, I'm here to stay and I'm afraid you have no choice in the matter.'

Lily sank into a chair and stared uncomprehendingly at him. How could he threaten to take her home away? She swallowed hard; her newfound security was vanishing like a mist before her eyes.

'But he left the house to me,' she said. 'I was

Tom's wife, you must know that. We were married all legal-like in the village church.'

'I'm sure you were.' James smiled not unsympathetically. 'But, you see, I am the only male heir. This is my property now.' He shrugged. 'I don't expect you to move out at once, of course, especially not at this time of night, so we'll just have to put up with each other for the time being.' He smiled and dimples appeared in his cheeks. 'Indeed, if you choose, you may stay here indefinitely, providing we find a live-in maid to satisfy the proprieties.'

Lily breathed a sigh of relief, at least she had time to think, time to consult Mr Brentford the solicitor who handled Tom's affairs.

'I'll make up the bed in the spare room with fresh sheets,' she said. 'The place isn't aired, of course. There's been no fire for some time in there but the weather has been warm enough, I dare say.'

'That's kind of you,' he said. 'That will do for tonight but when we are a little more organized, I'd like the main bedroom, the one that looks over the estuary. That was always a favourite of mine, that view, something you cannot buy.'

His cheek took her breath away but for the moment she held her tongue. Mr James Wesley might be the legal heir to Tom's possessions and he might not but, in any case, as the widow, Lily was sure she must have rights too.

Later, when she climbed into bed, it was strangely comforting to think of James asleep in the other room. On an impulse, she had put a vase of greenery on his window sill; tomorrow she would pick fresh flowers. She snuggled down under the sheets. Now that the shock was wearing off, she realized it might not be a bad idea to have a male protector about the place and James was a very personable young man. When she drifted off to sleep, it was with a smile on her lips as she dreamed of James slipping a gold band on to her finger.

Llinos was pleased with the revamped firebird designs. The bold tail feathers of the bird were painted large on the dinner service that was meant for one of the richer families of Swansea. To have her own pottery wares on the tables of the élite was something she had always dreamed of.

'You look better today, my love.' Joe had come into the room on silent feet. Her father used to say that Joe was creeping about the house but her husband was naturally quiet, his movements, his voice, his every action contained. Joe had an inner strength about him that made people respect him in spite of the superstition about his origins that still abounded among the townspeople.

'I am feeling better, Joe.' She held out her arms to him and he drew her close. She loved him and wanted him as much as she had on their wedding night. He would always thrill her, even when they were both old and grey he would always be handsome in her eyes.

'You are pleased with the new, bolder patterns, then?' Joe held her in his arms, his long silky hair brushed against her cheek like tender fingers.

'I think you are a man of vision, my husband,' she said softly. He smiled and put her away from him. He stood near the door, his hands thrust into his pockets.

'Ah, you think I can do no wrong. You are biased in my favour which is what a good wife should be.'

'And you have been everything a good husband should be.' Joe had been at her side constantly since she had lost the baby and yet she sensed something in him, a withdrawing of himself from her, and it troubled her. But she must let him be free; she could not tie him to her apron strings; Joe had never been that sort of man.

Llinos made up her mind, it was time she took charge of the pottery again. 'Tomorrow, I'll go back to work. Now I'm feeling so much better I need something to do with my time.'

Joe nodded his approval. 'That's what I wanted to hear, now I know you are on the mend and I can breathe easy.'

Llinos forced herself to smile; he seemed eager to go. 'And you can have a drink at the club with the men. Oh, don't think you fool me for one minute, Mr Mainwaring, you have been chafing at the bit these past weeks!'

'Of course I have!' He opened the door. 'I think it's about time I asserted myself. I shall go to the club tonight and there will be no complaints from you, madam!'

As Llinos watched from the window, Joe strolled along the drive, turning only once to wave to her. When he was out of sight, she returned to the drawings and took up a pencil. But she was thinking about Joe and how happy they had always been together. Was the death of their daughter going to change that? Perhaps she had taken everything for granted, had been too happy in her marriage. She shivered and bent over the paper, staring at it blankly. She was worrying about nothing. Joe loved her, would always love her. If nothing else in this world was safe, their love was.

CHAPTER TWO

The paint shed was quiet; the artists were engrossed in their work of decorating the china. Looking down the long table that was littered with pots of spirit and discarded colours, Llinos watched as Watt demonstrated to one of the newcomers how to fill in the latest designs. He worked with bold, confident strokes of the brush, bringing into being the riot of red and gold feathers of the firebird design.

Llinos, wrapped in a paint-stained apron, her sleeves rolled above her elbows, moved closer. 'You haven't lost your touch, Watt.'

He made a face at her as she went on past him. Llinos ignored him.

'Good morning, Pearl, how do you like the new designs?'

'Morning, Mrs Mainwaring.' Pearl was inclined to be formal when other, less senior, workers were in earshot. She brushed her face with the back of her hand and left a streak of rust paint across her cheek. She put her head on one side, examining her painting. 'Not a bad design, though some think birds are unlucky.'

'That's just silly talk!' Llinos smiled. 'The china is selling well, birds or not.'

'How's my Rosie shaping up as a maid?' Pearl asked. 'Pity the girl hasn't got her mam's talent with a brush, isn't it?' She laughed good-naturedly.

'Rosie's doing very well,' Llinos said. 'She's as good a worker as her mother any day. She has a much sweeter nature though!'

Pearl laughed, her head flung back, her dark hair escaping from her cap. She was not one whit offended by Llinos's jibe. They knew each other well; Pearl was a trusted overseer, her tongue sharp sometimes but her heart always kind.

'How are you keeping, Pearl?' Llinos did not need a reply. 'That's a silly question, you look fit as a fiddle.' It was true; Pearl was blooming with health. Her cheeks were full, her large breasts straining the material of her apron. She laid her hand on her rounded stomach.

'He's kicking like a mule today,' she said cheerfully. 'I'll be glad when he's out, I will indeed!'

'Gossiping again, Pearl!' Watt rested his hand on Pearl's shoulder. He caught Llinos's eye and winked. 'You shouldn't be so active in the nights, Pearl, you need to get some sleep at your age instead of fooling about with Will Shepherd all night!'

'Hey watch your tongue!' Pearl's eyes were full of humour. 'You're not too old to get a slap across the earhole, mind.'

'I think you asked for that, didn't you, Watt? Well, I'd better get on.'

'Excuse me, Llinos,' Pearl said quietly, 'can I just say it's good to see you back at work?

Mind, we're all that sorry you lost the little girl.'

At the mention of her baby, Llinos felt tears burn her eyes. She swallowed hard; she had cried enough, now it was time to get on with her life.

'Like everyone else, I must count my blessings, mustn't I?'

'Aye, you're right enough.' Pearl had been widowed over a year ago and the death of her husband had affected her deeply. But now Pearl was happy again, living openly with her man, declaring she would rather have a ring through her nose than on her finger.

As Llinos moved along the rows of tables examining the pottery she smelt the oxide and the tang of paint. Like Pearl, she was glad she was back at work.

Llinos was tired by the time she left the sheds. She made her way back across the yard longing to kick off her boots and rest. She glanced up at the sky. It was the end of September but the sun continued to shine with the warmth of high summer. She stood for a moment closing her eyes, thinking that her baby would never see the sunshine, never feel the breeze on her face.

Around her were the sounds of pottery life, men calling from the kilns, the chink of saggars being stacked, young voices of yard boys picking up the discarded clay. Llinos was trying to put on a brave face for the world but her arms felt empty and there was a hollow feeling inside her whenever she thought of the baby.

It was good to walk into the cool privacy of the house. She took off her apron and washed her hands in the china bowl in the kitchen before hurrying upstairs to the room where her son was having his lessons.

Lloyd looked up at her, a smile on his face. 'I can do my sums good now, Mammy.' He held up his book and showed her the rows of neat figures.

'He is a very bright boy, Mrs Mainwaring.' Eira was young to be a governess. She came from a good family and had been well educated but her parents had died within weeks of each other, leaving her orphaned and penniless. While Llinos had been confined to her bed, it had been Eira who had taken care of Lloyd.

'I have a favour to ask, Mrs Mainwaring,' Eira said brushing the chalk from her fingers. 'You know the family who used to work for my father before he died? Well they are feeling the pinch. Bryn Rees is sick, he can't find any other work and the children haven't got enough food to eat. I'd like to help them if I can.'

'What can I do, Eira?' Llinos said. 'You know I'll help in any way I can.'

'There seems to be a great deal of food wasted here,' Eira said. 'I wonder if I could take some of the leftovers to the Rees's, it would help a lot.'

'I'll speak to Cook about it.' Llinos rested her hand for a moment on Lloyd's head. Thank God he would never have to go hungry, not while she lived and breathed. 'You get on with your work now, Lloyd, your father will be proud of your progress; I'm sure he'll tell you himself when he comes home.'

But Joe did not come home that night. He sent a messenger to tell her he had decided to stay the night at the Gloucester Hotel in town. He was acting strangely since the baby died. But who could blame him?

Weary and heartsore, Llinos retired early. It was lonely in the large bed without Joe, she missed the warmth of his body against hers. She wanted him to take her in his arms and make love to her but he had not touched her since the death of their child. Llinos knew he stayed away from her out of consideration for her delicate condition but now she wanted life to return to normal and that meant becoming Joe's wife again in every way.

There was a letter on her plate in the morning. Llinos picked it up fearing it was from Joe. Quite what she expected him to say she was not sure but she had a feeling of apprehension that would not go.

But the letter was from the bank. The manager was asking her to call and see him on a matter of some urgency. Llinos threw it down, unconcerned about the matter but at least it gave her an excuse to go into town. She would call at the Gloucester Hotel and see Joe.

She asked for the carriage to be brought to the door for ten-thirty and, after breakfast with Lloyd, she dressed in her good clothes and stepped out into the yard. The carriage was waiting for her. The driver raised his hat to her and held open the door, holding her arm to help her up the small carriage steps.

She smiled her thanks. 'Morning, Kenneth, I need to go down to the bank.' She turned to look at him. 'It seems like we're in for another fine day.'

'Yes, Mrs Mainwaring, summer's going on

forever. The bees don't know what to do about it, the honeycombs are still overflowing.'

Llinos climbed into her seat, straightening her skirt. She was now the society woman dressed in the latest fashion, with her bonnet trimmed with glossy feathers. Once settled, Llinos looked back at the house and the buildings beyond.

Her father had built the pottery from nothing and at first it had been small with only the minimum of workers. Now it had expanded, grown richer, more profitable, employing more than three hundred men and women.

Beside it stood the larger Tawe Pottery that once belonged to Eynon Morton-Edwards but was now in the hands of a consortium of businessmen. Her own pottery, renamed since her father's day, would never rival the Tawe Pottery for production but, as for quality, the Merino was equal to any in the country.

The coach trip to town took her past the winding River Tawe, the rushing waters of which turned the wheel of the grinding house. The river was calm now in the dreaming sun but when winter came the waters could rise and rush, bringing chaos to the inhabitants of nearby houses.

The streets of Swansea were busy with traffic; small carts vied with large carriages for space at the roadside. Llinos looked out unseeingly, waiting for the driver to take her to her destination. She reached into her bag and drew out the crisp folded letter. She had read it several times but still did not know why the manager wanted to see her.

Llinos looked at the letter again but was still no wiser. One thing she was sure of however: she did not much like the abrupt tone of the request for her to call. But then the manager was new, young, eager to make a mark. She would reserve her judgement until she had spoken to him.

Llinos wondered if she should have seen Joe first and asked him to go with her but decided it was up to her to conduct her business alone. When she did see Joe they had some serious talking to do. She had made every effort to get over the loss of their baby, but had he?

She was kept waiting at the bank, something that would never have happened in the old days. She sat back in the uncomfortable chair, trying to relax, but with the thought of Joe's strange behaviour pressing in on her it was impossible. She pushed the thought away, determined to occupy her mind with other things.

Back at home, Lloyd would be at his lessons, his new art tutor struggling to teach him how to draw. Lloyd was impatient with the slow progress he was making, he preferred to be working with his hands, to fashion little figures and animals in wood, so realistic you felt they would bite if you got too close. He was a strange mixture, her son, practical like his grandfather and yet with something of Joe's intuitive way of thinking.

'Mrs Mainwaring, Mr Sparks will see you now.' The clerk held the door open for her and Llinos walked into the office, impatient to get the business over with as quickly as possible. She suddenly felt the need to be back home in familiar surroundings. Perhaps she would not try to find Joe at the hotel after all. It might be much better to talk to him in the privacy of their own home.

'Please sit down.' Mr Sparks was younger even than Llinos had imagined. His hair was slicked down close to his head making his nose appear more prominent than it really was. He was not an attractive man.

He flicked through some papers, keeping Llinos waiting. She was beginning to grow impatient; anyone would think she was here as a supplicant not as a successful businesswoman.

'Is there anything I can do for you, Mr Sparks?' she asked at last. 'I am rather busy you know, I do have a business to run.'

His head jerked up as though she had said something shocking. 'I am aware that your time is precious but then so is mine.' He sounded as aggrieved as he looked.

'Well then, shall we get on with it?' Llinos folded her hands in her lap and waited for him to gather his wits.

'I would normally deal with Mr Mainwaring,' he said, 'but in the circumstances . . .' He sighed and put the papers down, pressing out the creases with thin fingers.

'What circumstances are those?' Llinos was beginning to find the man offensive. She took a deep breath, trying to keep calm.

'Well the man is a foreigner.' Mr Sparks spoke abruptly and with such arrogance that Llinos wanted to hit him. Would people never accept Joe for what he was?

'I can see you are prejudiced against anyone not born in this country,' she said icily, 'though I cannot understand it.'

'It's not a case of prejudice but more of

expediency,' he said. 'I feel I might not make myself plain to someone from another culture.'

'My husband is doubtless more educated than you, Mr Sparks. He is certainly more considerate of the feelings of others. Another thing, he is probably far wealthier than you could ever hope to be.' She knew she was foolish to let the man goad her into defending Joe, he did not need defending to anyone.

'If you are not going to get to the point of this interview,' she said, 'I think I had better leave before I lose my temper completely.'

'No need for that,' Mr Sparks said hastily. 'It's just that one of my very good customers, and a dear friend into the bargain, is interested in your little pottery.' He beamed as if he had handed her a precious gift. 'My customer is very influential and he has made a fine offer.' He shuffled some papers on his desk. 'He is heading the consortium which owns the Tawe Pottery.'

Llinos was puzzled. She doubted Mr Sparks would have any friends, influential or otherwise. The man was simply a manager in a small town bank. 'What makes you think I want to sell my "little pottery"?' she asked icily.

'I have been instructed to give you a very good price.' He smiled ingratiatingly. 'There would be a little something in it for me of course. It makes perfect sense. The larger Tawe Pottery would absorb your business and most of your workers. We would all come out of the deal much the richer.'

Llinos stood up; her hands were trembling and it was an effort to keep them clenched at her sides.

Her very instinct was to strike out at the man's arrogant face.

'You must agree', he failed to see the warning signs, 'that the pottery business is not a suitable occupation for a lady.' He continued digging his own grave. 'I'm sure now that you are, well, a mature lady, you will wish to spend your time in a more feminine pursuit.'

'Don't say another word,' Llinos said in a low voice. 'I have no intention of selling the pottery. I don't know why you would even think such a thing.' She moved to the door. 'Furthermore, I object to you calling me in for such a trivial matter. It would have shown more courtesy on your part if you had sent me a communication in writing and then I would have been spared the irritation of this meeting.'

Mr Sparks was nonplussed; it seemed he had been expecting to meet a submissive little woman, to browbeat her, then to give her the benefit of his sage advice and expect her to snatch at it eagerly. He was grossly mistaken.

'I did not mean to irritate,' he said defensively. 'I thought you would be delighted at such a good offer for your business, more than it is actually worth in my opinion.' He hesitated. 'Wouldn't you even like to know the price that was offered?'

'No I would not. As for your opinion, it's hardly informed, is it?'

'But, madam, I am a bank manager, it is my business to be informed.' He coughed. 'I have taken the trouble to check your profits and losses accounts and your pottery is not so successful that you can turn down such a good deal out of hand.'

Llinos stood before the desk, her patience exhausted. She leaned forward and Mr Sparks jerked away from her as if frightened. 'You presume too much, you little upstart!' she said. 'Do you realize that my late father and the owner of this bank were great friends? One word from me and you would have no job.'

He was suddenly white-faced. He stood up, drawing himself up to his full height, and stared at her resentfully. 'There is no need for threats, Mrs Mainwaring,' he said. He had a point.

'You're right,' she said, 'but there is no need for you to patronize me just because I am a woman. I ran the pottery almost single-handed before you were even a clerk in the bank. Believe it or not, I know what I'm doing and my business is fine, thank you.'

'Well, let us hope it remains that way,' he said and Llinos looked at him long and hard. He shifted uncomfortably, fiddling with the inkpot on his desk, his eyes refusing to meet hers.

'Who is issuing threats, now, Mr Sparks?' Llinos let herself out of the office. She was blind with fury that she should be treated like a fool, patronized by a man who was so bigoted and prejudiced that he dared to look down on Joe. He was not fit to clean Joe's boots.

She could not face seeking out Joe at the hotel; she had suffered enough upset for one day. 'Take me straight home, Kenneth,' she said to her driver. She had a headache coming on, she was trembling, she had not fully recovered her strength. Mr Sparks had caught her off guard, piercing her normal reserve with his insolence. He had obviously been given a bribe to persuade her to sell and, bragging about his powers of persuasion, now he had fallen flat on his face. Llinos knew she had made an enemy that morning and, if she read Mr Sparks correctly, he would not hesitate to take his revenge if ever the opportunity arose.

Joe walked across the farmlands he had bought when his son was born. He had no need to work at anything; his father had left him so well provided for that he need never work again. But Joe was not used to being idle. Back home in America he had learned the ways of his tribe. He had helped, even as a child, to build stockades and repair the broken beams of the lodges. He had respected the laws of the Mandan tribe. Until he had married Llinos. Then he had smashed those laws into tiny pieces.

But he could never forget that part of him was white. He had been sent to an English school, he had learned new ways. He had learned his lessons well, both in the classroom and on the playing fields of the Merton School for Young Gentlemen. And then he had gone to war.

Joe had, in a strange way, enjoyed the fight against Napoleon Bonaparte. On the fields of France and Belgium he had been in his element, using his tracking skills and his native intuition to beat the man who single-handedly threatened the peace of Joe's world.

Joe had been batman to Lloyd Savage; they had become companions, forging a bond and a mutual respect for each other that rose above rank. But Lloyd had not wanted Joe as a son-in-law, indeed he had done everything he could to prevent the marriage. And yet, at the end, Lloyd had been happy enough that Joe would be there to look after Llinos when he had gone to his heaven.

Joe paused, looking down the hillside towards the rolling fields. The sea beyond sparkled like diamonds in the sun. Why did men seek material riches when there were riches all around in nature for them to enjoy?

He did not want to dwell too much on the past, on the days after Lloyd's death when he had been accused of his murder. Since then Joe had never used the herbs and spices used by the Mandan to treat sickness. That sort of medicine was not understood by so-called civilized people. He sighed, wondering if Lloyd would have approved of him now that his fortune had increased. It was strange the way money came to those who did not seek it. Fate had played a trick on him: here he was standing on the hills of Wales, staring out to sea, feeling proud that all the rolling greenery before him was his. Was he losing his Indian beliefs, the beliefs he had grown up with?

Among the men of the Mandan tribe, land was for everyone. No-one owned the earth, the sky or the waters. Perhaps he thought differently now that he was a husband and father. Now he wanted security for his wife and for his son. Was that the spur that drove men to toil in smoky sheds and pits?

He heard his name being called and looked downwards to where a tall figure was climbing the hill towards him.

'Eynon!' He held out his hand as the man drew

close. 'It's good to see you. We don't see enough of you since you sold the pottery.'

'I know.' Eynon sank onto the ground and took a small sketchbook from his pocket. 'I have become something of a recluse, I'm afraid. The only people I see these days are my servants and my old friend Father Martin.' His face lit up. 'I have my darling daughter, of course, my Jayne. She's become the centre of my universe.'

'I can understand that,' Joe crouched down beside Eynon, watching his slim fingers capture the curve of the hill and somehow, even in pencil, the sparkle of the sea. Eynon was a talented man.

'I'm sorry about the baby.' Eynon stared outwards, seeing the vista before him in a way that another man might never see it. Perhaps the reason they got on so well was that Eynon saw the land as Joe did, as the property of no man.

'We are coming to terms with the loss of our daughter,' Joe said. 'As for Lloyd, I think my son is sometimes lonely for the company of children his own age. Tutors are all well and good but being with adults doesn't teach a lad how to grow in the world of a child.'

'Perhaps I should bring Jayne over some time,' Eynon said. 'I suppose she should mix more with other children, too.' He glanced up at Joe. 'It's just that I'm afraid of losing her.' He chewed the end of his pencil. 'I suppose there's also the guilt about her mother, who died giving me my child.' Eynon sighed. 'I wish I could have loved her, just a little. Annabel was a good woman.'

He smiled suddenly. 'Of course it's all the fault

of that wife of yours. I've loved Llinos since the moment I first set eyes on her.'

'I know,' Joe said. 'And she loves you too in her way.' He watched the picture grow under Eynon's skilled hands; it showed the sea, the sky, the hills and the outline of a sailing ship on the horizon.

'That's very good. It's so full of life.'

Eynon shrugged. 'It's all right, I suppose, but I'll never make a real artist; my father wouldn't allow me to have the training.'

'I think natural talent outweighs any training,' Joe said quietly. 'In any case, why not hire an art tutor for your daughter and take lessons yourself?' He smiled. 'I expect you would find you knew more than the person supposed to be teaching you.'

'It's an idea,' Eynon said. 'Anyway, what are you doing up here on the hillside alone? Working something out in your head, if I know you.'

'There, you have answered your own question.' Joe smiled.

'Well, only half of it. Do you feel like telling me more?' Eynon closed his sketchbook and gave Joe his full attention. 'Is anything wrong?'

'Possibly,' Joe said. 'My mother is an elder now, I should go to America and see her.'

Eynon's fair hair covered his eyes for a moment but not before Joe saw the glint in them. 'That's not quite the whole truth, is it?'

'It's all I'm going to tell you.'

Eynon got to his feet. 'That's all right, old chap,' he said. 'But if you go, remember that I specialize in taking care of ladies deserted by their husbands.'

43

'So I've heard,' Joe said dryly. He could hardly fail to hear the gossip about Eynon and the wife of the new bank manager. 'Mrs Sparks is an attractive lady and her husband is not even absent I understand?'

'Not in body, perhaps,' Eynon said. 'But he is a dry stick for all that he's a young man and pompous to boot. I think his lady wife is glad of an escort to the balls at the assembly rooms.'

Joe had heard tales of Mr Sparks's pomposity from Llinos. When he had gone home last night she had been bursting with indignation. Mr Sparks thought he could dictate business terms to Llinos. He had actually advised her to sell the pottery. He was chancing his luck taking on a woman like Llinos.

Joe had been glad of the distraction. How could he have explained his absence for the night to his wife? He could hardly explain his reluctance to resume intimacy with Llinos to himself. Was it the loss of the child? Or perhaps it was the knowledge that Llinos was barren. It was not her fault of course; the prolonged birth had ruined her chances of ever conceiving a child again. He wanted to love her, to comfort her and yet he was almost afraid to touch her.

'You have met him?' Eynon asked. 'This man Sparks I mean.'

Joe's eyebrows lifted. 'No but I have heard of him all right! The man was foolish enough to try to tell my wife how to run her business. I believe he received the sharp edge of Llinos's tongue.'

'I can just imagine it.' Eynon laughed. 'But then Sparks is a small man in every way, small framed and smaller of mind. All the same, I think Mr Sparks will make a bad enemy.' He folded his sketchbook away. 'Are you going back towards the pottery now?'

Joe nodded. 'Aye, I'll walk so far with you. Finished your drawing then?'

'For today.' The breeze drifted in from the sea as they walked across the hills. It was Eynon who broke the companionable silence.

'I've seen a great deal of Watt Bevan lately but I don't mind because his presence makes my housekeeper very happy. Maura seems to have quite got over that husband of hers.' He glanced sideways at Joe. 'Some of us find our pleasures outside marriage, you see?'

Joe looked towards Eynon; he was smiling, he was a man who had flaunted all the codes of etiquette and enjoyed it.

'I think that Maura and her Watt are as respectable as any couple who walked down the aisle of a church,' Eynon continued. 'Though my friend Martin would be horrified by my attitude.' He paused. 'At least that's what he says.'

'And you don't believe him for one minute?'

'No, Joe, I don't believe him for one minute.'

The two men walked in silence for a time until the green of the hill led down to where the trail met the river.

'This is where our paths diverge,' Eynon said. 'Perhaps I can call over to see Llinos one evening? If she's up to visitors that is.'

'Llinos would like that. We both would like that.' Joe paused. 'Could I ask you a favour?'

'Anything.'

'When I go to America I would like you to take care of my family for me.'

'I would be honoured.' Eynon was suddenly serious. 'Something is wrong, isn't it?'

Joe looked away across the vast sky. There was a great deal wrong, his mind needed clearing. He had been troubled ever since the death of his baby daughter and now he was troubled about his mother. He had recurring dreams about Mint, dreams of her drowning in a river that flowed swiftly, taking away the very breath of life. He must go to her, for her days on earth were numbered.

There was more troubling him. He felt bewildered by his feelings for Llinos. He loved her still and yet he could not bring himself to go to her, to hold her in his arms and make love to her. While he lived in the same house as Llinos he would never find the answers to his problems.

He did not say as much to Eynon. 'It's just that I'll be gone for several months and I like to think of Llinos with a friend she can depend on.'

'You didn't really answer my question, Joe,' Eynon said. 'But I won't push you. Perhaps I will persuade Llinos to come with me to one of the balls; I will dance with her all night and pay her every attention.' He waved. 'Bye, Joe, take care.'

Joe watched as Eynon swung along the road towards where his house stood tall and golden in the evening sun. He waited until the other man was out of sight and then he turned and, with his head bowed, made his way home.

CHAPTER THREE

Lily was finding it more difficult every day to live in the same house as James Wesley. At first, she had thought to ingratiate herself with him, to seek his protection. She had even contemplated marrying him but it was becoming more and more obvious that he had no interest in her.

She watched now as he stretched out in the easy chair, his feet before the fire. The evenings were becoming chilly and Lily felt the cold badly. He glanced up and caught her eye and smiled. For once, there was no sarcasm in his voice when he spoke.

'We're like an old married couple here, aren't we?'

His words shocked her. 'Well, I don't know about that, I thought you hated me being here.'

'You are a foolish little lady! Of course I don't hate you being here. You are quiet and decent with none of the forwardness of some women I've met. All in all I find you a pleasant companion.'

Lily began to glow; her cramped inner feelings began to unfold a little. Being described as a pleasant companion was certainly not great praise but at least it was a start.

'Lily,' James said, 'are you a good needle-woman?'

'I'm not bad.' Lily had always mended her own clothes. Never rich, she had patched petticoats and sewn on buttons more times than she cared to remember.

'I wonder; would you do a little sewing for me?' He pointed towards the stairs. 'Up in my room, in the corner of the wardrobe, there's a good shirt. It's a little too large for me and needs to be altered. Could you tackle it for me?'

Lily was eager to please though she could see that the job would be a little more than sewing on buttons or doing some patching. 'I'll have a look at it.'

'Go on then, you little goose, go get it.'

Lily hesitated for a moment, not sure if she was being friendly or simply acting like James's servant. Then, with a shrug, she left the room. She was deep in thought as she climbed the winding stairs of the cottage. On the small landing, she paused to look out of the deep-silled window. It was dark in the garden with only a slant of moonlight to highlight the rose arbour.

She loved it here so much; the cottage had become her home, had given her a feeling of being in a safe haven. Even when her husband died, she had not been lonely, well only a little. Sometimes she missed Tom but mostly she felt relief that at last she was free. And then James had come along to destroy her dreams. But perhaps even now, she could rescue something from the situation. It seemed her hopes of a relationship with James might still come to fruition.

She lit the candles and opened the wardrobe door. There were suits and breeches, jackets and shirts. Lots of shirts. She took them out one by one, trying to judge which one needed altering. At last, she gave up. She went to the top of the stairs and called out to James.

'I can't find the shirt you want altered, will you come and show me?' She glanced around uneasily, was she wise inviting James to come up to the bedroom? The girl James had employed to clean and cook for him was asleep in the lean-to at the back of the cottage. If James meant to ravish Lily, there would be no-one to hear her screams.

But would she scream? Or would she let him have his way? Men once tasting the fruits of lust found it difficult to stop. Giving a man your body seemed to enslave him, at least in Lily's experience.

James came up the stairs reluctantly. He stood beside her and peered into the darkness of the wardrobe. He was very close; she could smell the clean scent of soap and she glanced up at him from under her lashes. He was quite a handsome man; she would not find his advances too distasteful, would she?

Lily had never enjoyed being with a man. The strange excitement that seemed to fill them when they took her had never affected her. She was unresponsive as a lover, she knew it and yet that had done nothing to deter the men in her life. Of course Tom had been an old man and grateful that she allowed him any intimacies at all.

'Fetch the candle over here, Lily,' James said. She did what he asked and he held it aloft moving the flame precariously close to the clothing. 'Ah, here we are.' Triumphantly, he held out the shirt. It hung limply in his hands, like a headless corpse in the candlelight.

'Where does it need to be altered then?' Lily asked.

'Ah, now I'm not quite sure. I'll try it on and then we shall see. Take the candle, Lily, there's a good girl.'

He stripped off his waistcoat and then his shirt and Lily saw he wore no undergarments. She turned her head away, strangely touched by the thinness of his chest. She felt that all this was leading up to a suggestion of intimacy and she dreaded the thought of him pouncing on her and throwing her on the bed. He did no such thing.

'There, Lily, see how big the shirt is, it hangs around me like the sails of a ship.' He smiled. 'If I went out in a strong breeze I'd fly up into the sky and you would never see me again. Would you like that, Lily?'

She was right; this was all leading up to coercing her into bed. He had enough shirts without fussing about this particular one. 'I'll need some pins, I'll fetch them from my sewing box.'

He stood still while she pinned the shirt at the seams and then looked down at her handiwork. 'Ah, that seems to be the answer, well done, Lily. Will it take you long?' He rested his hands on her shoulders and she felt the warmth of his fingers and braced herself. He bent towards her and kissed her lightly on both cheeks. 'There, you see, I'm not such an ogre am I?'

To her surprise, he turned away and lifted the shirt over his head. He dressed quickly and efficiently and moved to the door. 'I'm going to have a last small drink of porter and then I'll retire to bed. See you in the morning, Lily.'

She followed him onto the landing, even now suspecting his motives. 'As for you,' he said without turning, 'leave the shirt, you look all in.'

He left her alone, taking the candle with him, and she stood in the darkness, telling herself she would never understand the ways of men. In her own bedroom, she drew the curtains and pushed more coal onto the fire before lighting the candle.

Lily stood for a moment, looking down at her hands covered in coal dust, and wondered why, when she hated the advances of men, was she disappointed that James showed no interest in her?

Later, lying in bed, she began to plan her future. She would make herself indispensable to James; he would grow so used to having her around that he would never want her to leave. It was not an ideal way to live her life but it was a great deal better than being forced to find a home and employment somewhere else.

As she began to drowse towards sleep, Lily felt a warm glow remembering that James had noticed her. Had even spoken a few kind words to her. It was little enough but it was a beginning.

Llinos looked at the sleeping figure of Eynon's daughter. She was curled up in the big armchair like a sleeping cat, her legs tucked under her. Jayne was a pretty child, growing taller now with thin legs and a cloud of thick hair hanging loose from the ribbons.

'She feels the lack of a mother greatly,' Eynon said following Llinos's gaze.

'Well, she has more than enough love from you, Eynon, so don't fret, you are a wonderful father.'

'Thank you, kind lady.' He leaned forward. 'It's nice to see you come over to my house for a change, I'm always having to take the carriage to your place. You're a selfish hussy. That's what you are.'

'Me a hussy!' Llinos made a face at him. 'What's this scandal I hear about you then, Eynon? Walking out openly with a married woman? I thought you had more sense than to make your affair public.'

Llinos lifted her glass of cordial; it was pleasant to be in the airy drawing room and a change from the hustle and bustle of Pottery House. She loved teasing Eynon and he was always aware that behind her humour lay real affection.

Eynon played up to her. 'Ah, I'm to be scolded! Well, my excuse is that Mrs Sparks is a needy lady and her husband is not the affectionate kind.'

'I can vouch for that!' Llinos said dryly. 'Indeed, I found him a pompous, ill-mannered pig!'

'There we are then, imagine having to live with a man like that. I think I'm saving poor Alice Sparks from leading a very dreary life, don't you?' He smiled. 'I always try to do some good works, you know. I am such a charitable man that it grieves me to see a feisty young woman deprived of affection.'

Llinos tried to imagine Mr Sparks having a wife

with spirit and smiled. Perhaps Mrs Sparks had too much spirit and that might account for why her husband was so bad tempered.

'Be careful though, Eynon,' she said soberly. 'I don't trust that man, not one little bit. I think he would be the sort to do someone harm if he had the means.'

'Forget the Sparks family.' Eynon looked at her in concern. 'How are you feeling? I know you've had a bad time of it lately.'

'I've tried to put it all out of my mind now.' Llinos looked down at her hands; it was an effort to speak normally about so painful a subject. 'I know there won't be any more children.' She looked up. 'I feel so guilty about that and, to make it worse, the loss of our daughter affected Joe badly.'

Eynon took her hand. 'You have a fine son and you are a beautiful woman, what more could any man want?' As his eyes met hers, she read the love there and the longing. She squeezed his hand.

'You are always such a comfort to me. I know Joe had to go home, he's worried about his mother, but I needed him with me. Instead, I'm looking to you for comfort. Am I being unfair to you?'

He shook his head. 'Of course not!'

'Why do you still love me, Eynon?' she asked in a small voice. 'Why can't you find a woman who is single and free?'

'I can't love another woman when I love you so much.' Eynon looked away; if he looked into her eyes she would read too much of his pain.

'Oh, Eynon!' Llinos put her arms around him.

'You are my dearest friend in all the world, the only other man beside Joe I could possibly love.'

She felt his arms warm around her and she closed her eyes. It was so comforting to have a man hold her. If she was another sort of woman she might have given him the comfort of her body and taken comfort from his. But Llinos belonged heart and soul to her husband; she never wanted any man except Joe. The trouble was, he did not seem to want her.

'I'd better get back home,' she said, at last releasing herself from Eynon's embrace. 'My son will be missing me. Will I see you tomorrow?'

'I expect so.' With his arm around her shoulders he accompanied her through the hallway and onto the front step.

'Don't worry if you can't manage it, Eynon,' Llinos said quickly.

'Of course I can manage it! I can't wait to come over to your house and play games with that boy of yours.' He helped her into the carriage. 'Lloyd is so like his grandfather, sometimes I think he's inherited his soul.'

'Hush!' Llinos said. 'You sound like Joe!'

Eynon sighed. 'Do I?' he said wistfully. 'I wish I was half the man your husband is.'

'You are your own man, that's all you need to know,' she said.

As the carriage jerked into motion, she raised her fingers to her lips and blew him a kiss. She was aware of him watching as the carriage rolled down the tree-lined drive towards the road.

She leaned back against the cold leather seat, closing her eyes. She missed Joe so badly it was like toothache. She had cried at their parting, she felt bereft as though he was gone from her for ever and it frightened her.

'Come home, my darling,' she whispered but she was answered only by the creaking of the carriage and the rumble of wheels on the cobbles.

The journey from Eynon's house to her own took only little over half an hour. As the carriage turned into the yard, Llinos saw her son wave excitedly to her from the window of the house.

He leaned out over the sill, waving a letter at her. 'Daddy's written us a letter, Mamma,' he said. 'Hurry up, come and read it.'

In the drawing room, Lloyd had seated himself beside Charlotte on the large sofa, his legs, thin and gangly, hung over the edge and Llinos's heart contracted with love for him.

Charlotte smiled a welcome. 'Come and sit for goodness' sake and let's open the letter from my brother.' She ruffled Lloyd's hair. 'Put both of us out of our misery.'

Llinos tore the letter open with trembling fingers. 'It's bad news,' she said at last. 'Joe's mother has passed away.' She looked at her son, 'Your grandmother.' He had never met his grandmother, he would never know the sweetness of the woman, her age-old wisdom, her beauty.

'But Charlotte is my grandmother,' he said, puzzled.

'I know, darling, but you had another grandmother, her name was Mint, she lived in Daddy's land, in America.'

'Oh.' Lloyd looked crestfallen for a moment and then, childlike, he shrugged away the sadness in

55

his mother's voice. 'When is Daddy coming home?'

Llinos looked down at the letter. 'He will be back with us before Christmas,' she said. She should feel happy and yet her heart was heavy: Joe had to cross the great Atlantic sea that separated them; it was a hazardous journey at the best of times and now, with winter coming on, it would be even worse.

'Never mind, Mamma.' Lloyd had the same knack as his father of reading her thoughts. 'Daddy has the Great Spirit to keep him safe.' He slipped from the sofa and nestled his head against her knees. 'He'll be home before the snow comes, you'll see.'

Over his head, Llinos met Charlotte's eyes. 'He's like his father,' Charlotte said, 'he's a seer. If he says Joe will come home safely, then he will.'

'Of course he will,' Llinos replied and yet she knew she would not rest until Joe was safely in her arms again.

Binnie Dundee looked around the table in the sun-washed dining room and marvelled at his family of sons who were growing rapidly. The boys had strong limbs and glowing faces browned with the warmth of the American sun. He was a contented man.

He congratulated himself on shaking the dust of Swansea off his feet all those years ago and settling in America with a wonderful wife. Sometimes it troubled him that he and Hortense were not legally married, that he still had a wife back home. He had never kept in touch with Maura; once he made his decision to leave her he put her out of his mind. All he could do was to pray his secret was never discovered or Dan McCabe would have him hung, drawn and quartered for tricking his daughter into a sham marriage.

The boys were whispering together, no doubt planning some mischief. Binnie watched them fondly. No wonder Dan, Jerry and Matthew were the apple of their granddad's eye. If Dad McCabe favoured the child named *for* him it was only because Dan was the first-born and the image of him.

Binnie sighed, a contented sigh. West Troy was a fine place to live and Binnie was glad that he was not back in Swansea where the weather would be turning cold and rain beat incessantly against the window-panes.

'A penny for them.' His wife smiled across at him and Binnie felt a tug at his heart. He loved Hortense as much as he had done when they were first married. She would be so hurt if she knew the truth about him. He pulled himself up sharply. Why think about the past now? It was over and done with.

'I was remembering how dull the weather was back home,' he said. Hortense smiled and reached over to touch his hand.

'But this is your home now, Binnie my love.'

'I know.' He returned her smile. 'I know. I was just telling myself how lucky I am to be with the woman I love and to have three fine sons. I would give my life for you, my love, you know that.'

The sound of a carriage stopping outside the porch galvanized the boys into action. 'Grandma's here!' Dan said. 'See you later, Mom.'

Binnie stood in the doorway as Hortense followed her sons to where Mrs McCabe was waiting for them. He waved to his mother-in-law and she acknowledged him with a nod of her head.

When Hortense came back into the house she took Binnie's hand. 'Mom's angry, seems Daddy's off with one of the girls again.' She looked up at her husband. 'Thank the good Lord you are not like Daddy, spending your energy on other women.'

She was referring to Dan McCabe's habit of visiting his own houseful of girls; nubile dark-skinned girls whom he kept in style on McCabe land. The girls remained in the house for only a few years and then Dan would pension them off, giving each one enough money to make them rich beyond their wildest dreams.

'Even now he's past fifty, my father still acts like an old goat.' Hortense was disapproving and Binnie laughed out loud.

'Come on, now, Hortense, be sensible,' he said. 'Dan is a vigorous man and your mammy, she doesn't like – well, you know what I mean.'

'I know.' Hortense was suddenly flushed. 'And I am a different kettle of fish to Mammy, so why don't we take advantage of the fact that the boys are visiting with their grandmother and we have the afternoon free?'

'I thought John and Josephine were supposed to be coming for tea.'

'So? We have time enough, honey, come on.' She tugged at his hand, leading him towards the bedroom.

Quickly, she stripped off her clothes and stood

before him naked. Her waist had thickened a little since the birth of their last child but her breasts were full and her hips rounded and she was everything he would ever want in a woman.

It was wonderful to make love to his wife with the sun warming his back and splashing her face with light. She was a passionate responsive woman and he loved her so much that every time he made love to her was as good as the first time.

Afterwards, when they lay together in the large bed, naked as innocent babies, he reached for her hand. 'Never stop loving me, will you, Hortense?'

'Honey, while I've got breath in my body, I will love you, you can depend on that. As sure as the sun rises in the morning, I am yours until I die.'

Once showered and changed into a sparkling fresh shirt, Binnie prepared chilled cordial for the expected guests. Then he sat outside, rocking in the swing on the porch. The sun was high, the shadows of the trees deep and black. It was a good life, a better life than he had ever dared hope for.

He closed his eyes; perhaps there was time for a nap before John and Josephine arrived. They were a good couple and even though John, a Cornishman, had married one of the McCabe girls more from expediency than love, they had certainly made a go of it. John had worked hard and now, like Binnie, was a partner in the McCabe family potting business.

Binnie was drowsing, half-asleep when he heard the rumble of wagon wheels. He opened his eyes reluctantly and saw Jo waving at him, her bonnet hanging over her back, her hair ruffled by the breeze. She was a beautiful woman and had grown more beautiful since her marriage to John but she did not come anywhere near Hortense when it came to looks and sensuality.

'Our guests are here, Hortense!' he called. 'Get the maid to bring the drinks on to the porch, will you, honey?'

Josephine sat beside him on the swing, her skirts flowing from her slim waist. The couple had no children, even though they had been married for more than two years. But that did not seem to bother either of them. Perhaps it was the sort of life they had chosen for themselves, travelling about the country, seeking out the best potters as well as possible sites for new pottery buildings.

'How was the trip up country?' Binnie asked and John, who had settled himself in the rocking chair, looked up at him.

'I saw Joe, you know, the Indian fellow.'

Binnie felt his gut shrink. Joe, the husband Llinos had chosen for herself, knew of Binnie's past. He was aware that back on British shores Binnie had a wife, had once had a child. Had he spoken of it to John?

'Not much of a one for small talk, is he?' John's words were reassuring. Josephine leaned forward, her elbows resting on her knees tomboy fashion.

'The poor man had just lost his mammy, John, show a little charity, won't you, honey?'

'Didn't trust the man,' John said. 'Too tight-lipped for my liking and a half-breed to boot. What business has he got marrying into a respectable white family?'

'Isn't that rather a biased view, John?' Binnie said edgily. 'Joe has always been good to Llinos

60

and to her father. He nursed the captain as though the old man was his own father.'

'Aye and the gossip had it that he killed the captain to get his money, have you forgotten that, Binnie?' John was out of sorts, determined to be argumentative and Binnie, not caring to get involved, turned to Josephine.

'Glad to be home?'

'Well, sure, it's good to see Mammy and Daddy again but I don't think I could settle down here for the rest of my life the way you and Hortense have.'

'It's about time we thought of settling down, Josephine.' John's tone was sharp. 'After all, the time is slipping by. We should have a brood of kids round us by now.'

Ah so that was the rub, John wanted one way of life and Josephine another. Binnie suspected that John's wish to have children was born more from a wish to consolidate his position in the McCabe family than because he loved kids. He scarcely bothered with Binnie's sons, not even talking to them like human beings. But perhaps he was doing him an injustice; men like John who came from a privileged background felt that an heir was important.

Hortense came out onto the porch and hugged her sister. 'You're looking well.' She patted Josephine's stomach. 'Got a wee 'un in there yet?'

'No, sis, not yet.' Josephine looked away. 'Not for a while yet, if I have my way.' She lifted her arms above her head. 'I want to live a little, can't folks understand that?'

'I don't believe you!' Hortense pushed her sister playfully. 'I think John here is shirking his duty.'

61

'It's not me that's shirking my duty.' John was truculent. 'Tell my wife that it's a woman's place to provide her husband with a son.' He looked away across the dry grass beyond the house.

'And it's a husband's place to stay faithful to the woman he's supposed to love,' Josephine said. She moved away from the little group and stood at the rail of the veranda. 'If he stopped scattering his seed any place he could find a willing woman perhaps I would think about having children.'

The dark-skinned maid stepped out of the house, a tray of cordial in her strong hands. She placed the tray on the table and looked at Binnie.

'You need anything else, sir?'

'No, Justine, that's fine, thank you.' Binnie held out a drink to John before realizing that he was staring at the retreating back of the maid.

Justine was a beautiful young girl, her skin glowing with health, her dark eyes filled with laughter. She was good with the boys and unobtrusive around the house but Binnie had never looked at her in the way John was doing.

'You're too late,' he whispered in John's ear. 'Dan has already got his eye on her for that harem of his.'

'So what?' John said quietly. 'These girls are not above a bit of variety, especially when it's with a young, vigorous man.'

Binnie turned away. John sometimes disgusted him with his easy ways. At first, he had believed John to be a gentleman. The way he spoke was cultured, his table manners were impeccable but sometimes, as now, Binnie did not like him very much.

Hortense missed nothing of the exchange. She

was angry but Binnie knew her well enough to understand her silence. Hortense would never hurt her sister by lashing John with her tongue in public.

Josephine was no fool either; she looked at her husband knowingly. 'Fancying that little girl now, are you, John?' She spoke casually, as though nothing about her husband surprised her any longer.

'A man can look, Jo.' John sounded like a small boy caught with his hand in the cookie jar. 'Looking can't do any harm.'

'Putting your dirty thoughts into action can though, can't it?' Josephine sat beside her sister and changed the subject abruptly.

'Your boys are growing like sticks. When I saw them over at Mammy's they were like young gentlemen, so polite and considerate.' She touched her sister's arm. 'You must be so happy, Hortense, so pleased with all you've got. Don't ever let anything or anyone spoil it, you understand?'

Hortense looked puzzled. 'I sure won't, honey, but why should anything spoil what me and Binnie have here?'

'I'm just saying.' Josephine looked up at Binnie and he had the distinct impression she knew more about him than was comfortable. The women fell into desultory chatter about household affairs and John nodded to Binnie.

'Come down to the bar for a drink, I want to talk man-talk to you.' He looked at his wife. 'All this small talk is so boring.'

Binnie had no wish to go with John but

Hortense looked at him meaningfully. 'You go, hon, get away from the house for a while.' He knew she wanted to talk to her sister alone about the way John was treating her.

He sighed and picked up his hat. 'Right, let's just walk down to Maggie's place, it's not far.' The last thing he felt like was indulging John. In any case, he would rather drink in the comfort of his own home than put up with the other man's bad mood. Still, it would be a kindness to get him away from the women at least for a time.

'I've had enough of married life,' John said when they were out of earshot of the women. Binnie looked at him.

'I think I got that message loud and clear, so did the womenfolk.' He spoke in a level tone but anger was beginning to burn in his gut. 'Do you think you're wise showing it so openly? After all, your job, your home, your comfortable existence all rest on keeping Dan's girl happy.'

'Is that what you think about your marriage?' John asked. 'You pretend to care for Hortense because her father provides so well for you?'

'Hey, now don't go pushing me too far!' Binnie said. 'I love my wife and I work hard for her and my kids. Dan gave me a job and I earn every penny I get.'

'And I don't?' John said tersely.

'I'm not saying that.' Binnie told himself to calm down, there was no point in spoiling his day arguing with John when he was in such a foul mood. 'I'm saying be careful, that's all.'

'Like you are?' Something in the way John said the words made Binnie pause in his stride.

'What do you mean by that?'

'Come off it! I know you are living a lie. You're not married to Hortense at all, you are married to some Irish woman back home.'

Binnie's mouth was suddenly dry. 'Rubbish! Who told you that?' Binnie's mind was spinning. John had met up with Joe but the man was not the kind to indulge in malicious gossip.

'No, it wasn't Joe.' John had guessed his thoughts. 'It was one of the servants he had with him. The man knew you, knew, what's her name? Ah yes, Maura, that's it. I might have heard something about the marriage when I was back in Swansea but I never caught on about you until now.'

'Why would this man tell you anything about me?' Binnie asked.

John smiled. 'For a few dollars some people will do anything. Anyway, don't try to pull the wool over my eyes, Binnie, it's too late for that. I knew all along you were hiding something about your past and at last I've put two and two together.' He smiled but there was no humour in his face. 'Don't worry, old man, I won't say anything to spoil the luxury of your life out here though I might want you to cover up for me once in a while.'

'Cover up?'

'Yes, cover up. I've found a woman, someone I'm in love with and I'll need you to lie for me from time to time. As you say, it doesn't do to upset Dan McCabe.'

Binnie doubted John would ever love anyone except himself but at the moment he needed to be discreet, just until he had thought the matter through. Damn John Pendennis! He was trouble for anyone he came in contact with. Binnie pitied the woman John was supposed to love.

The two men continued the journey in silence. Binnie felt he was stuck in a cleft stick: he would have to lie for John because the alternative was too dreadful to think about.

'All right,' he said, though the words almost stuck in his throat. 'I'll cover up for you but I'm warning you, don't push me too far.'

'Or what?' John smiled. 'You've got no choice in the matter, Binnie my man, you are really and truly in the mire!'

In that moment, Binnie Dundee knew what it was like to want to kill with his bare hands. Instead, he glanced at John. 'I suppose there's no harm in you having yet another affair, it will all fizzle out in time.'

'No it won't,' John said. 'The other woman is Melia, Josephine's sister.'

Binnie looked at him aghast. 'Are you mad?'

John did not reply. Binnie frowned. Why on earth would John begin an affair with Melia? He could have married her in the first place if he had wished. But it was nothing to do with him; he had better keep out of it. The less he knew about the affair the better.

All the same, there was a bitter taste in his mouth. His future happiness, the life he treasured with Hortense and his sons could all be ended by one word from John Pendennis. The thought was like the knell of doom and Binnie turned his face away from John, ashamed of the tears that were blinding his eyes.

CHAPTER FOUR

Llinos was missing Joe so badly that she felt she would die of a broken heart if he did not come home soon. She was sitting in the dining room having a late breakfast with Charlotte and attempting to make bright conversation.

'It's a bit warmer today,' Llinos said. 'I think Lloyd will enjoy his walk.'

'Lloyd's gone out then?' Charlotte said, helping herself to more toast. 'I think it's a bit cold myself but my bones are old bones.'

'Nonsense!' Llinos refilled her cup with tea. 'A walk will do Lloyd good, he's indoors too much. Anyway, I suppose Eira finds it educational to show him the old buildings in the town.'

'She's a very careful girl, I'll give her that,' Charlotte said.

'Or else she's got a sweetheart,' Llinos said. 'I think the visit to the park later is not to feed the ducks but to meet up with a young man.'

The door opened and Watt peered round it anxiously. 'Am I too late to share some of that gorgeous smelling bacon?'

Llinos smiled. 'You're quite safe, we haven't eaten it all.'

He sat beside her and frowned in concern. 'You're looking a bit pale, Llinos, are you all right?'

'I'm fine, don't worry about me.' The truth was she felt tired this morning. No, not tired, worried sick about Joe. She longed for him to be back home with her. Until she had him safely in her arms she could not be sure she would ever see him again.

'More to the point, what's wrong with you, Watt?' She could read him like a book and recognized the line between his brows.

'I think you'd better stop Eira taking Lloyd out for walks, at least for a while.' He took a large helping of bacon and eggs; his worry, whatever it was, did not seem to put him off his food.

'Why?'

'You know the people who used to work for Eira's father, well the little girl has caught the whooping cough and it can be dangerous, especially to young children.'

Llinos felt a sharp pang of fear; Eira had been taking goodies to the family on a regular basis and she obviously intended to go visiting the family today.

'Whooping cough! Are you sure, Watt?' Llinos tried to swallow the dryness that was in her throat. She glanced at the clock. It was an hour since Eira had left the house, surely she would not stay out much longer.

'Don't worry,' Watt said. 'I'll try to find her and bring her home.' He rose to his feet, a slice of toast in his hand. 'I won't be long.'

Charlotte shook her head. 'As Watt said, don't worry, Llinos, I'm sure everything is going to be all right. Eira is a sensible girl.'

'I wish Joe was here.' Llinos sighed. 'I need him so much. Did you notice any change in him before he went away, Charlotte?'

'Well, I thought he was a little quiet after losing the baby. But that's nothing unusual, is it? Men grieve in a different way to we women.' Charlotte paused. 'Look, why don't you go and do some work, I'll call you if you're needed.'

'I couldn't work, not worrying about Lloyd as I do. I wish I had never agreed to him going out, as you said yourself, it's very cold today.'

'Well go into the drawing room, design some patterns, occupy your mind, Llinos, that's the best thing to do now.'

Rosie looked in round the door. 'Shall I clear the breakfast things away, Mrs Mainwaring?' she asked quietly.

'All right.' Llinos rose. 'I think everyone's finished now. Thank you, Rosie.' She watched Pearl's daughter neatly stacking dishes onto a tray. She was so pretty, not quite eighteen, small-boned with delicate colouring and features. She was very different from her mother. Pearl was big, robust, full of laughter. Rosie had a more serious side to her nature, a side that Llinos liked. Had her own daughter lived, she might have grown up to be just like Rosie.

'I think I'll go upstairs and read for a bit,' Llinos said. 'You'll be all right, Charlotte?'

'Of course I'll be all right! What do you think I do all day while you're at work? Go on with you, a rest will do you the world of good.'

Llinos kicked off her shoes and lay on the bed, the pillows propped beneath her head. She picked up a book but she could not concentrate on the words before her. She was worried about Lloyd and worried about Joe. Why did her life have to be so complicated?

She must have slept because she opened her eyes to the sound of someone knocking on the bedroom door.

'Mrs Mainwaring, it's me, Rosie.' She looked round the door. 'I've been sent to tell you that Eira's back.'

Llinos sat up at once. 'Where is Eira now?'

'She's upstairs. She was in the hall coughing her heart out and Mrs Marks sent her to bed.'

Llinos hurried down the stairs into the hall and Watt came to the door of the drawing room, Lloyd at his side.

'He's fine.' Watt touched Llinos's arm. 'Look, don't worry, there are a few chills and colds about now, Eira's cough might be nothing.'

Llinos wished again that Joe would come home; if Lloyd should fall sick she would be unable to cope alone. She put her hand on her son's shoulder. 'Did you take goodies to Eira's friends?'

'Yes, Mamma,' Lloyd said. 'They were all sick though so we didn't stay long.'

Llinos took a deep breath. 'We'll keep Eira in her room until we find out for sure what's wrong with her.' Her voice was calm, no-one would suspect her heart was beating swiftly with fear. 'And Watt, get one of the doctors up here, I want Lloyd examined.'

Llinos led Lloyd into the drawing room. 'Are

you feeling all right, Lloyd? Is your chest hurting or anything?'

'No, my chest doesn't hurt, can I go and play?'

Charlotte had followed them into the room; she caught Llinos's eye and nodded. 'Let him be, no point in alarming him is there?'

The doctor arrived within half an hour. He was young, new to the area and Llinos had never met him before. She only hoped he was familiar with the sicknesses that could rage through a small town and decimate half the population in a matter of weeks.

'I'm Peter Stafford.' He handed his hat and coat to the maid. 'Don't be too concerned, Mrs Mainwaring, there may be a serious sickness around but you are well served here for food and clean water.' He smiled deprecatingly. 'Of course, older doctors would think that a nonsense but I feel that cleanliness makes people much healthier and so they are able to fight off the sickness with more vigour.'

'Come into the drawing room, Dr Stafford,' Llinos said. 'Have you had much experience with this sort of illness?'

'If you mean do I know the symptoms of whooping cough, the answer is yes. I think I know something about the cause of such epidemics as well.'

'Oh?' Llinos looked at him, giving him her full attention. 'Then you must be a very clever young man.'

He half smiled and Llinos knew why; he was only a year or two younger than she was.

'The difficulty is that people are still drinking

water from the canal,' he said, rolling up his sleeves. 'The same canal water that men urinate in on their way home from the beer houses.' He looked at her. 'I am too much of a gentleman to describe all the other unclean things that are added daily to the canal. My point is that people gather at the canal. They wash themselves and their utensils in the same water. They huddle there cheek by jowl to wash clothing and to gossip and so the sickness passes from one to the other.'

'Not Eira though,' Llinos said thoughtfully. 'Still, I see you might have a point.' She took a deep breath. 'Now, Doctor, I want everyone in the household checked starting with my son. Then I'd like Eira to be examined. After that perhaps you will see the rest of my staff?'

His eyebrows lifted. 'And you?'

'All in good time,' Llinos said firmly.

'You've set me quite a task, Mrs Mainwaring. Please be sure your maid follows me with a bowl of hot water to wash my hands.'

Llinos was not as surprised as the doctor clearly expected her to be. 'My husband is scrupulously clean; he too believes in the power of soap and water.'

'Your husband is an American Indian gentleman I understand?'

'That is correct,' Llinos said dryly. It was clear that the doctor had been well informed about Llinos and her marriage to a foreigner.

'May I?' He examined Lloyd's chest, peered into his mouth. 'His throat seems a little red but that's nothing to worry about at this stage.' After a few moments, he straightened and smiled at Llinos.

'I think you have a fine healthy son here. Nothing much the matter with him.' Llinos sighed in relief. 'Now, let us look at all the other occupants of Pottery House, shall we?'

Peter Stafford proved to be methodical and thorough. His examinations took the best part of the day.

'I think you are all fit and healthy,' he said. 'All except Miss Eira. I think I had better take a look at her again before I leave.'

Eira's condition had deteriorated over the past few hours, that much was clear even to Llinos's untrained eye.

The doctor washed his hands and took so long about it that Llinos knew something was very wrong. Once outside the door, she looked the doctor in the eye.

'Is it the whooping cough?'

'I am afraid it is,' he said. 'I can only advise that you keep her isolated, give her plenty of water to drink, boiled water, if you please. She is a strong girl, she will probably get over this, given a week or so.'

'Do you think anyone else is going to get sick, Doctor?'

'I don't know.' He followed her downstairs, doing up his shirtsleeves. 'But I will call again tomorrow and check you all again.' At the door, he turned to her. 'Remember, people do survive these sicknesses.'

She watched him walk to his horse and carriage before returning to the drawing room. If only Joe was here, he would cure Eira for certain. He knew more about medicine than any trained doctor.

Watt was waiting for her near the drawing room door. 'I'll look after Eira for you, Llinos,' he said, 'I'm a big strong man and I've never had a day's sickness in my life.'

'I don't know, Watt.' Llinos rubbed her eyes. 'No, that's not going to work, I need you in the pottery. We must bring in a nurse.' She looked up at Watt. 'Any suggestions?'

'Mother Peters would do it.'

'Oh Watt, she's so old now she can hardly walk.'

'Nonsense! In any case, she wouldn't have to walk far, she could sleep in my room. I can sleep on the sofa downstairs, I've done it before.'

'All right.' Llinos rubbed her eyes; she had no better suggestion. 'Go ask her then, see how she feels about it.'

When Watt left, Llinos stared out of the window, her mind full of doubts and fears. From the music room, she could hear Lloyd's stumbling fingers on the pianoforte; his tutor must be giving him a music lesson. It all seemed so normal, surely there was nothing really to worry about?

She tried to calm herself but everything seemed to be piling up on top of her. She must not panic; she must deal with this sickness calmly and sensibly. But was she strong enough to handle it alone?

For a moment she allowed herself to wallow in self-pity. Her life had never been easy, not since the day her father had left Swansea and joined the fight against Bonaparte. Llinos had been left to run the pottery practically single-handedly but she had been strong then. She had been able to deal with all the extra problems of business, the

74

accounts, ordering stock, everything. She had saved the pottery then but where was her strength now?

She returned to her bedroom and sat near the window, staring out at the windswept garden. If only he could walk into the room right now she would have courage to face anything, but the room remained silent.

The sickness spread and, within two weeks, the pottery was running on half strength. Even Pearl, big healthy Pearl, had gone down with the whooping cough. But Llinos was grateful that Eira was on the mend. It seemed the young woman had only a mild dose of the illness and had managed to overcome the worst of it.

So far the rest of the household was unaffected. Lloyd had remained healthy and so had she. Llinos thanked God every day for that. She even prayed to Joe's Great Spirit, feeling she was hedging her bets in a most unworthy way. But she felt that whatever, whoever was out there, they were looking down at her kindly, keeping her little family safe.

She was back at work now, needed in the pottery because of the people off ill. She was looking through Joe's patterns for the firebird china when Watt barged into the small office. Llinos knew at once that something was badly wrong. She rose to her feet, the patterns fanning out on the floor where she dropped them. 'What is it, what's wrong?'

'It's Maura, I've got to go to her, Llinos.' He held up his hand as Llinos made a move towards him. 'No! Please, Llinos, stay away, I don't want you catching anything from me.' He shrugged. 'I should have known better, I've been going from this house to the Morton-Edwards's place not realizing I might carry the sickness with me.'

'Oh, Watt,' Llinos said, 'you can't blame yourself. As Dr Stafford said, none of us knows very much about how this sickness is spread.'

'You don't feel I'm deserting you?'

'You go and look after Maura and go with my blessing. Is Eynon all right?'

'He's fine. He's had Maura taken to his holiday cottage down by the sea. He feels the clean air will be good for her.' He paused. 'He's also worried that Jayne might get the whooping cough and I don't blame him.'

'Are we very selfish people, Watt?' Llinos asked wistfully. 'Worrying about our own, not caring too much so long as they are protected?'

'Now that Maura is sick, I know just how you feel,' he said despondently. 'I would do anything to save her from suffering.'

'Look, Watt, take anything you need from the house. I wish I could do more.'

'Eynon is very good,' Watt said. 'He's having the doctor call on Maura every day; he's brought in a nurse who is used to dealing with this sort of thing.' He hesitated. 'If only Joe was here, he'd save Maura's life, I know he would.'

Llinos felt her eyes mist with tears. 'I wish he was home too.'

Llinos watched from the window as Watt walked towards the stables. He was her right arm; he knew the pottery and loved it as much as she did. How was she going to manage without him?

She looked at her reflection in the glass of the window. She would manage, she would just have to.

'Joe,' she whispered, her breath misting the glass, 'if ever I needed you, it's now.'

'They're dying like flies and there's nothing I can do but offer them the last rites.' Father Martin was seated in Eynon's house staring dejectedly at the rich carpet under his feet.

Eynon touched his friend's arm. 'Look, Martin, you are doing everything you can. Stay a while, share some food and wine with me, it will make you feel better.'

Martin shook his head. 'I'm a vicar of this parish, I have a job to do and it's not about me feeling better.' He looked up briefly. 'If only our old vicar was still alive, he would tell me the things I should be saying, the words of comfort folk expect from a man of the cloth. I'm useless at it, Eynon.'

'No you are not!' Eynon said. 'I hear all around me of your courage, the way you go into houses where most of the family has died of the sickness. You are a man, Martin, not a god, you can only do your best and that is what you are doing.'

'Do you think so?' Martin looked at him hopefully. 'Do you really think I'm acquitting myself well?'

'I most certainly do. Now come on, have something to eat, I insist.'

'I dare not,' Martin said flatly. 'I have closed the eyes of the dead and I will not risk Jayne's health by sitting at the same table as her.' He smiled with a semblance of his old warmth. Even now he looked like an overgrown baby. His cheeks were pink and unlined; his hands dimpled like those of a child. It was only the lines around his eyes that gave away the strain he was under.

'I know what you could do, though,' he said, 'you could bring some food and wine out into the conservatory; it's too cold for a child at this time of year.'

'Good idea!' Eynon said. 'I'll do that.'

It was in a companionable silence that they ate their meal of cold ham and cheese and fresh baked bread warm from the oven. The butter had been churned early in the morning and drops of water slid from the yellow mound like tiny tears.

'Lovely salt butter,' Martin said appreciatively. 'But then, I always did enjoy your hospitality, Eynon.' He paused, a mouthful of bread lodged in the side of his cheek making him look even plumper. 'You are a good friend, Eynon, the best friend any man could want. If anything should happen to me, well, I just want you to know that I appreciate your loyalty and your support all these years.'

Eynon stared at him. 'You are not going to leave me your worldly wealth then?' he joked. 'Listen to me, Martin, you are not going to die of the whooping cough, I won't have it!'

'I think it's up to Him.' Martin pointed at the clouds. 'The man upstairs decides when it's time for me to go.'

Eynon rested his hand on Martin's arm. 'Right then, if we're going to be maudlin, I'll tell you that you are the closest thing to a brother any man could have. I won't do without you, you must survive, do you understand?'

Martin nodded and the two men sat in silence for a while. Martin ate no more of the crusty bread and the salt butter of which he was so fond. At last, he rose to his feet.

'I've got to go,' he said. 'I've other friends to visit.' He held out his hand but Eynon ignored it and pulled Martin close to him.

'You keep yourself safe, do you hear me?'

'I hear you.' As Martin walked away, his shoulders were bent. He was a man still in his twenties but he seemed aged by the sickness that had rampaged its way through the town. Eynon stared around him at the grassy garden beyond the glass of the conservatory, at the trees in the garden and the clouds hanging low in the sky.

'Dear God,' he said, 'if there is any justice you will bring Martin through this safe and well.'

He sighed heavily. 'I'm getting as daft as Martin, what God is going to listen to a sinner like me?'

Maura's eyes were bright with fever. She felt as though her head were filled with wool. She was aware that someone was bathing her face with tepid water, it felt good. She opened her eyes for a moment. Old Mother Peters was moving quietly about the room though it was clear that her limbs were gnarled with the bone ache. Her face was wizened but she was gentle, her ministrations welcome.

Maura was too tired to keep awake; she was

finding it difficult to breathe. Mother Peters placed a hot cloth with some sort of paste over her chest and back. It eased the congestion a little but then Maura began to cough. She was racked, her body ached, her head was bursting. Folk were doing their best for her but Maura knew that nothing would stop the pain.

She heard the door open but she was too weary to look up. She felt a movement at the side of the bed and opened her eyes with an effort. Watt took her hand, looking down at her with such love that, if she had the energy, she would have cried.

'Maura, you're looking a little bit better today.' He brushed his hand across her forehead. She tried to smile even though she knew he was fooling himself. Poor Watt, he had found love and now he was about to lose it again.

He raised her hand to his lips and kissed her fingers. She wanted to tell him to go away, to keep himself safe but she could not find the energy to speak.

'If only Joe was here,' Watt was saying. 'He is so wise, he would know how to cure this sickness.'

Perhaps, Maura thought, but then Joe was well out of it, away across the sea in America. America, she tried to imagine it, the place of sunshine and riches, so she had heard, the place where her lawful husband now lived unlawfully with another woman, calling her wife. What would Binnie Dundee think of Maura's death? He would be happy of course, released from the marriage vows he had held so lightly. Strange, she no longer felt bitterness towards him. She had lost her husband but she had found Watt. Together they had loved more in their short time together than most people love in a lifetime.

She struggled to talk. 'When I'm . . .' She paused for breath. 'Let Binnie know but don't upset things for him.' She began to cough. Watt held her upright as the coughing racked her. She felt as though her lungs were going to collapse but there were things she still needed to say.

'Don't talk,' Watt said pitifully. 'Please, Maura my love, save your strength.'

'Just don't spoil things for Binnie,' she said. 'You'll know how to tell him.' She sank back on the pillows; the room was growing dark. She reached for Watt's hand.

'Shall I fetch a priest, Maura?' He was crying, and she wished she could comfort him but she had no strength. She nodded her head and Watt moved to the window.

He called to the children in the street to fetch one of the fathers from St Joseph's. 'I'll give a sixpence to the one who can run the fastest,' he called.

He returned to the bedside and touched her face with his fingertips. It was so gentle, like the touch of a butterfly's wing.

'I love you, Watt,' she croaked. 'I'll love you always.'

She lapsed into unconsciousness and was awakened by the sound of the priest intoning the last rites. Her soul would go to God now; she would not rot in purgatory. She felt rather than heard the sound of the priest's voice recede. She was being drawn into the light where there was no cough to rack her body and no pain. And she was ready to go.

The funeral of Maura Dundee took place a week later. It was Watt who paid for the coffin maker and the gravedigger. The day was absurdly sunny, the sky above the cemetery cloudless even though the ground was covered in frost.

Watt looked down into the darkness of the earth and knew his life would never be the same again. The only other mourners were Eynon Morton-Edwards and Llinos Mainwaring. A few onlookers stood far enough away not to risk catching anything from the people at the graveside.

If Watt had raised his head, he would have seen that they were not the only ones burying their dead that day. One family carried nothing but a battered wooden door with a cloth-covered body on it. The coffin maker had been excessively busy and, in any case, good wooden caskets cost more money than most people could spare especially when there was likely to be more than one death in the family.

Eventually, the ordeal was over. Watt felt Llinos take his arm and draw him away from the fresh mound of earth. He looked beyond the grave, wanting everything to go away, wanting Maura to be alive.

'I'm alone.' He was not aware he had spoken the words out loud. Llinos hugged his arm to her side.

'No, you're not alone, Watt, you will always have me at your side.' She spoke with confidence, as though she knew the sickness could not reach her. He straightened his shoulders and walked with the small group away from the grave and away from the woman he had loved with all his heart.

It was several weeks later when Watt remembered Maura's dying request. He sat in his room, vacated now because Eira had made a complete recovery. For an instant, he longed to damn Eira to hell. Why should Maura die and Eira live? It just was not fair. He drew pen and paper towards him, he needed to couch his letter very carefully; Maura had made it plain that she wanted no trouble for Binnie.

He thought long and hard and in the end penned a short note telling Binnie that he, Watt, had lost the only woman he had ever really loved. That Maura was now laid in the cemetery up on the hill above Swansea. As he sealed it down, he knew that for Binnie this would be good news: he was a free man. As for Watt, he felt as though he was in prison and that he would never be free, ever again.

It was early one morning when Llinos heard the rumble of carriage wheels in the drive. She ran to the window, her heart fluttering like a trapped bird. Joe had come home.

She watched him alight from the carriage with tears in her eyes. He was even more bronzed now; his golden skin tanned a deeper gold by the hot American sun. She saw the worried look on his face; he knew, as he always knew, that there was trouble at home.

Llinos flung open the door and rushed out to meet him. He held her tenderly in his arms, careless of apprentices watching open-mouthed.

'Swansea is silent,' he said, 'the streets deserted. Is it the plague?' He held his arm around her as they walked together into the house.

'It's the whooping cough.' Llinos looked up at him, he was here, Joe was actually at her side, he was safe and he was home.

'Lloyd, is he well?'

Llinos smiled, though worry etched lines around her eyes.

'He's safe and well; so is Charlotte. Come inside, Joe, it's so cold out here.'

She rang for the maid; she wanted Joe to see his son, to see how Lloyd had grown in the time his father had been away.

Joe's face lit up when Lloyd ran into his arms, clinging to him as though he would never let him go.

'Rosie, fetch Mrs Marks, she's resting in her room, tell her that her brother is home.' She held onto Joe's arm. 'Now you are here everything will be all right, I just know it,' Llinos said softly. She was reluctant to move from her husband's side. All she wanted to do was to stay in Joe's arms for ever.

Charlotte cried out in delight when she saw Joe. She sat next to him on the deep sofa, her arm in his. 'I was so sorry to hear about your mother, Joe. I understand Mint was a remarkable woman.'

Lloyd was sitting cross-legged on the floor, watching them both. 'Grandmother Mint is dead. Are you sad, Daddy?'

'Yes, I am sad, Lloyd.' He ruffled his son's hair. 'I'm sad that you will never meet her.'

'Well, there's really no need to be too sad about that,' Lloyd said sagely. 'We still have Granny Charlotte. She's old but she will love us forever, she said so.'

'I expect she will.' Joe made a wry face at Charlotte. 'And she's not that old, you know.'

'And my other grandmother will look down from the clouds like a bright star to keep us safe, won't she?'

Lloyd looked up, peering doubtfully through the window. The clouds were dark now, racing across the sky. Soon, the heavens would open and the rain would tumble down into the garden. Lloyd moved closer to the window and pressed his face against the glass. After a few moments, sure enough, the rain came.

He sometimes wondered how he knew such things. He knew when the cuckoo was coming to put her baby in another bird's nest. He knew when the squirrels were going to come out in search of food.

'Why do I know things, Daddy?' he asked.

Joe did not need to ask what he meant; he answered as simply as he could.

'Some of us are born with keen senses, son. We are tuned into nature in the way that some people have an ear for music.'

'Doesn't everyone have keen senses, then?'

Joe shook his head. 'No, not everyone. We are gifted and very fortunate people and we must be kind to those less fortunate than we are.'

He turned to Llinos. 'Lord, I sound so pompous!' He caught her hand and kissed it. 'Is that what fatherhood does to a young man, turn him into an old preacher before his time?'

Later, when Lloyd and finally Charlotte had gone to bed, Llinos pressed herself into Joe's arms, her head against his heart. She listened to it beating, regular, strong.

After a moment, he held her away from him and crossed to the table to pour himself a glass of porter. Llinos frowned, wondering why he was not as eager as she was.

'Maura?' Joe said. 'She died of the sickness?'

Llinos nodded. 'She just faded away like a flower, Watt said. He would not let me go near her because of the danger but Watt and Eynon saw that everything was taken care of. Maura just could not fight the sickness.'

She moved closer to Joe. 'I don't know what to say to Watt. How can I comfort him when the woman he loved so much is gone from him forever?'

'You can't,' Joe said. 'He will have to come to terms with his loss in his own way. I'm going to bed,' he said. 'I've decided to sleep in the dressing room just for a while.' He refilled his glass. 'I'll take this with me.'

'But, Joe, why?' Llinos could not believe what she was hearing. Joe had been away for so long and now he did not want to share her bed. 'Something is wrong, isn't it?'

'We'll talk in the morning,' Joe said and then the door was closing behind him, shutting Llinos out of his life.

CHAPTER FIVE

Lily had settled into a routine that she thought suited her very well. She did a bit of sewing for James Wesley and turned her hand to cooking meals more suitable for a man. She had learned to cook meat pies running with rich gravy and delicious stews made tasty with herbs from the garden. But now, somehow it all seemed too tame for her, she wanted more, she wanted James to notice her as a woman. She did not fail to see the irony of her thoughts: she was Lily, the girl who shied away from physical intimacy with a man, and here she was longing for attention. She must be losing her mind. Or was she falling in love?

'Excuse me, miss.' The maid stood in the doorway and Lily gestured for her to come forward. It never ceased to thrill her that she had a servant to do the menial work; no scrubbing floors or washing up dirty pans for Lily. It was James who paid the girl but, all the same, Lily enjoyed playing the lady of the house.

'Yes, Betty, what is it?'

'It's the butcher, miss, he wants paying, he says his bill is overdue.'

'Then tell Mr Wesley, he'll pay the man.' James seemed to be a man of means; he would soon sort the matter of a measly overdue bill.

'I can't miss, he's gone out.'

Lily sighed. 'I won't be a minute.' She hurried upstairs to her bedroom and took her bag out of the cupboard. She still had some money from her husband's savings, money he had stored in an old tin. It was not much, it would not keep her in any sort of luxury and she begrudged paying the butcher out of her own little hoard.

She gave the maid some coins. 'Tell him if that's not enough, he'll have to come back when Mr Wesley is in.'

The maid returned after a few moments, she seemed agitated. 'He won't go away, miss, he says there's more money owing, much more.'

'We'll see.' Lily marched to the door, her colour high. 'Well, Stan Fellows, what's this then, think I'm going to run away for a few joints of meat, do you?'

The man looked at her with a smug grin. 'No, you can't run away, can you?' He laughed showing white, even teeth. He was a very handsome man but he was just not Lily's type. Was any man her type? she wondered.

'What do you mean I can't run away? Do you think I'm a prisoner here then?' she demanded. 'This is my home, the home my husband brought me to as a bride.'

'Ah but now you don't have a husband and no money, do you? Living in sin, so folks say.'

88

'Rubbish!' Lily stared at him. 'I am doing no such thing. Mr Wesley and I have separate rooms and we are well chaperoned by Betty.' She wondered why she was bothering to explain this to an ignorant tradesman.

'Aw, go on, pull the other one!' Stan said. 'But I'm broad-minded, see.' He put his arm around her shoulder in a gesture of familiarity that offended her. He smelled of stale meat and Lily was repulsed. 'If you give me a bit of what you gives him, I'll forget the rest of the bill.'

'How dare you. Go away!' She slammed the door and leaned against it trembling with anger. So the whole village thought she was living in sin, did they? She was suddenly annoyed with James; he should not put her in such an embarrassing position.

She stared through the window, watching the butcher walk away, his basket swinging on his arm. Just then, James came into view, striding purposefully towards the cottage. He was frowning; he did not seem in a very good mood. Perhaps she had better let the incident with the tradesman pass without mention. But on reflection, why should he get away with neglecting to pay his bills?

When he entered the room a few moments later, she stared up at him, her eyes steely. She faced him, her hands clasped together, wondering where to start.

'I have been insulted by a common butcher!' she said as James walked past her and sank into a chair. 'You owe him money, he's complaining that his bills haven't been paid.'

James looked up at her, his eyebrows raised.

'What am I, your own private bank?' He leaned forward and lifted the small brass bell to summon the maid. 'I have no money, you silly girl, why do you think I'm living here?'

'Ah, Betty, some hot cordial if you please. And you, Lily, sit down. Lily, I think it's time we had a talk.'

Lily obeyed him, she had never heard such a note of command in his voice before. She was trembling. What could he have to say that was so important?

'Lily, I am going to have to do some entertaining.'

She was bewildered by the triviality of his words. 'Entertaining, when you can't even pay the butcher. Isn't that a bit silly, James?'

'No, you don't understand. I have some friends, colleagues if you like, who are travelling men. They get lonely for a little bit of home comfort, you know what I mean?' He arched his eyebrows.

'Of course I know what you mean,' Lily snapped. 'They want some good home cooking and a bed for the night, that's what you mean, isn't it?'

'Good!' he seemed relieved. 'I thought you'd be angry because I'm penniless. That you wouldn't want to help me to make some money.'

'Well, I was misled, James, I understood you were comfortably placed.'

'Well, I'm not. Sorry. But together we can make a go of this plan of mine. You will help me then?'

'Of course. How many guests do you want me to cater for?'

He paused. 'Well, I think just one or two for a

start, don't you?' He smiled. 'I don't want to overwork you.' He stared at her with his strange eyes. 'They will pay well, Lily, we will make a packet, you and me. Then', he gestured expansively, 'we can be together always, wouldn't that be fine?'

'Oh, you won't overwork me, don't worry!' Lily said. 'I'll make sure of that. When can we expect these men, these colleagues?' She wanted to ask him about paying the butcher; if she was to cook fine meals she needed meat, but she held her tongue waiting for him to speak.

'Is tomorrow night too soon?'

'Well, no.' Lily thought quickly, there was some mutton in the cold pantry and mint in the garden. There was some beef waiting to be cooked; it was a small joint but supplemented with vegetables she could probably rustle up a meal for four.

'Good.' He rose to his feet and took her hands in his. 'Now go and sort out a pretty dress to wear to charm my friends. I like the one with the rose-sprigged muslin, it shows your fine figure off to great advantage.'

It did; her breasts jutted out of the bodice a little bit too far in Lily's opinion. But then she was flattered that James had noticed her at all. 'All right, if you think it will suit,' she said doubtfully. She would have to get the meal started and leave Betty to see to the final touches, otherwise Lily would arrive in the tiny dining room red from the heat of the fire.

It was late when Lily became aware of someone entering her bedroom. She sat up in alarm and saw James, holding a candle above his head. She could smell the porter on him and knew by the look on his face exactly what he wanted of her. He put down the candle and slid into bed and Lily stared at him, at a loss. Should she scream and push him out of her bed? Should she climb out herself and share Betty's room?

James put his arm around her. 'My lovely little Lily flower, do you know how much I want you, my darling?' He kissed her mouth and she tasted the ale on him. It was sweet and Lily felt herself relaxing. 'I've tried to fight it, Lily, I have no right to taste your sweetness when I have nothing to offer you except a roof over your head.'

She was flattered in spite of herself. 'Shouldn't we wait until we're married?' She felt it only proper to protest.

'We'll be married soon, my darling, no-one will know about this except me and you, will they?'

Lily had expected this after all; it was what all men wanted. His hair fell in soft curls against her cheek as he bent to kiss her neck and she felt a sort of tenderness for him that she had never felt for anyone before. He was like a little boy reaching out for the sweet jar.

'I need you, Lily, I want to make love to you. Please let me,' he whispered hoarsely, his hands pushed at her nightgown. With a sense of resignation, she slipped it off. 'And then, Lily, when we have made enough money out of my friends, we will have the finest wedding in all the land.'

'Yes, James.' She felt breathless as he pressed closer to her. It could not be wrong; James had said they would be together always and now he had told her he wanted to marry her. It did not matter that he was not as rich as she had first thought, they would make money with his scheme. Eventually perhaps they could buy a larger property and start up a real boarding house.

He heaved above her and she held her breath; she had never liked it, the way a man could take her and possess her body. It had always seemed like a violation to Lily but it was what men did and she just had to put up with it if she wanted the protection of a man. And yet somehow as she felt him close, his skin soft, the scent of him sweet, she felt a kindling of something that might be the stirrings of desire. Perhaps James was the man she had always needed to waken her passions. Slowly, her arms crept around his neck. She closed her eyes and held him close. He was wonderful, her love, she would never let him go.

All too soon, he flopped back on the bed beside her, his chest heaving. She had experienced three men: Saul, her first lover, her husband, an old man, and now James. James was different; with James she had found real love.

Lily thought of Polly, her old friend who she had not seen for a long time, the friend she had left behind in Swansea. Polly had liked lying with a man, had revelled in it, said she needed it like she needed water, to live. But to Lily the act

93

had always been a tiresome chore to be got over as quickly as possible. But not now. Now she felt warm and cherished, aroused for the first time in her life.

She felt James slip his hand along her stomach and tensed with excitement. He took her the second time with a gentleness that moved her. She cried a few tears as he whispered sweet words to her. He caught her nipple in his mouth and she tangled her fingers in the softness of his hair.

When he fell away from her she sighed with pleasure. James was kind and gentle and his touch pleased her.

He fell asleep almost immediately; in that he was no different from any other man. He lay beside her breathing evenly and, after a while, Lily curved into him enjoying the warmth of his body and, eventually, she too slept.

When she woke, James was gone. Betty was in the kitchen, her eyes downcast. 'The master's gone out,' she said unnecessarily. 'He's gone somewhere on business. I don't know where.'

'Why should you know where?' Lily demanded. 'The whereabouts of Mr Wesley has nothing at all to do with you, do you understand?'

'Yes, miss.' Betty glanced up at last and there seemed to be something like pity in her pale eyes. 'Want some hot milk, miss?'

Lily sank down at the kitchen table. 'I'll have some tea,' she said. The tea in the box was almost gone; it was an expensive item and one they might not be able to afford much longer. Still, it was as much her tea as James's and if she wanted it she would have it.

After breakfast, Lily asked Betty to boil up water for a bath. She felt unclean, as though she still had the smell of James about her.

Tonight, she would tell him in no uncertain terms that there would be no more creeping into her bed until they were safely married. He would respect her much more if she showed a proper modesty. While she soaped herself and let the hot water run over her body, she wondered if James would teach her to find fulfilment in lovemaking. She closed her eyes for a moment, wanting only to rest. But she had a meal to prepare, the table to set, wine to decant and, then, she would need to make herself look pleasant and charming to greet James's paying guests. With a sigh, she climbed out of the bath and began to dry herself.

Llinos watched as Joe talked with his son. They sat together and conversed like old men.

'The whooping cough is gone now, Father. Soon Eira will be able to take me out walking again. You can come with us if you like.' He sounded like a wise old sage and Llinos tugged at his hair and laughed.

'Your grandad will never be dead while you are alive, do you know that, Lloyd? When I named you after him I couldn't have chosen better. You are the spitting image of him.'

'I know, Mamma,' he said, 'you've told me that before, remember?' He looked out of the window. 'What time is Uncle Eynon coming over? I'm starving.'

'When are you ever any different?' Llinos

said. 'And for your information when Eynon does arrive he'll have Jayne with him, so on your best behaviour please.'

'Oh no!' Lloyd had the small boy's antipathy to little girls. That would change when he was older Llinos thought, watching him lovingly.

'Here he is!' Lloyd said excitedly. 'Can I go to meet him, Father?'

Joe looked at Llinos and shrugged. 'I suppose so though we all know you're after the gifts Uncle Eynon insists on bringing you, you little scamp.'

Eynon brought the coldness of the outdoors into the sitting room with him. He smiled at Joe and kissed Llinos lightly on both cheeks. He handed Lloyd a well-wrapped parcel and then gave Llinos a tiny box. 'For my best girl,' he said.

'You're very kind, Eynon. Where's Jayne? She's not sick is she?'

'No, she's not sick, thank God,' Eynon said. 'She's gone out with Mrs Sparks today, the dear lady has no children of her own and she took Jayne for company when she went shopping. She intends to bring her back to me later tonight.'

He spoke innocently but Llinos could tell by the gleam in his eyes that he was holding back a grin.

She unwrapped her gift; it was a jewel box painted with birds and flowers.

'It's lovely, Eynon! Thank you.' She kissed his cheek. 'And how is Mrs Sparks and that dear husband of hers?' Without waiting for an answer

Llinos spoke again. 'I still can't get over Mr Sparks's cheek in deciding I should sell the pottery.' She shook her head. 'The man is an arrogant fool.'

'I wonder where he got the idea you were going to sell?' Eynon said. 'I imagine someone with influence offered him a reward if he could persuade you to part with your business. That's the sort of man he is, always eager to take a bribe.'

'You could be right, he was so angry when I told him I had no intention of selling. I don't know the man very well and I wouldn't care to know him better!'

'I think Mrs Sparks shares your dislike of the man,' Eynon said quietly, glancing at Lloyd who had opened his parcel and was pulling the strings, quite efficiently, of the marionette Eynon had bought him.

'Then it's lucky she enjoys your company so very much,' Llinos said dryly. 'But, as I said, beware of that man, he may not be as much of a chicken heart as he looks.'

'Hey, you two!' Joe said. 'Stop gossiping! And you, Lloyd, isn't it time you were getting ready for bed?'

Later when Lloyd had left them, the conversation became desultory, not to say a little strained. And Llinos could not think why. She was relieved when the bell rang to announce that dinner was served.

They dined on a simple meal of rabbit pie, crusty bread and roast potatoes followed by a treacle pudding.

'That was wonderful,' Eynon said. 'My friend Martin would give his eye teeth to eat a meal like that.'

'How is Martin?' Llinos asked. 'I've heard a great deal about how brave he was visiting the sick.'

'It's true, I'm proud of him,' Eynon said. 'I don't think I could have done so well had I been in his shoes.'

Llinos got to her feet. 'Let's go into the drawing room, shall we?'

She was content to listen to the two men talk and she sank back in her chair, closing her eyes. Joe did not seem like his old self, he had changed since he came back from America. But then he had lost his mother; it had been a sad time for him. Perhaps she should just count her blessings and be happy because Joe was here, in Britain, in Pottery House, sitting only a few feet away from her.

The two men James brought to the house were well dressed and well mannered. By the look of their clothes, both were very wealthy. Lily took in the good cut of coat and trousers and the strong leather boots and smiled her most charming smile.

'This is Lily,' James said. 'Lily, meet Conrad and Clifford.' He put his hand on Lily's shoulder and his fingers were warm on her skin. She felt exposed in her low-cut gown and saw that the eyes of both men were drawn to the shadow between her breasts.

'We do not stand on ceremony here,' James was

saying as he led the way into the small dining room. 'Please, gentlemen, make yourselves at home.'

Betty carried in the tureen and ladled mutton broth into bowls. The smell rose invitingly and the two men began to eat with relish, Conrad dipping his bread into his bowl and sucking at it eagerly.

'You are an excellent cook, Lily,' Conrad said, soup dribbling unchecked down his chin. Lily averted her eyes.

'Thank you, Conrad, but I did have a little help.'

'Don't listen to her!' James said. 'She is the finest cook a man could ever wish to meet and quite a game little filly into the bargain.'

The men laughed and Lily felt uncomfortable. She glared at James, angry with him for being so crude especially in earshot of such fine gentlemen. Her eyes were drawn to the gold ring set with a large diamond that sparkled on Clifford's thin fingers. He was the smaller of the two men, his face a little gaunt to be called handsome but he had deep blue eyes that met Lily's whenever she glanced at him.

Conrad on the other hand was well built, his breeches stretched over his round stomach. He had a red, rather jolly face and a ready smile. Of the two of them, she preferred Conrad. Not that she needed to like either of the men, they were being entertained to supper, given a bed for the night and then, presumably, they would be off on their travels in the morning.

The beef was served and it sizzled with heat on the platter. Whole onions surrounded the joint and small roast potatoes and a garnish of herbs offset the smallness of the joint, the smell making the mouth water.

The wine flowed freely and Lily wondered how much the men were paying. It would have to be a great deal to cover the expense of the meat and the drink.

The pudding was steamed to perfection, the honey running over the sides melting into a golden glow.

'You have fallen on your feet with this little lady,' Conrad said, wiping his mouth on the napkin. Lily groaned inwardly; there would be a great deal of boiling of table linen tomorrow but, then, Betty could see to all that.

When the debris of the meal lay spread about the table, James replenished the wine glasses yet again and nodded in Lily's direction.

'Go along, Lily, we gentlemen wish to smoke, remember your manners now.' He slid an arm around her waist as, embarrassed at his tone, she rose abruptly. His hand tightened as she would have wriggled free.

He ran his other hand along her hip and let it rest for a moment on the curve of her buttocks. 'Go along then.' He released his grip. 'Go upstairs, I'll come to you when I need you.'

As Lily went into the bedroom, she wondered at James's parting words. What did he mean about needing her? Was he letting her know in advance that he wanted to come to her bed again? She sighed inwardly; she had wanted to hold him at bay, to make him more eager for marriage. But if entertaining was James's only idea of making money, they could never afford to get married; she felt they would make little or no profit out of his scheme. She had been well looked after by her late husband and had grown accustomed to depending on him for everything. James however seemed to have no head for business at all.

She was practically asleep when she heard the sound of ribald laughter from the hallway. Heavy feet stomped up the stairs and Lily held her breath, expecting James to come into her room at any moment. She was not mistaken.

'Ah, Lily, let's get some more light in here.' He lit the candles he had carried upstairs and, behind him, Conrad and Clifford stared at her as if she were another delicious morsel to be picked up and eaten. Lily drew the covers up to her chin.

The men crowded into the small room and Lily stared at them, waiting for James to bid them goodnight. He did no such thing.

'You see, gentlemen, she is as beautiful in bed as I promised you she would be.' He turned to wave his hand expansively. 'She is a lovely mistress, I can vouch for that. Now, which one of you gentlemen will go first?'

Lily stared at James in horror. She saw all too clearly now how he intended to make his money. He wanted to sell her to whatever man would pay for her. She felt an overwhelming sense of disappointment that was quickly followed by a rush of anger. How dare he treat her like a whore? But she must keep her temper; she realized she would have to think fast. She would never have the strength to fight the men off; she would have to use cunning if she was to get out of this situation with her pride intact.

'I'm sorry, James, I can't accommodate you tonight,' she said gloomily. 'My curses have come and I am in so much pain and discomfort that I dare not even move an inch. No-one would wish to share a bed with me now, you understand?'

'Hell and damnation, James, this is a fine kettle of fish,' Conrad said.

James hesitated and for a moment Lily thought he would tear aside the sheets. Bile rose to her throat but she forced herself to speak. 'Oh good heavens here come the pains again and the flooding. I am going to be in a dreadful state by morning.'

'We'll go to the village,' James said. 'All is not lost, gentlemen, I know some very willing ladies who will not be indisposed.' He glared at Lily before leaving the room and she lay quite still until the house fell silent.

Carefully she edged out of bed and dressed in her warmest clothes. Swiftly, in the light of the dying candles, she pushed her few possessions into a bag.

Her heart was in her mouth as she crept into the bedroom where the two guests had left their travelling bags. Silently, she took all the money she could find and pushed it into her bag.

Downstairs, Betty was sitting in the kitchen. 'Oh God, miss, I thought they had killed you!' she gasped. 'I hid in the garden until they went away. I knew what they was after, see.'

'Come on,' Lily said, 'we'd better get out of here as quickly as we can.'

Outside the cottage, Lily took stock of the situation. The two men had arrived in an open carriage but Lily doubted that she and Betty could harness the horses without any help.

'We'll ride,' she whispered. 'Get the saddles, Betty.'

Guiding the horses over the grasslands leading from the house, Lily held her breath as though afraid, even now, that James would catch her and drag her back to the cottage that had once been her home. She would never forgive him for what he had tried to do tonight.

She glanced back and saw the glow of flames rising from the roof of the cottage. 'The place is on fire!' she said.

'I did it, miss,' Betty said. 'That place belonged to old Tom, not to that young upstart. Why should we leave it all for him to live in?'

'Well done, Betty!' Lily said jubilantly. 'Now James will have nothing at all.'

Once away from the house, the two women began to ride swiftly. Betty brought her horse as close as she dared to the mount Lily was riding.

'We'll be branded thieves for this, you know that don't you?' she said breathlessly.

'I don't think so!' Lily shouted over the beat of hooves. 'Those fine gentlemen probably have wives. We could do them more harm than they could ever do us. Forget them, Betty, we're free.'

Although her body felt on fire and her head ached as though a hammer beat inside it, Lily was exultant. She had money in her pocket and she was going home.

CHAPTER SIX

Binnie read the letter for the umpteenth time, a mixture of feelings warring within him. His first reaction when the letter from Watt had arrived was one of profound relief. Then he realized that Maura, his wife, the mother of his child, who was still a young woman, was dead and a dreadful feeling of guilt flooded over him.

He had loved Maura once, when they had both been young and eager for life. Maura with her red-gold hair and her lovely smile had roused such feelings in him, feelings that vanished once they were married.

He turned to the letter again. It was tactful in the extreme. Watt had chosen his words carefully, not giving away anything that would incriminate Binnie. And yet Watt's own pain was plain for anyone to read.

'What's wrong, hon?' Hortense asked, looking over the breakfast table at him. 'You've been clutching that letter for ages, is it bad news?'

He swallowed hard. 'Yes, it is, a friend, an old friend of mine has died.' He looked down at his hands feeling like a Judas. He hated lying to his wife. But then Hortense was not his wife, not in the eyes of the church or the law at any rate. A thought struck him, that was something he could put right now, if only he could find a way.

'Remember Watt who came out here with John? Well his,' he hesitated, 'his wife died of the whooping cough. It seems the sickness has been running through the town like wildfire. Thank God we are out of it, my love, safe in America.'

'We get sicknesses here, too, honey,' Hortense said softly. 'No-one is ever sure what life can bring.'

'I know but this is a warm country, the sun shines more than it ever does back home.' He smiled. 'Here we don't have the dark, wet, miserable days I knew when I was a child.'

'Instead we have wild storms, great winds and fires that can run for days.' Hortense touched his cheek affectionately. 'You see America with rose-coloured glasses, Binnie.'

'Perhaps because everything I love is here,' Binnie said softly. 'I have you and the boys, you are all so precious to me. I've even come to think of Dan as the father I never had.'

He could not say the same about Mrs McCabe; she had never made him feel part of the family. The old lady loved the boys and respected Binnie for being a good worker but Binnie always felt she had reservations about him. It was almost as if she knew he had a secret past.

'By the way,' Hortense said, 'John's brought Jo into town.' She smiled. 'My sister is visiting with Mamma and Daddy, so Jo and me can have some real woman gossip. I'll enjoy that after having a stuffy old man like you around me all hours of the day.'

She was teasing and they both knew it but Binnie's heart sank. He liked it when John was safely up country supervising some of the other potteries Dan owned. Binnie rose from the table. 'I'd better do some work, I've got to check one of the kilns, I think there's a breach in the brickwork somewhere, the pots are not firing well.'

He kissed Hortense on the mouth; she tasted of honey and pancakes and he loved her so much he thought his heart would break whenever he looked into her eyes.

'Don't work too hard, Binnie.' She smiled the seductive smile that sent his pulses racing. 'You'll need some of your energy when you come home.'

He left her with a smile on his face and a lightness in his step, he was one lucky man to have a woman like Hortense at his side. Now, with Watt's letter tucked safely into his pocket, he could begin to feel more secure.

It was early evening when Binnie returned home. He bathed in the tub at the back of the house, cleaning the dust and clay from his hands. Above him, he could see the sky and he smiled. It was strange bathing in a shed with no roof.

Dressed in fresh clothes and with a glass of good whisky inside him, he sat down at the table to eat supper with his family. This was the life, the life he would do anything to preserve. The letter was burnt now but the words Watt had written continued to comfort him.

He was just finishing the delicious dish of roast

meat and potatoes cooked specially the way he liked it when his happiness faded.

The maid bobbed into the room and behind her was John, dressed for an evening out and Binnie's heart sank.

'You haven't forgotten you were coming out to do a bit of business with me, have you, Binnie?' John was all smiles, he looked big and sunburned and very handsome. Hortense welcomed him coolly. She was nobody's fool, Binnie thought with a pang of alarm.

'We had hoped for a quiet night in tonight, John,' she said. 'Can't this business wait until tomorrow?'

'Sorry.' John smiled charmingly but Hortense's gaze remained fixed. Hastily, Binnie put down his napkin.

'Sorry, love,' he kissed Hortense. 'I won't be too long and that's a promise.' He hustled John out of the house and began to walk rapidly towards the centre of town. He was angry, very angry. John was pushing his luck.

'What's wrong?' John asked. 'Little wifey wanted to take you to bed, did she? Oh, I forgot, she's not your wife, is she?'

Binnie turned on him, his shoulders tense. 'This is not going to work,' he said, the words forced through clenched teeth. 'Make this the last time you use me to cover up your tracks, do you understand?' He glared at John, ashamed that he had agreed to help the man in the first place.

'Hey, don't be so hasty, pal,' John said. 'I'm sorry, if I'd known you'd be so upset I wouldn't have asked you.' He shrugged. 'What I'm doing isn't so wrong, what married man doesn't get into these little flings; tell me that?' His words were barbed and Binnie knew it.

'Well I think you're playing with fire. In a small town like West Troy where everyone knows what undervest you're wearing before you do, you are bound to be found out sooner or later.'

'You haven't been found out.'

'Haven't I?'

'Well,' John smiled, 'only by me and I don't count, really, do I? It's man to man stuff that women just don't understand.'

Binnie looked at him steadily. 'Don't you love Josephine too much to play around and with her sister at that?'

John looked uncomfortable but only for a moment. 'Were you in love with the woman you married back home?'

'No, as a matter of fact I wasn't,' Binnie said. He stopped walking, he knew he couldn't put up with this any longer. He would not allow John to blackmail him and he would not help the man to deceive Josephine. Binnie had done enough wrong in his life without adding to it.

'I'm going home,' he said. John looked at him open-mouthed; he had walked on a few paces ahead and now he retraced his steps. 'Are you sure about that?'

'I'm sure,' Binnie said. He moved closer to John, his eyes hard and filled with such anger that John stepped back abruptly. Binnie realized he had been a fool; quite suddenly, it became clear to him that John was open to blackmail too. Look what he would lose if Binnie exposed him: his wife, his secure life in America, his easy living, all of it would vanish in a puff of smoke.

'If you speak of this to anyone, anyone at all, I'll kill you and that's a promise.'

'Well,' John said at last, 'you keep your mouth shut and I'll keep mine shut.' He walked away and left Binnie standing in the roadway, his mind seething with confused thoughts. If he returned home now Hortense would know there was something wrong. The last thing he wanted was to upset her. He dared not call in on Dan in case the old man asked questions. He began to retrace his steps towards home, there was nothing else for him to do.

An open wagon pulled up beside him. 'Hi, brother-in-law, want a lift?' Josephine was smiling down at him, her bonnet at the back of her head, her hair falling into unruly curls on her shoulders. She was a lovely girl, beautiful and intelligent, John was a fool risking all he had for a silly affair. 'I'm going to your place, as it happens.'

'It's no distance,' he said smiling back at her, 'less than a mile.'

'Oh, go on!' Josephine coaxed. 'Otherwise I'll think you're avoiding me.' She moved her skirts aside to make room for him and Binnie put his foot on the wheel and swung himself into the seat at her side.

They drove for a little while in silence. The roadway threw up dry dust from under the wheels and Binnie coughed. He felt uncomfortable, he wondered what Josephine was going to say, she certainly had something on her mind. Glancing at her face he could see that she was pensive, her eyes shadowed.

'I know what's going on,' she said at last.

His heart contracted with fear. Had John told her about Maura? He coughed again, playing for time.

'What do you mean, Jo?'

'I know my husband is playing around. You know it too, don't deny it, I can see by your face.'

'How do you know?' Binnie asked. His mind was racing, how much did she know about John, and, worse, what did she know about him?

'A woman always knows when her man is being unfaithful, there are signs you see, signs any wife would recognize.'

He breathed a little easier, she was only guessing. He must speak to John, warn him that he was teetering on the edge of the abyss.

'I don't think so,' Binnie said. 'Perhaps he's just restless, you know.'

'You've hit the nail on the head, Binnie, he's restless all right. He wants to come into town more often than is good for him. I had to insist on coming with him this time otherwise he would have left me at home again. Why?'

Binnie swallowed, his throat was dry. 'I'm sure it's not anything to worry about, Jo, men like the company of men sometimes just as you girls like to get together for a chin-wag.' He forced a smile though his tongue felt welded to the roof of his mouth.

'Just this morning, Hortense was telling me how glad she'd be of your company. Your visit is a good chance for her to talk to another woman instead of boring old me!'

Josephine glanced at him. 'You and Hortense

are so secure, she knows you love her too much to stray. Whatever you did in the past, you are her man now, through and through. I've never been sure of John and I don't think I ever will be.'

Binnie remained silent; he did not want to comment just in case he said the wrong thing.

Hortense had heard the wagon pull up and was waiting on the porch, a wide smile on her face. She hugged her sister and gave Binnie a look that meant he should make himself scarce. She did not seem at all surprised to see him home.

'I'm going to have a lie down,' he said. 'I'm tired and I could do with a nap.' Hortense nodded; it was clear she knew that her sister wanted to talk.

As Binnie walked up the stairs, his heart was heavy. He knew he could not keep his secret any longer, it was weighing too heavily on him. In any case, he felt sure that John had told Jo about him. Binnie's past was a strange thing to refer to when talking about an errant husband.

He stretched out on the bed and closed his eyes and, before he knew it, the silence had sent him off to sleep.

'I'm worried about Eynon.' Llinos was holding Joe's hand as together they climbed the stairs to the bedroom. 'He's playing a dangerous game.' He was at her side and yet he seemed so distant from her.

'Well don't worry, Eynon is a grown man, he knows what he's doing, he can look after himself.'

'But Mrs Sparks of all women, and her with a husband who would kill you with a look. I don't like it.'

'You can do nothing about it,' Joe said firmly as he led her into the bedroom. 'I agree it would be better if Eynon could meet an unattached lady and fall in love and get married and have a brood of children to keep Jayne company but life isn't as neat as that.'

Did his words have a hidden meaning? She examined his face but could read nothing from his expression.

'I know life isn't neat,' Llinos said. 'Will you unhook me?'

She leaned against Joe as he began to undo the back of her dress. He slipped it down over her shoulders and stepped away from her.

'Come to bed with me tonight,' Llinos said gently.

'I can't. Look, don't ask me to explain, I don't even understand what I feel myself but since our baby died, I just feel as if I've lost my sense of direction. Don't try to push me, Llinos, not now when I'm so confused.' He left the room and the door closed behind him with a snap of finality.

Llinos sat on the bed and tears flowed hot and bitter down her cheeks. She wanted Joe to thrill her as he used to. Joe loved her, didn't he? Why then had he ceased to desire her?

He used to make her feel beautiful and cherished. She would lie back on the bed and look at his lean, golden body. He was so wonderful, so handsome. But if he had changed when the baby died, he had changed more since he had come back from America.

He was out a great deal, sometimes he returned home in the early hours of the morning. She knew because she could not sleep until he was safely indoors. Even when she knew he was back she often lay awake wanting him.

'I love you, Joe,' she whispered. She imagined his silky hair brushing her face, his warm lips against hers. The bed was big and empty without him. 'Oh, Joe! What's wrong with us?'

She closed her eyes with a picture of Joe behind her lids. When he loved her it was beautiful, he made her body sing with happiness. Every time he made love to her was like the first time. The sensations transcended time and place, lifted her to the clouds, to fly with the eagles, to become one with him.

Afterwards, in the glow of their lovemaking, she would cling to him knowing if ever she lost him she would be only half a woman. But he would never betray her, she knew that. He would never stray to another woman's bed the way some men did. He belonged to Llinos body and soul and she to him. Why then was she so lost and lonely, why was she lying in her bed alone?

The next day, Llinos hardly saw Joe at all. He went out in the morning and stayed out all day. But towards suppertime, he came home. He looked tired, as though he had a great deal on his mind and Llinos would have gone to him, put her arms around him but he avoided her eyes.

'Joe, what's wrong?' she asked, her voice cracking with fear. He moved past her, his shoulders tense.

'Not now, Llinos, I'm in no mood for a quarrel.' He looked up with a smile as his sister came slowly down the stairs. He took her hand and led her into the dining room. He seemed to be his old self now, smiling and at ease. Llinos sighed softly. Something was very wrong and Joe would have to talk to her about it sooner or later.

As they sat at supper, Charlotte sprang a surprise on them both. 'I've made a will,' she said proudly. 'Well at least the solicitor wrote it up for me and I signed it.' She smiled at Joe, a sisterly smile and reached out to touch his hand.

'The money you gave me, Joe, and the money dear Sam left me, it must all go to Lloyd.'

'Charlotte! Don't even talk about such things!' Llinos said quickly. 'You are still young and sprightly.'

'Well, I am heading towards my three score years and ten, you know.' She smiled. 'You sometimes forget I'm a great deal older than Joe.'

Charlotte lifted a spoonful of soup to her mouth and then dabbed her lips with the pristine napkin. 'Anyway, why I want to leave it to Lloyd is because I want him to have the very best education and the best life any boy could ever want. I hope one day he'll find a fine girl to settle down with.' She held up her hand as Llinos opened her mouth to protest.

'Now, I know you two would never see your little boy go without and the bulk of your estate will go to Lloyd, that is right and natural, but I want to give him something too before I leave this earth. I love him as though he's my own son.'

'Hush, Charlotte!' Llinos said softly. 'You must do what you see fit with your own money but my advice is to enjoy it, spend it on yourself. Buy a new outfit, travel the world, anything.'

Charlotte smiled. 'What need have I for new clothes? I have more than I will ever wear as it is. As for travelling, my old bones would not allow it. No, I am content with my quiet, peaceful life here in Swansea. I have no wish to be anywhere else on earth. Except . . .' She broke off and looked directly at Joe. 'Except when I die I want to be buried at home, the home where I was born and brought up.'

She sighed. 'I loved our house on the edge of the River Wye, Joe. Can I go back there, to rest in peace, please?'

'Of course you can. We'll say no more about it,' Joe replied. Llinos looked at him sharply. Was he troubled about Charlotte's health? Was concern for his sister the source of his strange behaviour?

'Would you like me to carve you some beef, Charlotte?' Joe said, proceeding to do so without waiting for a reply. If nothing else, Charlotte had a good appetite and enjoyed her food enormously. She was still small and bird-like in spite of the puddings she tucked away.

Llinos looked at Charlotte carefully. She appeared well and strong, as if she would have many more years than the three score and ten she spoke of. But perhaps Joe knew something she did not about his sister's health.

Later, when Charlotte had retired, Llinos tackled him about his strange mood. 'What's wrong, love? Are you worried about Charlotte?'

He was silent for a long time and then he looked past Llinos towards the window where moonlight slanted into the room. 'No, not worried. I think she can see the end coming, though, she is an old woman now. She wants to put her affairs in order, make her wishes known while she has a clear head.' He put down his napkin and pushed back his chair. 'But I don't want you to worry about her, Charlotte will leave this world in the most peaceful of ways and when she goes it will be her time and she will be ready.'

Watt examined the glaze, he lifted a ladleful of the thick liquid and let it drop back into the pot. 'It looks fine, Pearl,' he said. 'We just need to watch the temperature in the kilns now not to spoil the load.' He rested his hand on her shoulder.

'Are you sure you're fit to be back at work? You are still very pale.'

Pearl nodded. 'I'm all right, Watt. I've got over the whooping cough and I'm fit and well again.'

She did not mention the baby she lost while she was in bed coughing her lungs up. But then Pearl was made of sterner stuff than most. She knew that life was uncompromising and if she did not bend with the cold winds she would break.

'I need to work, Watt,' she said simply. She peered into the glaze. 'I'm well pleased with this mix, it's going to look fine on the new lot of pottery we've got waiting.' She smiled though her eyes were shadowed.

'You just make sure the kilns are heated to the right temperature. That's not my responsibility, that's down to you, boss.' Her broad face crinkled into fine lines as she made a face at him.

Watt felt a rush of affection for her; Pearl was a good worker and had been a good friend to him especially since Maura's death. As if reading his thoughts, she sighed.

'Life's hard sometimes, Watt my love, and when sickness comes it gets even harder. Now, to change the subject, can you come over to my house? We're having a little "do" as it's my Rosie's birthday.'

'I didn't know that,' Watt said. 'How old is she then?'

'She'll be eighteen come Saturday.' Pearl fluttered her eyelashes at him in mock flirtation. 'I don't look old enough to have a girl that age, do I?'

'Good heavens!' Watt said. Rosie worked as Llinos's maid and he had not really taken a great deal of notice of the girl. She was polite and sweet and, if he had thought of her at all, he had thought of her as a child. By way of comparison to his lost dear Maura, Rosie was a child.

'No you don't look old enough,' he said quickly.

'Well? Will you come to the party then?'

Watt wanted to refuse; he was not ready for socializing, not yet. Pearl rested her hand on his shoulder.

'You can't grieve for the rest of your life, Watt, you have to get out there, face the world again. You've always been strong, you needed to be growing up without a mam or dad and I don't want to see you lose your courage now.'

He hesitated and Pearl pressed home her advantage. 'Our Rosie would be so pleased if you came, really she would. She admires you so much, she thinks the sun shines out of your . . .' She smiled. 'You know what I mean.'

That Rosie had even noticed him came as a surprise to Watt. He was sure Pearl was exaggerating in order to get her way. 'All right,' he said reluctantly, 'but you won't mind if I don't stay long, will you?' He patted her arm before moving away. Pearl meant well but Watt would much rather be alone now. Without Maura, life seemed to be empty. He supposed it was the thought that he had come full circle, he was alone again, without anyone who really cared if he lived or died.

He was being morbid and he knew it. Of course people cared, Llinos cared and so did Joe. His work-mates cared. 'But,' said a small voice in his head, 'you have no-one to call your very own.'

When he finished work, Watt looked around the sheds, putting away brushes, picking up a few shards of pottery. The smell of the broken pots reminded him of his childhood. Well, he had come a long way since then. He was now virtually in charge of the entire pottery. It was his job to see that everything worked well from the throwing to the painting and glazing and then to the firing. He had his finger on the pulse of it all, he breathed in the atmosphere and loved it.

Once he had considered living in America, making his own way with dreams of becoming his own boss. But now, a little older and wiser, Watt realized that not everyone was cut out to be an owner of a business. He was quite content now to be a large cog in the wheel of the pottery.

It was probably Maura who had made him see that a successful life was not about owning things but about loving and being loved. Now that had been taken away from him, but he should be grateful that once he had experienced a deep and fulfilling love with Maura, something that was not given to everyone.

But God how he missed her! Sometimes he thought he saw her, the red hair, the bright eyes filled with love. He thought he heard her voice, felt her touch in the night. Perhaps she was still there somewhere, looking after him. If she was, would she be telling him to pull himself up by his bootstraps and live his life? He smiled suddenly. She would have doubtless put it more strongly than that.

He made an effort for Rosie's party, dressing himself smartly in a crisp white shirt, dark trousers and fine leather boots. He stared at his reflection in the mirror, he was still a young man, not many years past twenty. Would he waste the long years that stretched out before him or would he try to make something out of the ruins of his emotions? It was up to him and he could hear Maura telling him that in no uncertain terms.

The little cottage where Pearl lived was about half a mile upriver from the potteries and Watt set out early, feeling that he would only need to pay his respects, stay a little while and then he would feel free to return home.

Her door, as were most of the doors in Fisherman's Row, was open and the burst of laughter coming from inside the front room made Watt feel more alone than ever.

'Come in, Watt!' Pearl had a huge smile on her face. 'My little girl had given up hope of seeing you. She's that thrilled you've come. Wasn't it kind of Llinos to give her the day off?' Pearl took his arm and led him into the parlour. There were several small children in the room accompanied by their parents and Watt immediately felt out of place. He waved his hand at Pearl's man Will. Will grimaced in sympathy and lifted the jug of beer to his lips as though determined to enjoy himself whatever the company.

'Rosie, come here, the boss has arrived!'

Watt swallowed his surprise. He had only seen Rosie dressed in her dark skirt and white apron with a cap on her head. Now she was beautiful in a sprigged-muslin gown that showed her figure to perfection. A neat jacket covered her slender arms. She no longer appeared the child he had thought her.

'Happy Birthday, Rosie.' He handed her the small bunch of flowers he had brought, it seemed an appropriate gift, not too personal, but now he felt a little mean.

'Isn't he sweet!' Pearl said and Watt raised his eyebrows at her. 'You obviously control your colourful language when you're at home,' he said dryly.

'Go on with you, stop teasing.' She put her hand on Rosie's shoulder, towering above her. 'Didn't I tell you that Watt was a wag? Now you talk to him while I see to the younger ones.'

Watt looked around in embarrassment. There was no sign of any other young men present, only older neighbours. It seemed that he had been fooled by Pearl, she was clearly trying to match-make. With the best of intentions, she was trying to get him interested in her daughter.

He glanced at Rosie; she was just as

uncomfortable as he was. She looked up briefly from under incredibly long, golden lashes. Why had he never noticed them before?

'I'm sorry,' she whispered. 'I know you've just had a bereavement and you must be feeling awful.' She sighed. 'Mam's a bit on the bossy side but she means well.'

'Of course she does. Come on, let's sit down and talk, make Pearl a happy woman, shall we?'

Rosie knew all about Maura and it was a relief for Watt to be himself, not to have to pretend he was 'getting over it' as people said. How could anyone get over losing the one they loved?

'Are you very lonely?' Rosie asked softly. She looked down at her hands clasped in her lap. 'Of course you are, what a stupid question.'

'Yes, I'm lonely,' Watt agreed. 'Sometimes I feel as if I'll never be happy again.'

Tears welled in Rosie's eyes; she got up and hurried out the room. Watt looked after her in bewilderment. Pearl came quickly to his side.

'She had just started courting one of the local boys,' she whispered. 'Didn't have a chance to see much of him, mind, her working up at Llinos's house, but she was getting quite fond of young Philip. Poor lad died in the whooping-cough epidemic.'

'I'm a selfish swine!' Watt said. 'There I am so busy feeling sorry for myself, not realizing that other people can be hurt too. I'll go after her.'

'She's out the back garden,' Pearl said. 'She needs some young company. Perhaps you two can help each other, be friends, fill in the emptiness. That's all I wanted when my dear husband died.'

She smiled. 'That's why I took up with old Willie there, he's a good man but he'll never replace what I had with my husband.'

It was sunny in the garden if a little chilly. A wash of light fell across Rosie's hair, turning it to gold. She was standing in the wild grass, tears rolling unchecked down her young face. Watt's heart contracted in pity. He took her hands in his.

'I know how you feel, Rosie, I really do. Perhaps we two unhappy people can be friends, can we?'

She nodded miserably and rubbed at her eyes with her fingertips. She looked so young and vulnerable that he longed to hold her in his arms and smooth back the hair that had tangled over her face.

'I would like to have a friend,' she said at last. 'I have my family but they don't really understand what I'm feeling. Everyone tells me I'll get over it as if I've lost a pet cat or something.' She glanced up at him. 'In any case, Mam has her own worries, she's not been right since she lost the baby. Can you see how pale and thin she is?'

'I have noticed,' he said. 'But Pearl is a strong lady, she'll be fine, you'll see.'

She looked directly at him then, her smooth cheeks blotched with red patches where she had rubbed at her tears. He took her arm. 'Let's sit down there on the wall for a bit, shall we?'

She allowed him to take her hand and lead her to the back of the garden where a rugged stone wall made a boundary between her own house and the one back to back with it.

'Your sweetheart, do you want to talk about

him?' He sounded like an old man he thought ruefully but he really felt for Rosie, he could understand her distress.

'Philip was so good to me.' Her voice broke. 'I'd known him since I was a little girl. He used to protect me from the other boys, he said he had always wanted to walk out with me.' She put her hands over her face. 'And then, when I saw him coughing up his very life, I couldn't bear it. I ran out and left him and he died without me there to hold his hand. I can never forgive myself for that.'

He drew her hands away from her face and pulled her to him. 'Look, Rosie, you did your very best for Philip and he wouldn't blame you for not wanting to see him die, I know he wouldn't.'

'How do you know?' Her voice was muffled against his chest.

'I know because I'm a man too and I would not want to put my loved one through such misery.' He smoothed her hair and somehow, the knot of pain that had stuck in his throat since he had put Maura in the ground began to dissolve, just a little.

'Come on!' He rose from the wall. 'Dry your eyes. You and me have got a party to go to.' As he took Rosie's hand and led her back into the house, a little light of hope lit within him, hope that one day he would find love again.

CHAPTER SEVEN

Llinos stared out of the window of the hotel and watched the sea rush in towards the shore. The coast of Cornwall was very much like that of Wales and she felt at home there, but she was missing her son badly.

Joe was sitting near the small table in the corner of the room, sipping a glass of lemon tea. 'I brought you here for a reason,' he said. 'I want to have you all to myself, to talk to you seriously about something that has been troubling me.'

She turned sharply. 'Couldn't we have talked at home?'

'No, we couldn't,' Joe said firmly. 'You are so busy with your business that you sometimes forget you have other obligations.'

'And you, my dear husband, are absent from home more than you are present!' She heard the sharpness of her tone and took a deep breath.

'I'm sorry, Joe.' She looked up at him anxiously. 'What's gone wrong between us?'

He hesitated and Llinos held her breath. 'When I was in America, when I buried my mother, it was all so painful. She asked a favour of me, a favour I couldn't refuse.'

'What sort of favour?' She spoke tersely. 'Surely it can't be anything important enough to come between you and me, can it?'

'Don't lose your temper,' he said gently. 'I'm trying to explain how I feel. Look, I know I am away a lot but when I am at home you are busy with your friends or your employees and we have no time to talk.'

'That's not fair!' Llinos said. 'I am not the one sleeping in another room. We used to talk in bed as well as make love. Remember what making love is?'

'Is that all that worries you, Llinos, that we don't sleep together? You can be so selfish at times!' He leaned forward. 'When I am there, I feel like a stranger in my own home.'

'So making love is something to be ashamed of now, is it?' She turned away from him, her shoulders stiff. 'I don't feel I've been neglecting you or our marriage. Indeed, it is the other way about, so why are you putting the blame on me? Aren't you big enough to shoulder some of the blame yourself?'

'Perhaps you'd better take a good look at yourself.' His tone sharpened. 'You are usually too tired to talk about my business, my feelings; it's you, you, you all the damned time!'

Llinos felt her colour recede. She had been neglecting her appearance lately but then if Joe loved her he would understand. 'I thought you of all people would accept my need to occupy myself with other things.' Had he forgotten that she had lost her baby and still felt the ache of it?

'You are obsessed with the business,' Joe said. 'You make sure you fully occupy yourself to the exclusion of everything else.'

'So I want my business, my father's business, to flourish. Is that a crime? You see, Joe, I am not just there for you to pick up and put down just as you please. So how dare you tell me I'm not a good wife?'

'At the moment you do not seem much like a wife at all.' He rose abruptly and put his glass carefully on the table. 'I don't want to argue with you, Llinos, but you are being stubborn; you're not even trying to see my point of view. I try to explain things to you and all you do is throw accusations at me and paint yourself as the neglected wife! You can't see any fault in yourself, only faults in me. Well I've had enough of it, I'm going to take a walk along the cliffs until my temper improves and my mind is clear.'

'Don't you dare walk out on me!' Llinos said to his retreating back. The door closed firmly and she was alone.

How could he treat her this way? Joe was usually so calm, so wise and now he was acting like a stranger. So she was not some foolish socialite of a woman who flattered and danced attendance on her man. If that's what Joe wanted he had married the wrong person.

She opened the door of the wardrobe and pulled out her bag and, with tears of anger burning her eyes, Llinos began to pack. To hell with Joe and his talks; if he only wanted to tell her how bad a wife she was she was not going to listen.

She felt her throat choked with tears. She loved Joe so much, she thought this trip would solve the differences between them. How wrong she had been. All she wanted now was the familiar surroundings of her own home. She longed to creep into bed and hide away from the world. And the one man who should be comforting her was Joe and he had failed her miserably.

'Talk to me, Binnie, tell me what's troubling you.' Hortense looked at her husband, at his white face, and fear began to churn in her stomach. He had been acting strangely for some time now. It was something to do with John Pendennis, she was sure of it. And if it took her all day, she meant to find out exactly what was going on.

The sweet scent of honeysuckle drifted through the window, the sun-warmed room was bathed in a refreshing breeze. She was alone with Binnie; the boys were on a trip with their grandfather, a trip Hortense had engineered in an attempt to get Binnie alone.

'Talk to me, Binnie.' Her voice held a note of urgency and he looked away from her.

'Hortense, love, do we have to discuss this now?' He got to his feet and stood at the window. Hortense stared at his rigid back and tried to remain calm.

'There is no putting me off, not this time. What are you hiding, Binnie? For the Lord's sake tell me, I'm going mad with the worry of it.'

She watched as he thrust his hands into his pockets and she noticed suddenly that he had lost weight. A shiver of apprehension ran along her spine.

'Are you sick, Binnie hon?' She could hear the tremble in her voice and when Binnie turned and shook his head, she knew he had heard it too.

'I'm not sick, my love.' He took her in his arms, pressing her close against him. 'Just sick at heart.'

'Just tell me the truth,' she said. 'Whatever it is we'll handle it together, just don't keep me in the dark.'

He released her. 'Sit down.' He swallowed hard and reluctantly she obeyed him. She stared up at him, trying to read the truth in his eyes.

'You don't look well, Binnie, you've lost weight and you're so pale. I'm that worried about you, hon.'

'I'm not ill, it's not that.' He cleared his throat. 'Look, the truth is John has been trying to blackmail me.' He did not meet her eyes; his head was bent so that she could not see his expression.

'What on earth could John blackmail you about, Binnie? Your life is an open book. You don't have women like Daddy does; you are a loyal faithful husband. Aren't you?'

'Yes, I am faithful to you, Hortense. I love you more than my own life and as for the boys, I would die for them, you know that.'

'So what is it then? Spit it out, Binnie, for God's sake!'

'I was married before.' The words were almost a whisper. 'I was married to an Irish girl back home in Swansea. We were only together a short time when I realized I didn't love her and I didn't want to spend the rest of my life with her.'

Hortense tried to absorb the shock; she felt physically sick, as though she had been punched. He had a woman before her, how could he? Anger and jealousy rushed through her like bubbling wine. She wanted to beat him with her fists for lying to her, for having another woman in his life.

'Oh my Lord, Binnie! I can't believe I'm hearing right.' She put her hands over her eyes as though she could shut out the pain. Binnie had been married, he had given his love to someone else. How could she ever trust him again? But then common sense reasserted itself. Binnie had come to her as a grown man; she could not expect him to have lived like a monk before he met her.

Startling though his confession was, she realized quite suddenly that she had not heard the full story. Why should John want to blackmail Binnie over something that happened years ago, long before the two men knew each other? A thought struck her, so dreadful that she could hardly bring herself to speak. Her hands fell limply into her lap; she stared at Binnie's bowed head and took a deep breath.

'And what happened to her, this wife of yours?'

'She's dead,' Binnie said flatly.

A feeling of relief poured through her, she had half expected him to say the woman was alive and well, perhaps planning to come to America to fetch him. The situation was bad enough but it could have been much worse.

'You were a widower when we married and, yes, you should have told me at the very beginning but what is so bad that John can hold it over you like a threat?' Hortense stared at him, willing him to look at her.

'Are you so afraid of me that you couldn't have told me all this before? I would have understood, you know.'

She watched him twisting his fingers together, like one of her boys caught in some misdemeanour. There was more to this than he had told her.

'Come on, Binnie, let me have it all. I know there's more you have to tell me so get on with it.' She was beginning to feel furious with him for his weakness. She felt the blood pound in her head. The question burst from her lips.

'When did she die this wife of yours?'

'Just a short while ago,' Binnie said. 'I was still married to Maura when I went through the ceremony with you.'

'No!' The word was almost a scream. She could not think, could not feel; she was numb with horror.

'We can put it right now, Hortense,' he said eagerly. 'We can get married in secret. No-one need ever know the truth. There's no harm done really, is there, Hortense?'

No harm done. He was a bigamist and she was a woman who had been made a fool of, a woman with three illegitimate sons to bring up. She suddenly felt as if the foundations of her life had given way and she was crashing to her doom.

She jumped up from her chair, pushing him away, and made for the door. It was open and outside the blossoms were on the trees, the fresh breeze perfumed with the scents of spring. It all seemed so normal and yet nothing in her life would ever be the same again.

Hortense spun round to face him, her eyes hard and angry.

'No harm done! My boys are bastards and you say there's no harm done! You must be crazy!' She felt crushed. She had heard of women dying of broken hearts and she wished in this moment that she could just lie down and die. But she needed to live to protect her sons.

He stared at her miserably. 'We can get married at once, there's nothing to stop us now.' He spoke pleadingly. 'I love you, Hortense, I've loved you from the day we first met, you know I've never looked at another woman since then.'

He loved her so much that he could not trust her; he had taken her to his bed, fathered three children on her and treated her like a weak gullible fool. Their entire relationship had been built on lies and deceit.

'John knows about all this!' she said bitterly. 'And no doubt Jo knows, and how many others, Binnie, ask yourself that. It will be all round the town by now.'

'No,' Binnie said. 'John won't say anything, he's not in a position to cast stones, he's not exactly the faithful sort, is he?'

'Two fine lads together, is that it? Fooling your women, behaving like children. You're worse than Daddy, do you know that? At least my father has the guts to be open about his affairs.'

'John won't say a word, he promised.'

'And you really expect a man like John

Pendennis to keep his promises? You're more of a fool than I thought.'

She was in full flood now, nothing could stop the bitterness and anger and the pain from pouring from her.

'He could tell my daddy all this and he would if it suited him. John Pendennis could tell the whole world about us living in sin. I'll be the laughing stock of West Troy and so will the boys. Another thing, what do you think Mammy will say? You'll be lucky if she don't take a meat cleaver to you.'

'I didn't mean to hurt anyone,' Binnie said. 'It was just that I couldn't stay with Maura because I didn't love her. I felt bad running out on her and the baby but—'

His sentence was never finished. Hortense ran at him, her fingers like talons, her nails raking his face. 'You had a *child*! You deserted your wife and your baby! You no good swine, you rotten waster!' She slapped his face hard and kept slapping him. When he tried to hold her back, she lashed out at him with her feet.

'I hate you, Binnie Dundee, I wish I had never set eyes on you! Get out of my house and out of my life before I take a knife to you.'

'Please, Hortense, listen to me!' He tried to catch her in his arms; incensed, she lifted a heavy jug from the table and crashed it down on his head.

'Get out!'

'Please, love, I'm sorry, more sorry than I can ever say. I wanted to tell you, I just couldn't find the right moment.'

'Don't lie!' she said fiercely. 'You've only told

me now because John forced it upon you.' Suddenly she felt the anger drain from her. This could not be happening, it was a bad dream. She looked at her husband and shook her head. Perhaps Binnie had never loved her, he was like John, looking for a meal ticket. How could she trust a man who had deserted his wife and child, a man who had lied to her all these years?

'Just get out of my sight, Binnie.' She saw there was blood trickling from a wound at the side of his head. She felt nothing. She stared at him, this man she had been married to for so long and saw a stranger.

'Surely you remember the good times, Hortense?' he asked. 'The times we made love, the times we marvelled over the boys?'

'It was all a sham, wasn't it?' she said in a low voice. 'You played your part well, I'll give you that. Now, get out. I want to keep this quiet until I've had a chance to think things through.'

He tried to speak but she held out her hand to stop him. 'You had better go before I kill you myself.'

'Please, Hortense.'

She turned her back on him. 'Get out of my life, you bastard!'

She heard him go upstairs, heard the sound of the cupboard doors opening and closing and she knew he was packing his clean clothes, looking out for himself to the last. Furious with him, she ran up the stairs, her skirts flying.

'Leave everything!' she shouted at him. 'You came to me with nothing, you can leave with nothing!'

'Be reasonable, Hortense,' he said. 'I have to have clothes and money otherwise where will I stay, what will I do?'

She dragged the shirt he was holding out of his hands, tearing at the cloth with her nails.

'You will work like everyone else in this country!' she said. 'Your soft living is gone, you will have to find out the hard way how difficult life can be in America with no-one behind you.'

'That's not fair!' he protested. 'I've worked hard for your father, I've improved the running of the pottery and—'

'And you've been well paid for it!' She glared at him. 'Now the free ride is over, so get out of my sight, you make me sick just to look at you.'

He left the room and she heard his hurried footsteps on the stairs. She thought she had seen the glint of tears in his eyes as he'd pleaded with her but her heart was full of grief for herself and her children, she had none to spare for him.

She heard the pounding of hooves outside and saw Binnie ride away at great speed. He could have the horse he had taken, he at least deserved that much. Call it severance pay, she thought bitterly.

She walked slowly down the stairs and into the hallway; the door was swinging open, there was no sign of Binnie. He was gone and all she could see was a cloud of dust thrown up from the hooves of his horse. Dust, that's what her life, in a few short moments, had become.

She longed to cry but what good would crying do? She went out onto the porch and sank onto the rocking chair. Around her, everything seemed silent, even the birds were quiet. It was as if the world had come to an end. Her world certainly had.

She tensed and sat upright. She could hear the beat of hooves on the dusty ground, the sound getting louder, was Binnie coming back to plead with her some more? But then she saw the open carriage and recognized her sister sitting in the driving seat.

'Oh Lord!' she said. 'How am I going to cope with it all?'

Josephine climbed down and hitched the horses to one of the rails. She looked pale and drawn and Hortense wondered if she had seen Binnie and knew what had happened. Josephine hugged her and sat on the facing swing, her eyes closed.

'Help me, Hortense, I can't bear it, John's being unfaithful to me *again*.' She dabbed her eyes with a scrap of lace and, for a moment, Hortense was confused.

'What?'

'Have you known about it all along, Hortense? Am I just a blind fool?'

Hortense rubbed her eyes. The whole world was going mad.

'How did you find out, Jo?' Hortense wondered if she could find the strength to comfort her younger sister when she was feeling as if the bottom had dropped out of her own world.

'I laid a trap for him and caught him in the act.' Josephine gave a short laugh. 'There he was, in the hotel in town where everyone knows him, knows me and knows our family.' She paused and dabbed at her eyes with the tiny scrap of lace. 'And guess who he was messing with?'

'I don't know,' Hortense said, not really caring who John was going to bed with. She had troubles of her own, big troubles.

Jo began to cry. 'Only Melia, our dear sister!'

'Oh, God!' Hortense said. 'Our family is falling apart and I don't think I can bear it.'

'I hit her,' Josephine said, not listening to a word Hortense was saying. 'I slapped her face, hard. She was lying there naked with him all over her and when she saw me she didn't even try to excuse herself. I hate her!'

'No, it's not her fault,' Hortense said. 'She was fooled by John's charm, we were all fooled. Men! None of them are to be trusted.'

Josephine really looked for the first time. 'You've been crying!' She took her sister's hand. 'What's wrong, hon? Don't tell me Binnie's been unfaithful too?'

'It's worse,' Hortense said. 'He was not free when he married me.'

'What do you mean "not free"?'

'I mean he had a wife at home. I am not his legal wife and my boys,' her voice broke, 'my boys are illegitimate. Don't tell me you didn't know. I'm sure John would have taken a delight in telling you that juicy titbit.'

Josephine hugged her. 'He said something about another woman back home but I didn't take a lot of notice. Binnie married! Oh hon, there was I blabbing on about my own troubles. Why have we been such fools?'

'I am a lot wiser now,' Hortense said harshly. 'Binnie Dundee will never set foot in my house again as long as I live, I'll see to that.'

Hortense stared out over the verandah, not seeing the dry earth or the dusty trail leading into town. She was seeing the face of the man she believed was her husband and the pain of his betrayal was dragging her down into an abyss. She had loved Binnie to distraction; now she despised him. Suddenly sobs racked her body and all she longed for was the comfort of her husband's arms around her.

Llinos was tired of the jolting of the carriage; her bones seemed to ache and she had a headache coming on. She had just left Joe behind at the hotel and instead of feeling righteous, she felt empty inside. The days had passed in a haze of pain but now she was on the last stage of the journey. Soon she would be home but the further she got from Cornwall and Joe the more she felt she had been a fool to walk out on her husband.

She wondered what he was doing now. What had he thought when he saw she was gone? Would he stay in Cornwall or would he take a mail and follow her home? She had no idea why she had allowed the argument to get out of hand. It had begun with nothing and escalated into a stupid row. She should have been more reasonable.

She and Joe scarcely ever had a cross word but then everyone quarrelled at some time; it was inevitable in any close relationship. But Joe's words had hurt her more than she believed possible. Had she been neglecting him? She did not think so. She had a young son to care for as well as a business. How could Joe expect her to be at his beck and call?

The pain in her head grew worse. She wished now that she had never embarked on this stupid holiday. She had been happy at home with her family around her; she had only agreed to the trip to please Joe. What a mistake it had been.

She felt the carriage jolt to a stop. She sat forward and leaned out of the window. 'What is it?' she called. The driver climbed down and looked at her doubtfully.

'There are two ladies up ahead, Mrs Mainwaring,' Kenneth said. 'It looks as if they are in trouble, one of them is lying at the side of the road.'

'We'd better help then,' Llinos said, her hand on the door but the driver stopped her, his hand held up in a warning gesture.

'It could be a trap, there could be robbers waiting in the trees, you never know what will happen on these lonely roads.'

Llinos pushed the door open and climbed from the carriage. She shaded her eyes and looked up ahead. One of the women was waving. She seemed small and defenceless, her clothes, though dusty, were respectable.

'Help us, please!' A voice called and Llinos stepped back a pace, her heart thumping. 'I know that voice,' she said quietly. 'It's Lily, she used to be a painter at the pottery.'

'It could still be a trap, Mrs Mainwaring. Is this Lily a trustworthy person?'

Llinos thought of the way Lily had plotted against herself and Joe and shook her head. Once, it seemed so long ago now, Lily, by her trouble-making, had almost led a riot, rousing the people of the town against Joe. She certainly was not to be trusted.

'Get into the driving seat,' Llinos said quickly. 'We'll drive past, see what happens.'

The carriage jerked into movement, one of the horses whinnied a protest at the sharp flick of the whip.

Llinos stared out of the window and, as she passed the women, she saw Lily look up at her pleadingly, her eyes shadowed, her face gaunt. The other woman, clearly a servant, was lying against a boulder, clutching her side; she appeared really sick. If she was playing a part, she was playing it very well.

Around the bend of the road, the carriage drew to a halt and Kenneth climbed down. Llinos watched as he wound his way back along the road-way and soon he was out of sight behind a cluster of trees. Llinos waited, feeling nervous; she wished again that she had not been so foolish as to leave Joe behind. Her pride had got the better of her good sense.

The driver appeared at the window so suddenly that Llinos started back in alarm. 'Sorry to startle you, Mrs Mainwaring, but they look genuine enough. Both of them are sitting on the ground now and there's no sign of anyone else.'

'All right,' Llinos said, 'turn around, we'll pick them up.' Lily might be an enemy but Llinos could not leave her to die at the roadside. Joe would have acted with kindness, she knew that, and he would expect her to do the same.

When the two women were seated opposite Llinos, Lily looked at her with large eyes. She was subdued; her arrogance that had been so much a part of her had vanished. She was beaten and helpless and Llinos could not help but feel sorry for her.

'Llinos . . . Mrs Mainwaring, I didn't know it was you but thanks for picking us up.' Lily's voice quivered with weakness.

'How is your companion?' Llinos asked, her voice cool.

Lily looked at the servant, who was grey with fatigue, and shook her head. 'If you hadn't come along Betty would have died,' she said humbly. 'And so would I. We haven't eaten for days nor had a drink of water since yesterday morning. We've been afraid to stop in case we were followed.'

'That's your business, I don't want to know anything about your problems. I might be letting you ride in my carriage but I don't want anything to do with you once we get into town.'

Llinos drew a basket from under the seat and, opening it, took out a bottle of water and a cup. 'Don't drink too much at first,' she warned, 'or it will make you sick.'

She expected Lily to take a drink herself first; Lily had always been selfish, not caring who she hurt so long as she was all right. She had changed because she held the cup to the serving woman's lips, supporting her head as she drank. Then Lily sipped a little water herself.

'I feel better now.' Lily licked the last vestige of water from her lips. 'Thank you for helping us,

Mrs Mainwaring. If I was you I wouldn't have stopped, not after the bad way I treated you.' She began to cry. 'If only you knew how much I suffered over that, I've been paid back a thousand times for my wickedness.'

'Where are you going now, which lodging house?' Llinos asked.

'I'll find somewhere once we're back in Swansea.' She looked down at her hands. 'Perhaps my friend Polly is still around, she'll take me in.'

Llinos sighed, she knew Lily was waiting for an offer of help but right now Llinos's patience was strained. She leaned back and closed her eyes, fighting back her unhappiness. The sight of Lily had brought back the past so vividly. The angry crowd outside the door, the sound of voices baying for blood, her blood as well as Joe's, and all because of the girl sitting opposite her.

'I know you must hate me,' Lily said. 'I don't blame you, I nearly got you killed. I realize now that Mr Mainwaring is a good man, the medicines he gave your father and old Mr Marks were only to do them good.'

Llinos opened her eyes. 'I don't want to talk about the past, if you don't mind.' She could not keep the note of anger from her voice. Lily went so pale that her eyelids looked blue and Llinos felt sorry for her. But once they were back in town, Lily was on her own.

It was silent except for the creaking of the carriage. The serving woman struggled to speak; she was slumped against the leather, scarcely able to open her swollen eyes.

'Don't be angry, Mrs,' she said. 'Lily's gone through the mill and she's a changed girl. Whatever she done, she's paid for it over and over.'

Lily remained quiet though tears rolled down her cheeks and her jaw quivered. She was a foolish, misguided girl and perhaps she had learnt her lesson, though Llinos doubted it.

'Try to rest, now,' she said. 'We will be back in Swansea before nightfall.'

Llinos pretended to sleep; she had no desire to talk and certainly not to Lily. She was sunk in her own misery thinking about Joe, alone in Cornwall. She wondered if he would ever come back to her or was their marriage over?

At last the smoke from the Swansea works drifted towards the carriage, bringing with it a sulphurous, unpleasant smell. Llinos opened her eyes warily.

'We're home,' Lily said quietly. She put her hands together and closed her eyes. 'Thank you God for bringing me back safely,' she whispered.

Llinos leaned out of the window. 'Kenneth,' she called, 'stop near Vaughan's lodging house and we'll drop them off there.'

'I haven't got any money, Mrs Mainwaring,' Lily said in panic. 'I can't stop there, not without a few sovereigns to pay the bill.'

Llinos opened her bag and took out some coins. 'I've brought you this far, Lily, but I don't want to see you again, do you understand?'

'Yes,' Lily said meekly. 'And thank you. Come on, Betty, we can rest in comfort tonight.'

It was good to be home but as Llinos stepped

into the hallway of Pottery House she knew that there would be questions asked, questions she was far too tired to answer.

The scents of the house, familiar smells of beeswax and flowers and from outside the ever present smell of baking clay made her happy and sad at the same time. She was home but she was alone. Was she going to be alone for the rest of her life?

life?

CHAPTER EIGHT

It was lonely at Pottery House without Joe. Since
Llinos had walked out on him, she had not heard
a word from him. She was frightened and yet she
felt she must put a brave face on things for
Charlotte and of course for Lloyd.

Eynon was a different kettle of fish; she wanted
to tell him the truth, to ask his advice. They were
sitting together in the drawing room of Pottery
House and Llinos stared at him, wondering how to
broach the subject.

'How's Jayne?' she asked lightly.

'I've told you once she's fine, my new business
is fine as well. I enjoy bringing china clay from
Dorset back to Swansea, it keeps me out of
mischief.'

'And Martin?'

'Martin is well and happy, fatter than ever. Now
cut all this chatter and get to the point.' He sat
back, a knowing look on his face. 'You are breaking your heart over Joe, aren't you, and too proud
to do anything about it.'

Llinos took a deep breath and then the words

poured from her lips like a flood. 'I don't know where he is. I walked out on him, Eynon. We had a row; he told me I was a bad wife. He's changed, Eynon, I don't think he's the same Joe I married. Where can he be staying? He's not at the hotel in Cornwall. Oh, I don't know anything any more!'

'Have you asked his sister where he is? Surely Charlotte must have heard from him?' Eynon said quietly.

'I think if Charlotte knew she would have told me by now.' Llinos looked miserably at the trees outside the window without seeing them. 'Charlotte is as worried as I am.'

'I'm sure he's as right as rain but I'll make some enquiries, if you like?'

'No!' she paused. 'Joe will come home when he's ready, if ever he *is* ready. It might be he's had enough of me. That was our first quarrel, it might well be our last.' She felt tears against her lids and tried to blink them away.

'I don't think Joe is the type of man to allow one disagreement to spoil the wonderful relationship he has with you.'

Llinos smiled. 'You are biased. Ask yourself, is his life so wonderful?'

'I don't know what you mean,' Eynon said evenly. 'He has his son, he has his own successful business to run and he has you. Joe has nothing to complain of, believe me.'

'He demands more of his wife's time and attention, it seems.'

'Is that what he said?' Eynon asked.

'That's what it comes to.' Llinos continued to stare at the trees as if they could give her answers to her questions. Joe was not content with their life as it was, he had made that quite clear. Now, sitting here in the sunlit room, Llinos could not believe that they had been so angry with each other. Surely, if she had been more understanding, had listened to him instead of being on the defensive, they could have worked it out? But she had indulged in her feelings of hurt pride and walked out on him. She had not even stopped to consider if Joe had a point.

'Anyway,' she said, 'I'm foolish pouring out my troubles to you. I don't know what I expect you to do about the mess I've got myself into.'

'I can support you and listen to you and perhaps even advise you,' Eynon said softly. 'Why not let Joe have his freedom for a while? He is trying to work something out in his head, if I know Joe. He is better off alone right now, you know, like a bear retreating into a cave? He has a different way of life from us, Llinos, just let him be, he'll come back to you all safe and sound again, you'll see.'

'Maybe,' Llinos said. 'Anyway, tell me about your exciting business venture, it sounds fascinating.' She forced a cheerful note into her voice. 'I knew you wouldn't be able to shake off your links with the pottery altogether.'

'Miss Clever Shoes!' Eynon said. 'All right, if you don't want to listen to my advice about Joe, then I'll humour you and change the subject.' His face was bright now, eager. 'I've bought three ships, good sound sailing ships, and I've hired experienced captains and crew.' He sat forward in his chair and Llinos realized that Eynon had needed a purpose; the life of the idle rich had never suited him.

'If I bring the clay up from Poole I will be making a good profit on it. I have plans for opening a new pottery myself, not a very big one and not yet a while but the idea is there buzzing around my head.'

'It sounds a wonderful idea.' Llinos was pleased for Eynon; it was about time he found a new interest instead of running around with married women.

'Jayne will be a very rich young woman one day if my plans work out,' Eynon said in satisfaction.

Llinos shook her head. 'She's not exactly poverty stricken now, is she? You are far richer than I am, Eynon. My pottery almost ran itself into bankruptcy once, remember? I'm very lucky to have survived those hard times.'

'Not lucky,' Eynon said softly, 'you are courageous, enterprising and damned hardworking. Those things have nothing to do with luck, Llinos.'

'You may be right.' She raised her eyebrows as Eynon put his head on one side.

'What?'

'I've at least stopped you looking at those damned trees, that's what!' He smiled at her. His teeth were fine and even and his hair was almost golden. He was a good-looking man and he loved her. How simple life would have been if she could have loved him in return.

The clock in the hall chimed the hour and Eynon stood up.

'I have to go,' he said. 'I'm meeting my secret mistress in a little over an hour and I've got to get ready.'

147

Llinos frowned. 'I wish you would be careful, Eynon. I don't like that man Sparks. I think he would be really vindictive if he caught you with his wife.'

'Then I shall have to make sure he doesn't catch me,' Eynon said lightly. He kissed her cheek and, on an impulse, she put her arms around him.

'You know how much I care about you, Eynon. Is this Mrs Sparks worth the risks you're taking?'

'I'm still a young man, Llinos,' he said quietly. 'I need a woman and as I can't have the one I love, I have to make do with one who is available.'

Llinos was still in Eynon's arms when the door opened and her son came into the room. He looked at Eynon disapprovingly.

'You shouldn't kiss my mamma,' he said accusingly, 'my father wouldn't like it.' He sat on the chair Eynon had just vacated, a mutinous expression on his face.

'But, Lloyd *bach*, Eynon and I are old friends, a kiss between us is just a sign of affection.'

'You don't love Father any more,' Lloyd said. 'Otherwise you wouldn't have come home without him.'

'That's silly!' Llinos's tone was sharp. 'And it's rude of you to interrupt. Now go to your room and stay there until you learn some manners.'

On his way out, Lloyd aimed a sly kick in the direction of Eynon's polished boots then slammed the door behind him.

'He's upset,' Eynon said. 'He's missing his father, he doesn't mean to be rude, he's just a child.'

'I know,' Llinos sighed heavily. 'Everything

seems so black and white when you're so young, doesn't it? Go on home, you've heard enough of my moaning for one day.'

She watched from the doorway of Pottery House as Eynon walked away along the row. He was a rich man, he could have ridden the several miles from his home on any one of a stable of horses. He could have ridden in the fine carriage with the Morton-Edwards crest emblazoned on the doors but Eynon loved to walk.

In his youth he had been something of a weakling; he had been bullied and once even beaten half to death. Now as a man, he was determined to keep himself in good shape, facing the world with his head high. He was a good friend and perhaps she should take his advice. He had told her to let Joe be, allow him to find his own way through his problems.

She sighed heavily. She had better leave Joe alone; he would come when he was ready. But why did he blame her for the rift that had opened between them? She had done nothing wrong, she had only cared for her family and for her business, surely she did not have to apologize for that?

Joe went away on business trips and she made no complaint about his long absences. Joe was his own man, he had money from his father's estate and need never work again but he could not be content with sitting around idling his life away in coffee houses and public inns. She respected Joe for that, why could he not respect her wish to work?

She shook off her feeling of gloom and went upstairs to Lloyd's room. Her son was sitting on the bed, swinging his legs, his feet connecting with the legs of his bedside table. 'Lloyd, please don't be such a crosspatch.' She sat on the bed beside him. 'I miss Daddy, too, but he'll come home when he's good and ready.' She smoothed back Lloyd's hair. 'You know he goes away on business quite a lot, you've never complained before.'

Lloyd looked at her. 'You've sent him away!' he said. 'You don't love my daddy any more.'

'That's not true, love.' She drew him into her arms. 'Look, your father and I had words. Everyone gets cross sometimes. I know I shouldn't have come home without Daddy but grown ups are silly sometimes, just like children.'

'I'm not silly,' Lloyd said. He was so serious, so unlike his amiable self that Llinos held him away from her.

'Lloyd, are you sick?' He was paler than usual, his eyes smudged with shadows. She had been so wrapped up in her own unhappiness that she had not taken enough notice of her son. Was this the sort of behaviour Joe had been complaining about?

She put her hand on Lloyd's forehead; it was hot and dry to touch. Could he be coming down with a fever? she wondered. It had not been long ago that whooping cough had swept through the town, the wet months of autumn turning into the cold of winter with little effect on the illness. Now, even with the coming of spring, there were still repercussions. Some of the children in the area had been left with a weak constitution after the epidemic.

'Where's Eira?' Llinos moved to the door and called out across the landing for the governess. Eira had suffered from the whooping cough herself, so she would know if Lloyd was sickening for it.

Eira came at once. 'What's wrong, Mrs Mainwaring?' she asked, her eyes going to the boy sitting on the bed. 'Is Lloyd expecting a lesson? I thought he was finished for the day.'

'I think he's sickening for something,' Llinos said. 'Take a look at him. I think it might be safer to call a doctor, anyone so long as it's not Dr Rogers.' Llinos shuddered; she still had not forgotten the man's coldness when her dear baby had died.

Eira felt Lloyd's brow in much the same way as Llinos had done and then took some cold water from the basin on the table and patted it over the boy's face.

'I'd give him a drink of soothing cordial,' she said. 'See how he is in the morning.' She shrugged. 'With children, a hot brow and a sickly feeling can be gone in a matter of hours.'

'You don't think it's the whooping cough?' Llinos asked. Eira smiled, shaking her head.

'If Lloyd had the whooping cough he'd be barking his head off by now. Don't worry, Mrs Mainwaring, you'll see, he'll be fine in the morning.'

But Lloyd was not fine. Llinos, awake early as always, looked in on her son before going down to breakfast. Lloyd was asleep but it was not a natural sleep. His breathing was ragged, his face mottled. He was a very sick child indeed.

'Joe! Where are you?' Her voice was full of anguish and it seemed to echo in the silence of the bedroom. Once he would have sensed her need, come to her; what had happened to the closeness between them? How could one foolish argument lead to this separation? As Llinos held Lloyd's hand, waiting for the doctor to call, she knew it was not as simple as that. The argument had just been the culmination of Joe's frustration. He was a deeply troubled man and she had been too selfish to notice it.

When the doctor came, he seemed young and presentable. He examined Lloyd and prescribed an hourly purge of the bowels and suggested that a warm fire be lit in the bedroom. 'It's just a childhood fever, dear lady,' he said. 'Nothing to worry about.'

Llinos thanked him, her heart heavy. She knew enough from Joe's teachings to realize what the doctor suggested would only make Lloyd worse.

When the doctor had gone, Llinos flung open the window to allow the fresh spring air into the room. She called Eira and told her to keep applying cold cloths to Lloyd's face and body.

'But, Mrs Mainwaring, the doctor said . . .'

'I know what the doctor said but I don't agree with him.' She looked at Lloyd: his eyes were still closed and his face flushed. 'Go back to your room, Eira,' Llinos said. 'I'll stay with my son.'

The day dragged on endlessly. Llinos kept Lloyd as cool as possible, bathing his head and body. She felt anxious because he was not able to eat but, following Joe's methods, she gave her son plenty of cool drinks.

Joe, why did her thoughts always come back to Joe? But she knew why, he was part of her, woven into the fabric of her being. She would always love him so why had she allowed a distance to grow between them? She closed her eyes and concentrated her mind towards him, begging him to come home. If there was a spark of the old Joe left in him, he would sense her need and come to her.

He did. It was evening when Llinos heard the rumble of wheels outside the house. She felt her heartbeat quicken, she knew without being told that Joe was home. She got to her feet as she heard his footsteps coming up the stairs, her hand pressed against her chest. And then he was there, taking her into his arms, holding her.

'It's Lloyd,' she said against his chest, 'he's sick.'

'I know but don't worry, he'll be all right.' Joe released her and sat on the bed beside his son. He touched the boy's face and neck and slid his lean golden hands over Lloyd's body. At last he looked at his wife.

'You have done a good job, our son is on the mend,' Joe said. And all Llinos could think of was that Joe had heard her silent plea and he had come home.

CHAPTER NINE

'Hortense, just let me speak to you, please!' Binnie stood in the doorway of his house, staring at his wife's set face. 'Can't I even explain how I loved you too much to tell you the truth? I was so scared of losing you. Can't you even try to forgive me?'

Hortense stared back at the man she had believed in for so long, the man she'd thought of as her husband. The knot of pain and anger was still there as she thought of the way he had deceived her. How could he dismiss it so lightly? He had sired three children with her, knowing they were illegitimate; how dare he come here snivelling to be forgiven? But she would have to speak to him; there were matters to be resolved between them.

'Come in,' she said but there was no welcome in her voice. He followed her into the shade of the house, nodding to the maid, looking around him as though he wanted to drink in everything that he had lost because of his lies. Hortense would have waited for him; if only he had told her the truth, they could have found a solution. Now, all she could do was to try to minimize the damage to her children.

'So far,' she said coldly, 'Daddy doesn't know what's going on here, all he knows is that we have had what he calls "a spat"!' She frowned. 'Some spat, Binnie,' she said. 'Do you know what you've done? You've ruined my life.'

'Hortense, please, honey . . .'

'Shut up!' she said harshly. She closed the door. 'Now listen to me, we are going up country, we are going to see a preacher and we're going to be wed, properly.' She held up her hand as he made a move towards her. 'No! I don't want you near me, Binnie, do you understand?' She paused for breath, fighting back her tears.

'I want my boys to have a legitimate father and that is the only reason I'm doing this. Once we're wed, you can get out of my life for good, do you understand?'

'I love you, Hortense,' he said and he sounded desperate. 'I've always loved you.' He stood hands to his side; he seemed lost, defeated. Was that an act too?

'I suppose you told your wife that, did you?'

He shuffled his feet and she stood waiting, not letting him off the hook. 'Well?'

He sighed heavily. 'It was a mistake.' He shook his head. 'I was young, I didn't really think things through. As soon as I got married I knew it was the wrong thing for me to do. I knew even then it would never work.'

'And what about the wife and child you deserted so callously?' It hurt unbearably to think of Binnie, her man, in the arms of another woman. She could picture him in the church, making vows he never intended to keep. He opened his mouth to speak.

'Don't talk about the past!' she said. 'It was never my intention to let you make excuses. All I want is to put things right. To be a legal wife not a whore.'

She sighed. 'For now,' she said, 'you can sleep in the back bedroom. If you stay down at Mammy's house folk will only talk.'

His face lit up but Hortense hardened her heart. 'That does not mean you are coming home to live like before.' She glared at him. 'You are not getting into my bed!' she said. 'You don't touch me, not ever again, understand?'

He was willing to agree to anything. Hortense felt a great sadness as she looked at him. She believed he loved her; she had felt his love wrap around her on nights that would have been cold and lonely without him. But to him she must have been a golden opportunity to live a life of ease. He had everything to gain, everything provided for him by his wife's daddy. But she was not his wife, she reminded herself numbly.

'In a few days you can go up river, find a preacher man who does not know me or my family.' She swallowed hard. 'It won't heal things between you and me so don't think that. Nothing alters the fact that you sired three bastards!'

Binnie was white-faced; he loved the boys, didn't he? And yet he could leave his legitimate child, walk away from his daughter without compunction. He was weak, a man ruled by greed, and she hated him.

A week later they were married. When they returned home from the trip the family were gathered to have a party. Food was spread out on the pristine cloth in the dining room and her family were done up in their Sunday best ready to greet the couple who had gone away to patch up their quarrel. If only they knew.

Jo hugged her. 'You've done the right thing,' she whispered. Josephine was the only one of her family who knew the truth but how long before John Pendennis got himself drunk and told the whole neighbourhood?

There was a flurry of greetings, kisses and hugs, and Hortense felt as though she was acting a part, the part of a happy wife. What a farce it all was. Melia was sitting quietly in the corner and John was on the other side of the room, as far away from her as he could get.

The rat! Hortense thought. He had sown his wild oats with Melia, had betrayed his wife, and now he was acting as if nothing had happened. Why hadn't Jo got shot of him?

'I can't,' Jo said reading her thoughts. 'I'm going to give him another chance.'

'Why?' Hortense asked, her voice low. Her parents were talking to Binnie, engrossed in conversation.

'I'm pregnant,' she said. 'It's what I've been longing for, you know that. Perhaps if we have a child together John will change.'

Hortense doubted it; being a father had made no difference to Binnie, none at all. But she smiled at her sister and squeezed her hand.

'You're right, hon, you stick it out. I'm sure John's had such a fright that he won't do anything like it again.'

Josephine smiled. 'I'm sure he won't,' she said.

'I've told him if he strays again I'll cut his balls off!'

Hortense found herself smiling in spite of her misery. She hoped Jo could tame John, could stop him running round after women like a stray tom-cat. But one thing that could be said in his favour, at least he had not committed bigamy. Men were men; look at her father. Perhaps she could have forgiven Binnie for a fling with another woman but his deceit went much deeper than that.

The boys were happy to see their mother and father together again. The younger ones came into the room and flung themselves at Binnie whooping with joy. Only Dan, the eldest, stood back, his expression guarded. He was a sober-minded boy, very adult for his age, and Hortense wondered how much of the situation Dan understood.

She ate very little of the party food and after a while she found the atmosphere stifling. She wandered out onto the porch and sank into the rocking chair. She felt like a very old woman, a woman whose life was over. She longed to cry but she had to keep up the pretence that she and Binnie were reconciled. She looked up when Mammy joined her.

'You're not a happy little girl, are you, hon?' Mrs McCabe was not a woman easily fooled.

'I'm all right, Mammy,' Hortense said. 'I suppose the honeymoon had to be over some time.' She looked at her mother. 'How did you feel the first time you knew about Daddy's women?'

'Ah, so that's what this is all about, Binnie been sowing some wild oats, has he?' She seemed quite relieved. 'Well, we women don't like it but they is men and men sometimes act like goats, you jest gotta get used to it.'

Hortense did not bother to correct her mother. 'But, Mammy, how can you bear to think of Daddy sleeping in the arms of another woman, deceiving you an' all?'

Her mother laughed. 'He never deceived me, not for one little ole minute, hon! I knowed what he was up to from the word go.'

'And you let him?'

'Sure I let him. How could I stop him? But I made sure the girls were clean, no sickness in them, you know what I mean? Those girls come from good families and when your daddy is tired of them, he gives them a nice little nest-egg to start up a new life.'

Hortense shook her head. 'Your ways are old-fashioned, Mammy,' she said. She thought of Josephine and her threat to cut off John's balls and smiled.

'What's tickling you, hon?' her mother asked.

'Just something Jo said. Come on, Mammy, we'd better go inside, otherwise they'll all be wondering where we've got to.'

'One thing,' Mrs McCabe said softly, 'your man is a good man and he loves *you*. Whoever he took to his bed, it meant nothing, it's what men do. The wife and children are the important things and anyone try to take that away and a man will fight to the death to protect them.'

'I'm sure you're right, Mammy.' Hortense took her mother's arm, knowing that her heart was broken, Binnie had feet of clay; their marriage would never be the same again. Perhaps she would grow to tolerate Binnie in time but never, never while she breathed would she forgive him for what he had done.

Llinos sat in the garden with Lloyd at her side. He was drawing pictures, his small face screwed up in concentration. He was still pale but his strength was coming back and he was improving from day to day.

He had quite a flair for drawing and, surreptitiously, Llinos looked over his shoulder. He had drawn a pattern of flowers, quite a good drawing for a child his age. Llinos sat quietly watching her son. He should have more art lessons. Eira was quite a good teacher but it might be a good idea for one of the factory artists to give Lloyd tuition.

She spoke to Joe about it that night as they prepared for bed. Since his return home, she felt he was softening towards her. True he had not come to her bed but, still, his smile was warmer, his tone kindly. Perhaps she had imagined it all. Now he seemed to be there in body but where was his spirit?

'Let the boy develop at his own pace, Llinos.'

It sounded like a rebuke. She stared at Joe, his face silvered by the moonlight. He was so handsome it hurt her to look at him.

'I can't do right for doing wrong, can I!' she demanded. 'Tell me, Joe, have you fallen out of love with me, is there someone else?'

'Yes, if you must know, there is someone else.' He kept his back to her.

'So you are being unfaithful to me!' The shock was like a physical blow. 'Who is it, Joe? Tell me.'

'I'm sorry, Llinos, I tried to explain things to you in Cornwall but I couldn't. I just knew you would never understand.'

Anger followed the shock, such anger as Llinos had never felt before. 'So you take another woman and the fault is mine, is that what you are saying?' Her voice rose and Joe turned to look at her.

'I have no intention of getting into a brawl with my wife!' he said. 'I'm going into the dressing room, I need to sleep.' He had put up a barrier once more and she knew she would never penetrate it. She wanted to beat at him with her fists, to make him take notice of her.

'Do you love her, this other woman, more than you love me?'

He did not reply. She saw his hair, long and sleek, hanging over his shoulders. He hesitated for a moment in the doorway.

'Joe, don't just ignore me, if you've anything to say then say it. Are you going to leave me?'

He stood tall and majestic washed in the light from the window. 'I've got nothing to say.' The door was closed quietly, shutting him away from her.

Llinos buried her face in the pillow, too hurt to cry. They had loved each other so much; what had gone wrong between them? She hardly slept; the rest of the night passed slowly, hour by hour while Llinos tried to come to terms with the fact that Joe was with another woman, making love to her. No wonder his absences from home had grown longer and more frequent.

In the morning, Llinos dragged herself from bed to find the dressing room empty and the sun poking through the curtains. She had slept late and her head felt heavy. Downstairs, she joined Charlotte in the dining room and picked at her food. There was no sign of Joe; he must have left the house early.

'What's wrong, Llinos?' Charlotte's voice broke into her thoughts and Llinos looked up quickly.

'Nothing, really. Lloyd is almost his old self. I'm thinking of getting someone to give him more art tuition. I would like him to try painting on chinaware.'

'I didn't ask about Lloyd,' Charlotte said quietly. 'I'm an old woman, Llinos, I found love late but Sam was the best thing that ever happened to me. Now I'm alone and I miss him every minute of every day. Don't throw away what you and Joe have because of a silly quarrel.'

'I am not throwing anything away!' Llinos said. 'I have tried my best to talk to Joe, to understand him but he just blocks me out of his life.' Llinos heard the note of despair in her own voice. 'The truth is, Charlotte, he has another woman.'

Charlotte shook her head. 'No, I don't believe that.' She looked down at her hands. 'Perhaps he's not very well or in a mood; men get like that sometimes, at least my father did.'

Llinos was silent. She did not want to inflict her own pain on Charlotte; Charlotte loved Joe, could believe no wrong of him. It was not fair to disillusion her.

'Did you see him this morning? Did he say anything before he left the house?'

Charlotte shook her head. 'No, he'd left by the time I got up. Still perhaps it's just as well, he probably needs some time alone to think. Men can be so difficult. My father was a difficult man; he couldn't talk about his troubles. His feelings were kept tightly locked inside him. I know Joe seems different but perhaps there is more of Father in him than I thought.'

Llinos sighed. There was no point in going on with the conversation, Charlotte knew no more about Joe than she did.

Later, Llinos called Watt into the house. 'Sit down, love.' She smiled affectionately at him. 'I have to talk to you.'

'Is anything wrong?' Watt looked concerned.

'No, not wrong.' She hesitated. 'I just want to take a back seat in the business, be here with my family more than I have been.' She tried to smile. 'So Watt, my boy, you are now in charge of the pottery, completely in charge. I know you can handle it so don't look so worried.'

Watt rubbed his fingers through his hair. 'I'm not worried about handling the pottery,' he said. 'I live and breathe the pottery. No, it's you I'm worried about. I've never heard you talk like that before, the pottery has always been so important to you.'

'Not so important that I can risk losing Joe over it,' she said quietly. Watt stared at her for a long time. It was clear he was trying to think of the right thing to say.

'Am I losing him, Watt? You're a man, can you tell me what I've done to turn Joe away from me?' She could not even mention to Watt the fact that Joe had another woman; it was far too painful.

'Nothing!' Watt said quickly. 'If Joe has problems they are his problems.' He held out his hands to her. 'Look, Llinos, we always hurt the one we love, you know that. If Joe is worried he'll take it out on his nearest and dearest, even Joe's human, *cariad*.'

She smiled involuntarily. 'It's a long time since you've called me "sweetheart" and in Welsh too!'

'Well, I love you like a sister, you know that, Llinos. But stop worrying, let your man work out things for himself.' He smiled apologetically. 'That's the trouble with women, they try to see inside us, try to turn us inside out. It just doesn't work.'

'I suppose you're right.' Llinos suddenly felt a little better. Everyone seemed to be telling her she was not at fault, that Joe would be back given time. Perhaps he would get this other woman out of his system and then he would realize that it was Llinos he loved.

'Thank you, Watt,' Llinos said. 'Now go and be boss and make sure my pottery flourishes, right?'

'Right.' He let himself out and Llinos could hear him whistling as he walked down the drive. At least she had made Watt feel better; the work gave him something to think about, something to take his mind off Maura.

Maura was dead and gone, out of reach for ever. Joe was still alive and well and so long as they both breathed, Llinos knew she and Joe would never be able to live apart. One day he would come home and then he would be hers again.

CHAPTER TEN

'So you're a big boss, now?' Rosie was looking up at him with something like awe in her young face. Watt smiled and ruffled her hair.

'That's just a name, love, I'm doing the same job but for more pay, that's the truth of it.'

'Get away from here!' Rosie said. 'You're an important man, Watt Bevan, and don't pretend to be ordinary like me, 'cos I don't believe you.'

They were walking along the river-bank towards the place where the waters of the Tawe ran into the sea. The long stretch of the bay reached from Swansea to Mumbles and there the grey rocks crouched like old men dipping their toes in the sea. It was a lovely summer day and Watt felt glad to be alive. And then he felt guilty because Maura was dead. He could picture her now, so beautiful with her red hair tangled over her shoulders and her sensuous mouth inviting his kiss. Maura had given him a taste of what real loving was all about. They should have been together for ever, instead death had snatched her away from him.

'That woman is staring at you,' Rosie said nudging him. 'See, she can't take her eyes off you.'

Watt looked at the woman and a shock ran through him like a burst of strong wine.

'Hello, Watt, remember me?' She looked up at him, her mouth curving into a smile.

'Lily! I thought you'd left Swansea to get married?'

She looked tired. Her eyes were shadowed and she was much thinner than he remembered. Once he had been in love with her, the love of a green youth, but he had got over that a long time ago.

'My husband died, Watt, so I've come home.'

'So I see.' His tone was dry; he had no intention of renewing their relationship. Not that they had had a relationship. He had wanted her, lusted after her perhaps. She had wanted, well, he had never been sure what she had wanted.

Lily seemed to be waiting for him to say something more and Watt felt uncomfortable. 'What are you doing now, still painting pottery?' he asked, more from a need to break the silence than because he was really interested.

Lily shook her head. 'No, I thought I'd have a change. I've started work at Howell's grocery store, I'm on my way there now.'

'Oh, that's a pity, you were always such a talented painter.' He spoke before he had time to think. Lily blushed and looked down at her hands. The tips were browned by potato dust. 'Thank you, Watt, you don't know how much it means to me to hear you say that.'

'Well, I'd better be off then.' Watt became aware

of Rosie at his side, moving restlessly from one foot to the other.

'Sorry, I've been keeping you,' Lily said quickly. She was so different, so beaten that Watt felt sorry for her.

'Look,' he said, 'where are you lodging? I'll try to come to see you, shall I? Perhaps we can find you a better job, something more suited to your talents.'

'I'm at Dai Vaughan's lodging house, just until I find something better,' Lily said. She must have seen Watt's frown because she sounded defensive when she spoke again.

'It's just temporary, like. I'll get somewhere better when I earn enough money to pay for it.'

'So, Lily, have you learned a lot from your past mistakes, then?' Watt said softly. 'No-one gives you anything for nothing, in this life we all have to work for what we have.'

'I know.' Her meekness was out of character and it was also very appealing. Watt told himself he was a fool but as he took Rosie's arm and walked away, he felt a lightness in his heart that had been absent since Maura died.

'You should stay away from that woman!' Rosie had sensed his feelings. She looked up at him, her mouth a prim line of disapproval. 'My mam told me about Lily. She acted so high and mighty and then caused nothing but trouble for Mrs Mainwaring.'

'That's all in the past,' Watt said. 'Pearl and Lily never got on, your mother resented it when I praised Lily's work. But she *is* really talented, it's a pity to see such talent going to waste.'

'Well she looks too old for you, Watt, she's all skin and bone and shadows.'

Watt hid a smile, Rosie was jealous of Lily. 'I did think I loved Lily once,' he said, 'but that was a long time ago. Now I know better.'

'Go on!' she said and Watt noticed her tone was acid. 'I saw the way you looked at her, you fancy her, don't deny it!'

'I don't!' he protested. 'I'm not the young fool I was. I'm more mature now.'

Rosie smiled, her eyes lighting up with laughter. 'Do you want to know a joke?' she said.

'Aye, go on then.'

'What's the difference between a man and a cheese?'

'I don't know.' Watt humoured her. 'But I suppose you are going to tell me.'

'A cheese matures!' Rosie pushed Watt's arm and giggled like the young girl she was. She was so sweet, so unspoiled, and he had to agree that compared to Rosie's fresh, youthful appearance Lily had looked careworn and sickly. Still, he had felt something stir within him, something of the old attraction. It had been a dangerous attraction though and he was not going to fall into that trap again.

Llinos watched as Joe sank into his chair. She handed him a glass of port and he took it, swirling the ruby drink around and peering into its depths as if he could read his future there. Being Joe, perhaps he could.

'I'm so glad you came to see us, Joe.'

He nodded but did not reply. He appeared

worried, as unsure about the future as she was. He was obviously unhappy and Llinos wanted to force him to talk to her about the other woman in his life but she dare not. What if he told her the marriage was over, that he had tired of her and wanted a different sort of life for himself? What if he walked out of her life never to come back?

She swallowed her pain. 'Had a good business trip?' He had been away for days and it was like a knife turning within her as she thought of him with another woman. He had bathed and changed his dusty clothes before joining Llinos and Charlotte for the meal but, since then, he had been uncommunicative, unwilling or unable to talk to her.

He sighed and looked across the room into the fire. 'It went all right, I suppose.'

She wanted him to say it was good to be back home, that his madness was over but he did no such thing. 'Aren't you going to look in on your son?' she asked, forcing a note of brightness into her tone. 'Lloyd has missed you very much, Joe.'

She knew what she was doing; she was trying to bind him to her with his love for Lloyd. It was the act of a desperate woman and she admitted to herself that she was desperate.

'I looked in on him when I bathed,' he said and tipped up the glass, sipping a little of his drink.

They sat in silence for a while and then Llinos took a deep breath. 'I've asked Watt to take more responsibility for the pottery.' She spoke softly, wanting him to look at her with love as he used to. She needed his love like she needed water to live, what had she done to lose it?

'Good.' He was not really listening to what she

was saying. She had tried to please him, tried to do what he wanted in spite of her own feelings, and he was not even listening! Suddenly she was furious with him.

'I've had enough of this!' She rose to her feet, glad that Charlotte had decided to go to bed early. She was so incensed by Joe's attitude that she must tell him so or she would break up into thousands of little pieces.

'You are away most of the time, leaving me to bring up our son alone. When you *are* here you look as if you would prefer to be somewhere else, so why don't you go?'

'Not now, Llinos,' he said. 'I'm not in the mood for a row.'

'And I'm not in the mood to be ignored any longer.' She wanted to slap his handsome, golden face. In that moment, she felt she hated him. What she really hated was his indifference to her.

'Why don't you go and stay with that other woman, Joe?' she demanded. He rose to his feet and moved to pour himself another drink.

'I can't explain about her, you wouldn't understand, but being with her is something I just can't help.'

'Ah, that's what they all say, isn't it, the men who cheat on their wives. They hide their guilt by pretending the woman is to blame in some way. You are hateful Joe! I can't bear to look at you, do you know that?'

He spun round to face her. 'Stop it, Llinos!' She had never seen Joe so angry with her. His eyes blazed like fires. 'If you have finished telling me how low you think I've sunk in your estimation then I'll take my drink and go to bed.'

'Aye, go to bed; you never share mine any more, do you?'

He strode to the door, his dark hair swinging on his shoulders, his drink trembling in the glass.

'Don't walk out on me, Joe Mainwaring!' But he did just that, closing the door in her outraged face. Llinos picked up a glass and threw it and it shattered, the pieces falling like diamonds onto the carpet. She put her hands over her face, trying to hold back the tears but they came anyway, hot and bitter and, sinking into a chair, she sobbed as though her heart was broken.

Later, as she tried to sleep in the large bed without the warmth from Joe's body to comfort her, she tried yet again to understand what had gone wrong.

'Fool!' she whispered. He had another woman, that was what had gone wrong. He had never lied to her before but then nor had he shut her out of his life the way he was doing now.

On an impulse, she got up from bed and slipped into the dressing room. She heard sounds of his regular breathing and knew he was asleep. How could he sleep, how dare he sleep when she was so overwrought? She hesitated, wondering if she should slip into bed beside him. But what if he rejected her? Feeling worse than ever, she made her way back to her own bed.

She ordered breakfast in her room. She felt unable to face the day, her eyes were red from weeping and the pain inside her would not go away. Rosie carried in the tray and set it on the table, looking at Llinos with a frown.

'Are you all right, Mrs Mainwaring?'

'I'm just fine, Rosie. Go on, back downstairs, have your own breakfast, I'm sure you must be hungry by now.'

Llinos ate very little of the toasted bread and sizzling bacon but was comforted by the warmth of the tea. Last night, she had lost her temper and all she had achieved was to drive the wedge deeper between Joe and her.

Eira brought Lloyd to kiss her good morning and Llinos realized that her son was dressed for the outdoors.

'Where are you going, Lloyd? Walking with Eira again?'

'Father is taking me out today. Are you feeling sickly, Mamma?' he asked, resting his head against her breast. 'Father says you need to rest a lot and I'm not to bother you.'

'You don't bother me!' Llinos said hugging her son. 'I love you so much, Lloyd, do you know that? Now, if you want to go out you may go but as it's raining today, wouldn't you prefer to stay indoors and let Eira give you some painting lessons?'

'Lloyd needs a change from lessons, Mrs Mainwaring,' Eira said. 'I think he should go out more. So long as he wraps up well the rain won't hurt him.'

'Perhaps you're right, Eira.' Llinos wished Eira was older, married and as used to the ways of men as she was to children, then she could have asked her advice about Joe. Strange, Llinos had never felt the lack of a female companion before; she had been content in her marriage and her motherhood and her work. Eynon had been the only friend she had ever wanted. Now even he was otherwise occupied and with a married woman at that. Were all men born womanizers?

Eira led Lloyd towards the door; she paused and looked back at Llinos. 'Mr Mainwaring has sent the other tutor away,' she said. 'He thinks that, between us, he and I can do the job just as well.'

The door closed behind Eira before Llinos had time to take in what she had said. How dare Joe take matters into his own hands? It was she who arranged Lloyd's lessons, she who should hire and fire his tutors. But a small warm glow lit within her; Joe clearly intended to spend a great deal of his time at home in future.

Llinos slipped out of bed and began to wash. The water in the jug had gone a little cold but it would have to do. As she dressed, Llinos wondered how she could talk to Pearl about Joe. Pearl was wise and perhaps a little cynical about men and outspoken with it. She would not hesitate to offer an opinion. But then Pearl had not been well lately and she had her own troubles. Llinos sighed. She had no right to burden others with her problems.

Perhaps she should just face facts; Joe had grown tired of her, their old closeness was gone. The magical quality they shared of knowing each other's thoughts had vanished like the mists off the river when the sun came out. He was preoccupied with thoughts of another woman and the pain of it was almost physical.

Charlotte poked her head round the bedroom door. 'Aren't you well, Llinos, my dear?' Charlotte still could not pronounce the double 'L' in Llinos's name. 'I must say you look as if you've had a terrible night. Did I hear raised voices when I was in bed?'

She sat down on the chair near the window. 'Tell me to mind my own business if you like, what *is* wrong between you and Joe?'

The gentle sympathy in Charlotte's tone was enough to bring the tears flooding to Llinos's eyes.

'Don't cry, there's nothing that can't be solved when two people love each other the way you and Joe do.'

Llinos looked at Charlotte frowning worriedly and held her tongue. How could Llinos tell his sister that Joe, the perfect brother, was being unfaithful to his wife? She tried to wipe away the tears.

'Come on, talk to me about it, I'm an old woman, I might just be able to help you.'

Charlotte patted Llinos's back, treating her like a little girl. It was a good feeling to be mothered. Llinos, the strong independent business woman, was at her weakest now.

'It's Joe,' she said at last. 'I think . . . . Oh, I don't know, he's changed.' She looked up at her sister-in-law. 'I'm worried about him.'

'There's nothing wrong with him. He still loves you, any fool can see that,' Charlotte said firmly.

A glimmer of hope entered Llinos's heart. 'What is it then? He won't talk to me and I can't seem to get through to him any more.'

Charlotte shook her head. 'Joe is a strong healthy man, whatever is wrong it's not his health. Could he be having business problems?'

Llinos shook her head. 'Joe is very rich and very clever with his money, you know that, Charlotte.'

'Even clever people can lose their fortunes, my dear, it's happened many times before and will happen again I've no doubt.'

'That could be it, I suppose.' Llinos could not look Charlotte in the eyes; she hated to deceive her.

'I would just sit tight and bide my time if I were you,' Charlotte said. 'A man needs his own thinking time, especially a man like Joe.' She smiled. 'He is still the Mandan Indian, you know, he's American Indian in spite of the blood of his white father running in him. Don't try to understand him, not just now. And remember, the last thing a man wants is to face a barrage of questions.'

Llinos forced a smile. 'Have you seen Joe this morning?'

'I saw him go out with Lloyd,' Charlotte said. 'Those two look so good together. Just be patient, my dear, let Joe sort out his own problems and be waiting to take him into your arms when he does.' She rose to her feet.

'Now, why don't you spend the day resting in your room? Try to take things easy for a change. It's not that long since you went through a very trying time losing that sweet baby. Joe is affected by all that too, I'm sure; you both need time to recover properly.' She looked at the barely touched tray on the bedside table.

'And you must eat, do you understand?'

'Yes, Mother,' Llinos said in an attempt at lightness. 'I'll be a good girl and do as you say and perhaps things will come right.' But even as she spoke, Llinos had very little hope that her optimistic words held any real meaning. Joe had gone far away from her and she felt she would never get him back.

'What's wrong, Mam, have you got a bad head again?' Rosie put the heavy basket on the kitchen table with a sigh of relief.

'You're awful pale, Mam, are you sure you're not sickening for something?' She looked down at her mother, a worried expression on her face. 'Why don't you have the day off? Mrs Mainwaring will understand, you know how kind she is. She's sent you these things, look.' She removed the snow-white cloth from over the basket. 'Fresh butter, some eggs and some veg. The pottery won't fall to bits without you, Mam, you should stay home if your head is bad.'

'It's only a bit of a chill, *cariad*, and I have to go to work. What would they do if Pearl wasn't there to chivvy them along? Anyway, we need the money, don't we?'

'Well, it's a bit better now, Mam. I bring in money as well.'

'Aye and talking about that, you'd better get back up to the big house. Tell Mrs Mainwaring that I'm grateful for her trouble but I'll be all right once I get myself together.'

'I'll wait for you,' Rosie said. 'We'll walk down the hill together.'

'Aye, all right then, perhaps the fresh air will do me good.' She sniffed. 'Not that it's very fresh round here, mind, not with the works spewing out filth day and night.'

They walked away from the crowded huddle of houses on Greenhill arm-in-arm. They were two very different women, Pearl, large, buxom, and Rosie tiny, delicate.

The empty basket bumped against Rosie's side as she walked but she was happy. She thought of Watt, she was thinking of him a great deal lately, ever since he had come to her birthday party. He had looked so different from when he was in work, younger somehow. He was so handsome, so self-assured but then he was older than she was. Not much, just enough. It was a pity that she had sensed something between him and the awful woman they had met in town.

'Mam, do you remember that woman named Lily? She used to paint pots alongside you? Skinny type, plain as a pikestaff.'

Pearl sniffed. She had more colour now; the air, smelly or not, seemed to be doing her good.

'Who could forget that trollop! I remember her well, trouble she was to everyone she met. Nearly got Mrs Mainwaring killed with her goings on.' Pearl looked down at Rosie. 'Why, don't tell me she's back in Swansea?'

'Me and Watt met her the other day, she seemed to know Watt very well.' She waited with bated breath for her mother's next words.

'Oh aye, Lily had her sights set on our Watt but once a man came along who she thought had more money she dropped Watt like a hot cake.'

'Did they . . .' Rosie was not sure how far to go; her mam was pretty easygoing and had fun at work with the men but she did not like her children to be too forward. 'I mean was they . . .' She stopped, unable to go on, a rich blush stained her cheeks and she felt the heat run down to her small breasts.

'I don't think he ever went to her bed, if that's what you mean.' Pearl laughed. 'No fear, not our Lily, she didn't like a man to touch her, funny girl.'

Rosie smiled. 'Well, she's not much to look at and she looks fair worn out as if she'd been selling herself on the streets or something.'

'What do you know about such things?' Pearl's voice was sharp and Rosie bit her lip.

'Nothing, Mam, just that you sees them women waiting, like, for a man to come and pay them. They all seem bone weary of life, you know what I mean.'

'Aye, love, I know what you mean and you just thank the good Lord that you and me are respectable women with decent jobs.'

Rosie hid a smile; her mother chose to ignore the fact that she went to Willie's bed whenever she had the chance. Willie had thrown a lifeline to Pearl when she was widowed suddenly. He was a good man, a little slow of wit but he took care of Pearl and Rosie liked him for it.

'Aye, good thing we don't have to stand on street corners like those women. But you mustn't scorn them, Rosie. Our Lord forgave that Mary who was with men all the time so don't you be a judge now.'

Rosie digested this in silence, it was not like her mother to be so charitable. When Dad was caught with one of them hussies, Mam had hit him with the good copper saucepan, giving him a sore head for weeks. But Dad was gone now, dead and in his grave, past the sins of the flesh.

'Was this Lily any good with the painting?' she asked, still consumed with curiosity about the woman. There had definitely been something between Lily and Watt and it disturbed Rosie to think about it.

'Not bad, good enough I suppose. When she worked at the pottery, Lily was a fussy little madam, full of herself and Watt fancied getting inside her drawers but she wasn't having none of it.'

Pearl laughed. 'Sorry, *cariad*, I shouldn't say such things to my little girl but then you will have to learn about men sooner or later and it might as well be sooner.'

Rosie knew she was in for a lecture, she tried to deflect her mother, whose bad head seemed to have gone away, but it was no use.

'Remember this, Rosie, however nice a man is, however kind and polite, he will want to do things with you, things you shouldn't do until you got a ring on your finger.'

Rosie hid her face and smiled. Now her mother had started, she might just as well tease her along.

'What things do you mean, Mam?'

'Well.' Pearl seemed at a loss. 'A man starts by feeling you in certain places, you know.'

'My chest, Mam?'

'Aye, that's right.' Pearl sounded relieved. 'Now that's all very well if you are courting properly, like, but make sure a man's intentions are the church and the ring not just the bed.'

The sound of the River Tawe rushing to the sea heralded the closeness of the potteries and Pearl smiled. 'All I'm going to say to you, Rosie, is be a good girl and don't let any man take liberties.'

'Not even Watt Bevan?' Rosie did not look at her mother.

'Especially not Watt; he's a fine man but he's a man like any other and will take his pleasure of you if it's offered for free.'

Pearl stopped walking. 'Well, talk of the devil!' Watt was near the pottery gates, talking to one of the delivery men. Piles of bags weighted the cart, which dipped perilously at the back, threatening to discharge the load into the roadway.

'Day to you, Watt,' Pearl said, 'got some more clay, have we? About time too, the stocks are getting pretty low.'

'Better, Pearl?' Watt came towards them, a sheaf of papers in his hands. He peered at Pearl and shook his head. 'You don't look well to me, a bit white around the gills.' He smiled. 'Why didn't you take the day off?'

'I told her that,' Rosie said. 'But mam's stubborn, she won't listen to nobody, especially me.'

Watt smiled at her. 'You'd better get up to the house, Rosie,' he said pulling a curl of her hair, 'Mrs Mainwaring might be needing you.'

'Well it's Mrs Mainwaring who sent me to our mam's, so there!' She liked Watt but she did not intend to take orders from him. 'Don't you try to be all bossy with me, Watt Bevan.' She smiled up at him and he made a face at her. Rosie tried to imagine him touching her breasts, taking liberties with her and the thought brought rich colour to her face.

'Why are you blushing, Rosie?' Watt teased.

'Seen a young lad you fancy, have you?' He looked around as though expecting to see one of the apprentices, knowing full well that Rosie's attention was fixed on him.

'Clever boots!' She flounced past him. 'See you after, Mam,' she said as she made her way towards the house, her colour still high. She was becoming a woman and she was beginning to feel the stirrings of passion except that, being young, she mistook them for love.

CHAPTER ELEVEN

'I want to leave him!' Alice Sparks was a woman in her prime. Her hair was styled with a middle parting, curling at the sides of her face. Her clothes were cut from the best cloth and her boots had the sheen of the best leather. She stared up at Eynon, her eyes large.

'I don't think I can stand Edward's meanness for a moment longer. You see the clothes I'm wearing? He has bought none of them. My father gives me an allowance from which I have to see to all my needs.'

They were seated in a back room of one of the inns in Parkmill, several miles away from Swansea. It was a place that was made for clandestine meetings. The windows were small, the panes filled with thick glass making it difficult to look inside. There were private corners where lovers could have comparative privacy. 'Edward is so mean that he makes me live in that dreadful little house he rents. Apart from which he's a spiteful man and he hates everyone, including me.'

Alice looked very beautiful in the half-light. Her

dark hair sprang in curls around her fine-boned face and her small hands were clasped together on the table top. Even Eynon himself could not be unaware that she looked very much like Llinos Mainwaring.

'There would be a scandal if you left him,' Eynon warned. 'I doubt if any of the "proper" women of the area would ever welcome you into their homes again.'

Alice tossed her head. 'I don't care a fig for that sort of woman.' The slender column of her throat was enhanced by the low-cut neck of the gown. The waist was nipped in just below her white breasts. She was a beautiful, spirited woman and yet the last thing Eynon wanted was to be responsible for her. To live with her was not in his scheme of things. In any case, there would be such a scandal they would have to leave Swansea and Eynon had no intention of doing that.

Alice seemed to sense something of his feelings; she tried to push Eynon into a decision. 'You must do something soon, Eynon,' she said. 'I have a nasty suspicion I've fallen for a baby, your baby.' She looked at him, archly anticipating his questions. 'I know it must be yours because I've been turning Mr Sparks away from my bed these past months.'

That was a lie. The reason she had taken a lover in the first place was because Mr Sparks did not care for bedroom activities. Eynon knew that as well as she did.

'Are you sure, Alice?' There was a constriction in his throat; he had a sense of history repeating itself. His first wife had come to him with just such a claim. He had married her and in due course the child was born. He liked to think that Jayne was his own flesh and blood; he loved her dearly but he would never be sure if he was her natural father.

'I'll do my best to help out financially, of course,' he said. And that he felt was his duty done. Alice Sparks was a married woman; a woman he would hate to live with on a permanent basis.

'But, Eynon, I want to be with you, to share our child with you, don't you understand that?'

'Might I suggest you would be better off sticking it out with the man you married.' He spoke so firmly that Alice looked at him in surprise. 'I think I'm right in saying that your child is Edward's, at least in law,' he added.

She seemed nonplussed. 'You don't want to live with me?'

'Not to live with forever. It's best to be honest about these things, isn't it?' He waited for her to speak but she remained silent.

'You see, Alice, I'm in love with someone else, someone I can never have.' He shrugged. 'Any other woman pales into insignificance beside Llinos Mainwaring.' The moment he said her name, he knew it was a mistake. Alice pounced on it as if the knowledge was a weapon she might be able to use sometime.

'The wife of that half-breed? I don't believe it! Heavens, Eynon, haven't you more pride?'

'Pride, what can you mean?'

'She's been to bed with that . . . that foreigner! How could you be in love with her? It's not proper.'

'It's no worse than going to bed with you,'

Eynon challenged. Alice looked at him frostily.

'At least my marriage is a respectable one,' she said huffily. 'Mr Sparks is a particular man, he takes good care of his health and he washes regularly.'

Eynon could have laughed if the matter were not so serious. 'Meaning that Joe doesn't? Look, Alice, Joe is a rich man in his own right; he is an educated, cultured man. He is well respected by the more intelligent members of society.'

'That's not what I heard. At least Mr Sparks does not indulge in affairs, he has too much respect for himself, unlike you and your friend the Indian!' Alice did not see the trap she was making for herself.

'Well then, if I have no respect for myself, where does that leave you? I think you had better follow my suggestion and go back to Mr Sparks.'

'Well from what I heard, the dear sweet Llinos Mainwaring has been discarded in favour of another woman.' Alice's tone was spiteful.

'I would not take kitchen gossip too seriously, Alice, because more often than not you are the subject of it.'

'Take me home!' She snatched up her gloves and waved them in her face in an effort to cool the hot colour that had turned her cheeks an un-attractive shade of red. 'I will not spend one more minute in your company, Mr Morton-Edwards!'

'Well,' he almost smiled, 'you will have to if we are to share my carriage, for I have no intention of walking back to Swansea.'

On the way home, he was aware of Alice fuming beside him. She refused to look at him and did not reply to any of his remarks. 'Stop here!' she commanded and Eynon tapped his stick at the driver.

'You are still a little way from the centre of Swansea,' Eynon warned. 'It will be a long walk, I hope you understand that?'

'I understand more than you think,' she said waspishly. 'Good day to you, Mr Morton-Edwards.'

He watched for a moment as she stalked away, her skirts swaying beneath her coat. He wondered where on earth she had got the story about Joe and another woman. Still, she was not to be taken seriously. He wondered briefly if she was having a child. He doubted it; her sort of woman would stop at nothing to get what they wanted.

He told the driver to get under way and settled back in his seat closing his eyes. It seemed his little peccadillo with Alice Sparks was over and done with and for his own part, it was not a moment too soon.

Watt held Rosie's hand as they walked along the river-bank. The sun was shining, the birds were singing in the leafy trees and the sound of the water was like a melody. It was good to be with a nice-looking girl who made no demands on him.

Watt still missed Maura; it seemed only the other day that he had buried her in the cemetery on the hill. He sometimes felt he would never get over her but, for all that, he needed company. And Rosie was good company, she made him laugh.

'It's nice here, I like you to bring me down by the river,' Rosie said. 'It's quiet and we can be on our own without a crowd around us.'

Watt nodded without speaking. He liked the river too; the soothing sound of it over the stones at the water's edge seemed to ease the ache inside him.

'My mam don't mind us courting,' Rosie said and her words brought Watt up sharp. He stopped walking and looked down at her. She smiled her cheeky, dimpled smile. 'It's all right, don't start running away, "courting" is Mam's word, not mine. She doesn't mean anything by it, Watt, it's just that she knows she can trust you to behave, not to play fast and loose with a girl.'

'Rosie,' Watt said softly, 'I was in love with Maura, I suppose I still love her. I'm just not ready for anything serious, not yet.'

'Neither am I!' Rosie laughed and pushed him away. 'I'm young and free and you're an old man, Watt Bevan.'

He smiled as she ran away from him beneath the trees. He supposed he was an old man compared to Rosie and him still in his early twenties. But then he had gained a great deal of experience in his short life. He had been an orphan, had worked from the age of nine at the pottery. He had travelled the great Atlantic Ocean and most important of all, he had loved and lost. All of it together made for a mature mind, so he liked to think.

He saw Rosie peep out from behind some bushes, like some woodland creature. She was so pretty, her skin freshened by the breeze to a becoming pink and her eyes shining with fun. She was good for him, there was no doubt about that, but was he good for her?

He pretended he had not spotted her and strolled past the bushes, hands in pockets, gazing up at the fluffy clouds. He heard a rustle and then she pounced on him, her momentum and the flurry of her arms and legs bearing him to the ground.

'Help!' he called, 'I'm being attacked by villains! Call the constable someone.'

'Hush!' Rosie put her hand over his mouth. 'Don't be so daft, people will hear you and come running and what will they think then?'

'They'll think why is that hoyden lying on that poor defenceless man?' Watt said enjoying the soft weight of her body a little more than he should.

She scrambled away from him, holding out her hand to help him up. He tugged and she fell in a heap against him. He kissed her. Her lips were soft and warm and responsive. He let his mouth linger on hers, it was not what he meant to happen, he was acting like a heel and yet, as her warm arms wound round him, he was tempted to allow the kiss to go on.

'Hey!' He pulled himself away from her. 'What's this wanton woman doing leading me astray?' He addressed the tree tops and the clouds. 'There's me taking an innocent walk and I'm attacked by a hussy. I ask you, trees, is it safe for a young man to take a walk these days?'

'Stop being daft!' Rosie smoothed down her coat and ran her hands through her hair. Her bonnet lay on the ground and she picked it up, dusting it against her sleeve. 'Come on, Watt, Mam's expecting us for tea and she don't like to be kept waiting, mind.'

'Oh I know Pearl of old!' Watt said ruefully. 'Rules the paint shop with a rod of iron does your mam and the Lord help anyone who crosses her. She even frightens me!'

'Liar!' Rosie said, her eyes shining with laughter. 'Last one home fetches in the coal!' Her hair flying, she raced back the way she had come and, more slowly, Watt followed her.

Pearl had a good fire burning in the grate and the house smelt of freshly baked bread. Watt followed Rosie into the kitchen where Pearl was brewing a pot of tea. Willie was dozing in the chair beside the fire, his fiddle across his lap. Pearl dug him in the ribs.

'Wake up, Willie, we've got company.' She was looking pale and drawn but she smiled happily at the couple. 'About time you came home, we're all starving waiting for you.'

Watt sat in the chair Pearl pulled out for him and looked at the snow-white cloth, the dish of raspberry jam and the thin slices of buttered bread. 'This looks like a feast for a starving man,' he said warmly. He liked Pearl, he was comfortable with her. She understood the pottery, knew the work better than most. Pearl was a woman he could rely on.

'It's not much, Watt.' Pearl put the pot on the stand. 'But it's all good home-made food and you're welcome to share it with us.' She turned her head. 'Willie, come on, boy, take your place at the table or do you want me fetching and carrying for you?'

Willie nodded good-naturedly and did as he was told. He always did. Rosie sat down beside Watt.

'Where are the boys, Mam?' she asked, her interest centred on the slice of bread she was transferring to her plate.

'When I saw you and Watt were going to be late I sent them over to Aunt Vi's. She called over the back wall to say they were having tea there, thank goodness.'

Pearl still looked far from well, Watt thought; there were shadows under her eyes and she seemed to be thinner about the face.

'You all right, Pearl?' he asked quietly and Pearl nodded. Watt glanced at Rosie, she seemed oblivious to her mother's tiredness. She lifted the slice of bread and bit into it with obvious delight, her white teeth making indentations in the soft jam. Over her jam-stained mouth, her eyes sparkled at Watt.

'Are you sure you're all right?' Watt asked and Pearl threw her daughter a swift glance before answering.

'I'm just a bit worried, love, but I'll talk to you about it at work, it doesn't concern anyone else, see?'

He did see; Pearl had a problem she did not want to discuss in front of Rosie or Willie. He nodded. 'Aye, fair enough.'

When they had eaten all the bread and jam and emptied the teapot twice over, Rosie cleared away the dishes.

'Remember to put the butter on the cold slab, now,' Pearl admonished, 'and cover the dish to keep the creatures off it.' She took the pristine cloth from the table and folded it, careful to keep to the same creases. 'Saves on the ironing,' she said.

After tea, Willie took up the fiddle and played a haunting tune that reminded Watt of Maura. He was glad of the dimness of the candles as moist tears came to his eyes. He could almost see her, smell the scent of her; would he ever forget her?

It was almost dark when Pearl's sons returned to the house. The kitchen suddenly seemed crowded, the boys arguing who should drag in the tin bath. Watt guessed it was time he left.

'Thanks for keeping me company.' He kissed Rosie. 'Are you coming back to the house now or shall I go on ahead?'

'I'll stay with Mam for a bit,' Rosie said. 'Help her to get the boys to bed. If you see Mrs Mainwaring though, tell her I won't be long.'

Watt patted Pearl's shoulder. 'Now if you don't feel better tomorrow, take time off, no-one will mind.'

As he made his way back to the house he wondered if he was becoming too friendly with Rosie, giving her false hopes. But then she was a sensible girl, look how she had stayed to help her mother. Anyway, she knew he was still pining for Maura, he had told her often enough. He gazed up at the sky, darker now, and felt tears smart in his eyes. 'Maura, if you are looking down at me from heaven, I want you to know I miss you like hell!'

As if in reply, the clouds parted momentarily and a shaft of moonlight illuminated his face. Then it was gone, back behind the clouds from where it had come. 'Thank you, my love,' he said softly.

'I do not understand what you are saying, Alice.'

Edward Sparks sat in the stuffy drawing room of the small terraced house he was so proud of. His chair was nearest the fire, he liked to think he was master in his own home.

'I'm telling you that Eynon Morton-Edwards and that Llinos Mainwaring woman are, well *sleeping* together.' She was seated opposite him, her feet – small slender feet – propped up on a cushioned stool.

'Sleeping together?' he said as though the words were foreign and he had never heard them before. He could be so obtuse at times.

'Fornicating!' She almost shouted the word at him. 'Is that clear enough for you, Mr Sparks?'

'Language!' he said. 'No need for vulgarity, Alice, I know what you mean by sleeping together, I was merely questioning the veracity of your statement.'

'I was in the glove shop, you know I've become quite friendly with Mrs Morgan the proprietor, she told me about it.' Friendly was too strong a word for the association she shared with Mrs Morgan but the woman was a good source of gossip, meeting everyone from ladies to maidservants as she did.

'Mrs Morgan saw them together, said they were looking into each other's eyes in the way that lovers do. Another thing, that Indian man, the husband, he has a new lady love, out of town somewhere. Their maid was sent to Swansea to pick up some linen cloths; it seems the girl was more than willing to gossip about the strange ways of her master.'

Edward rubbed his chin thoughtfully. 'I can't

say I'm surprised. The Mainwaring woman thought she was a cut above me. I did not like her attitude at all. You know she actually insulted me.' He sniffed. 'No-one insults Edward Sparks and gets away with it. There I was, trying to guide her, as a good bank manager should, expecting her to accept a very good price for the pottery. Do you know, my dear, the woman was too stupid to see it.'

He looked over his wife's head. 'I do agree with you about one thing, Alice, for that woman to marry a foreigner tells us a lot about her lack of moral rightness.'

It was something that her husband was actually agreeing with her. Alice looked at him, seeing the balding head, the mean mouth and narrowed eyes and wondered if she had ever disliked a man so much in her entire life. And she had a problem. She was with child. It was not Edward's child.

She was well aware that Eynon Morton-Edwards chose not to believe her but the truth was her husband had not come to her bed for many months. It was not through any lack of trying on her part but Edward seemed not to need the physical release that played so important a part in her own make-up.

She looked at him carefully; somehow, she had to lure him to her bed, he had to believe the child she was carrying was his. Perhaps at supper she could urge him to drink a little more than usual in the hope of rousing his dormant libido. She sighed inwardly, libido was too strong a word for it, Edward's attempts at sex were fumbling, inept. No sooner had he started than he finished, leaving her frustrated and sleepless.

That evening Alice took care with her appearance. Mr Sparks did not like displays of vulgarity, as he called the fashion for low-cut bodices. The gowns she wore for him had to be made with excessive modesty, too high across the bodice to be elegant. So perhaps a little guile was called for.

At the supper table, Alice kept surreptitiously filling her husband's glass, careful not to overdo it; she did not want him falling asleep half-way through his duties. She smiled and flattered him until even she felt she was flattering him too much but, being a vain man, he drank it all in, a superior smile on his face.

'I don't think it will take you long to be top dog at the bank,' she said, her eyes wide with feigned admiration.

'Senior manager, Alice. The use of the words "top dog" are vulgar and are a careless use of the English language. As wife to a bank manager, you must be circumspect at all times, please remember that.'

'I will, Edward,' she said humbly. She paused for a moment, watching him drink the mediocre wine that he insisted went well with the beef dish they were eating. He was so pompous, so lacking in real style. A man from poor beginnings who had made a good marriage, that's all he was and he dared to teach her how to behave. Still, she needed to keep her acidity in check, at least for now.

'I wonder, Edward,' she said softly, 'if you would be considered more suitable as a senior manager if you were a father.' She looked down in false modesty at her hands. 'I know you don't like me to speak of such things, it is not delicate, but

194

I do think that to father a child gives a man standing in the community.'

He was silent for a long time, considering her words. She did not look up, afraid that the habitual look of displeasure that crossed his face whenever she mentioned anything remotely sexual would put her off the act itself. She must think of it as a necessary chore, something that must be done for her own self-preservation.

Damn Eynon Morton-Edwards! If he had been an honest man he would have swooped her up and run off with her, treated her to a much more luxurious life than Mr Sparks could ever provide. But she would miss him, no doubt about it. Eynon was a good, considerate lover, always thinking of her needs before his own.

Her husband's voice startled her. 'I think you have a point, Alice.' His tone was cold, he had no real interest in her and she knew it. She knew she was too much for him, her drive too strong. He needed a woman who would be grateful for a quick coupling, who wanted no more than her husband's release. Well, he had chosen a red-blooded woman and that was his mistake.

'I would be obliged if you would come to my room tonight, Alice.' He rushed the words out as if in themselves they were dirty. He emptied his glass and gestured for her to leave him. 'We shall retire early.'

Alice left the dining room and wandered into the kitchen. The house Edward had rented for them was small and the kitchen reflected that fact. There was the cook and one maid, no men servants and, coming from a well-to-do home,

Alice felt that she had come down in the world.

'Evening, Mrs Sparks.' Cook looked up from her task of rolling pastry for next day's pies. 'Can I get you anything?'

In her father's house Alice never associated with the servants but here, in the cramped conditions of the misnamed Pleasant Row, she had no-one else to talk to.

'A glass of sherry would go down nicely, Cook,' Alice said. Cook looked over her shoulder and addressed the girl standing at the sink.

'Did you hear, Martha? Fetch the bottle out for Mrs Sparks and be sharp about it.'

'All right, Mrs Johns, I'm going as quick as I can.'

Cook grimaced as the girl went into the pantry. 'Not very bright but works 'ard,' she confided. 'Special occasion, is it?' She nodded to the bottle that Martha placed on the table. 'The sherry, it's not like you to drink strong liquor, if you don't mind me saying.' She looked at Martha. 'Well, get a glass, you stupid girl! Mrs Sparks can't drink it without.'

Alice looked at the cook; she was a woman of about fifty with grey hair and a careworn expression. On her plump finger she wore a gold band; she had been married once, had enjoyed the sins of the flesh no doubt. Alice shook her head.

'Mr Sparks is in a happy mood tonight.'

'Oh I see.' Cook frowned. 'I spects you need fortifying then.'

Alice sighed inwardly. It was Edward not she who needed the courage found in a glass. He was always anxious to get the act over and done with.

He was a strange, pinched man and Alice would never have married him if her father had not given her an ultimatum. It was either marry or go live on the streets. Her father was tired of her wild ways and vowed never to give her another penny unless she made a respectable marriage.

As the wife of Edward Sparks, Alice's father gladly paid her an allowance, enough at least to keep her out of his way.

She finished her sherry. 'Well, I suppose I'd better go and see to Mr Sparks.'

Once upstairs, Alice searched for her most modest night attire. She knew Edward by now; he would lift the hem of her gown, climb upon her and carry out his task as coldly as if he was filling in a balance sheet. There would be no pleasure in it for her, except the pleasure of knowing she was fooling her husband.

She crossed the landing into Edward's room. It was larger than her own room with a big window facing the shallow valley below. At one time the view might have been, as the name of the row suggested, pleasant. Now the outlook was ruined by a coal shaft cutting across the greenery like a scar.

Edward came into the bedroom smelling of porter. He divested himself of his clothes and slid into the bed beside her. His feet were cold as they touched her flesh and she resisted the urge to draw away from him and call off the whole silly episode. She resented him taking his quick release at her expense. But it was necessary, she must just grit her teeth and put up with it, her one consolation being it would not last long.

He was so predictable. He lifted her gown to just above her waist, not touching her breasts in the way Eynon did. Eynon enjoyed her breasts; he told her they were beautiful. Edward would never know, he never got that far.

He jerked away above her in his usual ragged manner and she scarcely knew he was there. He must be so small a man in every way that his efforts made no impression. Mr Pencil, she should call him instead of Mr Sparks. The thought made her want to laugh but she stifled the feeling, squeezing her eyes tightly shut. And then, he was falling away from her, panting as if he had run a marathon.

He never asked her if it had been good for her and that was just as well or she might have been tempted to tell him the truth. She made to slip out of the bed but his hand on her arm stopped her.

'Stay,' he said and it sounded as if he were commanding a disobedient puppy. 'I might want to try again later. I think it would be just as well to make sure that you get with child, the sooner the better.'

Alice stared up into the darkness. Edward never made love by candlelight, it was not modest. 'Very well, Edward,' she said meekly. Then she turned her face into the pillow. Edward could do what he liked; even if she was asleep it would make little difference, she would not even stir. Once she had safely delivered the child, there would be no more. From now on, Alice Sparks would please herself regarding what she did and with whom.

CHAPTER TWELVE

Joe's absences from home grew more frequent. Sometimes Llinos thought he had taken her cutting words at face value and moved in with the other woman. She had tried to appease him and, on his brief visits home, to talk to him but nothing Llinos said or did made any difference to the way he behaved.

Llinos spent more time at home, leaving the pottery in Watt's capable hands but even that seemed pointless now. She missed her work. At least it had helped to fill the days that were becoming increasingly empty without Joe. Even Charlotte was running out of excuses for her brother.

The evenings had fallen into a pattern: with Lloyd in bed, Llinos would sit with Charlotte sewing or drawing, both of them making desultory conversation avoiding the topic that was uppermost in both their minds. Llinos found it a strange life for a woman used to working and to sharing her life with her husband.

It was when Charlotte found Llinos crying one

evening that she broached the subject of Joe's strange behaviour. Even then, her words were guarded.

'Joe will be able to explain himself, just give him time.' She rested her hand on Llinos's shoulder. 'I know it's difficult for you to understand but Joe is not like other men.'

'Not capable of being faithful to his wife, you mean?' She stopped speaking abruptly, there was little point in upsetting Charlotte.

'It can't be another woman,' Charlotte said but there was no conviction in her words. 'Joe loves you, he loves his son, too. He's never shown the slightest interest in anyone else. In any case, who could it be, ask yourself that?'

'You must admit he's changed, Charlotte,' she said. 'Ever since I lost the baby things have not been right between us. These days Joe seems a different man to the one I married.' Llinos stared into the fire. 'Do you think he blames me for the baby's death, Charlotte?'

Charlotte coughed to hide the tears that were forming a knot in her throat. 'It was a terrible thing you losing your little girl but I don't see how Joe can blame you. He's upset, he's recently buried his mother and that coming on top of the loss of the baby must have affected him deeply. Perhaps we should make allowances for him, Llinos.'

Llinos put down her drawing pad and walked to the window. She parted the curtains and stared into the darkness of the night. The pottery towers loomed in ghostly silhouette against the moonlit sky. A soft rain had begun to fall and ran like tears along the window-panes.

'Perhaps I'm not prepared to make allowances any longer,' she said. 'A woman needs the support of her husband when a tragedy happens. Joe has done just the opposite, he's left me to wallow in despair alone.'

'I don't know.' Charlotte looked desperately unhappy. 'I just don't know what to say to you. I don't understand Joe any more than you do but he's an honourable man, we both know that.'

'Honourable or not, the next time he comes home I'll make him talk, make him tell me what is going on. He'll have to give me some straight answers or our marriage is finished.'

'No!' Charlotte said quickly. 'Please don't issue ultimatums to Joe, I don't think he would take kindly to that.'

Llinos turned to look at her. 'And I don't take kindly to being a deserted wife!' Her tone was sharp and she immediately regretted it. 'Oh, Charlotte, I'm sorry, I shouldn't take it out on you.' She put her arms around the older woman. 'Please take no notice of me. I'm a jealous, spiteful woman and right now I don't like myself very much.'

'Be careful.' Charlotte held her hand. 'Don't push things too far with Joe, you might ruin what you have with him.'

Llinos returned to her chair. 'At the moment, Charlotte, I have very little with him, surely you can see that?'

'I know.' Charlotte nodded. 'Just be patient a little while longer, that's all I'm saying.' She got up with painful slowness, the wet weather was making her bone ache worse. 'I'm going to my bed.' She tried to smile and Llinos realized how fragile Charlotte really was.

'I'll come with you.' She took her sister-in-law's arm and helped her up the staircase towards the bedrooms.

Llinos was only half-asleep when she heard the bedroom door open. She was immediately alert, breathing in the familiar scent of Joe with a wash of longing. She tried to speak to him, to beg him to love her again but pride held her silent as he crossed the room, walking past the bed without pausing.

The door of the dressing room closed behind him and Llinos let out her breath. It was over; her marriage was dead and it was high time it was buried.

Lily stared out of the window into the small garden of the house in Pleasant Row and watched the rain running down the window-panes. She was grateful to Watt Bevan; he had been kind to her. She knew he did not forgive her for her past mistakes but nevertheless he had found her work at one of the nice houses in Pleasant Row off Broad Street. Lily sniffed; working as maid to the bank manager's wife was not much suited to her talents but Watt had put in a word for her at the Tawe Pottery and as soon as a vacancy occurred she would be employed there as a painter.

Lily did not like Mrs Sparks; she found her to be a difficult mistress, a woman with a very high opinion of herself. She was expecting a baby and anyone would think no woman had ever carried a child before.

Lily wanted nothing more than to shake the dust of the Sparks's household off her feet but for now she needed a roof over her head and regular food to put in her stomach. All things considered, coming to Pleasant Row had proved a good move especially as her small store of money was running out.

She had become weary of sharing a damp room with Betty in the run-down lodging house on the edge of town. Betty had cried as Lily packed her small bag and, just for a moment, Lily had felt a pang of guilt at the thought of leaving her there. But still she could not hold herself responsible for the girl; Betty had to make her own way in life.

Lily thought of her bedroom in the Sparks's house, it was sparsely furnished but at least it was warm and dry and the air did not stink of stale urine and men.

'Lily, wake up, girl!' Cook was holding out a basket towards her. 'You're supposed to be going shopping down the market, why are you standing there like you was made of stone?'

Lily felt like telling Cook what she could do with her shopping basket but thought better of it. Mrs Johns could make her life difficult if she had a mind to. Lily took the basket and moved to the door just as the bell in the scullery rang out the strident summons. She looked back and hesitated and the bell rang again.

'Better answer it, girl,' Mrs Johns called, her voice sharp. 'Mrs Sparks don't like to be kept waiting.'

Cook had told Lily how Alice Sparks had come down in the world, pushed into a loveless marriage by a father who could not handle her wild ways. Well, Mrs high-and-mighty Sparks was not a toff now, she was just the wife of a very ordinary man who owned nothing but a position in the bank.

With a sigh, Lily slipped off her coat and walked through the passage to the sitting room. The house was not very big, not much better than Lily's own marital home had been but that did not stop Mrs Sparks putting on airs and graces.

'Lily.' Mrs Sparks sounded petulant. Her condition was not yet showing, her waist as slim as Lily's, but she was acting as though she was the most delicate of invalids. 'Bring a footstool for me, there's a good girl.'

Lily hid her irritation; the woman had called her back for a trivial task that she could easily have done herself. It was Lily's afternoon off and she still had the shopping to do before she was free to please herself. How she hated the job of waiting on such a spoiled brat of a woman.

'Lily,' Alice Sparks said, 'tell me, why do you look so sad and weary all the time, have you had a difficult life?' She did not wait for a reply. 'You're a widow I understand?'

'Yes.' Lily was surprised; Mrs Sparks had not taken much interest in her personal life in the few weeks she had worked there.

'Yes, Mrs Sparks, sadly, I am a widow.'

'Well, then, didn't your husband leave you provided for?'

Lily shook her head. 'No. He thought he had,' she said, coming quickly to the defence of her late husband. 'Then a long lost relative turned up, a male relative.'

'Oh, dear, did he turn you out?'

'I left of my own accord.' Lily forgot her usual reserve in her anger. 'He wanted me to behave like a whore!'

'Oh dear!' Mrs Sparks appeared shocked and yet there was a strange sparkle in her eyes almost as if she found it all too amusing for words.

'I don't think James intended to make money out of me,' Lily said, but, on reflection, that was just what James *had* intended. Lily was to sleep with men for money, to prostitute herself for James's benefit. There was a bitter taste of anger in her mouth.

'Men are mean and cruel, they don't know the meaning of love. They think you are just there to satisfy their wicked lust,' she said bitterly.

'Oh, I don't think you are being fair, Lily,' Alice protested. 'I'm sure the gentleman intended to treat you with respect.'

Lily was about to speak but stopped herself abruptly. There was no sense in letting her tongue run away with her. 'Well, I felt I had no choice but to leave,' she said, her head down.

'Isn't that always the way?' Alice said dryly. 'We women always bear the brunt of a man's foolish actions.'

Lily imagined Mrs Sparks was talking about her delicate condition. Still, in Lily's eyes Mrs Sparks was a pampered rich woman with too much time on her hands.

'Sometimes I think I hate my husband.' Mrs Sparks's tone was bitter and Lily was shocked; Mrs Sparks should know better than talking like that about the man who provided her with a home and respectability. Lily longed to be out of the house, to be free for an hour or so. She had agreed to meet Betty; they were going for a rare treat of coffee at one of the houses near the seashore.

'I don't suppose your husband left you any inheritance at all then, did he?'

Lily thought of the dwindling store of money she had stolen from James and his companions. 'I do have a little money,' she said proudly.

'Then you should allow my husband to invest it for you,' Alice said. 'Perhaps in some worthy charity. I confess to being a little bored with Mr Sparks but, as a bank manager, he has his uses.' She laughed and Lily thought again how like a cat she looked with her tiny pointed teeth and her green eyes.

'Think about it, Lily, your little bit of money, wisely invested, could make you rich. Now run along, I need to rest.'

Lily was late for her meeting and Betty was already seated in the window of the coffee house, waiting anxiously for her to appear. Betty's broad face broke into a smile when she caught sight of Lily and she warmed to her. Betty was not so bad, a little dull perhaps but she had a good heart. Lily took off her gloves and sat down opposite Betty, leaning forward across the white cloth on the table:

'Wait until you hear what I've got to tell you!' she said in a sibilant whisper. 'I don't think that Mrs Sparks is the lady she makes herself out to be! She told me she hates her husband.'

Betty shrugged. 'Nothing new in that, love, it's what most women feel.'

Lily was disappointed, she thought Betty would be interested in a little malicious gossiping but Betty was already looking at the bill of fare, her eyes glowing in anticipation of a fresh hot cake and a mug of coffee.

Alice had been toying with Lily; the girl was so gullible that she had been an easy target. She had been married once but had found the experience most distasteful. Silly girl, she did not know what she was missing.

Still, it would be useful if Lily were to hand over her money. The last thing Alice would do was to give it to Edward. She wanted to amass a store of funds so that she could be independent of her husband. If she waited for Edward to provide the luxuries of life she would wait a long time.

Eynon Morton-Edwards need not think he had got off lightly either; he must be made to pay for his fun. He had got her pregnant and whether he liked it or not she needed help from him. The trick was to find an excuse to get out to see him. Edward thought a woman's place was in the home, especially a woman in her condition.

When Edward returned home that night, he slumped into his chair and, at once, Alice brought him a drink of porter. He looked at her in surprise. She rarely stirred out of her chair, usually waiting for Edward to ring for the maid.

'I'm a little restless, darling,' she said. 'I think I need something to fill my time.' She saw him look at her with suspicion; Edward was beginning to know her. 'Perhaps I could do some charity work. It would at least get me out of the house and I might make some influential friends into the bargain.'

She saw him frown as if considering the matter; his thought processes were so slow she could almost see the wheels turning inside his head. He rubbed his chin and looked at her.

'What sort of charity work did you have in mind? Nothing too heavy, I hope, not with you in such a delicate condition.' He could not conceal his pride; he thought his inept fumblings had got her pregnant, the fool.

'Well, what about a charity for destitute women?' She stared at him impatiently. 'That should make me some friends.'

He digested her words. She felt like kicking him: was making a decision so difficult for him? Heaven help his customers.

'All right in theory but such things cost money and I am in no position to fund a venture of that sort.'

'Oh I would not expect you to, Edward. No, the idea is to bring money in, not hand it out. I mean to approach prominent citizens of the town and involve them in the work. With my family connections, I'm sure I could fund the whole thing most adequately with donations from the rich. Think how good it would look for you, it would surely advance your position in the bank. The rich men who get girls into trouble will pay handsomely to have them taken off their hands.'

There was silence for what seemed an eternity and then Edward Sparks actually smiled. 'Do you know, I think you have something there.' He looked at her in admiration. 'We could make quite a good profit from the scheme, legitimate expenses for the administrators of the charity, of course.'

She clapped her hands. 'How clever of you, darling!' She was well aware of the 'we' he used. Still, she was pleased with her story. If she did manage to get Eynon to pay up, the charity idea would serve her very nicely. She was not above creaming off a little of the donations for her own use.

'You approve then, Edward?' she asked demurely. She saw the light of the fanatic in his eyes; nothing was more dear to him than the prospect of becoming rich. But he spoke calmly.

'Just so long as you do not overstrain yourself, my dear.' He smiled, something he did not do too often. 'I wouldn't like you to put at risk the son you carry for me.'

'I would never do that, Edward,' she said softly, her eyes lowered. She wondered if he would suggest taking her to bed, something he only attempted when he was particularly pleased with life. But this time he made no suggestion, he was too wrapped up in his thoughts of climbing up the social ladder. Not that any self-respecting member of high society would countenance him for a moment. Alice bit her lip in frustration. She was tied to an imbecile but only for now. One day she would leave Edward, she would think only of herself and he could go to hell his own way. Until then, she would run her little scheme, mix with the gentry and hopefully make a nice little profit into the bargain.

Betty was looking at Lily with wide eyes. They

were walking back along the Strand; the night was closing in and Lily was nervous about being alone in the dark. Betty walked confidently at her side but then Betty was a resilient young woman, of larger stature than Lily and with something of the peasant about her.

'Well, I don't know,' Betty said. 'Does this Mr Sparks know what he's doing? You don't want to lose the little bit of security you've got, do you?'

'No but he is a bank manager. With a bit of money behind me and a good job at the Tawe Pottery I could even rent a house for us to share. You'd like that wouldn't you, Betty?' She was growing fond of Betty in spite of her crude manners.

'It would be wonderful, much better than cleaning up that scruffy place all day. But do you trust Mr Sparks then?'

Lily did not like Edward Sparks; he had a mean look about his eyes but at least he made no attempt to be familiar with her. 'I'm sure he's all right with money,' she said. 'He wouldn't be employed in a bank otherwise, would he?'

'You going to see that lovely Watt Bevan again?' Betty changed the subject. She was not a woman to count her chickens before they were hatched and she felt Lily's enthusiasm was a little misplaced. 'Nice, well set-up fellow, could do you a bit of good if he had a mind.'

'I'm not interested,' Lily said airily. 'Watt is nothing to me, just a friend, that's all past history you could say.'

'Anyway, perhaps you're too old for him, he's courting that pretty little girl Rosie, isn't he?' Betty knew how to stick the knife in. 'Seen them together a lot I have.'

'Rosie's common,' Lily said. 'Her mother's the big woman who works in the paint shed, Pearl they call her. She's as common as muck too. Her husband was hardly cold in his grave when she found herself a lover.' She sniffed haughtily.

'Mrs Johns, the cook, said that Pearl was the talk of the neighbourhood and serve her right! I never did like her.'

'You don't like many people, do you?' Betty asked, her broad face shining with perspiration. Lily realized they had been walking uphill away from the town. She must have been instinctively heading towards Pottery Row.

'I like you, Betty,' Lily said sharply. 'Otherwise I wouldn't be offering you a home rent free, would I?'

Betty remained silent and Lily stared at her challengingly. 'Didn't I bring you with me to Swansea? I could have left you behind and made my own way back. Finding a place for one of us would have been much cheaper than for two.'

'Aye, I suppose so.' Betty shivered. 'We're well away from that James Wesley and his friends and I got you to thank for that.'

Lily did not like to remember anything about that night. She had put up with James's pestering, hoping to get a wedding ring out of it. All he had done was to humiliate her. She never had liked intimacy of any kind and that last episode with James had put her off men for good.

'I wouldn't take a man to my bed, not if you gilded him in gold leaf,' she said. 'Look we'd better turn back, we're just getting further away from town.'

'Aye, you're right, I'm tired.' Betty's tone was full of self-pity. 'I've worked hard scrubbing floors all day, I'm not tucked up in a nice cosy job like you. Easy you got it and me with poor knees that thinks they are dish mops.'

'I used to be a painter,' Lily reminded her. 'I am wasting my talent pandering to the likes of the Sparks family.'

'Keep in with that Mrs Sparks, I would. She's got some good ideas from what you told me. She might even make you rich, you never know.'

Lily brightened. 'You could be right.'

The return downhill did not take long and Lily took her leave of Betty at Broad Street and turned into the narrow Pleasant Row. 'You'll be all right in the lodging house until I get us a place?' Lily called over her shoulder.

'Aye, course I will,' Betty called back. 'It 'ud be a brave man who took Betty on.'

Looking at her, tall and broad-shouldered in the growing dark of evening, it was easy to believe her and yet Betty did not have the sense she was born with.

The Sparks's house sported one candle in one of the windows. That Mr Sparks was a mean man but then if he made money for her what did she care?

'You are late, Lily.' Mr Sparks stood near the back door, the poker in his hand. He looked as if he had been expecting burglars not the return of the maid.

'Am I? Sorry, Mr Sparks.' Lily wanted to smack

his thin face; he was looking at her as if she were something the cat had dragged in.

'I hope you haven't been out with any of the local lads, Lily,' he said, his eyes running over her. Lily smoothed down her skirts, her chin lifted.

'I am not that sort of girl, Mr Sparks,' she said haughtily. 'I don't allow anyone to take liberties with me.'

He still looked doubtful. He was barring her way to the stairs and she longed to get up to her room and climb into bed. 'You're out late for a decent young woman though, you must admit,' he said.

'I've been out with a lady friend,' Lily said. 'We had a drink in the Mansel coffee house and then took a stroll. I will swear to that on the Bible if you will fetch me one.'

Her indignant tone convinced him. 'There will be no need for that, Lily. But please come in before dark next time my wife is good enough to give you time off from your duties, is that understood?'

'Yes, sir,' Lily said. To her relief, he stepped aside but as she made to climb the stairs, the bell rang summoning her.

'My dear wife needs you, Lily. First go and wash your hands and then report to her bedroom, there's a good girl.' He turned away from her. 'Oh, and when your duties are completed, make sure the fires are damped down and the candles extinguished.'

'But that's not my job,' Lily said.

'Well in that case make sure you are home at a decent time and then the other girl will be up and about to see to those things.'

Alice Sparks was in bed. She had the best bedroom in the house on the first landing facing the park at the back of the property. She did not share her husband's bed and Lily did not blame her. Sparks was a mean-faced prig and what's more he was always sweating in the most unsavoury way.

'You said nothing to Mr Sparks about investing your money?' Alice asked abruptly. 'I'll need to broach the matter when he's in a good mood.'

'Of course not, Mrs Sparks,' Lily said. 'I keep my own counsel, don't you worry about that.' She almost smiled. 'I know Mr Sparks is your husband but I don't confide in any man. Secrets are best kept from them.'

'At least until the time is ripe, Lily.' Alice actually smiled. 'Until then, we must play our cards very close to our chest.' She clasped her full bosom. 'I hope you will remember that.'

'I will, Mrs Sparks.'

'Perhaps this would be a good time to bring me your money,' Alice said. 'I will not tell Edward that it's your investment; I'll pretend it comes from one of the wealthy families who live in the west end of the town.' She smiled. 'He'll try all the harder to gain a good profit for you.'

'Right, Mrs Mainwaring.' Lily would have liked more time to think about the scheme but she was too timid to say so.

The small store of money was kept in a bag under her bed. Lily drew it out and looked at the coins inside. It was not much but it was all she had. She hesitated for a moment and then took the money downstairs and into the main bedroom.

'It's not very much,' she said apologetically.

Alice looked into the bag and nodded her head. 'I see what you mean. Never mind, we can probably do something with it.' She tucked the bag under the pillow and closed her eyes.

'You may go.' Alice dismissed her and, as Lily left her room, she was frowning. Alice Sparks might think she was very clever but Lily was no fool either. She would watch and wait and eventually she would find out all about Alice's activities and, when she did, she would make sure she used the information to her own advantage.

CHAPTER THIRTEEN

'Well?' Hortense looked at Binnie as he stood in the doorway of the house, twisting his hat between his fingers. If only she could hate him. If only she could wipe him out of her life for ever. But so far that was something she had failed miserably to do. She had lived with him for too long, had grown used to him, to every curve of him, to the way he breathed when he was asleep and to the look in his eyes when he wanted to make love to her.

She had made him go up country on the pretext of checking the other potteries her father owned. She did not trust herself to be with him too much or she would surely weaken and take him back into her life as before.

'Please, can we just talk?' he said. 'I've stayed out of your way as you asked but I can't bear it, Hortense, I ache to be with you and the boys. Please just talk to me.'

'What is there to talk about? You've lied and cheated me, wormed your way into my heart and home. What is there to say?'

'I can't go on making excuses for spending time

away from home, can I?' he asked quietly. 'People are beginning to ask questions.'

'Well, that's just too bad, isn't it?' She stared at him, glad the boys were not at home. They missed their father, the three of them kept asking her where he was.

'Come in.' She held the door open resisting the urge to throw herself into his arms, to cling to his broad shoulders and cry away all her unhappiness and pain. 'Come into the backyard, we won't be overheard there.'

They sat together and yet so far apart. Hortense was afraid to look at him. She wanted him so badly, wanted his love and the feel of his body close to hers. He was silent, miserable, waiting for her to speak.

She risked a glance at him; his head was bent, his hair flopping over his brow. Her heart ached with love for him.

'Don't you miss me, just a bit, Hortense?' His voice was hoarse. 'I miss you like hell!' He sounded distraught. 'Hortense, honey, I shouldn't have lied to you. I know I did wrong but I loved you from the first moment I set eyes on you. I love you more than my own life. I swear I have never even looked at another woman, not since you and I were wed.'

She gave a short laugh. 'But we weren't wed, were we?' Bitterness welled up within her again. The pain was sharp; the hurt had gone too deep to be washed away by protestations of love.

'I know, I know.' He tried to take her hand but she snatched it away from him. 'You were married!' She almost spat the words at him. 'You had a child by another woman and you tell me you're sorry!'

She felt crazed with anger, jealousy welled up and blinded her. She slapped his face, hard. Binnie did not flinch. In a frenzy, she beat him about the face with her fists, wanting to hurt him as he had hurt her. 'I hate you, Binnie Dundee, don't you understand, I can never trust you again!'

At last, exhausted, she stood back from him. His hair was tangled, his face red from her blows. There were tears in his eyes. He stood for a moment in silent misery and then began to walk back towards the house.

'Binnie!' She called his name but he took no notice. He disappeared from sight and Hortense sank onto the garden seat, her head in her hands. She hated him and she loved him. She wanted him so badly and she remembered all that was good about him. It was true he had never looked at another woman, never embarrassed her the way John Pendennis embarrassed Josephine. Binnie was a good father to his sons. Now, she had driven him away for good and she felt wretched.

It was a week later when Josephine came to call. John helped her down from the carriage and then, without so much as a glance at Hortense, whipped the horses into motion and drove away.

'He's afraid he'll get the sharp edge of your tongue,' Josephine said ruefully. The sisters sat in the coolness of the sitting room drinking ice-cold cordial.

'How are you feeling, Jo?' Hortense tried to appear composed; she was not given to airing her grief and pain.

'My health is excellent.' Josephine smiled. 'The baby is making me grow fatter by the day.'

'I don't mean that, hon,' Hortense said softly.

'I know. John is a waster, he will never change but at least I've put a stop to his cavorting with Melia.'

Hortense had not seen Melia for several weeks; Melia was keeping out of the way, knowing her eldest sister would have some harsh words for her.

'There's talk that Melia is allowing one of the townies to call on her,' Josephine said. 'He's rough by McCabe standards but he's got money and that was always very important to Melia.'

She looked at Hortense, her gaze level. 'I know she played around with John who had nothing except what Daddy handed him on a plate, but that was just to satisfy her lust. She would never have married him, I only hope he realizes that.' She paused and looked down at her hands. 'Perhaps when she marries this man she'll move far away from here, I never want to set eyes on the bitch again.'

It was not like Jo to be so bitter but Hortense knew something of what she must be going through. 'I can understand that,' she said softly. 'But blood is thicker than water, hon, and Melia is your sister.'

'Why didn't she think of that when she took my man!' Josephine took her hand. 'I know Binnie did you wrong, Hortense, but he's never once strayed, not since he met you. Now isn't that the truth?'

Hortense swallowed hard. 'I know all that, Jo.' She spoke with difficulty. 'But he made my boys illegitimate, how can I forget or forgive that?'

'What would you have done if he had told you the truth in the beginning?' Josephine asked quietly. Hortense thought about it, what would she have done? Jo answered the question for her.

'You would have missed out on some of the happiest years of your life that's what. At least now you are legally wed, isn't that good enough for you?'

'I don't know.' Hortense sighed. 'I want him like hell and yet there's a pain inside me that won't shift.'

'Do you want to live the rest of your life without him?' Josephine asked. 'Think carefully about that, Hortense.'

Hortense bit her lip. The prospect of forever being alone without Binnie was terrible and yet he needed to be punished for what he had done. 'I suppose not,' she said at last.

'Well, then, you'd better move yourself because John told me that Binnie is going to book a passage back home to England.' Josephine spoke sharply.

Hortense felt as if a great void had opened up before her. She stared out of the window, trying to control the rising tide of panic that threatened to choke her. Binnie, gone, out of her life, out of the country. She could not bear the thought.

'Oh my Lord!' She put her hands over her face. 'What am I going to do?'

'Go to him before it's too late, tell him that you will try to make a go of it,' Josephine said gently. 'Give him and your marriage a chance before it's too late. Now come on, let's have tea, I'm starving.' She patted her stomach and smiled. 'I am eating for two, if the old wives' tales are to be believed.'

She sighed. 'You two were so happy, you were the envy of all of us. Just think about what I've said, hon, and get him back before it's too late. You can't do anything tonight but tomorrow, go see Binnie, talk to him.'

They had tea together, small crusts of freshly baked bread and a bowl of Mexican chilli. Hortense hardly ate anything; her thoughts were on Binnie packing his few belongings and making for England. Just to think of it twisted her stomach into knots.

'You're lucky with Justine,' Josephine said, her mouth full of meat and beans. 'I wish I could get a cook like her.' She smiled ruefully. 'But then I wouldn't trust John to be in the same house as her, she's a beautiful girl.'

'You're right,' she said, putting down her fork, her food tasted like sawdust anyway. 'I will see Binnie and tell him we'll try again.' She felt suddenly released, free and almost happy. 'I don't say I won't give him hell whenever we have a showdown over something but I will try to heal the breach between us.'

'Good!' Josephine said warmly. 'I'm really glad, sis, you and Binnie go together like two sides of the same coin. Unlike me and John.'

'But is he behaving better now?' Hortense asked and Josephine looked up and met her eyes.

'I doubt it but at least he is being more discreet.' She smiled. 'And I think he is pleased there's a baby on the way, it's good for his manly pride you know.' She looked up at the dust trail appearing at the end of the street. 'Talk of the devil, here he comes if I'm not mistaken.' Jo led the way onto the veranda and Hortense went to stand beside her sister, her arm around her waist.

John drew the horses to a halt and to Hortense's surprise he jumped down from the carriage and strode towards the house. 'Something's wrong,' Josephine said softly, 'he always looks like that when he's bringing bad news.'

'Got something I think you'd like to hear.' He spoke directly to Hortense and she felt fear clutch at her stomach.

'What?' She tried to sound calm but it was as though a thousand birds were twittering inside her head.

'Binnie's gone.'

'Gone, what do you mean?'

'He didn't see any point in staying any longer. He sailed for England last night and by now he's out in the Atlantic Ocean. Aren't you pleased?'

'John! Why didn't you say something before!' Josephine said hotly. 'You must have known all along about Binnie's plans, why keep it to yourself?'

'Binnie asked me to, that's why. Now are you coming home or what?'

'I'll see you soon, hon.' Josephine held Hortense and kissed her cheek. 'Try not to fret, it might all be a mistake.' She did not think so and neither did Hortense. She turned away from John's hateful smiling face and entered the house. Blindly, she stumbled up the stairs and straight into her room. She leaned against the closed door, pain and fear swamping all reason. Binnie had gone;

she had lost him for ever and it was her own fault.

Pearl walked slowly away from Pottery Row, her back ached and she felt ill. She had tried to hide it from the rest of the people working in the paint shed but she knew she could not keep her secret for much longer. She was sick, very sick. She had tried desperately to talk to Watt about it but so far there had been no opportunity. In any case, perhaps it was better not to burden him with her worries. Watt was the sort of man who took other folk's troubles on himself.

It was a relief when she reached the small house and let herself indoors. Pearl was pleased to see that the fire was lit and the table was laid for supper. 'Rosie!' Pearl hugged her daughter. 'What are you doing here?'

Rosie smiled and pushed the kettle onto the fire. 'Hello, Mam, I've got the day off so I thought I'd come and make tea for you.

'Watt's here, he's supposed to be helping so I've sent him to fetch coal for the fire. There's no sign of Willie or the boys.'

'Willie said he'd take the boys over to his sisters, I expect he's still there.' Pearl watched her daughter's face change as Watt came in the back door, a bucket of coal in his hand. Her face was radiant and Pearl suddenly felt anxious; Rosie was falling in love. Watt was a good man but he was older than Rosie and more experienced in the ways of the world. He had even travelled across the sea to America once. How long would he be content with a young untried local girl?

'You're a lucky pair getting time off whenever

you want it,' Pearl said as she slumped into a chair. 'Mrs Mainwaring must be very fond of you both.'

'Well she is and doesn't that show what good judgement she has?' Watt said, looking down at Rosie's smiling face. Pearl saw her daughter as Watt must see her. She looked good enough to eat, her cheeks flushed, her hair curling around her brow.

'Hey, how about making your mam a cup of tea?' She shrugged off her shawl feeling the sweat breaking out on her brow. '*Duw*, it's hot in here.' She began to cough and once started she could not stop.

'Are you all right, Pearl?' Watt's voice seemed to be coming from a long distance off. She tried to gather her wits but it was a losing battle. The last thing she remembered was Rosie crying out her name.

She came to and found herself lying on the floor, a pillow under her head. Her neighbour Mrs Grove was kneeling beside her, still in her nurse's apron.

'Could be the change, Pearl love,' she said, looking thoughtful. 'Do you think you're on the change?' Pearl struggled to sit up.

'I suppose so.' She struggled to her feet, Watt's hand around her waist. Rosie looked at her mother, her face white. Pearl let Watt guide her to the chair and took the cup of tea Rosie held out with shaking hands.

'Or,' Mrs Grove said slowly, 'you could be going down with the lung sickness from breathing in pot dust all day. Your chest is rattling like stones in a tin can.'

'Thank you for coming, Mrs Grove,' Pearl said hastily. 'It was very kind indeed but I feel all right now.'

'Been feeling faint have you?' Mrs Grove asked briskly. She looked at Pearl. 'Could still be the change, mind,' she said helpfully. 'You coming up to forty if I'm not mistaken. Could be you're expecting of course, stranger things have happened.'

'No,' Pearl said. 'I'm not expecting. I know the signs, I've had enough children to recognize how I'm looking and feeling now. I wish that's all it was.'

'If it is the lung sickness you won't have long for this world,' Mrs Grove said gloomily.

It was Rosie who took charge. 'I'm very grateful to you for coming in to help, Mrs Grove, but this is a family matter and we'd like it kept that way. I'm sure Mam will be fine once she's had a good rest. All she needs is a tonic, I'm sure of it.'

'Well I never!' Mrs Grove sniffed, not bothering to conceal the fact that she had taken offence. Watt attempted to pour oil on troubled waters.

'You're a very good midwife, excellent from what I hear but you must admit you don't know much about any other condition, Mrs Grove. We don't want to alarm people unnecessarily, do we, so I think it might be best if we leave any diagnosis to a doctor.' He pressed some coins into her hands.

'I'm sure you'll be discreet about all this, you are a professional woman after all.'

'Aye, you're right there, Watt Bevan,' Mrs Grove said. 'If I blabbed about everyone's business there would be all hell let loose in the place.' She moved to the door. 'Now if you are sure you can manage without me, I'll get back to my own fireside. Take it easy, Pearl, there's a good girl, we don't want you falling into a dead faint in the middle of traffic in the High Street, do we?'

When she had gone, Rosie sat beside her mother. 'How long have you had this cough, Mam?'

'I'm not sure.' Pearl rubbed her eyes tiredly. 'What am I going to do? If I can't work the boys will have to go into the workhouse.' There were tears in her eyes and Rosie hugged her mother.

'We'll be all right, Mam,' she said quickly. 'I earn a bit, don't I? I can help out with food and that and Mrs Mainwaring is very kind, I know if I ask her she'll send you all the leftovers instead of giving them to Eira's friends.'

'That's all very well, love, but how will we pay the rent? What you earn as a maid won't keep us lot for long.'

'Don't worry, Pearl,' Watt broke in. 'We'll think of something and we'll be able to keep your job open for you until you're better.'

'Oh Lord, but how about the boys, who will look after them? I can't die, I can't!'

Rosie seemed to grow in stature. 'We'll be all right, I tell you.' She looked at Watt. 'Perhaps one of my brothers can get work at the pottery as an apprentice or something. Dom is old enough, isn't he? And there's Willie, he'll help out, won't he?'

Pearl shook her head. 'You know as well as I do that Willie can't help out, he and me, well we have an understanding: he helps his sister and I, well, take care of myself.' Pearl knew that Willie's family depended on him. It took all the meagre wages he earned as a fiddler at weddings and funerals to care for his widowed sister and her brood of children.

Rosie began to cry and Watt put his arm around her. Pearl watched for a moment, a bitter taste in her mouth. Then she forced herself to speak.

'It will be all right, Rosie, don't you worry, we'll all pull together.' Watt met her eyes and Pearl knew what he had in mind almost before he spoke. He wanted to bring money into the house and the only way he could do that was to marry into the family.

Like Pearl, he had seen Rosie's love for him blossom and, given time, that love might have been returned but now was not the right time. Pearl knew that and surely Watt knew it too.

'Pearl, Rosie,' Watt smiled, 'perhaps this is not the right time to say this and then again maybe it's exactly the right time.'

'Our worries are not yours, Watt,' Pearl said quickly. 'You mustn't feel responsible for us, you do enough to help as it is.'

'Be quiet for once,' he said. 'I'm not taking your troubles. I'm asking Rosie to make me the happiest man on earth and marry me.'

'What?' Rosie was still pale; she stood in the circle of Watt's arms and looked up at him. 'What did you say?'

'You heard. I'm asking you to marry me, Rosie.' He spoke soberly.

Pearl took a ragged breath, waiting for Rosie to speak. Rosie's face seemed suddenly lit from within. If Watt had any doubts about her love for him, about being impetuous, Rosie's smile was enough to drive the doubts away. 'Will you have me, Rosie?'

'Oh, Watt, my lovely!' Rosie buried her face in his shoulder, suddenly shy. 'I want to be your wife more than anything in the world.'

'I'll move in here, if that's all right, Pearl.' He smiled. 'Everything can go on as normal except that Rosie won't have to work any more. And you, Pearl, you can take your time and get fit again instead of worrying so much!'

'But I am worried,' Pearl said. 'Are you sure of your feelings, Watt? It's not that long since you lost Maura.'

'I loved Maura,' Watt said, 'I can't deny it. But I'm a young man, Pearl, I need a wife and a family. I can't live alone for the rest of my life, can I?'

'No, I suppose not.' Pearl knew that Watt had come up with the perfect answer. After all, he would be gaining a lovely young girl for a wife, a girl who adored him. Pearl looked at her daughter's radiant expression and then smiled. 'Come here, my lovely girl, let your mam give you a kiss!'

Pearl closed her eyes and hugged her daughter and any worries she had about Watt's love for Rosie were pushed to the back of her mind. Her immediate problems of money were solved; Rosie would give up her job and stay at home to look after the boys. It would all work out for the best and as for her bad chest it might be nothing at all. Mrs Grove was no doctor. In any case, it did not do to brood on such things.

'Let's celebrate,' she said. 'Bring out the black-currant wine, Rosie, it isn't every day I'm asked for my daughter's hand in marriage.'

'Binnie!' Llinos looked at the man standing in the hallway. 'Binnie Dundee, is it really you?' She put her arms around him and hugged him warmly and then held him at arm's length. '*Duw!*' she said lapsing into the Welsh. 'You look so brown, so handsome and haven't you filled out! I hardly recognized you.'

She took him into the sitting room. 'Do you want a drink, Binnie, are you hungry, what would you like? Oh,' she put her hands to her face, 'I'm so happy to see you after all this time! Tell me all about your life, what's been happening to you out in America?'

He released himself from her embrace and sank tiredly into a chair. Llinos looked at him carefully; beneath the tanned skin and the fairness, where the sun had bleached his hair, he did not look happy.

'I'll tell you about me, first, shall I?' she said to help him out. 'I'm leaving a lot of work to Watt now. I needed to spend more time with my family you see.' She looked around her, the house was silent, giving lie to her words. Lloyd was outdoors with Eira and Charlotte was resting in her room. Where Joe was she had no idea. He had stayed for one night and in the morning he had been gone.

'Joe is away on business.' It was the wrong time to tell him of her problems; it was clearer with each passing moment that he had come home, come to his old friend Llinos to talk about his own worries. 'Come,' she said, 'let's talk.'

Slowly, in a halting voice, tinged now with an American accent, he told her about his life. The rumours she might have heard were true, he had married bigamously, had three sons and a wonderful wife. He sighed heavily.

'It all fell apart, Llinos,' he said. 'I suppose Hortense was bound to find out sometime but I lived in a fool's paradise believing I could keep up the lies forever.'

'But your wife, can't she forgive you?'

He looked up at her, shaking his head. 'I can't blame her for hating me. I tried to make it right by marrying her secretly but I know Hortense only agreed to it so that the boys wouldn't be shamed by the stigma of illegitimacy.' He looked wretched. 'We're both hoping that no-one finds out about my past, but she can never trust me again and who can blame her?'

'Binnie,' Llinos said slowly. 'Love does not just die like that, whatever you did, you were a good husband and father, weren't you?'

'I think so.' He rubbed his fingers through his hair. 'Can I take you up on your offer to stay for a while, Llinos?'

'Of course you can.' She rang the bell and Rosie came at once, looking at the American visitor with curiosity.

'Bring some tea and sandwiches and some fruit cake, Rosie, there's a good girl,' she said, not taking her eyes from Binnie's face. He had tired lines around his eyes but even though he was older by several years than Llinos, he seemed to have retained his youthful looks and vitality. Living in America suited him.

He drank the tea thirstily but ate little. Llinos understood his pain, knew that where he really wanted to be was back with his family.

'Is it really over, Binnie, are you sure about that?'

'She's told me so,' he replied. 'I have never seen Hortense so angry, so hurt. I can't bear to think what harm I've done her.'

'Women say all sorts of things when they're hurting, Binnie,' she said softly. 'When I am angry with Joe, if I think he's been neglecting me for his business, I can be a witch! I don't mean any of it and I'm sure your Hortense is crying her eyes out this very minute because you've left the country.'

'I wish I could believe that,' Binnie said. 'I'd be on the next ship back across the Atlantic if I thought there was a chance my wife would forgive me.' He looked at her. 'But I don't believe there is any chance, none at all.'

He closed his eyes for a second. 'All that I have I owe to Hortense and her family, they took me in, gave me work and treated me like a son and I betrayed them.'

'Binnie!' Llinos spoke sharply. 'Knowing you I'm sure you worked hard for what you got. You always were a good potter, you know most of the jobs inside out. You would be a valuable asset to anyone's business.'

'So you'll give me work?' he asked, looking down at the floor. 'I'm sorry to come cap in hand to you, Llinos, but I had nowhere else to go. You and the pottery have always meant home to me. I don't know anything but potting.'

'Speak to Watt, he's in charge now and I'm sure

he'll find you something. And Binnie, write to your wife, tell her how you feel and ask her to give you another chance to make a go of the marriage, it might work.'

Binnie began to cry, tears rolling along his tanned cheeks and his big shoulders shaking. Llinos went to him and cradled his head against her breast, patting his shoulder as though she was his mother, not a friend he had not seen for years.

It was at that moment the door to the sitting room opened and Joe walked into the room. He took one look at the embracing couple and without a word turned and left, closing the door quietly behind him.

CHAPTER FOURTEEN

Lily was standing at the vegetable stall in the market, examining a box of cabbages with a critical eye. Mrs Sparks was partial to fresh vegetables and none came fresher than the ones brought from the farms of Port Eynon and Gower. Lily paid for the cabbage and tucked it into her basket. It was time she was getting back.

Alice had been extra friendly that morning, pleased that Lily had handed over her small supply of money. Lily had watched her put the bag of coins away and felt a dart of apprehension; that money was all she had in the world.

'Well I'll be blown down by a feather, if it isn't my old friend Lily!' The voice at her side startled her and Lily spun round prepared to be reproving of such familiarity.

'Polly!' She stared at the girl with whom she had once shared all her secrets, not sure if she was happy or alarmed to see her again. Since coming to Swansea, Lily had thought better of contacting Polly. Dealing with Polly usually spelled trouble.

In any case, with Watt's help she had managed just fine on her own.

'You're looking well,' Lily said, her eyes running over her friend's good clothes and fashionable hairstyle. Polly must have found a rich admirer.

'I am very well. Come and have a cuppa something with me, I'll pay.' That was a turn up for the book, Polly never used to have money, she had spent it as soon as she got it.

Lily looked around anxiously. 'I don't know. I should be getting back, I'm a working girl, mind.'

'Oh, come on!' Polly pulled at her arm. 'Half an hour won't hurt one way or the other. It's a long time since I had anyone to talk to.'

Lily followed her into the Market Inn and the two girls seated themselves in the tiny snug designed for the use of ladies. And Polly did look every inch the lady. Gone was the tangled hair and the shabby clothes. Polly was wearing a well-cut, high-waisted dress in a blue organza and over it a small neat jacket. Her hair was clean, drawn back from her face with two curls hanging beside her cheeks. It looked as if Polly's fortunes had risen just as surely as Lily's own fortunes had fallen.

'Where you working then?' Polly asked. 'Not back at the pottery, I'll warrant!' She giggled. 'Wouldn't want you there, not after the trouble you caused.'

'Come on, Polly, all I did was fall in love with the wrong man. Saul Marks was a bad influence on me, you know that.' She paused for breath, settling more comfortably on the wooden seat.

'Anyway, I'm working for a Mrs Sparks, she's the wife of the bank manager.' She tried to make the job sound grand but wearing her cloak over a voluminous apron did nothing to hide her humble occupation of maid.

'Not that old harridan! You must be mad!'

Lily looked away. 'Beggars can't be choosers.'

Polly ordered cordial for the both of them and put some coins on the table. 'Please be quick about it, landlord, a lady could die of thirst waiting to be served.' She dropped the coarse manner of speech she normally used and spoke as though she had been bred to privilege and riches.

'You've come up in the world, Polly, what are you doing?' Lily whispered.

'I'm married.' Polly held out her hand and showed the gold band and the diamond-encrusted ring beside it. 'Jem is an old fool but I give him a bit of life in the bedroom, know what I mean?' Her rough speech had returned, she obviously did not feel the need to put on an act with Lily.

'You've fallen on your feet then,' Lily said enviously. 'I was married as well, Tom was a good man and when he died I thought I'd be safe for life. I had a lovely cottage and enough money to live on and then James turned up.'

'James?'

'Yes, Tom's heir, so he claimed. I thought him a real gent until the night he came to my room and . . .' She broke off, not sure how much she should tell Polly.

'And what?' Polly's eyes were wide. 'Did he force you, or what?'

'Well, not exactly,' Lily said. 'I was quite happy to give him some womanly comforts but then he thought he'd make a business out of me.'

'How do you mean?' Polly was leaning forward, practically licking her lips, but then she had always been common, a hussy willing to go with any man.

'He brought in some friends.' She decided she might as well tell Polly the whole story, she was not the sort to be shocked, that was something in her favour. 'There was I thinking they wanted supper and a bed for the night and they had different ideas.' She sniffed. 'They thought I was part of the bargain.'

'Oh, sounds like a bit of a laugh.' Polly giggled. 'I can't imagine you having men flocking around you, you always seemed a bit, well, not interested in it if you know what I mean.'

'They didn't care if I was interested or not!' Lily said acidly. 'They would have been content to take what they wanted regardless of my feelings. Well, I wasn't having that, I took off in the middle of the night.'

'So you didn't get anything out of the deal then? That's a shame.'

'Oh, I made sure I got some money.' Lily smiled, her tension relaxing. 'I robbed the lot of them, took every penny I could find including what James had in his pockets.'

'Good for you!' Polly slapped her knee in delight. 'You learned somethin' from Polly then, never give anything for nothing. What you done with it, your money, I mean?'

'I gave it to Mrs Sparks, she promised to invest it for me.' Lily looked up as the landlord brought a jug and some cups. She could see that Polly had no intention of pouring the cordial so she poured it herself. Polly was looking at her thoughtfully.

'That's the last you'll see of that money! You didn't learn enough from me, my girl!'

Lily shook her head. 'Alice Sparks thinks she's a cut above everyone, she treats me like a slave not a maid. Sometimes I feel I could slap her smug face. As for *him*, well Mr Sparks walks about the place as if there's a bad smell under his nose but I don't think they'd steal my little investment.'

'Forget your money and Mrs Sparks and come to work for me,' Polly said. 'You could live better in my house than you've ever done in the Sparks's little place.'

'It's very kind of you, Polly, but I'd have to give in my notice.' Lily was not at all sure she wanted to work for Polly. Polly was the sort to have men around the place, men with no good intentions. In any case, she needed to keep her eye on the money Alice was investing for her. Polly was just being her usual nasty self; Mrs Sparks would see her money was invested and, with luck, Lily might well become as rich as Polly.

'Don't be daft!' Polly laughed. 'Just tell that old battleaxe that you've got something better. Think about it, you just have to pack your things and come over to me. You know where I live, don't you?'

'No.' Lily was mystified; why should she know where Polly lived?

'You don't know nothing, do you?' Polly pushed her arm. 'My old man owns the Tawe Pottery! Along with a few other old geezers, that is. I live in the big house that used to belong to the Morton-Edwardses until the place was sold. What do you think, me in the big house, is that a turn up for the book or what?'

Lily could not believe it. 'You are living in the house that belonged to the Morton-Edwards family? You have come up in the world!'

'There you are then.' Polly was delighted at Lily's surprise. 'Didn't think I'd done that well, did you?'

Lily felt the sour taste of jealousy in her mouth. Polly of all people living in the lap of luxury; it just was not fair. There was she, Lily, a talented painter, wasting her time serving people like the Sparkses and her friend Polly, who had no manners, was lording it about in a big posh house.

'No, I can't say I did.' Lily did her best to smile. 'You've done well, Polly, you really have and I congratulate you.'

'There we are then, it's settled, you get your things and when you're ready come up the house and we'll settle you in. You never know, I might be able to introduce you to some other foolish old man who's more interested in what's under the skirts than what's in your brain.' She picked up her bag and got to her feet.

'Better go,' she said. 'We're having visitors this afternoon, they'll have tea with us and then my old man will take them off to his den and booze with his mates and tell them all what a stud he is. Can I give you a lift anywhere? I told the driver to pick me up just along by the beginning of Market Street.'

Lily shook her head. 'I'll walk with you to the end of the road, though.' She was not sure that she quite believed Polly's story and yet her clothes and jewellery looked fine enough. Together, they left the inn and Lily's basket of vegetables weighed heavily on her arm. Seeing them together, people would think that Polly was the mistress and Lily the servant; it was not a thought Lily relished.

The carriage was waiting as Polly had predicted and, when he saw her, the driver leapt down to open the door. The coat of arms gleamed in the sunlight; the brass-work shone like gold and the driver was liveried and respectful.

'Day to you, Mrs Boucher, I hope you've had a pleasant time of it in town.'

Polly touched his arm. 'I thank you, Dave.' She allowed him to help her into the carriage and his hand lingered a little too long on her waist. Polly was still up to her old tricks by the look of it.

'Bye then, Lily, see you soon, mind.'

The carriage jolted into motion, the horses, grandly bedecked, setting off at a spanking pace along the road. Lily watched for a moment and then, her head bent in despair, she began to walk towards home.

Llinos looked down at Lloyd asleep in his bed. Her son was a handsome boy, especially now when he was rosy with sleep. Standing beside his bed, Llinos suddenly felt that she had grown old overnight. It was as if her body had become barren since losing the baby.

She saw again the small form of her daughter, saw Joe lifting the baby up in his arms, a look of grief on his face. Since that day Joe had changed, but so had she. Llinos crossed the room and looked into the mirror, surprised to see the familiar unlined face, the same tangle of dark hair. It was the eyes that were different, they were heavy lidded, lacking lustre.

'Oh, Joe!' she whispered. He had come home to find her in the arms of her old friend Binnie Dundee. He had looked at the two of them, a long hard look, and then turned and left the room. He had spent a few hours with his son and his sister the next day, never even looking at Llinos. Did Joe really believe she was being unfaithful, and with Binnie, her dear old friend?

The old Joe, the loving, intuitive Joe, would have read the event for what it was. He would have seen Binnie's pain and Llinos's compassion and would have understood everything at a glance. Instead, he had chosen to use it against her, to blame her for some unknown sin. Joe was a man with a guilty conscience. Llinos was becoming more angry with every passing slight; every stab of pain was driving a wedge between her and the love she had once held for her husband.

Rosie knocked on the door and Llinos composed herself, tucking a stray curl behind her ear.

'Scuse me, Mrs Mainwaring, but Watt is downstairs, he's asking to see you, if you have a minute.'

'I'll come down straight away,' Llinos said. Watt was waiting in the small sitting room. He smiled warmly when he saw her and she wanted to hug him, at least Watt had not changed, he was a good man, still grieving over the loss of his love Maura.

'Sit down, Watt, is anything wrong?' She tried to speak lightly. Watt knew her from childhood and he could usually read her moods. Now, however, he seemed more intent on his own troubles.

'In a way.' He looked up at Llinos. 'It's Pearl, she's very sick.' He shook his head. 'It's her lungs the nurse said and I'm afraid she's right. Anyway,

I've told Pearl to take time off.' He bowed his head. 'I don't think she'll ever be able to work again. I said I'd pay her at least for now. Did I do the right thing?'

Llinos looked at him in surprise. Pearl so sick that she was giving up work? It was difficult to believe. Pearl was a big, strong woman; she had always seemed so robust. But by now she must be almost forty, she was getting old.

She frowned. 'Poor Pearl, I'm so sorry and of course you did the right thing. Anything else I can do to help?'

Watt's expression softened. 'I'm taking care of things. I know you've enough on your plate as it is, without worrying about Pearl. I just wanted to talk to you about it, to prepare you, but I've got everything in hand, don't worry.'

He did not wait for her to reply. 'Binnie's back now, he can cover for Pearl. I'll see everything runs smoothly, don't you worry your head about that.'

'I know,' Llinos said. She sighed heavily. 'Anyway, it's about time I shook myself out of my apathy and took an interest in the pottery again. What's the point of being here in the house all the time when Joe doesn't appreciate it anyway?'

He looked down at his hands as though he had not heard her. 'I told Rosie to stay at home, do you mind?' He smiled. 'I'm sorry for interfering in your household arrangements, Llinos.'

'Don't keep apologizing!' Llinos said. 'I told you to take charge and you have. I'm grateful to you, Watt.' She moved out into the hall and Watt followed her. 'I'll fetch my coat and then I'll take a walk down to Pearl's cottage and have a word with her.'

'I've promised to keep her job open for when she recovers.' He looked away and stared through the window, swallowing hard. 'I know you'll be discreet.'

'Of course and, Watt, I would have made exactly the same decisions as you.' Llinos looked up at him expectantly as he walked across the room and opened the door for her. She sensed there was more he wanted to say. 'What is it?'

'It's Rosie, I've asked her to marry me.'

'You've done what?' She took his arm and almost marched him through the front door towards the gates of the pottery until they were well out of earshot of any of the servants. 'Are you out of your mind? You know you're still grieving for Maura, how could you bring yourself to marry someone else?'

'It's difficult,' Watt said. 'I'm very fond of Rosie and . . . well, she needs me to take care of her, to take care of the whole family come to that. With Pearl out of work it will be a struggle for them just to survive.'

'But marriage, Watt, aren't you sacrificing your own happiness for the sake of doing a good deed?' She buttoned up her coat. 'We're all fond of Pearl and I can pay her a small retainer; they would still have more than most families live on.'

'I've given my word and I won't go back on it. In any case, Llinos, what have I got in my life to look forward to now Maura's gone? At least with Rosie I'll have a wife who loves me and a family to call my own. Can't you see how important that is to me?'

Llinos could see his need to belong. Watt had been orphaned at an early age, the people of the pottery had been the only family he had ever known.

'Well, if you're sure Rosie is what you want then you have my blessing. I won't ask if you love her, that's your business.' She paused. 'Do you love her?'

'I think love can grow,' Watt said. 'I care for Rosie, she's pretty and funny and . . . well, I care for her.'

'I see.' Llinos did see. 'Right then, go back to work and I'll walk down to the village.' She smiled. 'Don't worry, I won't say a word out of turn. If Pearl wants to talk to me I'll listen, otherwise, I'll just pretend to think she's just a bit off colour.'

Watt hugged her arm to his side. 'I knew I could depend on you, Llinos. I couldn't love you more if you were my own sister. I would do anything for you.'

'Go on with you, don't get all mushy now or I'll think you're after something.' She paused near the painting sheds. The smell was familiar, the oxide, the tallow, the pungent scent of the glaze; it was her life. And it was all changing, everything was changing and Llinos did not much like it.

'I won't be long and, when I come back, I'll talk to one of the better painters to see if between us we can come up with some fresh designs.'

'Change the firebird emblem on the china, is that what you mean?'

'That's exactly what I mean. Joe is no longer interested in the pottery or in me and it's about time I accepted that and acted accordingly.'

She knew she sounded bright and confident but, as she walked away from the pottery, her vision was blurred. Angrily she wiped away the tears that misted her eyes. Crying had never solved her problems in the past and it would not solve them now. She had to wake up and face the facts, Joe and she were finished, their marriage was over.

'I have some news for you, Edward, my love.' Alice was reclining in her favourite chair after eating a hearty dinner of beef and kidney pie laced with oysters. She was holding a glass of port in her hand, watching the light from the fire reflecting in the ruby wine.

'My news first, my dear.' He sat down the same way as he did everything, with small precise movements. 'I have been working hard at the bank and my endeavours have been recognized.' He smiled with self-satisfaction. 'I have been made senior manager of the Swansea branch, now what do you think of that then?'

'How wonderful, haven't I a clever husband?' she enthused. 'I knew you could do it, my darling.' She looked at him from under her lashes. 'And there is something else you have done successfully.' She smiled at him. 'Can you guess what it is?'

He frowned. 'I'm not given to such childish games, Alice, you know that. If you have something to tell me then say it.'

She swallowed the angry retort that sprang to her lips. He could be such a conceited buffoon at times. 'You have done wonderfully well, the midwife thinks we are to have twins.'

His eyebrows shot up into his hairline. 'Good heavens!' he said. 'Two more mouths to feed.'

Alice hid her anger. 'Ah well, you must be particularly virile, my darling,' she said. 'And we did try exceptionally hard to get a baby.' She glanced at him from under her lashes. 'I shall have to be extra careful, twins tend to be born prematurely.' It was a good ploy, with luck Edward would never realize that the babies would arrive too early for him to be the father.

'So it's twins then?' Edward looked suddenly pleased with himself. He clearly saw himself as a man of great physical prowess. 'Well, that is good news.' He did not sound sure. 'Not quite necessary now that I've been given a senior position anyway.'

'Well it can't be undone!' Alice said and then softened her tone. 'Excuse me, dear, women are sometimes a little out of sorts at such times.' She forced herself to smile at him though she felt more like slapping him across his smug face.

'Look at it this way, a man of experience like you, and a solid family man to boot, can look higher than Swansea. You could be promoted to Cardiff or even to London or Bristol, wouldn't that be wonderful?'

After a few moments' consideration he nodded sagely. 'I must confess, dear, that I had not thought that far. You are quite right as usual. You are an asset to me, Alice.'

This was praise indeed coming from Edward. She pressed home her advantage. 'Edward, I understand you have visits from area bank officials occasionally, is that so?'

'It is. Why?'

'Well then we must entertain them in style when they come to visit, impress them with our hospitality and our breeding.'

This was sometimes a sore point with Edward that Alice came from a better class of family than he did. Now, however, he saw the advantages and decided to play them for all he was worth. Edward Sparks was a very ambitious man.

'What, invite them here, you mean?' Edward sounded doubtful. He looked around the small rooms, seeing the place with fresh eyes. Alice smiled to herself.

'It would be nice if we had a larger house, of course,' Alice said. 'Something in a better area.' She waited for Edward to digest this latest idea. He stroked his chin and looked down at his highly polished boots.

'But could we afford it, Alice? Would your father help us, do you think?'

Alice doubted it; her father had been glad to get rid of her. However, Eynon Morton-Edwards could be induced to put some money her way, especially when she convinced him that the twins she was carrying were his.

'You go ahead and arrange it, Edward, darling,' she said. 'Leave the financial side of it to me.'

He appeared doubtful. Alice knew he liked to be in control of anything to do with money. Methodical he might be but an entrepreneur he was not. 'Once Daddy knows there are grand-children on the way, he'll give in and increase my allowance. He might even be generous enough to buy us a better house. If he does, I'll leave it all to you to handle, I promise.' He seemed satisfied. He poured himself a full measure of port, a sure sign that he was congratulating himself on his cleverness.

All that remained was for her to see Eynon and to convince him it was in his best interests to help her. She already had a small store of money handed over to her by Lily. The girl was a fool; she would never get it back. As soon as was possible, Alice would find a way of dismissing Lily. And thinking further ahead, perhaps she would really go to see her father. There might be something in this grandchildren business.

She smiled to herself, she was really doing quite well, the small store of money Lily had given her would be enough for a down payment on a property, a gesture of goodwill until the real money came in. And come in it would, Alice intended to rise again to the station from which she was born. She was tired of medi-ocrity, tired of making do with out-of-fashion garments. If her husband was incapable of making their fortune then it was up to her to see to it and see to it she would.

CHAPTER FIFTEEN

'I can't believe he's gone, left me like this without a word.' Hortense was walking in the garden with her mother, arms linked, closer than they had been in some years. In the background, she could hear the raised voices of her children as they climbed through the trees, shouting to each other as they played, unaware that anything was wrong. All Hortense had told them was that Binnie needed to go away for a while on a trip.

This morning, unable to keep silent any longer, she had dragged her mother away from her household duties and had told her everything. She explained about Binnie's marriage, about his lies and deceit and about her own belated wedding to him. Now, she was waiting for the tirade of abuse against Binnie that must surely come. Her mother surprised her.

'Why all the fuss, hon? A man's a man, you never expected him to be pure like the driven snow, did you? You're not that much of a fool. At least he never strayed when he was with you and that's more than can be said about your father!'

'But, Mammy, he lied to me! The boys were born out of wedlock, they're bastards, can't you see that?'

'But who's to know, Hortense? You and Binnie are legally married now and the boys will grow up thinking everything is fine and dandy. Look how many Americans living as respectable folks was born on the wrong side of the blanket, more than a few, I'll bet.'

Hortense could think of nothing to say. She stared out across the open scrubland behind the house, prime land on which a town would one day flourish and grow. America was becoming rich in assets, industries were springing up, folks from across the sea were coming to America in shiploads. It was the land of opportunity and her sons would be part of it. But what of her husband?

'Your silly pride might have lost you the best man you are ever likely to find, honey,' her mother said. 'And all because of some nonsense that happened before he met you.' She slipped her arm around Hortense in a rare show of affection.

'You know I grieve for my Josephine whose man can't keep his buttons done up. Then there's poor Melia with no man of her own to love but you, Hortense, I was always happy about you.'

She paused to pick a dead head from one of the flowering shrubs, throwing it onto the ground and staring at it as though the answers to all her questions lay in the dried-up petals.

'You are my first-born,' she said, 'and it did my heart good to see you happy, cared for by a good man. Now you've let your damned pride drive him away. Get him back, Hortense, honey, write him a letter, tell him you wants him home before he meets some English girl and forgets all about you.'

Hortense felt a pang of fear. Binnie loved her, she had no doubt about that but she had struck out at him, spitting out fury and anger, and he had left America thinking she had finished with him for good. He was a good man but he was a young vigorous man and before long he would need a woman to fulfil his needs.

'I think you're right, Mammy. I've been a fool driving him away like that but perhaps it's not too late.' Hortense brightened. The day seemed to glow around her; her mother had made her see sense. She wanted Binnie back in her life and, even if she had to travel to England to do it, she would win her husband back in the end.

Josephine threw down her bonnet and slipped out of her light jacket, happy to be indoors away from the glare of the sun. She had a headache coming on; she seemed to be getting headaches a lot lately. The coolness of the house welcomed her and she was glad she had decided to return early from her shopping trip in town.

The house seemed to dream in a soft silence, outside the birds were singing and the leaves on the trees rustled in the warm breeze. It was good to be at home, in the house Daddy had given them. Her pregnancy had given her the ideal excuse to stop traipsing around the countryside with John. It was time they settled now that there was a child on the way. John settle? Pigs might fly.

Josephine rubbed her hand over her eyes; the headache was persisting, perhaps something to eat would help and a warm cup of coffee. She looked around for the maid. Veenie was usually in the kitchen preparing food. But the kitchen was empty. Josephine wandered outside to the back of the house and heard sounds coming from the washhouse. Veenie was probably up to her elbows in water. She was and she looked up startled when she saw Josephine.

'Mrs Pendennis, you home early,' she said. 'Do you want me to git you anything? You looks hot and flustered.'

'A nice cup of coffee would be wonderful,' Josephine said. 'Where's Mr Pendennis, gone out has he?'

Veenie appeared flustered. 'I don rightly know, miss.' Veenie rubbed her big arms against her apron. 'I'll put the coffee on right away.'

She really should get another couple of servants, Josephine thought. Now that she was going to be staying in Troy she could establish a permanent staff. A cook would be a necessity and a young girl to do the menial tasks. But not too pretty a young girl, she thought ruefully.

Veenie made an inordinate amount of noise, bustling about the kitchen, banging pots even singing a little to herself. Josephine considered asking what had got into her but she was too tired and her skirts felt suddenly tight around her expanding middle. Better to get upstairs and change.

'Mrs Pendennis!' Veenie followed her into the hall. 'I should have asked you before but I needs a day off next week.' Her voice was unnaturally loud. 'Any day will do. I just needs to see my sister, she ain't been well an I said I'd go over and give her a hand.'

Josephine stared at Veenie: why was she getting so excited at a simple request for time off? She heard it then, the sound of movement from upstairs. She heard a laugh, low and very feminine, a woman's laugh. Veenie bit her lip and twisted her apron around her long fingers. 'Sorry, Mrs Pendennis, I tried . . .'

'My Lord!' Josephine said. 'He's got a woman up there, in my bed, the bastard!' She picked up her skirts and made her way upstairs, her heart thumping, the pain in her head worse. She pushed open the bedroom door and stood looking at them, her husband and the woman he was embracing. 'Melia!'

For a long moment, no-one spoke. The silence was intense. Josephine ignored her sister and stared, eyes narrowed at John. 'You lying cheating bastard!' She spoke in a low voice. 'I thought you were going to reform, give up your wild ways now that you are going to be a father. Instead I find you in bed and with my *sister*! How low could a man sink?'

John stared up at her, his colour high, it was clear he had been drinking. 'A man needs some fun and some variety in his life. You wouldn't give me either so I looked elsewhere.'

'And you!' Josephine stared at Melia. 'How could you do this to me?'

'Oh, look, hon, it doesn't mean anything.' Melia pushed aside the sheets and stood up beside the bed. Her breasts were firm and small, her hips rounded. Her skin had the sheen of sweat on it and her mouth was still damp from John's kisses.

Rage such as she had never known before filled Josephine. She lunged forward and smacked Melia full in the face. Melia staggered away from her but Josephine followed and smacked her again, harder. Melia turned towards the open French doors. Outside, the balcony shimmered with colour and light but Josephine saw none of it; all she could see was John, her husband, in the arms of her sister, making love to her in the same bed he shared with his wife.

'You slut!' Josephine advanced on Melia, her hands reaching out to scratch the smooth skin. 'You whore!' She lashed out again at Melia and her sister looked at her with open scorn.

'And you are a miserable, jealous woman and you're fat and ugly into the bargain, why would a man like John want you?'

Enraged, Josephine flung herself at Melia. They were both on the balcony, struggling and lashing out at each other. The soft air brushed Josephine's hot cheeks but she did not even feel it. The old boards of the balcony creaked beneath her feet. A small table was pushed against the rail as the two women struggled.

'You brazen whore!' Josephine pushed Melia away, hating her. Melia struggled to keep her balance, her arms flung wide. Then, as if in slow motion, she fell against the wooden handrail of the balcony.

The old wood groaned under the sudden weight. Melia clung to the rail but it cracked with a sound like a gunshot. And then Melia was crashing through the wooden balustrade and spiralling downwards, her bare limbs gleaming in the sunlight. It seemed to Josephine that the seconds became hours as she saw her sister screaming and twisting downwards, her arms flung wide, her mouth open.

Melia hit the dusty garden below with a dull thud and lay there, unmoving.

'What have you done, you maniac!' John was pulling on his trousers. 'You've killed her, you've killed your own sister.'

He saw Veenie standing in the doorway. 'Run and fetch Mr McCabe,' he shouted. 'Git!'

Josephine could not move. She stared down at her sister, spread-eagled against the dusty ground, her limbs very white in the bright sunshine. Josephine could not believe her own eyes. She had pushed Melia to her death.

She stood there unable to move as John rushed down the stairs and out of the house. She saw him bend over Melia and lift her wrist in his brown hands, hands that moments before had been caressing Melia's flesh. When he released her wrist, Melia's arm fell limply back onto the ground.

Josephine clung to the door-frame, staring out, unable to move and she was there when her father came into the garden. He looked up at her and then went to Melia's side. Josephine heard the sound of his voice giving instructions and then John was lifting Melia and carrying her into the house.

It was like a bad dream being enacted before her eyes. As if in a nightmare, Josephine stood in the circle of her father's arm and watched as Veenie and John dressed Melia and tied up her hair. Melia was still, unmoving, there was no doubt she was dead.

'Now. Veenie, listen to me, this is what happened here,' Dan McCabe spoke firmly, his tone clipped. 'The girls was going to have some tea on the balcony.' He frowned in concentration. 'You must go now and fetch a tray up here with a bite to eat.'

Veenie disappeared promptly, her eyes wide with fear. Josephine felt her father hug her tightly. 'Come on, honey, pull yourself together, we must cover this up best we can. Fetch her slippers, John.' He barked the command and John moved swiftly.

Josephine felt John lift her feet one by one and help her change her shoes. She watched speechless as Veenie returned with a tray and a cloth and set the small table for tea. The maid was edgy and kept well away from the broken spars of wood that dangled over the garden below, glancing every now and again at Josephine with tears of sympathy in her dark eyes.

'Now then,' Dan said, 'this is what took place: the girls were going to have tea, as I said, then Melia stumbled against the balcony rail. The wood gave way and she fell. Simple as that and no-one could save her.' He looked at his daughter. 'That's what happened, isn't it, Jo?' He squeezed her shoulder again.

'I hit her,' Josephine said, 'she was in bed with my husband, I was blinded with anger and so I hit her. It's my fault she's dead, my fault.'

'No, you got that wrong,' Dan said. 'It's nobody's fault, she slipped, the wood must have been rotten to break like that anyway.' There was a catch in his throat. 'I've lost one daughter, I do not intend to lose another. Now have you all got the story straight before I call the sheriff?'

Josephine nodded, her father always knew what to do, she was safe with him. He led her to the sun-filled sitting room and she waited there feeling as though she was living in a nightmare world. It was a strangely unreal world where people came and went, questions were asked and lies were told.

At last, Melia's body was taken away and Josephine was alone with John. She could not look at him. Not even when he came and knelt beside her and took her hand and begged her forgiveness. When she was so weary that she could not bear it, she asked Veenie to move her things into the spare bedroom. Then, without even bothering to take off her dress, she crawled into bed and fell into a fitful sleep.

The next morning, Josephine Pendennis miscarried her child and she knew then that the nightmare was real and would stay with her for the rest of her life.

'Are you settling in now, Binnie?' Even as Llinos asked the question she felt she already knew the answer. Binnie was like a fish out of water, pining for his family back in America.

'I'm doing my best, Llinos.' He had a bit of an American accent now, he even looked American with his brown skin and sun-bleached hair. He was different from the young man who had left Swansea to escape an unhappy marriage. But his past had caught up with him and here he was back where he had started, working in the potteries as a casual hand.

'I'm sorry, Binnie,' Llinos said. 'I would have liked to make you manager but you can see how things are. Watt is in charge now, he's been very good to me and I can't take that away from him, can I?'

'I'm not complaining, Llinos,' Binnie said, rolling his sleeves above his elbows as he prepared to dip a tray of pots into the already-prepared glaze.

'No, but in America you were the boss,' Llinos said softly. 'You had a position of responsibility. Here you are just another worker.'

'It's no more than I deserve,' he said. 'I cheated and lied my way through life and I should have known I would have to pay for it one day.'

Llinos wondered how much she should tell him about Maura and Watt. She might be making matters worse if she meddled. And yet Binnie looked so beaten, so lost, surely there was something she could say to comfort him?

'She was happy, mind,' she said at last. 'Maura was in love and even though she couldn't get married, she enjoyed her life, you can be sure of that.'

'No thanks to me though.' Binnie dipped a pot, turning it in the glaze, allowing the liquid to run evenly over the handle and the lip of the pot. He held it aloft for the excess to drain away before placing the pot on a stand. Then he looked up at Llinos, his eyes shadowed.

'Do you know my first reaction when I got Watt's letter telling me Maura was dead?' He paused, taking a deep breath. 'It was relief, I was actually pleased that the woman who I married, who had borne my child, was dead. I don't deserve sympathy, I deserve a good whipping.'

'You are too hard on yourself,' Llinos said. 'You were young, it was too soon for you to take on a family. You have to forgive yourself, Binnie.'

'How can I?' he asked. 'I've ruined so many lives by my selfishness. I have lost the only woman I ever really loved because I was afraid to tell her the truth about my past. I have been weak and irresponsible, there's no-one to blame but myself.'

He dipped another pot and spoke without looking at her. 'And you, Llinos, I expected to find you blissfully happy. Instead you have shadowed eyes. Where's your husband, have you parted from him?'

It was as though he had stuck a knife in her heart. 'I didn't realize how perceptive you were, Binnie,' she said. She sighed. 'I don't know where Joe goes to, he tells me he's away on business but I know different. Even when he's home, he's not the Joe I married. My marriage to Joe is as good as finished.'

'I can't believe that.'

'Believe it. Oh, Joe won't desert me entirely, at least I don't think so, we have a son and though Joe might walk out on me, he would never turn his back on his Lloyd.'

'Well, whatever's troubling him, let him work it out by himself. Sometimes pushing too hard has the opposite effect to the one you were hoping for.'

'Everyone tells me that. But I hurt inside, Binnie, I hurt so much.' Llinos stared at Binnie for a long moment as if he could provide the answers she was so desperate for. He shook his head sadly.

'We each have to work out our own problems, Llinos,' he said. 'No-one's life is free of pain.'

'I know,' Llinos said softly. She left the shed, with its smell of oxide and tallow, and crossed the yard to the house, a house empty of Joe, the man she loved. Suddenly there were tears in her eyes.

Binnie dipped another pot into the glaze, and watching the thick liquid running over every part of the pot brought a certain satisfaction. At least here in the shed he felt alive, as though somehow working at the pottery brought him closer to his life back home in America. And yet it was an illusion, an illusion that vanished the minute he stepped outside into the cool of the evening.

He missed the sunshine of America, the wild grasses that grew around his house, the smell of honeysuckle, the smell of baking and the singing of the maid at work in the kitchen. If he closed his eyes he could see it all, his home, his garden and the world beyond, the world of West Troy, the place he had grown to love, the place that now meant home. And most of all, he missed his wife and his sons.

Tonight, when he finished work, he would go back to the cheap lodging house, eat a meal of meat cuts and over-boiled potatoes. And then he would spend a lonely night sitting in his room, staring around him at the faded curtains and the worn carpet placed over a loose floorboard. Finally, he would crawl into bed, a cold, empty bed. He had left behind him a world of light and luxury and love and now he wondered if life was worth living at all.

'Hey, why so glum!' Watt Bevan touched him on the shoulder and Binnie looked up sharply. Watt was taller than him by several inches; the Watt Bevan who had been little more than a stripling when Binnie left for America was now a mature man.

On his brief visit to America Watt had seemed to be unsure of his future, undecided if he would stay in West Troy or return home to Swansea. It seemed he had made the right decision because now he looked happy and fulfilled.

'Homesick, I guess,' Binnie said, placing the last pot of the batch onto a stand ready to be taken to the kiln.

'I suppose you're not used to being on your own so much,' Watt said. 'So come and have supper with me and my girl Rosie tonight. Pearl, you remember Pearl, well she's making one of her huge hotpots.'

Binnie toyed with the idea. Though his first instinct was to refuse the invitation, he decided anything was better than spending another night in his room staring at the four walls.

'That's good of you, Watt, I'll be happy to accept your hospitality.' He wiped his hands and arms on a rag dipped in turpentine. The gloss had run into the material of his shirt and he stared at it in an effort to force away the sense of despair that washed over him. He did not feel like socializing and yet what was the alternative?

'Yeah, sure, tell me what time and I'll be there.' He made an effort to smile. 'It will be good to eat supper among cheerful company.'

'Come any time you like. At Pearl's it's open house, more like the feeding of the five thousand than anything else but at least you won't be bored,' Watt said. 'I tell you what, I'll pick you up at your lodgings and take you to Pearl's house myself, otherwise you might change your mind.' Watt frowned. 'I know it's hard for you coming back here like this. I could break John Pendennis's neck for him, I never thought he would turn out to be such a bastard.'

The word made Binnie shudder, he could hear again the sound of Hortense's voice as she accused him of fathering bastard sons on her. And she was right, God help him, she was right!

'I'm grateful to you, Watt,' he said, his voice thick. 'Without this job and the kindness of my friends I don't think I could survive.'

'Look,' Watt said, 'why don't you write a letter home?' He paused. 'By now, your wife will have cooled down, she will be missing you as much as you are missing her. At least give it a shot, isn't it worth it?'

Watt was right it would be worth one more effort. Tonight, after supper with Watt, Binnie would go back to the lodging house. He would sit by the rickety table in his room and he would write to Hortense begging her to forgive him. His heart warmed with hope. He would ask her to take him back. He would tell her he would do anything so long as she gave him a second chance. As Watt pointed out, she might have had time to think things out by now.

Supper at Pearl's house was a noisy affair. The

younger children quarrelled over where they would sit at the big scrubbed table. Pearl, who appeared paler and thinner than Binnie remembered, cuffed one of the more boisterous boys and pushed him aside to make room for the large pot she was putting in the middle of the table.

'Nice to see you looking so well, Binnie lad,' she said. 'That man there,' she nodded to Willie who was plucking the strings of his fiddle, 'that's Willie Sharp, say hello then, Willie, where are your manners?'

Willie nodded politely and Binnie smiled to himself, trust Pearl to find another man to love her.

'Now, you children,' Pearl's voice boomed out, 'let the visitors help themselves first, do you hear?' Pearl smiled at Binnie, 'Go on, lad, get some food while it's hot.'

Watt was helping Pearl's daughter bring in plates piled with bread. The smell was mouth-watering and Binnie began to feel a little better, here he was among old friends. He saw Rosie sit beside Watt and gaze up at him with naked love in her eyes. A lump came to Binnie's throat, his own Hortense had looked at him in much the same way, once.

He managed to eat his meal and even to make a few pleasantries about the food but he came alive when one of the younger boys asked him about America.

'It's a vast country,' Binnie said. 'The sun seems to always be shining and even when it rains, the rain is soft and fragrant. The grasses grow tall and, in the summer, a riot of flowers grow wild and strong with no help from anything but nature.'

'Is it the land of milk and honey it's supposed to be then?' Pearl asked. Binnie looked at her; she was older now but she had the same bright look in her eyes, the same verve for life that had picked her out from the crowd working at the pottery in the old days.

'All I can say is that I love it there,' Binnie spoke quietly.

'Why don't you go back there, then?' one of the boys asked innocently. Binnie stared at him and then began to smile.

'I just might do that, son,' he said. 'Now how about another helping of that delicious hotpot, Pearl?'

That night, he sat in his room and stared out of the window. To hell with writing letters! He would take the chance and go back to America and even if Hortense wanted nothing to do with him, he would be near his sons, see them growing up, and make his home in the adopted country that he had grown to love.

CHAPTER SIXTEEN

Rosie sat patiently at the kitchen table as her mother wound a coronet of paper flowers in her hair. It was her wedding day and Rosie could hardly believe it. She stared into the speckled mirror, seeing her pale face, eyes wide with anticipation, and gave an involuntary smile. She knew she looked her best. Watt would be proud of her.

'Keep still, love!' Pearl teased Rosie's fair hair into tendrils around her cheeks and stood back to admire her handiwork. 'Is this lovely girl my little Rosie then?' Pearl wiped her eyes. '*Duw*, there's beautiful you look.' She bent over her daughter and kissed her cheek. 'That Watt Bevan is a lucky man and I only hope he realizes it!'

'I'm lucky too, Mam,' Rosie said gently. 'Watt is very handsome, he could have any woman he likes.'

'Well, he likes you, so there!' Pearl rubbed her chest with her hand, as though attempting to rub away the pain. 'You sure you want me at the church and me in my condition? I might spoil things by coughing all over the place.'

Rosie turned to look up at her mother. 'Of course I want you there, Mam!' she said indignantly. 'It wouldn't be a wedding without you and the boys around me.' She pulled at one of her curls.

'Watt will have Llinos Mainwaring and all the folks from the pottery on his side of the church.' She smiled happily. 'And Binnie Dundee is standing up for him as groomsman even though he's leaving for the docks straight after the wedding.'

'Ah,' Pearl said, looking shamefaced. 'And you only got me and the boys. Mind, you do need a man to give you away, don't you?' She did not meet her daughter's eyes.

'Well, it's not all that important is it, Mam? One of the boys can do it, can't they?' She looked at her brothers neatly dressed in their Sunday clothes, boots polished, hair slicked down with water and smiled. 'Dom is a big boy now, at fifteen he's taller than most men twice his age.'

Dom stared down at his boots. 'I don't want to stand up in no church, it's bad enough going there when it's not even Sunday.'

'Well, love.' Pearl hesitated. 'I've asked Willie Sharp to do it. I hope you don't mind love but he's been a good friend to me.'

Rosie shrugged. 'More than a friend, Mam. Well, I'm happy about it if you are.'

'Are you sure, love?' Pearl sounded wistful. 'I know Willie is really proud that I asked him but if you prefer . . .'

Rosie smiled suddenly. What did it matter? 'Willie shall give me away, it's settled.' What did any of the wedding arrangements really matter?

She was going to be Mrs Watt Bevan, she would have a gold ring on her finger and a man to love and cherish her. Nothing was going to spoil her wedding day.

'Thank you for everything, Mam,' she said warmly. 'You and Willie have done a lovely job of the bedroom, what with the windows painted and the pots of poppies all over the place.' She blushed at the thought of the bed, made up ready for the night with clean sheets and the best patchwork quilt.

What would it be like having a man make love to you? She dared not ask her mother in case Pearl boxed her around the ears for her forwardness.

Pearl seemed to sense something of what she was thinking. She rested her hand on Rosie's shoulder and leaned forward to whisper to her. 'Nothing to fright you, having a man, mind.' She smiled and patted her stomach. 'Otherwise I wouldn't have got so many babies would I?'

She sighed softly. 'Though there's nothing like your first love, nothing on earth or in heaven. I loved your father until the day he died.' She wiped her eyes. 'I'm just all tearful because you're getting married, love. Take no notice of me.' She dabbed at her cheeks with a scrap of linen.

'Now, what was I saying? Oh yes you just let Watt take the lead, he'll know what to do and you'll just enjoy being the wife of a good man.'

Rosie's colour was high, her mother's talk was embarrassing her, so were the feelings rushing through her. She felt damp with desire for Watt's touch. He had kissed her, of course, held her hand and when, last night, before saying goodnight, he held her in his arms, she had felt him hard against her and knew he desired her too.

'I'll be all right, Mam,' she said shyly. 'I know Watt will take care of everything.'

In the silence that followed Rosie heard the rumble of wheels on the cobbled street and her heartbeats quickened.

'The horse and trap's here,' Pearl said, the excitement evident in her voice. 'Come on then, you lot, outside with you, we'd better not keep the groom waiting.'

Rosie, seated in the front seat of the flower-bedecked cart, drawn by two horses, felt the sun on her face and smiled at the neighbours clustered around the doorways of their houses. Greenhill might not be a posh place to live but Rosie would not change the warmth and kindness of the people who lived there for anything.

She was glad Watt was going to make his home there, at least for the time being. Later, once Mam was well again and was settled back in work, Rosie could think about a place of her own, somewhere nearby so Rosie could keep an eye on Mam and the boys.

Pearl was wearing a full-skirted dress, her Sunday best. Over it, she had thrown a fine lace shawl so that her too-thin body was concealed as much as possible from prying eyes.

The church was bathed in sunlight, the cross over the door gleaming like gold. Father Martin stood ready to greet them and his gaze rested for a moment on Pearl's white face before giving his attention to Rosie.

'You sure about this, Rosie?' he asked in his

jocular way. Rosie liked Father Martin. He was pink and plump with kind eyes and a soft voice. He never judged people the way some men of the cloth did.

'I'm sure, Father,' she said smiling. 'Sure as I'll ever be.'

'Right then, let's get on with the show.'

Watt looked very tall as he stood waiting for her with Binnie Dundee at his side. Rosie could see the sadness in Binnie's eyes. He must be remembering his own wedding and the woman he had left behind in America.

Watt smiled down at her and held out his hand to take hers and everything else went from her mind except the man she was about to marry. His fingers closed around hers and any flutter of nerves she felt vanished as love for him flowed through her.

She had meant to enjoy every minute of the ceremony but she hardly heard the words that joined her in matrimony to Watt Bevan. And then he was putting the ring on her finger, bending forward to kiss her lips in a brief salute.

'Hello, husband,' she whispered. The organ music swelled and tears came to Rosie's eyes but they were tears of happiness. People kissed her and hugged her and heaped flower petals and salt and rice on her, congratulating her and wishing her a long and happy marriage. It all passed in a haze and before she knew it she was seated beside Watt on the cart heading back towards Greenhill.

Pearl had coaxed Willie into playing the fiddle and the beer flowed, spilling onto the flagged floor of the kitchen and soaking the thin mats in the parlour, and the party atmosphere was almost too much to bear. Rosie thought she would burst with the joy of it all.

Pearl took the fiddle from Willie and handed it to one of her sons. 'Come on, me lad, it's time you danced with me!' She held onto Willie, twirling around as though she was a young girl again, careless of the pain in her chest.

'I'll be glad when we can get away,' Watt said. 'I feel as if I'm the star turn at the circus.'

Rosie felt a shadow fall over her happiness. She touched Watt's cheek, her eyes misted with tears. 'Aren't you happy, love?'

Suddenly the music stopped. Rosie looked up to see Pearl doubled over in pain. 'It's nothing!' she gasped. 'I'm just too old for all this dancing.'

Rosie was frightened by the pallor on her mother's face. Pearl staggered and would have fallen if Willie had not been close enough to support her.

'Mam!' Rosie rushed to her mother's side. What's wrong, Mam?'

Pearl had difficulty speaking. 'Take me upstairs,' she whispered and Rosie took her arm, leading her towards the door. Rosie could feel her mother trembling as she helped her upstairs. The freshly painted room, the clean patchwork quilt and the vases of flowers appeared incongruous now as Pearl moaned in pain, falling onto the bed, the terrible coughing convulsing her thin body.

'Get the doctor.' Rosie spoke as calmly as she could and Watt, standing nervously in the bedroom, nodded to Dom. The boy, his face as white as his mother's, clattered back down the stairs.

'*Duw!*' Pearl gasped. 'I don't need no doctor, love. I'll be right as rain in a minute.'

The pain caught her again and Pearl gasped, holding tightly to Rosie's hand. 'Sorry, love, I'm spoiling your wedding night.'

'Hush about that!' Rosie looked up and caught Watt's eyes; he shook his head sadly. Rosie felt fear rush through her. Was Mammy going to die?

Watt was at her side, his arm supporting her. 'The doctor will be here soon and then everything will be all right.'

Rosie felt a sense of panic flood through her; looking at Pearl's grey face and haunted eyes, Rosie wondered if anything would ever be right again.

Binnie had left the small house in Greenhill while the music was still loud and the celebrations were in full swing. Good old Pearl had kissed him and wished him well in America and he had smiled as she swung into a dance with her man.

He hoisted his small bag of possessions higher onto his shoulder and strode down the hill, seeing the gleam of the sea on the horizon. Soon he would be on the water, sailing back across the wide Atlantic Ocean. The thought thrilled him. A horse and cart rattled past and Binnie looked up at the driver, there was a medical bag at his side attesting to the fact that he was a doctor. Some poor soul was sick but in the huddle of streets in Greenhill that was nothing unusual.

A voice called out behind him, bringing him to

a halt. 'Binnie Dundee back from America, well well, it's a long time since you showed your face round here.'

Binnie turned to see the outline of a woman in the brightness of the moonlight.

'You should be too ashamed to show your face around these parts. Binnie Dundee, the rat from the gutter!'

'Are you drunk?' Binnie asked evenly. 'What sort of woman accosts a man in the street at this time of night?'

The woman drew nearer. 'You no good wretch! How could you leave my niece Maura the way you did?' He recognized the voice, knew that the insult was intended to anger him. All it did was to drive the knife of guilt deeper into his heart.

He raised his hat. 'Goodnight to you, Mrs O'Brian, shouldn't you be indoors by now?' He tried to walk away but a thin hand grabbed him, holding onto his coat sleeve.

Kate O'Brian stood solidly in front of him, peering up into his face, trying to see his expression in the darkness.

'You killed her, that's what, you and your faithless ways put our Maura into an early grave.'

He felt weary to the bone, too disheartened to argue with the woman. Swansea, it seemed, held nothing for him but recriminations and bitter memories.

'Anything you say, Mrs O'Brian, now let me go on my way if you please.' He shook off her hand and walked away, knowing that tears were running unchecked down his cheeks. He would not sleep that night; as he began his journey home he would try in the hours of darkness to exorcize his guilt, to pray to God for forgiveness for hurting the only two women who had ever been important to him.

He quickened his step; the sooner he was on board the *White Dove* the better. The only person in the whole of Swansea who would be sorry that he was leaving was Llinos Mainwaring. She had been so kind, so understanding when he told her of his decision to return to America. She hugged him and handed him his wages with a handsome bonus included.

He heard the rumble of wheels and stepped to the side to make way for the carriage and pair that was coming towards him. 'Want a ride the rest of the way?' Llinos was leaning out of the window. 'Come on, Binnie, climb in, I want to wave you off properly.'

'Llinos, you shouldn't be out at night alone, not in this sort of district,' Binnie said.

'I'm not alone, Eynon is here too.' Eynon Morton-Edwards pushed open the carriage door and Binnie nodded. 'Thank you, Mr Morton-Edwards, I'll be glad of the ride.'

He sat beside Llinos and she took his hand. 'I hope you'll find happiness in America,' she said. 'But, whatever happens, I know you are doing the right thing going back there.'

'I feel it's right, too.' He smoothed her fingers. 'And you, Llinos, will you be happy?' She did not reply and he tried to see her expression in the darkness.

'I can see something is wrong between you and Joe.' He hesitated. 'Is it anything to do with the Indian girl Joe brought from America with him?'

'Indian girl?' Llinos said faintly.

He realized at once that he had made a mistake. Llinos had known nothing about the Indian girl.

'I'm sorry,' Binnie spoke quickly. 'It was just gossip, I expect. I'm forever getting the wrong end of the stick, take no notice of what I say.'

'It must be Sho Ka,' Llinos said and Binnie heard the tremble in her voice. 'You remember, Binnie, we saw her that time we went to America? Joe was betrothed to her before he met me. She's so very lovely, how can I compete with her?'

Binnie held her hands. 'Look, Llinos, don't jump to conclusions and don't throw everything away like I did. If you love Joe, talk to him. I'm sure he can explain everything.'

'I expect so.' She did not sound convinced. 'Now you go back to your wife. Once you're home, everything will be all right for you, I feel it in my bones.'

'Take care of yourself, Llinos, and thank you for all you've done,' Binnie said. He slid from the seat as the carriage rumbled to a stop on the dockside where the sailing ships bobbed on an eager tide. 'Look after yourself, Llinos.'

Binnie looked back once at the folding hills around the huddled town and then up at the stars twinkling overhead. He knew in that moment that he was leaving his past behind him for good. His ghosts were exorcized.

He walked swiftly now towards the ship that was to carry him across the Atlantic and back to West Troy and suddenly Binnie's heart was light. He was going home.

* * *

273

Rosie was managing the house more efficiently than Pearl ever had. Pearl sat in the old armchair in the kitchen and looked around her, admiring her daughter's handiwork. The place was spotless. Rosie cooked with little fuss and the washing and ironing were done to perfection. But Rosie was not happy and it troubled Pearl.

Pearl had been housebound since her lung sickness had flared up and she had more time to think. Now she lived vicariously through the lives of her children. Willie came to see her often but his heartiness and good health wearied her.

She spent very little time out of her bedroom, the room that should have been Rosie's and Watt's. But when she did venture downstairs her sharp eyes missed nothing. Pearl saw that Rosie did not smile much any more and as for Watt, well, she had grave doubts about Watt. He seemed agreeable enough as he praised his wife's cooking and complimented her on the pristine whiteness of his shirts but there was a hint of unhappiness in his eyes which Pearl, even with her new-found sensitivity, could not understand.

Pearl looked out of the window, wishing she had the strength to walk in the backyard, to touch the washing blowing in the breeze. But her days were numbered, she knew that better than anyone.

She left the window and sank into a chair with a sigh of relief; she was tired, weary to the bone. She got tired very easily these days and the tears were never far from her eyes. It seemed as if, without her noticing, old age had caught her in his trap.

'Hello, Mam, you look all washed out.' Rosie had been to the market and, as she put the basket of vegetables on the table, the smell of fresh leeks made Pearl feel hungry.

'I'll make you a nice cup of tea now, love.' Pearl made to get up but Rosie waved her back into her chair.

'You just sit down by the fire and I'll make the tea.'

Pearl watched her daughter as she poured boiling water into the brown earthenware pot and felt a glow of pride. They were one of the few families who could afford tea in the whole of Greenhill. Watt's wages made for a good easy living, something Pearl had never experienced before.

Pearl rubbed her eyes worriedly; she sometimes felt that Watt's marriage had been forced on him by her illness. He had been lonely, too, missing Maura, and Rosie was sweet enough to turn any man's head. And she had been his for the asking. Still, marriages had been based on less.

Her own marriage had been one of convenience at first, arranged for her by her overbearing father. Pearl's protests that she did not love the man had been brushed aside. But love had grown and together Pearl and her husband had made a fine upstanding family life for their children so there were no regrets.

Pearl sipped her tea, the heat of it stung her gums where she had teeth missing but her stomach gurgled in appreciation. 'Lovely cuppa, Rosie.' She held the cup between both her hands. Her fingers were no longer stained with paint and glaze but were unnaturally white against the china.

She wondered about the new patterns Llinos had designed, nice paintings with pretty tea roses sticking out of bunches of wild flowers. More in keeping, Pearl thought, than the bright firebird designs the pottery had been using.

'Strange really,' she said out loud, 'I never thought anything would go wrong between those two.' She saw Rosie look at her, eyebrows touching her hairline.

'What are you going on about, Mam?'

Pearl smiled. 'Oh, just thinking out loud, love. Llinos and her man, well they don't seem to be together much lately, that's all.'

'But they're an old married couple now,' Rosie said reasonably. 'I don't suppose they want to live in each other's pocket any more, do they?'

Pearl looked at her darkly. 'You got a lot to learn about love, girl.' She held out her cup for more tea and Rosie obliged by lifting the china pot from the hob.

'I suppose you're right.' She sat opposite her mother. 'I love Watt more than I thought I ever could love a man. It's just like you said, Mam, I want him by me day and night.' She hesitated. 'Only I don't think he feels the same way.'

The conversation was taking a turn Pearl did not like. 'Men are different,' she said quickly. 'They have their work and their pals down at the beer house and their woman is only ever a part of their life, it's a quirk of nature, love.'

Rosie sighed. 'I suppose so.'

Pearl leaned across the table. 'He's good to you, in bed I mean?'

Rosie blushed and looked down at her hands shyly. 'Just being with him makes me feel good.'

'Then he's doing right by you,' Pearl said. 'And

you leave him be. The more a woman nags a man the more time he'll spend out of her sight.'

'Is that what's wrong with Llinos and her husband then?' Rosie asked. 'Does she nag him, do you think?'

Pearl shook her head. 'I don't think so, love, Llinos don't seem the kind of woman to nag, but something is wrong and that's for sure. But then the threads that bind a man and woman together are very frail, they could be broken by a careless word.'

Pearl looked closely at her daughter. 'My only advice to you, love, is to keep Watt happy in the bedroom,' she said. 'I know you're not asking me but I'm telling you anyway, a man happy with his wife in between the sheets rarely strays.'

Rosie looked down at her hands. 'Watt wouldn't do that,' she said. 'I know I haven't been married to him for long but he's an honest man. Don't you think so, Mam?'

'Honest he may be,' Pearl said. 'But it don't pay to be too sure about anything when it comes to men. Any man could be tempted, even an honest man.' She paused. 'Take Llinos and Joe, lovers from heaven once.'

'You think Joe . . . Mr Mainwaring has got another woman then?'

Pearl shook her head. 'It's only a feeling, love, but yes, the signs are all there.' And they were. Joe away most of the time and Llinos going about with a long face. And now the change in the patterns for the china. Oh, yes, the signs were there all right and Pearl had the strongest feeling that Llinos had read them loud and clear.

Well, it was nothing to do with her any more. Pearl's days at the pottery were over and done with. She had to be content now to sit by her fireside and make the most of the days she had left. They were not many according to the doctor who saw her on Rosie's wedding day.

Pearl looked out into the sunlit yard and prayed to God in his heaven to let her live a little while longer. Just a few more months, time enough for Watt to get Rosie in the family way. She spoke her thoughts aloud.

'When are you going to give me a grandchild, Rosie?' Pearl watched her daughter's face and saw that Rosie was near to tears.

'Never the way things are going on between me and Watt!' Rosie rushed from the room and Pearl heard the floorboards above her creak. She put her hand to her eyes.

'Silly girl.' She comforted herself. 'Her old man probably forgot to kiss her good morning before he left for work.'

She settled back into the rocking chair, adjusting the cushion behind her head and, with the sunlight on her face, she slept.

CHAPTER SEVENTEEN

Alice Sparks was enjoying herself. She picked up a bolt of rich curtain material and held it up to the light slanting in from the shop doorway. The shades of blue striped with beige would look good against the high windows in the new house.

'I'll have the whole bolt,' she said. 'Please deliver it to this address.' She handed the obsequious salesman her card, proud of the gold lettering that spelt out her name and her new address.

Highmoor was built in the prestigious Mount Pleasant area of Swansea, sited on a hillside facing the sea. It was an old house of mellow stone, built to last. It was quite large, not as elegant as the home in which she had spent her childhood but a great improvement on the house in Pleasant Row.

At the thought of Pleasant Row she frowned. It had been too small to house a family and the new servants. Now, however, she felt her position had improved and the new servants were fitting in quite well.

Lily, the stupid girl, had given in her notice,

making some absurd excuse that she was to be engaged as a companion to a wealthy lady. Even when Alice had told her of the move to a better location, a nicer house, she could not be persuaded to stay.

Alice had demanded to know the name of this mysterious lady and had gasped with shock when Lily said she was going to work for Polly Boucher. Alice sniffed at the thought; Polly's husband might be very wealthy, almost as wealthy as Alice's father, but for all that he had married a common little trollop who had climbed up the social scale only by making an advantageous marriage. The likes of Polly Boucher would never be welcomed at Alice's new home.

As for Lily, she had shown base ingratitude by leaving Alice in the lurch the way she had. But then what could you expect of a girl from the lower orders? Alice smiled. Lily's small 'investment' had served very well. Come to think of it, Lily was better off where she was because she would never see her money again and would be in no position to protest about it.

'Is there anything else, madam?' the salesman was practically rubbing his hands, no doubt he would receive a handsome commission on the purchases she had made.

'You could bring me a chair and a cup of iced lemon cordial and then show me to the furniture department,' she said haughtily. 'You can see I'm in a delicate condition, can't you?'

'I do beg your pardon, madam.' He hastily fetched a chair and Alice sank into it with a sigh of relief. Her ankles were beginning to swell, something she had not bargained for when she became pregnant.

As she drank her iced lemon she thought of Edward, but only briefly. His objections to her spending were constant and she had decided to pay them little attention. He was a thorn in her side, the only disagreeable aspect of her improved lifestyle. Still, for the moment he was a necessity and she would have to put up with him.

Why could she not have found a man who was her social equal? Alice was from a long line of landowners. Her father owned acres of rolling meadows and dense woodlands. The house she had been born in was a cut above anything that Swansea could offer. It boasted grand architecture and a whole host of servants. Highmoor might be a step in the right direction but, while she was married to a lowly bank manager, Alice would never take her rightful place in society.

Eynon Morton-Edwards was part of the cream of Swansea's gentry. Although his father had been in trade, he had been of good stock. Eynon was highly educated and above all he was a gentleman. It was a great pity she had not met him before she tied herself to Mr Sparks.

It was high time she had a reply to her letter urging Eynon to see her. She had risked everything on her expectations of Eynon handing her a large sum of money once he knew the truth about the twins. She would just have to convince him that he was the father, otherwise her wonderful new lifestyle would vanish before her eyes. Still, it might be worthwhile speaking to him again and failing that she would have to throw herself on her father's mercy.

The furniture department was busy and Alice brushed people aside, claiming the attention of the manager by her imperious manner. She ordered a fine dining suite and a large comfortable sofa and then decided to call it a day.

She arrived home exhausted by her shopping trip but happy in the knowledge that, soon, all the empty spaces in the large house would be filled with good, tasteful furnishings. Had she left the matter to Edward, she would have landed up with the cheapest pieces of furniture and the most tasteless drapes he could find.

The new cook she had employed was young and fresh but used to cooking for quality. Mrs Clare, as she was called for reasons of civility, was pretty, very pretty indeed, but Alice had no fears about her being a temptation to Edward. Most masters of the house would have readily availed themselves of Mrs Clare's charms but Edward Sparks was not a man who enjoyed the sins of the flesh. He was made of ice, neglecting his husbandly duties now that he felt his job was done.

Alice smiled to herself; little did he know that the babies she carried were the progeny of a rich man, a man who could hold up his head in any society. She was glad her children would have a father who was respected, wealthy and handsome. Eynon had a daughter but should Alice give birth to sons, Eynon would one day leave them his fortune. The thought made her very happy.

Alice heard the sound of the front door opening and then Edward's voice echoed through the hall. He was in a bad mood, that much was clear from the high-pitched tone he used to the unfortunate maid. When he entered the room, he looked at his wife, his expression cold.

'Alice, you are spending far too much money, my account is almost empty. You must stop this extravagance right now, do you hear me?'

'How could I not hear you, Edward? I think the entire neighbourhood must have heard you. Kindly lower your voice and sit down. Now, tell me calmly just what it is I have done wrong.'

He mopped his face with his handkerchief; sweat beaded his prominent nose and ran along the sides of his thin cheeks. Alice wondered how she could bear to have him touch her. Well, from now on, that was just not going to happen. He would not dream of coming to her bed while she was pregnant and she would make sure he never bothered her after the twins were born.

'You know what is wrong!' He paced towards the window; his brow was furrowed and he seemed about to burst into tears. 'How do you think it looks when the senior manager of the bank cannot even keep his own accounts in order? Tell me that, Alice, just tell me that!'

She sighed heavily. 'My father has promised me some more money.' The lie came easily to her lips. Edward was such a fool. Alice shook her head, despairing of this weakling she had married. 'You worry too much, dear Edward. Haven't I said I will take care of everything?'

'Well then,' he lowered his voice a fraction, 'you'd better get on with it before I end up in trouble with the bank.'

'I will write to my father at once.' Alice rose to her feet, tired of Edward's moaning. 'I shall go to my room now and compose a letter. In the meantime, perhaps you would be good enough to summon the maid and order a cooling drink.' She frowned at him. 'It doesn't do to get overwrought, Edward, you'll suffer an apoplexy and then where will I be? And me with twins on the way.'

She was glad of the peaceful silence of her room. She sat in the light from the window and drew a sheet of paper towards her. It was high time that Eynon took some serious responsibility for the children he had spawned on her. She would write to him again, threaten to go to his house and confront him. He would have to see her if he wished to avoid an unpleasant scene. After all, facing Eynon was far better than facing her irate and disapproving father.

Lily was better placed now she was with Polly; she certainly felt more secure though she found the big house somewhat intimidating. Several times she had got lost in the maze of passages joining the lower rooms and had needed to ask the servants for help.

She was in a strange position, neither servant nor mistress, and as she sat with Polly in the drawing room of the big house she stared out at the neat gardens and wondered what else fate held in store for her.

She had become what Polly laughingly called a companion housekeeper and was dressed in a good silk gown and a matching jacket. That they were Polly's cast-offs rankled more than a little but anything was better than the rough calico Lily had become accustomed to while working for Alice Sparks.

'Jem was at it again last night, he's a real scream when he gets randy!' Polly kicked her legs in the air in glee. 'You should see him, Lil, his nightshirt standing out in front as if he had a poker up there! He's a real laugh and no mistake!'

Lily was disgusted at the very thought. Jem Boucher might be a gent but he was so old. His cheeks were sagging and his beard hung in grey straggles down the front of his waistcoat. The thought of going to bed with the man made her want to retch.

Polly read her expression well. 'He's not half bad for an old guy, mind,' she said. 'Better than some young 'uns who turn out to be one-minute wonders.' She smiled as she saw Lily's blank stare. 'You *know*, in and out so quick you got no time to draw breath.'

Lily remained silent; she could not think of anything to say. Polly, sensing her disapproval, shook her head in amusement.

'At least I had the sense to get myself out of the gutter!' she said. 'Sometimes, Lily, you annoy me! You act all superior but didn't you marry a man just to get yourself a comfortable bed and food in your belly?'

Lily lowered her head; she could not deny what Polly was saying. But then her husband had been a normal man, a man who liked his comforts but not a man to make a show of them the way Jem did. Jem was an old lecher who eyed every woman as though she were a morsel of food on a plate to be devoured at will. Lily kept well out of his way.

'I'm sorry, Polly.' She forced herself to speak gently. If Polly should lose patience with her she

285

would be out on the road again. 'It's just that I've never liked that sort of thing, you know that.'

'Aye, I know, right stick-in-the-mud you are, Lily, I just don't understand you. Lying with a man is *fun*, it's not dirty the way you think it is.'

Lily looked up at her friend's earnest face and wished she could be like her. She spoke her thoughts out loud. 'You are so easy with men, Polly, and I'm so awkward with them.' She sighed. 'I don't think any decent man will look at me now, I'm getting too old.' She rose and looked in the mirror over the fireplace. She saw a pretty girl with large eyes and small, neat features. She had put on a little weight and it suited her. Her skin was unlined, her hair softly curling around her forehead. 'Well,' she said, 'I feel old, inside, you know what I mean.'

'What I do know is that what you need is some fun, girl.' Polly sat up straight. 'Ring the bell for the maid, Lil, let's get the carriage into town and buy some clothes, is it?'

Lily knew what that meant. Polly would buy gowns and perhaps some bonnets and even several pairs of shoes but not for her. Oh, no. Polly would have the new clothes and pass her old dresses on to Lily. Still, anything was better than sitting here in the house like a prisoner.

Sometimes Lily missed the pottery, missed the smell of oxide and tallow and missed the company of her fellow workers. Once she had thought she was above them. She had looked down on Pearl. She had even scorned Watt Bevan who had offered her a respectable marriage. If only she had taken him up on his offer she would be her own woman now, comfortable and respected in the community. Instead she was little more than a lady's maid, pandering to Polly's every whim.

'Fetch the coats then, Lily,' Polly said. 'And for goodness' sake cheer up, I might have a surprise for you later.'

'What sort of surprise?' Lily was suspicious; sometimes Polly's surprises were not welcome ones. Like the time she had arranged for them to go to the musical evening in the town hall. The music was fine, it was the company of the two young gentlemen that Lily objected to. All they wanted was a good time and the evening had ended up with Polly giving it to them while Lily sat in the coach in a fever of impatience to be home and warm in her bed.

'Don't worry, we are not going out on the town tonight. No, this surprise is going to happen right here and I guarantee that you'll like it,' Polly said. Lily could only hope so.

It was a fine day, a little chilly but with a pale sun lighting the roadway ahead of them. The coach was a comfortable one; it should be, it had once belonged to the Morton-Edwards family and was made from the finest materials money could buy. Jem had purchased it from Eynon Morton-Edwards after Polly admired the family crest. Lily supposed that a man as rich as Eynon would have several coaches in his stables; he could well do without one of them.

The town was busy and, as Lily stepped out onto the cobbled roadway, she saw Alice Sparks going into the best clothing emporium in Swansea. Polly gestured towards the ornate doorway.

'There's the woman you used to work for, uppity bitch! Come on, let's go in after her!' Polly hugged Lily's arm. 'We'll show the old madam a thing or two, you'll see. Thinks she's made of better stuff than me but money talks louder than any posh voice.'

Her heart sinking into her boots, Lily followed Polly inside the store. The air was heavy with the scent of rosewater and, if the rich drapes at the windows were a little dusty, it was difficult to tell in the dimness of the light.

Alice Sparks was at the millinery counter. The hat she was trying was far too large for her small face but she turned this way and that, admiring herself in the long mirror. Polly tapped her hand on the polished counter and the sales assistant gave her a long look, assessing her clothes, her good jewellery, and immediately bowed to Alice, begging to be excused.

'Bring me your most expensive hats.' Polly had adopted the fine accent she had learned from her husband. 'And you can send the bill to Jem Boucher, pottery owner.'

'Yes, madam, at once.' The woman fetched an armful of boxes and placed them on the counter and Polly remained still, waiting. Eagerly, the assistant opened the hatboxes, spreading hats across the counter.

'Take your time, madam,' she said. 'I will be back with you in a moment.'

'Wait!' Polly ordered and the assistant stopped in her tracks. 'I want you to show me the hats not to simply hand them to me as disrespectfully as if I was some street girl.'

'But, madam, I have another customer.'

'Yes!' Alice Sparks called. 'I *was* here first.'

'How is that bank-manager husband of yours, Mrs Sparks?' Polly said innocently. Lily watched in admiration; Polly was cleverly putting Alice in her place as the wife of a humble manager of the bank at which Jem Boucher deposited his great wealth.

The assistant looked from one to the other and then Polly attempted to clinch the matter. 'I am in rather a hurry, I have other purchases to make, so perhaps you would serve me first?'

'But I want *seven* new hats.' Alice made a last-ditch attempt to win the day. 'I need a new one for every day, you see.' She smiled sweetly. 'My dear father has left me his fortune and I intend to spend as much of it here in the emporium as I can.'

'In that case,' Polly said sweetly, 'your need is greater than mine. My companion and I will take a seat until you are finished.'

She hustled Lily to the side of the room. 'Now the old bitch will have to buy seven hats or risk looking a fool! This is going to be a right scream, Lil.'

'But if her father has left her money she can afford seven hats.' Lily was bewildered; it was not like Polly to stand aside for anyone.

'Don't be daft!' Polly said scathingly. 'Them Sparks haven't got two half-pennies to rub together.' She giggled. 'My Jem knows everything about the bank and Mrs high-and-mighty Sparks is in for a nasty surprise any day now. She can't afford one hat let alone seven.'

Alice was pale-faced by the time her packages

were being put aside for delivery. She looked briefly at Polly, her eyes cold.

'Day to you, Mrs Sparks,' Polly said brightly, 'hope you enjoy your nice new hats.'

As Alice swept past them, Lily felt sorry for her. She was a bitch as Polly put it, but it was sad to see any woman brought low because of a man. Lily wondered uneasily if she had been a fool to trust Alice with her money. Still, there was little point in brooding about that now.

The hours passed quickly and, to Lily's surprise, she left the emporium with a brand-new gown, two pairs of evening slippers and a fine pure-wool wrap. Polly's own purchases were too numerous to carry and would be delivered later.

'You got to look your best for this evening, see.' Polly hugged her arm as the two women returned to the coach. 'And don't look so worried, I wouldn't do anything to hurt you, would I now?'

Lily was not too sure about that but she smiled; at least she had some new clothes of her very own. She felt a dart of happiness as she thought of the pale blue muslin dress that showed her slim figure to advantage. The pale white wool of the wrap brought out the colour in her cheeks and she had felt for a moment like the well-dressed lady about town that she had always wanted to be.

It was with mixed feelings that she dressed for supper that night. She looked her best and she knew it but she was suspicious. Polly had something up her sleeve. Lily could only hope that her friend's plans did not include any more eager young men.

But when she entered the large, pleasant dining

room, her fears were allayed by the sight of Jem seated at the head of the table, his grey hair highlighted in the flickering light from the candles, his eyes sparkling as he lifted his glass to greet her. At his side was another man, not quite as old as Jem but old enough to be circumspect.

'Come in, my dear Lily.' Jem spoke with unaccustomed warmth and though Lily was used to leering smiles from him she was surprised at the pleasant way he greeted her now.

'Come and sit here, between me and our guest.' Jem indicated the empty chair beside him and Polly winked at Lily. So this was her surprise, a man as old as Jem but much more handsome with startlingly bright blue eyes.

'Let's get the formalities over quickly.' Jem smiled. 'Matthew Starky, meet our little friend Lily.'

Her fingers were grasped in a warm handshake and smiling eyes looked into hers.

'And very beautiful you are too, Lily, if I may say so.' His voice was warm with a West Country accent and Lily found herself liking him on sight. Quite what he expected of her she did not dare to think but, for now, he was just a fellow guest at the dinner table of Jem Boucher and it would not hurt to be kind to him.

The meal was more sumptuous than usual. Rich soup was followed by a fish course and then the main course was carried in by a bevy of servants. Chicken carved into fine slices decorated the edges of the meat charger. At the centre of the plate, a huge joint of beef, still sizzling from the oven, took pride of place on the polished table. Lily did not have an enormous appetite but she enjoyed every mouthful of the dinner.

Matthew was a good companion; he kept the company regaled with anecdotes about his life as a tea merchant, a business that clearly kept him in great style judging by the rich cloth of his coat and the gold stud sparkling at his shirt front.

When the ladies took their leave of the gentlemen and retired to the drawing room, Lily looked at Polly, her eyebrows raised. 'Well,' she said, 'Matthew is a very nice man but what does he want of me?'

'Don't be so silly!' Polly said. 'He wants to set you up in a fine house at the edge of town and shower gifts on you.'

'So he is looking for a mistress.' Lily felt inordinately disappointed; she had found herself hoping for marriage to an old man who would one day die and leave her his wealth.

Polly sank into a chair and fanned her face with her hand. 'Yes, my love, he wants a mistress, what else?'

'Nothing else,' Lily said flatly. 'You know I don't like that sort of thing, Polly. I don't know why you put me in such a position. Now I'll have to refuse him and he'll be hurt.'

Polly leaned forward. 'Play your cards right, Lil,' she said earnestly. 'Matt has got no children, his wife is ancient, older than he is even. When she pops her clogs he'll probably want to make an honest woman of you.' A wicked smile curved her lips. 'If you can be a good enough actress to persuade him you love him, love all the things he does for you, he'll be at your mercy. Men are such fools!'

She spread her hands wide. 'In any case, what have you got to lose? You and me can still see each other every day but instead of having my cast-offs you can buy your own clothes. Matt is a generous man, he'll make you a good allowance.'

'And in return I must sleep with him whenever he wants me.'

'Lily! You exasperate me at times. Can't you see what a fine opportunity this is? Matt could have any young girl he wanted.'

'Exactly, so why does he want me when he doesn't even know me?'

'He's seen you about town with me, he thought you were a lady of quality. He couldn't believe his luck when he learned you were a working girl without the protection of a man.'

'So you offered me to him like a bargain package then?' Lily felt weary; how could she face a liaison with another man? And yet what was the alternative? She could stay with Polly, keep accepting her generosity, but how much nicer it would be if she had a place of her own and an allowance to spend as she pleased.

'I would want the house in my name,' she said flatly. 'I've been cheated out of one home by a long-lost relative. I don't want that to happen again.'

Polly sank back in her chair. 'I think Matthew would be glad to give you a house.' She smiled, dropping her cultured accent. 'You're not half a bad stick you know, in the looks department I mean.' Polly sat back and assessed Lily. 'Nice bosoms, small waist, good ankles.' She laughed. 'All the things a man wants in a mistress.'

'No,' Lily said, 'not all the things. A man wants a mistress to be passionate, to look forward to going to his bed. I can never be like that.'

'But you can pretend, you dumb cluck!' Polly said. 'Just moan a bit when he takes you to bed. Wriggle about a bit like you're enjoying it.' She grinned impishly. 'He thinks he's getting a virgin so if you're a bit slow, like, he'll put it all down to your modesty.'

'Oh, Polly!' Lily found herself smiling, appreciating the trouble her friend had gone to for her. And perhaps it would not be too bad, Matthew was old, he had a wife, surely Lily could put up with a bit of unpleasantness once in a while?

'But, doesn't he know I was married once?' she asked quickly as the sound of laughter drifted in from the hall and Polly smiled. 'I lied to him about that, made him keep off you, see? He's thrilled to think he can give his business friend an untried girl.'

That would not be difficult, Lily thought ruefully, she knew hardly anything of the passion that drove other women.

The two men entered the room, the aura of cigar smoke hanging around them like a mark of wealth. Matthew took a seat beside Lily and smiled at her. She tried to respond as she had done earlier, laughing at his jokes and looking up into his eyes but she felt stifled by the thought that sooner or later, she would have to go to this man's bed. Still, she had endured life with Tom for very little reward. If she gave herself to Matthew Starky, she would make sure that she benefited handsomely from the arrangement.

'You are very sweet, Lily, do you know that?'
Matthew took her hand and kissed the softness of
her palm. Lily lowered her eyes, the colour rising
to her cheeks. Matthew spoke again.

'I have admired you from afar for some time.
I'm so happy that my dear friends have arranged
this meeting.' Lily did not reply. 'Such a shy little
miss,' Matthew said. 'I promise you one thing,
Lily, I will be very good to you.'

Lily looked up at him. 'Will you offer me
security, Mr Starky?'

'I will offer you anything, my dear Lily.'

'Once I become your . . . your lady friend, my
prospects of making a respectable marriage would
be gone. So I would like a house of my very own,
somewhere I can sit in the window and watch the
world go by. I need to be safe, do you understand
that?'

'I do understand, completely. I have many
houses, you can take your pick, Lily. Once you
have chosen I will have my lawyer chap draw up
the proper papers.'

He slipped his arm around her waist. 'Don't be
shy, I will not rush you. Indeed, I will woo you like
a young man with his first love. I will dress you in
silks and shower you in gems. I will be so good to
you that you will think every day is your birthday.'

She sighed as she leaned against him; at least
now she had a protector, a man who would be
generous with his gifts who would not ill treat her.
Lily smiled at Polly, her friend had served her well,
she had found Lily a good man. Matthew Starky
was a real gentleman and quite handsome in spite
of his age. If the arrangement turned out as Lily

hoped she need never worry about money again. Which was just as well because it looked as if the money she had given Alice Sparks to invest was lost for ever. For the first time since she had returned to Swansea, Lily felt secure and cared for and it was a feeling she very much enjoyed.

CHAPTER EIGHTEEN

Binnie Dundee had arrived at the coast of America early in the morning. It was good to stand on the deck of the ship and watch the land he had come to love draw nearer. The sun was just beginning to bring warmth to earth, sky and sea and Binnie felt his heart lift in anticipation. Soon, very soon, he would be home where he belonged.

As soon as he disembarked from the ship he walked into town to buy some supplies for the journey. The store smelled of coffee beans and tobacco, sacks of meal jostled with bottles of home-made beer and Binnie breathed in the atmosphere, knowing that he was really home.

He bought a horse from the storekeeper. The animal was overpriced, an old mare with little fire in her belly but she would do to carry him home to West Troy.

He travelled by day, stopping only to eat and drink, and rested at night. But, now, his bones ached and the horse, head nodding towards the earth, was as weary as he was. Binnie took a deep breath; he would need to rest soon. He covered his eyes with his hand and realized that the sun was at its zenith. Later, it would turn into a ball of brilliant reds and oranges and sink towards the horizon. But the skyline of West Troy was in sight and his heart bounded with happiness.

'Nearly there.' He drew the sweating animal to a stop and patted the heaving flanks. 'We'll rest up a bit. Come on, old girl, let's get under the shade for a while, shall we?'

It was good to stand on familiar soil and Binnie drank in the warmth and the flavour of America. Soon he would see Hortense's lovely face, he would hear the laughter of his sons. For a moment, his sense of optimism faded. What if his wife refused to take him back?

The horse wickered softly and Binnie rubbed the animal's neck. 'Soon be home, old girl,' he said. 'I'll take you to a stream of fresh clean water and you can drink to your heart's content.'

He was impatient to resume his journey but when he remounted the horse he had to coax the tired animal onward. 'Good girl, come on, not much further now.' He sat back in the saddle and stared ahead of him wondering what his reception would be. He prayed that by now Hortense would have forgiven him or at least be prepared to try again to make their marriage work.

He closed his eyes, remembering the softness of her, the scent of her skin, the way her eyes lit up when they saw him. Abruptly, the picture came to him of their last encounter when Hortense had attacked him, raining blows on him, her face white with pain, her eyes darkly shadowed. How could he have hurt her so badly?

'Oh, God, be kind, let my wife forgive me,' he said out loud.

The sun was setting as he entered the streets of West Troy; the buildings bathed in a red-gold glow seemed to welcome him home. He felt his spirits lift as he passed the house where the McCabe family lived. All seemed quiet and he did not stop.

He stood for a long time outside his own house. The windows were open, the soft rise and fall of voices drifted to him from inside. He felt his heartbeat quicken as he knocked timidly on the open front door.

Justine's eyes widened as they rested on him. She darted back into the house calling out loudly, 'The master's come home! Miss Hortense, the master's come home.'

He stood on the porch, his heart pounding with fear. What if his Hortense turned him away? His life would be over, there would be nothing left to hope for. He could not settle in Swansea, America was in his blood, but without his wife and family even the land that had become dear to him held little appeal.

She came running out of the drawing room, her eyes alight, her cheeks red. When she saw him she stopped for a moment as though unable to believe he was really there. Then she was flinging herself into his arms, her tears wet against his neck. He held her close, breathless with the joy of holding her again, unable to believe that she wanted him, that she was clinging to him as tightly as he was clinging to her.

She was sobbing in his arms and he swallowed his own tears as he bent to kiss her trembling mouth. How he loved her, she turned his blood to water with love. He felt her soft arms around him and he sent up a prayer of thanks.

'Come in,' she said at last. 'Come in, my darling, you look worn out.' She drew him into the house and waved her hand at the gaping maid.

'Go get the bath ready, there's a good girl,' she said.

Binnie walked across the hall with a sense of unreality. He felt the coolness of the house, his home, close welcomingly around him. His wife was clinging to his arm. She was radiant with happiness and Binnie wanted to hold onto her, to make sure she did not vanish like an illusion conjured from his need of her.

'Hortense, my lovely, I couldn't stay away. I've dreamed of holding you in my arms, I've cried a million tears.' His voice broke.

'I didn't know if you'd want me back, I was so frightened you'd send me away again.' He kissed her, drinking in her sweetness. 'Hortense, I love you more than my own life, I can't live without you. Can you forgive me, Hortense?'

Hortense held his hand and drew him into the drawing room. She pushed the door shut and pressed herself into his arms again, her head against his chest.

'I've been such a fool.' Tears ran down her cheeks like dew. 'I only know that I want you whatever you've done.' There was a catch in her voice. 'Life's so short, too short, my darling, for us to be apart.'

He did not remember how long they stood holding each other but, at last, Hortense drew away.

He put his hands on her cheeks and looked into her eyes. 'I love you, Hortense. I will never hurt you again. I give you my solemn promise that my life will be spent making up to you for what I've done.'

Hortense made an effort to compose herself. 'Never mind all that now, you're home and you smell like a horse!' She smiled. 'I'll put out some clean clothes for you. And then you must eat something, you're so thin I can feel your bones.'

'How are the boys?' He looked into her face, catching something from her expression that made him apprehensive. 'They're all right, aren't they?'

'The boys are fine.'

'But something is wrong?' he said and she nodded.

'Have your bath and a good meal and then we'll talk.' She pushed him gently towards the door. 'The water will be nice and hot, freshen yourself up then you'll look more like my handsome Binnie, my dearest husband.'

There was no bitterness in her voice and Binnie sent up a silent prayer. She had forgiven him for deceiving her. He caught her to him again and bent his face into the warmth of her neck. She was warm and clean and the softness of her breasts against his chest made him long to taste her sweetness. He touched her softly and she looked up into his eyes.

'I love you, Binnie.' She slapped his hand away. 'Now, I won't tell you again, go and get cleaned up then we'll talk.' She followed him to the outhouse and watched as he stripped off his clothes. She laughed as she saw that he was aroused.

'You'll never change!' she said chidingly but there was a gleam of happiness in her eyes that made him feel ten feet tall.

He bathed swiftly, enjoying the feel of hot water against his dusty skin. The water was scented with roses and the moonlight shone in through the outhouse window. He sighed with happiness; he was home, Hortense wanted him, she was giving him a second chance. What more could any man ask of life?

Llinos stared into the coals burning low in the grate and her eyes blurred with tears. She was so lonely for Joe. She prayed every night for him to come home to her so that they could talk but he never came. Was he making love to the Indian right now? It did not bear thinking about.

Binnie's words ran through her mind like a haunting tune. He had not meant to add fuel to the flames by telling her about the Indian girl Joe had brought home with him. But, now, the other woman in Joe's life had become a reality. Every time she thought of Joe with the beautiful Sho Ka it brought Llinos to the edge of despair.

She had tried to think the matter through rationally; perhaps when Joe went to America to see his mother he had met Sho Ka again and realized that he loved her more than he loved his wife.

Llinos needed him to be honest and tell her face to face that their marriage was over. She wanted to hear about Sho Ka from his own lips. And yet if he walked into the room right now her courage would fail her, she was sure of it.

At last, she called the new maid to damp down the embers of the fire. She rubbed her eyes wearily; she would go to bed but she would not sleep. She would lie awake, tossing and turning in the darkness. Her life was in chaos; she was not being fair to Charlotte or to Lloyd or even to herself. She must stop agonizing over Joe and get on with her life.

When at last she crawled into bed, Llinos curled herself into the pillows for comfort. She felt tears burn in her eyes and cursed herself for a fool. She had learned a long time ago that self-pity was a waste of time.

In the morning, as Llinos got ready for work, she was determined to rebuild her life. She rolled up her sleeves and wrapped an apron around her waist. After she had checked that Lloyd was with Eira, busily engaged in his lessons, she would spend the day in the sheds, overseeing the painting of the new patterns. At least she could occupy her mind during the day. It was the long evenings and the lonely nights when she missed Joe most.

Lloyd seemed more boisterous than usual, running around the study with a toy horse and cart in his hand.

Eira was doing her best to get him ready for his lessons. 'Come on, Master Lloyd, what will your father think of us if you don't learn to read and write and make sums?'

Lloyd looked up mutinously as his mother came into the room. 'Where is my father, why isn't he here?' he demanded.

Llinos felt her stomach turn over. 'Daddy has to work, lovely, just like other fathers.'

'But he's away all the time,' Lloyd said. 'Doesn't he want to be with us any more?'

Llinos hugged him. 'Of course he does!' she said emphatically. 'He loves you very much.' She was not aware that she had put the emphasis on 'you' until she caught Eira's solemn look.

Lloyd wriggled away from her embrace. 'And he loves you too, Mummy. So why doesn't he come home to us?'

'I don't know.' Llinos felt suddenly weary. 'Be good now and learn your lessons, I've got to do some work.'

Lloyd dropped his toy on the floor and kicked it across the room. 'You're always working and Daddy's always away, I hate you!'

Llinos left the room, resisting the urge to slap her son. It was not Lloyd's fault that he was misbehaving. He was bewildered by his father's neglect and so was she; neither of them deserved such cavalier treatment.

Llinos made her way downstairs and through the back of the house to the yard. The bottle kilns rose high into the sky and the heat and smell from them was strangely comforting. This was her life, the pottery, it was what she knew and if Joe did not want to be part of it then she would just have to get on with it alone.

Pearl, against all opposition, had come back to work but she looked pale and drawn and the light of fun had gone from her. She no longer teased the younger women or flirted with the men; she was subdued by the cough that constantly racked her.

'Are you sure you're fit enough to be working?'

Llinos touched Pearl's forearm, daubed now with paint. 'You still look so pale and tired.'

'Don't you start, Llinos,' Pearl said with an attempt at jocularity. 'I've had enough nagging from Rosie and Watt as it is.'

She leaned closer to Llinos. 'I want to work, Llinos, love.' Pearl's eyes filled with tears. 'I'm an old fool I know but the thought of sitting in a corner to die drives me out of my mind. I'll just take my time, paint a few pots if that's all right by you.'

Llinos rested her hand on Pearl's shoulder, feeling the bones through the material of her dress. Pearl was wasting away and the thought was like a blow. Everything Llinos had known and loved was vanishing before her eyes.

'You live your life, Llinos, live it to the full,' Pearl said, 'because it has a way of drowning you in years and making you old.'

She looked down at the pot she was painting. 'If your man don't love you any more then find one as does. That's my advice and I mean it from a kind heart.'

'I know.' Llinos walked away, clasping her hands together to stop them from trembling. So even Pearl had noticed that Joe was no longer home. Pearl, who was older and wiser than Llinos, was telling her to find another man. Did everyone know that Llinos was a rejected wife then?

Llinos looked at the patterns developing on the china and felt a tug at her heart. Gone were the bold designs of the firebird, gone were the sweeping tail feathers and the eager head poised as though for flight. In their place were the cool colours of wild flowers, the softness of rose petals, the azure of the bluebells. It was all more fitting than the Indian designs and yet Llinos felt as though abandoning them was abandoning Joe.

Watt joined her as she watched one of the new artists brush in a variety of foliage for the backdrop of flowers.

'Pearl's come back to work then?' Llinos led him out of earshot of the new girl. 'She looks so dreadfully ill.'

He shrugged. 'I know but try telling her that. I suppose she feels anything is better than brooding over what no-one can change.'

Llinos looked up at him. He did not look a happy man. 'Is marriage suiting you, Watt?' she asked quietly.

He smiled. 'I am content, Llinos; don't you worry about me.'

'I do worry about you, though.' She took his hand and squeezed it. 'I want you to be happy, Watt, you're very dear to me.'

'I am happy,' he said quickly. 'Rosie is a good wife, she is full of fun. And she's a good cook into the bargain, what more could any man ask?'

'I'm glad to see you smiling again. I know you can't have got over Maura in just a few months but at least you are not alone.'

'And you are.' Watt walked with Llinos into the yard, which was littered with discarded shards of pottery. Watt kicked at a piece of clay and looked around him in disgust. 'I'll have to have a strong word with the younger boys, the yard never looked this untidy when I was cleaning it up.' He did not look at her. 'About Joe.'

'Don't!' Llinos said. 'You were always a good worker and a good friend but please, Watt, don't talk about Joe. I know you mean well and you are concerned about me but this is something I have to sort out for myself.'

'Maybe,' Watt sounded doubtful, 'but if you need to find him, I know where he is. In the event of an emergency you should be able to get hold of him.'

Her heart quickened. She stared up at Watt, torn between wanting to know and fear of what she would learn. At last, she took a deep breath. 'I suppose you'd better tell me then.'

'He's got a house, it's in the Vale of Neath, a lovely place with a stream and a waterfall and trees everywhere.' Watt looked down at her. 'He's there with a woman. She's called Sho Ka.' He smiled ruefully. 'The locals call them "foreigners" but then everyone is a foreigner to them except someone born in the vale.'

'How do you know all this?' Llinos asked, the pain making her voice almost unrecognizable.

'Rosie's folks from Neath came to visit. David is her cousin, a widower with two small daughters. He talked a great deal about Joe. He didn't have any idea Joe was your husband, of course. I'm sorry, Llinos.'

'I knew he had a woman,' Llinos said listlessly. 'I didn't know who it was until Binnie let the cat out of the bag. Before he went away he told me Joe had brought an Indian girl back here with him. I knew it had to be Sho Ka.'

'Look, Llinos,' Watt put his arms around Llinos's shoulders and walked her towards the house, 'take time off, think this thing through and don't jump to conclusions. Joe is not the sort of man to forget his marriage vows.'

'But then is any man the sort?' Llinos asked. 'Look at Binnie, he married Maura and soon learned it was a mistake. His marriage vows didn't stop him from running off to America, did they?'

'I know.' Watt looked downcast. 'I never thought it of Joe, though, he had such principles, he adored you. I just can't understand him going off to live with another woman.'

'Well, we're all fallible, I suppose.' She spoke calmly but she was so hurt she felt she would die. The image of Joe with the beautiful Sho Ka in his arms was almost too much to bear. But bear it she would. What else could she do?

The moon was making patterns on the timbers of the ceiling as Binnie climbed into bed beside his wife. Hortense reached towards him, pressing her lips into his neck and he felt the cool of her tears against his skin. His heart leapt with hope; she had missed him as much as he had missed her.

Tentatively, he took her into his arms; he wanted her with an urgency that was greater than any physical need. He had to make her his own again, to stamp himself upon her, to affirm that they were truly man and wife.

She had crept into the bed wearing her cotton nightgown but she slipped out of it, tossing it on the floor. Her breasts were pressing against him, full warm breasts that had suckled his children. How he loved her.

Her passion excited him and he lost himself in

the sweetness of her. Desire flamed within him now, blocking out thought. All he knew was that beneath him lay his wife, his Hortense, and together they were reaching new heights in happiness and joy.

In the morning, Binnie's sons greeted him with bright eager faces and warm arms.

'Dan,' Binnie said, his voice thick with emotion, 'have you helped your mom while I've been away?' Dan nodded. 'Sure, Dad, I brought in the kindling for the fire and, oh, lots of things.' He nestled close to his father. 'But, Daddy, I'm sure glad you're home.'

They ate breakfast together, a proper family once more, and Binnie could hardly contain the joy that poured through him like wine. And yet, there was a sadness about his wife that bothered him. She had refused to discuss it last night, not wanting to spoil their first moments together but now she would have to talk to him.

Later, Hortense sat with Binnie, her face white, her hands shaking. 'It's hard to know where to begin, honey.' She swallowed hard and, little by little, the story of the tragedy unfolded.

'There was such a fight. Melia fell, the balcony was rotten, Jo didn't mean to kill her.' Hortense's face crumpled and Binnie took her in his arms, smoothing back her hair.

'It's all right, honey,' he said soothingly. 'It's not Jo's fault.' It was all down to John Pendennis. That man ruined everything he touched.

'It was awful, hon. Melia's funeral was a nightmare.' Hortense gulped back her tears. 'Jo lost her baby and Mamma and Daddy shut themselves away and I was alone with no-one to hold me. I longed for you then, Binnie. I saw what a fool I'd been to drive you away. Thank God you've come home.'

He kissed her hair, muttering soothing words but in his heart anger burned against John Pendennis. John had managed to wreck the happiness of the entire McCabe family single-handedly. 'Damn John to hell!' he said bitterly.

'Hortense, my lovely girl,' he cupped her face in his hands, love turning his blood to water, 'I'm here now and I'll never leave you again.'

'I'll tell you something, Binnie Dundee,' Hortense said, 'there's no chance of you leaving because I'll never let you out of my sight again.'

He kissed his wife's soft lips, knowing that he was the luckiest man on God's earth. He was home again, home with his family. Hortense had forgiven him and from now on, he would make her the happiest woman on earth or he would die in the attempt.

CHAPTER NINETEEN

Rosie looked up into Watt's face trying to read his expression. Tentative questions hovered on her lips but when she tried to speak her courage deserted her. Watt was acting as though their wedding had never taken place and Rosie was reluctant to ask him why. Perhaps she already knew the answer but it hurt to think even for a moment that Watt might not really love her.

In the company of Pearl and the boys, he was his usual smiling self. He drove Pearl and Dom to the pottery every day as usual but his evenings were spent out of the house on some pretext or other.

At first Rosie had comforted herself with the thought that once her mother was well again everything would be all right. The wedding night had been postponed out of necessity; what should have been a joyful event had turned into a nightmare. But even though Pearl was on the mend now Watt still acted like a stranger. If just once he would take Rosie in his arms and tell her he loved her she would be content. But he never did.

When they were alone in the bedroom, he avoided her eyes. They made love in the dark and, untried though she was, inexperienced in the ways of men, Rosie recognized that their swift coupling was born out of physical need rather than love.

Rosie put the pot of rabbit soup rich with vegetables on the table and rubbed her hands against her apron. She must talk to Watt, make him tell her what was wrong. Was he disappointed in her? Did he regret the marriage? She opened her mouth to speak but just then the door burst open and her brothers came rushing into the kitchen, boots clattering on the red flags she had polished so industriously just this morning.

'Sit down you lot and be quiet!' Rosie said. 'I'll spill the soup if you don't keep still. And leave the bread alone a minute, will you?' She threw an exasperated look at Watt. 'My brothers don't know how to behave at table, they're little pigs!'

He nodded but it was clear he was not paying much attention. Rosie felt a dart of unease, was her family getting too much for him? The boys were boisterous, wild sometimes, but they were just behaving like normal youngsters.

She poured the soup and then cut some thick slices of bread and offered them round to the boys. 'All right then, you can start now.' She sat at the table and picked up her spoon. Watt was half hidden behind his paper, she could not see his expression clearly but he seemed engrossed in what he was reading.

The soup was hot and nourishing, Rosie congratulated herself on her cooking and it gave her pleasure to see Watt eating heartily. Her spirits lifted; he had promised to take her to the fair in Neath tonight. She would see a bit of life, hear the music of the carousel and mingle with the crowds of other young people enjoying themselves. Then when she and Watt were nicely relaxed she would talk to him about his strange moods.

'You've started without me! I hope there's some food left, you lot are such gluttons!' Pearl came into the room smelling of soap and water. Freshly washed, Pearl should have looked well, her colour should have been good, but her skin was parchment thin, sagging into lines around her mouth and eyes. She was far from well and yet she insisted on going to the pottery each day.

'Are you all right, Mam?' Rosie asked. 'You look awful tired.'

'Course I'm all right, love.' Pearl sank into a chair. 'I'll have a bit of supper and then get off to bed. You don't mind seeing to the boys, do you, Rosie? Dom's trews have to be mended for work tomorrow.' She smiled at her son. 'You're settling in well, aren't you, boy *bach*? We'll make a potter out of you yet.'

A feeling of resentment brought colour to Rosie's cheeks. She was being treated like a paid help, head cook and bottle washer. She was young; she needed to have some fun in life.

'I was going out with Watt, to the fair, Mam.' She ladled stew into her mother's bowl. 'Can't Dom mend his own trews?'

'I'm sorry, love, I'd do it but I just feel so damn tired all the time.' Pearl dipped her spoon into the stew but she was not eating very much. Rosie looked at Watt pushing some bread into his bowl, his head bent; he seemed far away. As her husband, he should have come to her rescue, insisting that she have a night off. Rosie sighed in exasperation.

'Rosie, can I have some more bread, please?' Fred, the youngest of the boys was looking at the empty plate with disgust. He was a big lad for his age, almost nine years old. He attended the new school on the outskirts of Swansea and was turning out to be a good little scholar. Rosie loved him dearly but right now she felt like slapping him.

'What did your last servant die of?' she demanded. 'Hard work, was it?'

There was a sudden silence and Rosie was aware of Watt staring at her, his eyebrows raised.

'Are you all right, Rosie?' he asked, suddenly giving her his full attention. 'Come to think of it, you're looking a bit pale. Perhaps we should give the fair a miss until another time.'

She shook her head. 'I'm just fine apart from being worked to death round here,' she said. 'Being a maid up at the Mainwaring house was easy compared to this!'

How could she tell Watt she felt sick and miserable, bitterly disappointed by his attitude? He was her husband, he should be looking out for her. Didn't he realize she had been looking forward to the fair all day?

'I'm sorry,' she said, her resentment fading. 'I'm just tired, I suppose.'

Pearl pushed away her bowl. 'No, love, I didn't think. I've been putting on you too much. I'm sorry, love.' She peered into Rosie's face. 'You're not expecting are you?'

314

Rosie shook her head. 'No, Mam, I'm not expecting.' She thought of the way Watt withdrew himself from her when they made love. He was like the man in the Bible who spilled his seed onto the ground. In any case, how could she bring a baby up in the overcrowded house in Greenhill?

She sighed. 'But I do feel a bit poorly, Mam, I think I'll go to lie down for a while.'

She just had to get out of the room before the tears flowed but Fred's voice followed her. 'I'm sorry, Rosie, I'm a lazy slug. I should be getting my own bread like I did when you was working.'

Rosie made for the stairs and Pearl called after her, 'The boys will help you a bit more and so will I, Rosie. I'm real thoughtless putting so much on your shoulders and you just wed. Look, I'll ask for some time off and you can have a lovely rest, how's that?'

Rosie hurried upstairs without replying. She felt a sense of despair creeping over her. A rest was not what she wanted; she wanted a home of her own, to have her husband to herself and the chance to cradle her own child in her arms. She loved her mother and the boys but she loved Watt more and already the family had come between them. Why else was Watt acting as though she was nothing more to him than a paid servant?

In her room, she lit several candles, not wanting to be alone in the darkness. She lay across the bed, her eyes closed against the shimmering light. She had expected so much from her marriage but somehow everything was going wrong. Unless they were in bed and he needed relief, Watt was indifferent to her and as for Mam, well, she simply treated Rosie like a servant and a convenient nursemaid for the boys.

The tears flowed down her cheeks and she held the pillow against her for comfort. She knew she was feeling sorry for herself but she had the right. She would be old and tired soon enough, now she just wanted to live a bit. Was that too much to ask?

She heard footsteps on the stairs and then Watt was in the room, bending over her, touching her cheek with his fingers.

'Are you sick, Rosie?' He sat on the edge of the bed looking at her anxiously. She wanted him to take her in his arms, to hold her and kiss her and tell her she was the most beautiful girl in the world and that he loved her.

'I know we all seem to be taking advantage of you,' he said. 'But you must be patient, Pearl is sick, really sick, she shouldn't even be working. I'm worried about her.'

Rosie sat up. 'That's just it, you worry about everyone except me!' She brushed her eyes with the back of her hand. 'I'm getting old before my time, do you realize that?' Once she had begun she could not stop.

'I'm in by the fire most nights sewing the boys' shirts and mending ripped trews while you go out and Mam either goes over to Willie's house or takes to her bed.'

She swallowed hard. 'I didn't get married to live by myself, Watt. I want a proper marriage. You take your pleasure not thinking of mine and then your back is turned on me without even a kiss goodnight. What sort of marriage is that?'

He seemed dazed. 'I'm sorry, Rosie. Give it

time, be patient.' His face was turned from her. 'I don't suppose I'm really over Maura yet and when Pearl fell sick, well, it brought the nightmare of Maura's death flooding back. I'm sorry, Rosie.'

'Oh yes, everyone's sorry!' She shook her head. 'But I'm more sorry than any of you.' She turned her face away from him, was he too concerned about himself to realize how unhappy his words had made her?

'Well, what do you want to do then?' he said. 'Do you want to go out as we planned or shall I stay in with you this evening?' He touched her hand briefly. 'I know this isn't an ideal arrangement, us living with Pearl and you taking care of things in the house but that's why we decided to get married, wasn't it?'

She felt a pain as though he had stabbed her with a knife. 'Was it?' she said quietly. 'So our marriage was an act of charity thought up by you to help Mam out. Well what about me? I want to be loved and cared for. Don't you love me even a little bit, Watt?'

'Of course I love you, Rosie,' he said but his words lacked conviction. 'You needed me, all of you. I thought I was doing the right thing.'

'The right thing! Is that all our marriage means to you?' Fresh tears welled in her eyes. Watt tried to take her in his arms but she pushed him away.

'Leave me be!' she gasped. 'I hate you, Watt Bevan! How dare you marry me out of pity?'

'But I didn't marry you out of pity!' She waited, hoping he would say he married her because he loved her. He remained silent. Suddenly calm,

317

Rosie sat up and looked him full in the face. 'If you didn't marry me out of pity then why did you marry me?' She glared at him through her tears. 'Did you want everyone to think what a good man you were taking on Rosie and her entire family? You saw yourself as our saviour, is that it?'

'Don't be melodramatic, Rosie!' He was growing angry. 'I'm faithful to you, aren't I? When I go out, it's only to the public bar with the other men. I work hard and I bring home good wages for you, isn't that enough?'

'No, it's not enough,' Rosie said. 'In any case how do I know you're faithful to me? You are out every night, you could be sleeping with all the harlots in the streets of Swansea for all I know.' She paused. 'It's not enough for me, Watt.'

Watt moved away from her. 'Well, it will have to do,' he said. 'I can't promise undying love, Rosie, I'm sorry.'

'Go away,' Rosie said. 'Just leave me alone. I need to think things out.'

Watt hesitated in the doorway. 'You're acting like a spoilt child, Rosie, there are more important things at stake here than just your hurt pride.'

'Go away,' she said. 'Just go away.' She turned her face to the wall.

'To hell with you then!' he said. She heard the door slam and knew that, yet again, Watt was going out to drown his sorrows and the thought was like a knife turning in her heart.

Rosie drew her legs under her and sat against the pillows, staring at the wall. The shadows thrown from the flickering light of the candles danced like grotesque monsters but they were nothing compared to the monsters in her head. She had to face the truth: her husband did not love her, had never loved her. He had married her out of pity for the family. What sort of foundation was that on which to build a relationship?

There was the sound of slow footsteps on the stairs. Pearl paused on the landing coughing as though she would never stop. Rosie closed her eyes; she did not want to see anyone, she wanted to be alone with her misery.

'Can I come in, love?' Pearl peered round the door. 'Oh, Rosie love, don't cry, everyone argues.' Pearl took Rosie in her arms and they clung together. Rosie could feel the rattle in her mother's thin chest and for a moment guilt flooded through her.

'What is it, love?' Pearl asked anxiously. 'Why were you rowing with Watt?'

Rosie shook her head. How could she explain to her mother that Watt had married her simply to take care of the family? Pearl would feel she was to blame and her mother had enough to contend with as it was.

'Well don't worry about it, whatever it is, rows happen to everyone. You know your dad and me used to shout at each other all the time, it didn't mean we loved each other any the less. Watt is a good man and he loves you, *cariad*.'

'No!' Rosie released herself from her mother's arms. 'He doesn't love me. He never calls me *cariad*, he scarcely calls me by name, let alone call me his sweetheart.'

'Ah but men are not so soft as us. And, remember, they say things in anger that they don't mean,

319

we all do.' She brushed Rosie's hair away from her face. 'Give it a chance, love.' She smiled. 'I don't think men and women will ever understand each other so we just have to make the best of things.'

'I know, Mam.' Rosie was confused. She did not want to think of Watt any more; she would prefer to put him out of her mind but the look on his face haunted her. He would never love her as he had loved Maura Dundee. Rosie was second best and she did not think she could live her life like that.

'You rest now, love,' Pearl said. 'I can sew our Dom's trews. Watt will calm down, everything will be just fine in the morning, you'll see.'

'I think I will stay up here, Mam,' Rosie said. 'I could do with an early night.'

'You're not sick, are you, love?' Pearl asked anxiously. Rosie shook her head.

'No, Mam, I've got a bit of a headache, that's all.'

'Oh, that's all right then.' Pearl sounded relieved. She crept towards the door and paused there; in the half-light she looked gaunt, ghost-like. Rosie felt a qualm of fear.

'Mam, you are better, aren't you?' she asked. Pearl smiled but her teeth seemed overlarge for her face.

'Of course I am, why else would I be working again? Now go to sleep, you've got enough to think of without worrying about me.'

The door closed and Rosie undressed quickly and quenched the flames of the candles, wanting to lose herself in the soft darkness. Her mother was all right, as she said, she would not be going back to work if she was still ill. And Rosie could not deal with anyone else's pain just now, she had enough of her own.

Rosie was on the edge of sleep when Watt crept into the bedroom. She kept her eyes closed, not wanting to talk to him. She was tired and disheartened. He did not love her; the thought was like a chant running through her mind.

He climbed into bed beside her and put his arm around her waist, drawing her back against him. His breath smelled of beer as he put his face close to hers; his hand crept round to rest on her breast.

'You're beautiful, Rosie,' he said. She could tell he was aroused but she was unmoved. If it took a bellyful of ale to make him want her then she did not want him.

She sat up, anger running through her like wine. 'How dare you come to me like this?' She was whispering; the last thing she wanted to do was wake Mam and the boys. 'You tell me you don't love me, that I have to take the crumbs you offer and then you want to make love to me.' Her voice rose in spite of herself.

'Don't start!' Watt said.

'Don't start?' she repeated. 'Am I supposed to fall into your arms like a whore then?'

'At least a whore would know how to please a man!' Watt said. Rosie felt as though she were shrinking into herself.

'So I am a disappointment to you in every way then, is that it? Well don't worry, you'll be free of me soon.'

'Don't talk rubbish!' Watt turned over and pulled the bedclothes up to his chin. 'Go to sleep, there's a good girl.'

She wanted to kill him right then. She sat staring into the darkness, pain searing her. She could not even cry. She became aware that Watt was breathing deeply and she knew he was asleep. How dare he sleep when her world was in ruins?

She lay awake for a long time, her head spinning with thoughts, but by the morning she had made up her mind. She would find another job where she could live in. At least when she worked as a maid she had some free time as well as the company of girls her own age. Now she was just a drudge. She would not be leaving her mother in the lurch, between them Mam and Watt brought in enough wages to pay for someone else to wait on them.

Rosie had had a restless night, tossing and turning, trying to come to terms with the humiliating knowledge that Watt did not love her. She got out of bed in the grey light of early morning and lit the fires as usual and made the breakfast, acting as though nothing was wrong.

Watt kissed her cheek before leaving for work and Pearl stood with him in the doorway.

'Come on, Dom lad,' she said, 'don't make us all late.' She glanced at Rosie but said no more about taking time off. 'You'll see our Fred off to school, won't you, Rosie?' she said.

'Don't I always?' Rosie said but the door closing drowned out her words. She sent her brother on his way with a packed sandwich for his dinner and then cleared the dishes away. She stood for a moment in the warmth of the kitchen and looked around her. It would be hard to leave her home and even harder to say goodbye to Watt and their marriage. But then it was not a marriage at all, it was a sham.

She swallowed her tears and ran up the stairs. It took her only a few minutes to get dressed for outdoors. She threw some clothes into a bag and took all the money from the housekeeping jar. Out in the street, she looked back at the house where she had hoped for so much happiness and then, after a moment, she began to walk briskly towards the town.

Alice Sparks was beginning to despair of ever finding a suitable lady's maid. She had put a notice in the local paper but so far without any response. She was stretched out on her chair, relaxing after breakfast, when Cook knocked on the door.

'Excuse me, Mrs Sparks, but there's a girl here looking for a position.' Alice roused herself and sat up in her chair. 'What does she look like? Is she respectable?'

'Oh yes, Mrs Sparks,' Cook said quickly. 'It's Rosie, she's been working up at Pottery House for Mrs Mainwaring.' Cook would say anything, she was tired of fetching and carrying for Alice.

'All right bring her in, let's have a look at her.' Alice was tired; the heat of the fire had made her sleepy. The last thing she wanted to do was conduct an interview but she needed someone to tend to her personal needs and the sooner the better.

The girl was neatly dressed, her hair combed and pinned back from her face. She looked clean and neat and very capable.

'Come in.' Alice gestured for the girl to come

closer. She studied her from head to foot and was pleased with the girl's demeanour.

'I see you wear a wedding ring, widowed are you?' Alice was not really interested but it was better that the maid had no ties. The girl nodded briefly.

'I'm looking to live in. I'm used to housework and I'm strong and healthy.' She looked it. Her skin was radiant, her eyes clear. There were no wrinkles on the smooth face but then the girl had suffered no hardship, that much was clear.

'How did you know I was looking for a maid?' Alice asked. 'Did you read it in the newspaper?'

'Yes, miss.'

'Madam, I prefer you to call me madam. And you worked for Llinos Mainwaring I understand?' Alice said. 'Would she give you a reference?'

'I'm sure she would.' The girl replied. 'I left to get married, she was sorry to lose me.'

Alice wondered what she could prise out of the girl by way of information about Llinos Mainwaring. 'Very well, I'll give you a month's trial.' She waved her hand, dismissing the girl. 'Cook will show you to your room.'

A thought struck her. 'Oh, I'll need you to help me dress for an outing this afternoon and I shall require you to come with me.'

The girl nodded. 'Yes, madam.' She was quick to learn, Alice gave her that much. Rosie could well prove to be an asset, that was if Alice could keep her temper in check. She had lost her last maid and Cook had threatened to walk out more than once and was only calmed down with the promise of an extra bonus in her wages.

'Off you go then.' When the door closed behind the girl, Alice got to her feet and stared at her reflection in the mirror. She was looking well, a little on the plump side but that was only to be expected. She tweaked a curl into place, it was important that she looked her best as she was going to see Eynon.

The visit was not before time; the bills were mounting and the rest of the mortgage had to be paid by the end of the month. Still, she had a feeling that when he saw her he would take her word for it that the twins were his. He was vain like any other man and Alice knew exactly how to play on that vanity.

The afternoon was sunny, the road dappled with light. Alice sat in the cab feeling confident and happy. Rosie was at her side, demure in her coat and bonnet, her work-roughened hands folded in her lap. The girl had a pleasing way with her and Alice congratulated herself that at last she had found a good servant.

'Once we are in the big house where Mr Morton-Edwards lives you must go to the kitchen with the other servants,' Alice said quietly. 'My visit is very private and I trust you will speak of it to no-one.'

'You can depend on me, madam,' Rosie said earnestly. Alice found herself warming to the girl; she was going to be good company as well as discreet, exactly the sort of maid that Alice needed.

Eynon was standing before the fire in the large, comfortable drawing room. He looked more handsome than ever, his pale hair shining in the sunlight.

'Good lord!' he said when he saw her. 'You have grown large! Come along, you'd better sit down.' He helped her to a chair, placing a cushion behind her back. 'Are you keeping well, Alice?'

'I am very well,' she said running her hands over her stomach. 'I have your sons in here, Eynon, I'm having twins.'

'Good Lord!' he said again. He sat down opposite her and watched her carefully. 'How can you be sure I am the father?' he asked, his expression earnest.

Alice was encouraged by his manner; now he could see she was really pregnant he was at least prepared to listen to her. She leaned forward.

'I did not sleep with Edward until I was almost two months late,' she said. 'Eynon, I'm telling you, hand on heart, these twins are yours. I swear it on my own life.' She smiled at him. 'Aren't you proud? You could be the father of two fine sons in a few months' time.'

'Perhaps,' Eynon said. 'But I don't know what to think and that's the truth.'

'Look, Eynon,' she said. 'You can bring your friend Father Martin here and I'll swear it on the Bible in his presence if you like.'

'All right, suppose I accept the truth of what you say, what do you expect me to do about it?' Eynon rose and stood in front of the fire, his hand resting on the mantelpiece. 'Just tell me what it is you want.'

'I want money to buy the house I'm living in,' Alice said. 'If you will put a little extra funds my way I will see you are not bothered again.' She glanced up at him from under her lashes. 'Unless you wish to be.'

326

He thought about it in silence and Alice watched his expression with a warm feeling that he was softening towards her.

'At least give me the benefit of the doubt, Eynon,' she said gently. 'If the twins are yours you surely want them to have the security of a roof over their heads, don't you?'

He sighed in resignation. 'All right, Alice, I suppose I owe you that much. First thing in the morning I'll go to the bank and see to it.'

'Thank you, Eynon.' Alice felt a surge of triumph. 'I will take good care of the twins, you can be sure of that, and you can see them any time you like.'

'What about Edward?'

'Oh, him!' Alice dismissed her husband with a wave of her hand. 'Edward thinks I'm spending my time doing charitable works. But then he's a fool.' She laughed. 'And he has not even the grace to be good in bed!'

Eynon smiled. 'You are incorrigible, Alice, and you soon to be a mother.' He rang the bell for the servants. 'Now, you'll take some tea with me?'

'I'd be delighted.' Alice relaxed now that she had won Eynon over. 'Then I will have to go back home to face that miserable husband of mine. Why couldn't I have married someone like you, Eynon?'

'Because someone like me would have far too much sense to take you on!' he replied crisply.

It was early evening when Alice returned home and it was to find Edward there before her. She handed her hat and coat to Rosie and the girl hurried upstairs to put them away. Alice thanked her lucky stars that she had found someone who did not need to be told every little thing.

'You're early, Edward,' she said. 'Didn't you have much work today?' She sank into a chair and watched as her husband closed the door and leaned against it.

'Alice,' he said, his voice full of doom, 'you have to help me.'

'Why, dearest, what's wrong?' Alice could afford to be magnanimous now that she had the promise of money from Eynon.

'I'm in trouble with the bank,' he said. 'Deep trouble.'

Alice sighed, he really was a pathetic creature. 'Do sit down, Edward. You worry too much. This very day my father has promised to pay off the mortgage for us. That's where I've been now, Edward, sorting out our problems.'

He sank down in a chair, his hand over his eyes. 'You don't understand, the auditors have been called in and I've been taking money from customers' accounts to fund your fancy lifestyle. I'm ruined Alice, ruined now, do you understand?'

For a moment she felt her stomach lurch with fright. 'How did you let that happen, Edward?' she said sharply.

She sank into a chair and thought carefully about the situation. Whatever happened to Edward, her own future would be secure, provided Eynon kept his word. She relaxed.

'Don't worry, Daddy won't let anything dreadful happen,' she said reassuringly. She sighed, wishing her husband would vanish into thin air. He was becoming a liability. In any case, she had always known she had married beneath her and this last little episode proved it.

'You will get us out of this won't you, Alice?' He was like a child asking for reassurance. 'Otherwise I could well end up in prison.'

'Of course I'll get us out of it,' she said but her thoughts were already drifting. She was imagining a life without Edward and the prospect was such a pleasant one that she settled back in her chair and closed her eyes, effectively shutting Edward out of her sight. Yes, a husband in prison would arouse more sympathy than censure amongst the towns-people. The gossips would say how sad that poor Mrs Sparks married a man who betrayed the trust of his customers. All in all, matters were turning out very well, very well indeed.

CHAPTER TWENTY

Llinos sat in the carriage, staring out at the lovely Vale of Neath. The hills were verdant, the trees flourished everywhere along the river banks and the sun dappled the grass with gold. But her thoughts were not in tune with the brightness of the day. She felt a lump in her throat; Joe had chosen a beautiful place to bring his mistress.

She leaned back, feeling the cold of the leather seat through her thin coat. She shivered, wondering if she should turn back, go home; live for a little while longer in her dream world where one day Joe would come back to her and everything would be wonderful again.

She wished for a moment that she had asked Charlotte to go with her but her sister-in-law was getting old. In any case this was something she must face on her own. Llinos swayed as the driver turned the horses along a small track that led uphill towards the top of the valley. There, on the hill, stood the house where Joe lived with his mistress. It was an ugly house, squat and rambling, but it commanded a fine view of the valley and the river and the wild rolling country-side beyond.

'Whoa there, lovely girls.' Kenneth coaxed the horses to stop just short of the house as Llinos had instructed. She was scarcely aware of him helping her down onto the dusty path, her gaze was focused on the doorway which stood open, the sunlight spilling inside.

'Wait here, I won't be very long.' She was surprised how normal her voice sounded. The driver touched his hat and mumbled into his beard.

'I'll take the girls to the soft ground over there, let them rest their feet for a bit.' Another time, Llinos would have been amused at the way Kenneth treated the animals like human beings but now she was too tense to think of anything but what might lie ahead of her.

Her shoulders were erect, her head high as she walked towards the house but for a moment she hesitated, summoning all her courage, then she knocked on the old oak of the door and stood back, resisting the urge to run away.

A rosy-cheeked maid, her plump form wrapped in a spotless apron, came hurrying from the back of the house. She looked at Llinos in surprise.

'Yes, miss?' She brushed flour from her hands and stood waiting for Llinos to speak.

'Mr Mainwaring, is he at home?' Her voice was unbelievably pompous, her tone clipped, angry and the girl stepped back a pace. Perhaps she was aware that her master had a wife as well as a mistress.

'No, miss, he's not here just now, sorry.' She

looked behind her fearfully. 'The lady of the house is here if you want to talk to her.'

'Yes, thank you,' Llinos said. 'I want to talk to her.'

Sho Ka was sitting in the garden at the rear of the house. She looked up as Llinos emerged from the back door and her eyes widened. The Indian girl was just as beautiful as she had been when Llinos first met her in America, long before she and Joe were married.

'Yes, Sho Ka, it's me, Joe's wife.' Llinos made an effort to keep her voice steady. 'You look well.'

Sho Ka stood up; she was taller than Llinos by several inches and held herself like a queen. She looked more than well; she was beautiful in a sprigged muslin gown. The pale ivory shawl over her shoulders emphasized the golden colour of her skin and the dark sheen of her hair. Llinos felt her stomach contract. How could she blame Joe for wanting someone as lovely as Sho Ka?

'Where is he?'

'Joe?'

'Of course.' Llinos swallowed her anger. 'Who else would I be asking for?'

'He's ridden over to one of the farms, he's fetching us some butter and eggs.' Sho Ka's voice faded as Llinos winced. The 'us' had hurt, it confirmed that the two of them were a couple, that Joe and Sho Ka were lovers.

'I'll wait.' Llinos looked round for somewhere to sit and finally chose a wooden bench standing in the shade of a huge oak. Sho Ka looked at her uneasily, her eyebrows raised in an unspoken question. Llinos remained silent. What she had to say she would say to her husband, not to the woman who was his concubine.

The little Welsh maid came to the back door. 'Shall I fetch some tea, miss?' she said in Welsh and Llinos was about to reply when she saw Sho Ka nodding.

'Please do, Bronwen, and bring some of your *Teison Lap* cake as well.'

It was a double shock to Llinos to hear Sho Ka speak in the Welsh tongue and worse, to be speaking as mistress of the house.

'I had forgotten that the Mandans had some Welsh,' she said almost absently. She twisted her hands in her lap, staring at her fingers through a haze of tears. Every moment she sat with Sho Ka reinforced her belief that the Indian girl had usurped her position as Joe's wife.

'It comes in useful now I am in Wales,' Sho Ka said. 'Look, Llinos, things are not always what they seem.'

Llinos looked up challengingly. 'So you are not sleeping with my husband then, is that what you mean?'

The colour swept into Sho Ka's face and the last vestige of hope faded from Llinos's heart.

'I'm sorry,' Sho Ka said. She paced around the small patch of lawn, walking silently, as Joe did. The shawl slipped from her shoulders and Llinos felt her stomach twist into knots.

'Sho Ka, you're pregnant!' Llinos felt sick. For a moment she was blinded with jealousy. She wanted to hit the Indian girl, to hurt her as she had been hurt.

'You have ruined my life!' Llinos said. 'You have

333

stolen my husband from me. How can you face yourself in the mirror?' She turned away blind with anger and walked through the kitchen past the startled maid.

Kenneth was waiting patiently, his hand smoothing the mane of the nearest horse. He looked up when he heard her footsteps. 'All ready to go, Mrs Mainwaring?' he asked.

'Yes please, Kenneth, take me home.' He helped her into the coach and she sat back against the hard leather, her hands covering her face. She felt diminished, defeated. She longed to scream out her anger, to confront Joe with a torrent of abuse. She closed her eyes, wondering if she would ever erase from her mind the sight of Sho Ka, beautiful with child.

By the time she reached home, Llinos felt as though all her senses had been blunted by pain. She went directly to her room and fell onto the bed, fully dressed. 'Joe,' she whispered into the pillows, 'I hate you for what you have done to me.' But she did not hate him, she loved him and if he came to her now and asked her forgiveness she would take him back without hesitation. But she was fooling herself, he was not coming back. She had lost Joe for ever.

'So Binnie, you're back.' Dan McCabe looked heavy-eyed, his hair was whiter than Binnie remembered and he seemed to have lost weight. 'I'm glad to have another man about the place and I don't deny it.' He sank down into the chair on the porch and waved to Binnie to join him.

'I've lost one of my girls,' he said, 'and nothing

334

in the world is going to bring her back but I still have my grandsons and that's thanks to you, Binnie my boy.'

'I'm sorry for all that's happened,' Binnie said. 'I feel I've added to your worries.'

Dan waved his hand. 'You did wrong not telling us all the truth right up front, but I can understand that. You had a wife, a wrong 'un for you as it turned out, and then you found my Hortense.' He half smiled. 'I think I'd have shut my mouth too, if I was in your place.'

'I do love her, Dan,' Binnie said. 'I'd lay down my life for her if I had to.'

'I know that, son.' Dan touched his arm. 'You're not cut from the same cloth as that bastard Pendennis!' He looked up, his brow furrowed. 'You know he ran off with a bag full of my money, don't you?' He slapped his hand on the arm of his chair. 'The low-down skunk caused a whirlwind of trouble in my family and then robbed me into the bargain. I hope he rots in hell!'

'Where's he gone?' Binnie asked.

'As far away from me as he could run,' Dan said. 'He knows I'd have a noose waiting over a tall tree for him if I ever came across him again.'

He fell silent as Josephine came out of the house. She was pale and subdued. The brightness, the laughter in her eyes that had been her charm had gone.

'Hello, Binnie.' She sank limply into the seat beside him. 'Glad you've come home.' A little warmth came into her face. 'At least our Hortense is happy now.'

'Jo,' he said, 'I'm so sorry.' He rubbed his hand

through his hair. 'I feel it's my fault somehow, I brought John here.'

'I knew he was no good from the moment I married him,' Jo said softly. 'I fooled myself into thinking everything would be all right when there was a baby on the way. Now,' she spread her thin hands wide, 'now I have nothing.'

'Don't say that, honey,' Dan said. 'You'll meet someone else, you're young yet.'

'Sure I will, Daddy,' she said. 'Don't you go worrying about me, now.' She gave Binnie a swift look and he knew that Josephine was too damaged to ever trust a man again.

Mrs McCabe bustled out onto the porch with a maid behind her carrying a tray of cool drinks. 'Welcome home, Binnie.' She looked at him with narrowed eyes. 'I'm a plain-speaking woman and I don't agree with what you did to my girl. You lied and you cheated and you made her unhappy. But I knowed you loved her from the first.' She nodded, her chins trembling. 'I'm prepared to forgive and forget but don't you be doing anything else sneaky or I'll take a gun to you myself, do you hear?'

'I hear,' Binnie said.

'Now, we'll say no more about it. Welcome back into the family, Binnie Dundee, you are the man of the house after my Dan and I know you'll take the responsibility should you be called upon.'

As she sipped her drink, she looked grey and beaten and Binnie felt his heart contract with pity. What if his sons grew to manhood only to give pain to their mother? It did not bear thinking about.

He stayed a little while longer and then, with a sense of relief, took his leave of the McCabe family. They were good people, honest souls who did not deserve the treatment that both he and John had handed out to them.

As he rode back along the street towards his own home, Binnie thanked God in his heaven for allowing him a second chance. He would worship Hortense; he would never look at another woman so long as he lived.

As he neared his house, the light was fading and the gleam of lamplight in the windows welcomed him home. He found Hortense in the parlour and when she saw him her eyes lit with happiness.

'Well, what did Mamma and Daddy have to say?' She put down the shirt she was mending and came to him. 'Have they forgiven you?'

'They have.' He kissed her. 'Even your mother welcomed me back after giving me the sharp end of her tongue!'

'Well,' Hortense wound her arms around him and nestled her head against his chest, 'if Mammy gave you the sharp end of her tongue, I'd say you were well and truly one of the family now.' She kissed him and her eyes closed as he touched her breast. Binnie's heart overflowed with happiness. 'I want to take you to bed, my love,' he whispered.

'What's stopping you, hon?' she asked.

Binnie carried her upstairs and into the bedroom and, his heart beating with desire for his wife, he kicked the door shut.

Llinos sat alone in the drawing room staring unseeingly at the flicker of the candlelight. Sho Ka was having a child, Joe's child. After they had lost their own little girl, how could Joe betray her in that way? She clenched her hands together in a burst of anger; she had adored Joe, she had never looked at another man. She had borne Joe a fine healthy son and none of it had been enough for him.

Perhaps, in the Indian culture, it was acceptable for a man to have more than one woman but it would not do here in Swansea. The whole town must be talking about Llinos Mainwaring, the woman who had been abandoned by her husband.

Llinos looked up sharply, startled by the sudden rapping on the door.

'Mr Morton-Edwards is here to see you, Mrs Mainwaring.' The maid bobbed a curtsey.

Eynon crossed the room in rapid steps and took her hands.

'Llinos, my dear girl, I came as soon as I got your message. What's wrong, are you sick?'

She shook her head. 'Sit down, Eynon, and talk to me.' She took his hand. 'It's Joe, he's taken a mistress, she's expecting his child and I can't bear it.' She leaned against his shoulder. 'What did I do wrong? You are a man, can you tell me why Joe went away?'

Eynon shook his head and his pale golden hair fell over his brow. For a moment, he looked like the young boy Llinos had first met on the road to Swansea. She had been in trouble; he had helped her then, perhaps he could help her now.

'You have done nothing wrong, get that idea out of your head right now!' He sounded angry. Llinos took a deep breath.

338

'You knew he'd left me for another woman?'

'I had heard gossip but it was all very vague.' Eynon was not about to commit himself. Even if he knew the whole story, he would not hurt her by telling her so.

'Her name is Sho Ka.' Her voice broke. 'She's a beautiful Indian girl and Joe must love her very much.'

Eynon put his arm around her. She leaned against his shoulder and, though he was her dear friend, it was not Eynon she wanted to hold her but Joe. She could close her eyes and feel the silk of Joe's hair against her cheek, breathe in the scent of him. She drew away from Eynon.

'What can I do to get him back, Eynon?' Even to her own ears her voice sounded weak, pathetic.

Eynon read her thoughts. 'Is this my little Llinos, my dear friend who ran a pottery single-handedly?' He shook his head. 'It is not. You were strong then, draw on that strength now and be dignified about all this. As a man I can tell you that there is nothing worse than a woman clinging like a vine.'

'Do you think I should just let Joe go then?' Llinos felt ill; her last hope was vanishing before her eyes. She had wanted answers from Eynon, answers he clearly could not give her. Eynon looked away from her without answering.

'You're right,' she said forcing a cheerful note into her voice. 'There is nothing worse than a woman holding on to a man who no longer wants her.'

'I didn't say that exactly,' Eynon spoke softly. 'And I know you're not the sort to indulge in

339

self-pity. I just want to see again the spirited Llinos I've always known and loved.'

'Right then, that's enough about my troubles. Tell me what you are up to now, are you still involved with the insatiable Mrs Sparks?'

Eynon nodded. 'In a way,' he said. 'While I am no longer enjoying the sins of the flesh with her, I am still involved.' He ran his hand through his hair. 'She claims she is having twins and that I am the father.' He looked directly at Llinos. 'I am inclined to believe her, don't ask me why.'

'Because you are as vain as all the rest of the male population!' Llinos said. 'You like to think you're a real man about town and what more proof do you need than to be the father of twins!'

'Maybe.' Eynon smiled wickedly. 'I would love a son and two would be even better.'

'So, what are you going to do about it? Marriage is out of the question, Mrs Sparks already has a husband.'

'I don't know,' Eynon said truthfully. 'But if the twins are mine I want to provide for them.' He sighed. 'I don't think Edward Sparks is capable of looking after himself let alone a family.'

'You could be right.' Llinos smiled as she tried to imagine the miserable bank manager coping with children running round him. 'So Mrs Sparks wants money from you, I take it?'

'That's the idea,' Eynon said.

'And you've given it to her?'

'No fear!' he said emphatically. 'I've bought the house she lives in. I will give her the deeds so she can pass the property on to her children. Call it a gift for services rendered.'

340

'I see.' Llinos sank back in her chair thinking about Mr Sparks. He had not approached her lately; he must have dropped his idea of getting her to sell the pottery. Perhaps whoever was behind the venture had lost interest in it. Still, it had made Mr Sparks inordinately angry when she had dismissed the idea out of hand. He must have lost a handsome bribe because of her refusal to sell.

'He's an odd man, Mr Sparks.' She voiced her thoughts out loud. 'There's just something about him I don't like.'

Eynon looked at her questioningly. 'What do you mean?'

'I mean I don't trust him with financial matters.' Llinos leaned back against the cushions and rubbed her forehead thoughtfully. 'He is not astute enough to run a bank. His advice to me to sell the pottery was foolish. The price offered was a good one but not good enough.' She shook her head. 'I don't think he's capable of handling large transactions and I would certainly never trust him with anything of mine.'

'In that case why don't you move your assets elsewhere?' Eynon said sensibly. 'There are other banks in Swansea you know, beside the one Sparks manages.'

'I know. It's just that my father always dealt with that bank, it's a sort of loyalty, I suppose.'

'Well, don't take loyalty too far, that's my advice. Think of yourself first in all matters financial.'

'I might just do that.' Llinos smiled. 'But come on, what will you do if Mrs Sparks has these babies and they are the image of you?'

'I don't know,' Eynon said. 'I hadn't thought that far ahead.' He rubbed his eyes. 'Anyway, let's change the subject.' He grinned. 'I'm going to be a real gossip monger now and tell you about Lily, you know, the girl who—'

'I know Lily!' Llinos said. How could she ever forget the girl who had caused so much trouble in her life? 'I picked her up when I was travelling back to Swansea a few months ago. What's she done now?'

'She's become the mistress of one of the town's richest men, Matthew Starky. You may know him, he's a tea merchant.'

Llinos shook her head. 'I've heard of him but I don't know him personally. I met his wife once and she seemed to be a very sweet old lady.'

How could these men do such things? How could a man claim to love his wife and then sleep with another woman? Eynon read her thoughts.

'It happens, Llinos,' he said softly. 'Look at me, I love you with all my heart but I have needs and so I go to bed with other women.' He shrugged. 'It's the nature of the beast, Llinos, face it.'

'But Joe had me, why did he want Sho Ka as well?' It was a plaintive cry and suddenly, in spite of all her resolutions to be strong, she broke down and sobbed on Eynon's shoulder.

He held her gently and wiped away her tears with his fingers. 'Come on, Llinos, love, let it all out once and for all and then get on with your life. It's a harsh world where not many of us get what we want.'

She nodded; she knew that only too well. After a while, she moved away from him and stood before the window staring into the garden. The kilns shimmered and a heat haze danced around the yard. This was her world, a world she had saved from bankruptcy. Eynon was right, she must pull herself together and get on with her life.

He came and stood beside her. 'Look,' he said gently, 'why don't you put your heart into the pottery again? Start a new line perhaps, expand the business?' He touched her shoulder. 'The china clay was always part of you, in your blood. You were never half hearted about it as I was.'

'You're right, Eynon but it's so hard to be without Joe.' She looked up at him. 'I thought we would be together for always, how could I have been so wrong? Anyway.' She smoothed down her dress. 'I think I'll start going out and about more. Perhaps you will escort me to the symposium at the Assembly Rooms next week?'

'I would be honoured, my dear Llinos,' Eynon said. 'But you do realize our appearing in public together will give the gossips a field day?'

'Well, Eynon, what's sauce for the goose is sauce for the gander, isn't that what they say?'

Later, when Eynon had gone, Llinos thought over the things he had said. He had not actually told her she was indulging in self-pity but that was what he meant and he was right. Where was her spirit, her dignity? She was not the first wife to be scorned for another woman and she would not be the last.

Llinos went to the drawer and took out her sketch pad and pencil. It was time she began to take a real interest in the pottery again; it was her livelihood and her son's future. If Joe decided to stay with Sho Ka and have another family Lloyd would take second place.

The thought angered her. She could just about accept that Joe would leave her but how could he abandon his child? He knew only too well the damage that was done by such a rejection. It had taken him years to be reconciled with his father; was that the future he wanted for Lloyd?

Resolutely, Llinos pushed all thoughts of Joe out of her mind and began to make rough sketches on the paper. She drew a picture of a jug and basin and sketched a woman at a well drawing water. All was quiet in the house. Llinos looked around the room; it was growing dark, candles would need to be lit soon.

She sensed the emptiness of the house, the silence, the absence of the man she loved and her head sank down onto the sketch pad in front of her. Tomorrow she would face life, she would be strong, but for now she wanted to grieve for the love she had lost.

CHAPTER TWENTY-ONE

Alice waited until Edward had closed the drawing room door. He had come home for lunch but he would not have much appetite once he heard what she had to say.

'I'm sorry, Edward, I just couldn't get a penny from my father, he flatly refuses to help me.' She had not even seen her father; she was reserving that option in case of an emergency. 'I shall ask him again, of course, if I can find him in a better mood but, as of now, I'm afraid you're on your own.'

'Alice, your father is Dennis Carrington, he is very rich and very influential. He imports and exports large cargoes every day, he's not going to want a son-in-law who is serving time in prison, is he?'

He smiled at her obvious discomfort. 'You see, Alice, if I'm lost then so are you, Alice, please remember that.'

She shrugged, the deeds of Highmoor were safely stowed in her drawer and she felt protected from the worst that fate could throw at her.

Whatever Edward did now, if he lost everything, even if he went to prison, she and her children would always have a roof over their heads. Still, he had a point, her father would not like a scandal in the family that's why he had urged her to marry Sparks in the first place.

'And don't shrug your shoulders at me, madam,' Edward said. 'Remember I am master in my own house.'

'Really?' Sarcasm laced Alice's tone. 'My father says that any man worth his salt should make a good living for his wife and family.' If she ever did ask her father for money it would be for herself not for Edward. On the other hand, she would have to try to put matters right if only to preserve the good name of the Carrington family.

Alice felt a sense of relief when she thought of her meeting with Eynon. She hoped he would hand her a bag of money as well as the deeds to the house but he was a cautious man. But at least she'd succeeded in convincing him the children were his. That was a step in the right direction.

Edward put his hand to his eyes. 'Dear God in heaven what can I do?' he said and Alice pursed her lips in disgust.

'You can do what any other man does in this life and work harder.' She saw him take his hands away from his face and for the first time she realized how sick he looked. Sweat beaded his face and his cheekbones stood out prominently in his drawn face.

'Edward, is there something more, something you are not telling me?' she demanded. Her hands resting on her stomach felt the babies kick as though in protest that their mother was being worried in this way.

Edward sank into the armchair facing her. 'I am ruined!' he gasped as tears poured down his face. 'You, Alice, have ruined me.'

'What have I done?' she asked. 'Only provide you with a comfortable home worthy of your position in the bank.'

'You have spent money we haven't got!' He spat out the words. 'You have put me in a debtors' prison, that's what you have done.' He stared at her as if he hated her.

'Good God, woman, just look at your own foolishness. Remember the day you bought seven new hats, hats I could not pay for?'

Alice felt uncomfortable; she had forgotten about the hats, they had been bought in a spirit of bravado. But then she had no choice; she could not allow herself to be bested by that common piece who was no better than she should be.

'You worry too much, Edward,' she said flatly. 'Surely a few hats will not break the bank but if it's such a big problem I'll return them to the shop.'

'Try to understand what I've been telling you, woman!' He was almost whispering. 'You know I have been taking funds from the customers' accounts to pay our bills.' He rubbed his hand through his hair. 'I thought I could replace the money, I felt sure your father would help us out. You convinced me of it.'

Alice really was not interested in Edward's petty pilfering; even that he had failed to do effectively. 'Edward, you're a fool. Haven't you thought of a way to cover up the discrepancies? Why not transfer funds from the richer accounts?' She leaned forward, all pretence of respecting her husband gone.

He looked at her with haunted eyes. 'Tell me how?' He was pleading with her to help him. She was silent for a moment, annoyed that she had to do Edward's thinking for him.

'Surely you can divert incoming funds to clear the deficit? People expect delays when money is being transferred or bills being paid.'

Edward chewed his lip; he was pondering the matter in his usual slow-witted way. 'It would buy us a little time, wouldn't it?'

She watched him sweating and could not even summon enough feeling for him to hate him. Perhaps she should take a holiday, put some distance between them. She could go home at least until the children were born. She thought of her enormous bedroom in her father's house and the way the servants rushed to do her bidding. At home she had been cosseted, respected, now she was the wife of a not-very-bright bank manager, it was so humiliating.

What if she showed Father the deeds of Highmoor and assured him that she was going up in the world? That would impress him and Alice felt a strange need to impress her father. And surely he would not turn her away when he had grandchildren to consider? Edward's whining voice interrupted her thoughts.

'It might work.' He was still chewing over her advice, still considering shifting money about to suit himself. 'But only for a time. Sooner or later, if I don't return the money, the discrepancies will be discovered.'

'Well, Edward, put it out of your mind for now.' She smiled in what she hoped was a reassuring manner. 'I'll speak to Father again, I'll do my best to get us out of this scrape which is of your making, remember.'

Her words were unfair but Edward was so grateful for her help that he failed to notice the blame laid squarely on his shoulders. Alice frowned; she had enough to worry about without Edward whining on about his problems at work. She was an expectant mother and should be cared for, not troubled by petty money matters.

She would write a letter home, ask Father if she could stay a while. No-one would think it strange that a woman wanted her family around her when her children were born. She closed her eyes with a feeling of well-being. Later, she would visit Eynon, ask his advice about Edward's predicament. She would have to put her husband's misdeeds in the best possible light, of course. If nothing else she could prepare the ground for Edward's 'mismanagement' to be exposed. Alice smiled to herself. Now that Eynon believed her about the twins he would take the trouble to listen to her complaints about her swollen legs and the pain that constantly nagged at her side. He was a kind considerate man, what a pity he was not her husband instead of Mr Sparks.

She stretched, easing her back, perhaps she would have a little doze before lunch and then, when she had eaten, Rosie could help her dress in her latest outfit. She liked to look smart for her

349

meetings with her lover. And Eynon would be sure to offer his carriage if Alice did travel to her father's estate. She closed her eyes, shutting Edward out of her mind; she had more important things to think about like her own well-being and that of her children.

It was late afternoon when she called at Eynon's house. The maid who opened the door recognized her and stood back to allow her entry into the hall. It was a very grand hall with a sweeping staircase and beautiful windows above the landing. Elegant, highly polished furniture stood discreetly against silk-hung walls.

Once Alice would not have noticed anything of the grandeur, she had been brought up in a house that was much larger than this with rolling acres of land as far as the eye could see.

'Is Mr Eynon expecting you?' the maid asked quietly. Alice waved her hand dismissively.

'Of course he's expecting me, girl! Rosie, you go into the kitchen, I'll send for you when I'm ready to go home.'

To Alice's consternation, Eynon was entertaining guests. Her heart sank when she recognized the pert face of Polly Boucher and beside her the aged man who was her husband.

'I do apologize, Eynon.' Alice made an effort to conceal her irritation. 'If I'd realized you had company, I would not have intruded.'

'Nonsense!' Eynon smiled; he seemed in a good mood. 'Jem and I have concluded our business and I'm sure Polly here will be glad of some female company.'

Men could be so obtuse. Alice stared sourly at

Polly who smiled patronizingly and twitched her good silk jacket into place around her slender waist. Alice felt at a disadvantage, heavily pregnant, it was difficult to dress with any sort of style.

'Day to you, Mrs Sparks,' Polly said disarmingly. The girl was a good actress, no-one would ever know there had been friction between them. Alice decided to play Polly at her own game. She sat close to her and smiled as warmly as she could.

'It's so nice to see you again, Mrs Boucher,' she said, accepting a cordial from the maid. 'Did you enjoy your shopping spree the other day?'

'I most certainly did.' Polly winked at the old man who was her husband. 'Jem is a very generous man, he spoils me, don't you, my darling?'

Jem nodded but his eyes resting on Alice were cold. 'How is your husband, Mrs Sparks?' he asked grimly. Alice swallowed some cordial, there was a constriction in her throat, she wondered uneasily if Edward's foolish scheme had been found out.

'He hasn't been very well lately,' she said. 'I do think he needs a long rest from business.' She paused for effect. 'He seems a little under the weather, you know? Not quite his composed self. He sometimes becomes quite confused, I do worry about him.'

It seemed a good idea to scatter some doubt about Edward's state of mind to anyone who would listen. Perhaps if his misdeeds were discovered the problem could be put down to ill health.

'Oh dear, I am sorry,' Polly said, her twinkling eyes belying her words. 'It must be so difficult to have a husband who has to work all day with no time for play.' She winked at her husband again. 'We have plenty of time to play, don't we, Jem?'

'Aye, indeed,' Jem said, 'we play so much I'm quite worn out with playing.' He rose to his feet. 'Thank you for your hospitality, Eynon, and I'm glad we had this little chat. Perhaps we can meet up again to discuss developments?'

Polly smiled at Alice. 'There you are, you can have dear Mr Morton-Edwards all to yourself now.' Her smile widened. 'I don't think you'll need a chaperone, will you, not in your condition.' She paused before delivering her parting shot. 'We might meet again though I doubt it, we do not move in the same social circles, do we? Bye, Mrs Sparks.'

Alice's cheeks began to burn; once she would have slapped a common slut like Polly for her insolence. But then she had been rich, the daughter of a successful man. Now the roles were reversed, Polly was the rich one and that hurt.

When he had shown his guests out, Eynon returned to the room and sat beside her. 'What can I do for you, Alice?' He seemed a little distant and Alice was worried in case Edward had been foolish enough to make his 'mistakes' too obvious. Suddenly she felt desperate.

'I need to confide in you, to ask your advice,' Alice said. 'I'm very troubled, I didn't want to say too much in front of Mr Boucher but I think Edward has been making serious mistakes in the bank. He really is not a well man.'

She slanted her eyes towards him. 'I know

you've given me the house, Eynon, and it's just as well under the circumstances, don't you think? I mean with Edward so confused and all.'

'I'm afraid I know nothing about banking,' Eynon said. 'And I don't particularly want to. On such matters I cannot offer any advice. However I will ensure that you are adequately looked after.'

'What do you mean?'

'I intend to pay for the doctor and the midwife and all the trappings of childbirth.' He smiled. 'Yes, Alice, I am willing to put some funds at your disposal.' He rose and took a key from his pocket. Alice watched with bated breath as he unlocked a drawer.

'Here, Alice, this should be enough to see you through. When the children are born we'll talk again. In the meantime, I'd take that husband of yours to a doctor if he's as confused as you say he is.'

Alice looked uneasily at Eynon. 'Do you know something I don't?' she asked. 'Please, Eynon, as a friend, if you know anything about the affairs of the bank, tell me.'

Eynon nodded. 'All right, the auditors are to investigate sooner than we thought, the books will be audited before the end of the month. If any problem shows up I'm afraid your husband will be in serious trouble.'

'Oh, dear, what am I going to do?' Alice said, hoping her pretence at being worried was convincing. 'In my condition I can't stand any upsets.'

He stared at her and then smiled. 'You needn't force any tears, Alice, and I expect your claims that your husband is sick will be taken into consideration. However, I suggest you persuade your husband to offer his resignation forthwith.'

Alice sighed with relief. The purse Eynon had given her was heavy, she would have to sacrifice it so that Edward could pay off the debts, save himself from disgrace. He could retire from the bank offering his health as an excuse.

Once the twins were born everything would be all right. Eynon would continue to support her and so, no doubt, would her father. He had always wanted grandchildren and when he saw two beautiful babies he would soften. He might even insist the twins be given the Carrington name.

She smiled secretly, she might even confide the truth of the twins' parentage to her father. He would not be shocked, he was well used to her flighty ways and would cluck his disapproval but in the end he would be pleased that the twins were not the offspring of a lowly bank manager but a man of property and wealth. Her father was nothing if not a snob.

'Don't worry, Alice,' Eynon said gently, 'I'll speak to the owners of the bank, if necessary I'll offer to pay off the debts incurred by the "mistake". Then it's up to that husband of yours to get out of a job that he patently is not suited for.'

This was even better than Alice could have hoped for: Eynon would put things right with the bank and then, once the babies were born, he would want to make love to her again; she would be happy and indulgent and he would adore her. The pity of it was that she was still married to Edward Sparks. Still, she would have to make the best of it, already things were looking brighter for her.

'Thank you, Eynon, I'm very grateful for all your kindness.' And once she had her figure back she would be happy to prove to Eynon just how grateful she could be.

Llinos left the paint shed and made her way across the yard, hearing the cheery sound of voices as the workers streamed towards the gates. Another day was over and she faced a long, lonely night. Still, there was one bright spot, the new designs were working splendidly. Her 'Maidens at the Well' pattern had proved far more popular than she had ever imagined. There was no doubt about it, times were changing and customers wanted refined, well-decorated pottery products to put on their tables.

Watt followed her across to the house. 'Can I speak to you, Llinos?' he asked and she beckoned to him to come inside. He looked lean and tired and she wondered how he was coping with married life. Much better than she was no doubt.

'Llinos,' Watt said, 'I have something to explain to you.' He stood in the hallway and kicked off his clay-stained boots.

'What's wrong?' He followed her into the drawing room and Llinos closed the door. 'Is it Pearl?'

'No.' He looked down at his feet. 'It's Rosie, she's left me.'

Llinos sank into a chair, shaking her head. 'But I thought everything was going right for you at last.'

'It's all my fault, I let her know I'd married her

out of concern for the family and now she's gone. I heard she's working as a maid somewhere or other. I just don't know what to do about it.' He ran his hand through his hair, sending a shower of dust onto the carpet.

'Oh, Watt!' Llinos looked at his drawn face. 'Don't you love Rosie then?' She wondered what was happening to the world, was everyone going mad?

'I don't know.' He shook his head. 'I don't know anything any more.'

'Well,' Llinos sighed, 'you'll have to sort yourself out before it's too late. Can you imagine how much you must have hurt Rosie?' She thought of her own feelings of pain and betrayal and her sympathy at that moment was with Rosie. The poor girl had married Watt in a haze of happiness. She loved him to distraction, anyone could see that, and he had let her down.

'Well, no-one can advise you,' she said, 'you have to sort this out on your own I'm afraid.'

'There's another problem, something to do with the pottery.' Watt straightened his shoulders, once again in charge of his emotions.

'I sent for more china clay but the Dorset Company said we had not settled our last bill.'

Llinos rubbed her eyes; she could do without problems of business right now. She was tired and downhearted; she felt like an abandoned wife and she supposed that was just what she was.

'Perhaps it was an oversight.' She pushed back the few stray curls that hung over her face. 'Perhaps we'd better check with the bank.'

'I have.' Watt looked grave. 'I don't know what's

happening, Llinos. Our profits are up and yet there are insufficient funds in the bank to meet our commitments. I don't understand it.'

Llinos frowned and with a sigh took the account books out of the desk drawer. She had kept her own accounts since the early days when the pottery had been running on a shoestring and she had not seen any reason to relax her vigilance over the years.

'According to my figures we should have a healthy balance,' she said. 'Indeed, we're better off than we've been for some time. I think that might be due to the popularity of the new designs we've been using.'

Watt leaned over her and ran his finger down both the credit and debit columns. 'No mistakes there,' he said. 'Look, I'd better call at the bank tomorrow and sort this out, there's obviously been some mistake.'

Llinos agreed with him, there were no money problems for them to face whatever the Dorset China Clay Company said. She closed the books and put them away. She was worried enough without the bank making silly errors.

'It's probably Mr Sparks's fault,' she said. 'I never did trust the man to get things right, he's an incompetent. I did promise Eynon I would think about moving my account elsewhere but I haven't got round to it.'

'Well perhaps you'd better think harder.' He paused. 'I've heard talk, I don't like to repeat gossip but it seems that his wife has been overspending at the shops. She returned no less than seven hats to the emporium in the High Street.

That doesn't go down well with the people of the town, I can tell you.'

'That's their business,' Llinos said tiredly. 'All I care about is my own affairs, I just want this silly nonsense sorted out as soon as possible.'

Watt walked to the door and paused. 'Llinos, what's happening, between you and Joe, I mean? Is he ever coming back?'

'I don't know, in any case I don't want to talk about Joe.' Llinos felt tears come to her eyes, she thought of Joe, of his lean, strong body, his golden skin, his silky hair. She could hear his voice vibrant with love but it had been a long time since he had spoken to her of love. When had it gone wrong? Had the death of their baby changed the way Joe felt about her or had he just grown tired of her?

'Is there anything I can do?' Watt asked. 'Should I go to speak to him?'

'You know he's with another woman. What could you say to him to bring him back to me, Watt?'

He looked down at his feet and shook his head. 'Perhaps being a man he'll talk to me, tell me what is going on.'

'I doubt it.' Llinos pushed back her hair.

'Well,' Watt persisted, 'I could tell him about the problem with the bank, he should be the one sorting it out not me.'

'No,' Llinos said. 'I don't want to bring Joe back because he feels sorry for me.' Her words were brave but did she mean them? Sometimes she felt she would have him back on any terms.

'Don't worry about me.' She made an effort to smile. 'I'll go to the bank myself. You know I can handle my own affairs. I did just that when my father was away, didn't I?'

'I suppose so.' Watt sounded doubtful. He hesitated in the doorway for a moment as though reluctant to leave her. 'Look, don't worry about the bank, I'll go to town in the morning, see what is going on, shall I?'

She nodded. 'All right then. It might be for the best, I don't think I could keep my temper with Mr Sparks if I went myself.'

'I'll get off home now.' Watt still hesitated. 'If you are sure there's nothing else.'

'Go!' Llinos said. 'Go before I throw something at you!' She sank back in her chair and closed her eyes. The distant sounds from the kitchen were somehow comforting; it was good to know she was not completely alone. Upstairs, Lloyd would be preparing for bed with Eira fussing over him like a mother hen. Later, when she had rested, Llinos would go up and tuck him in for the night.

She heard the sound of the front-door bell then the maid's voice, high-pitched with surprise. The door to the drawing room was flung open and suddenly Joe was standing there, his hair flowing to his shoulders, his blue eyes looking into hers.

Her heart leapt with hope; had he come home to her? Her mouth was suddenly dry. His first words sent her spirits plummeting.

'Why did you come to the house and upset Sho Ka?' He spoke in clipped tones. 'You could see she's in a delicate condition, she's just not up to facing a confrontation with you right now.'

Llinos looked at him in astonishment and then a fierce anger blazed through her with the heat of a forest fire. She had found Joe's mistress big with child and *he* had the gall to talk as if Llinos was at fault.

'I didn't upset her!' Why, she wondered, was she bothering to defend herself. She faced him, her cheeks flushed, her hands clenched into fists. They stood close together, so close she could smell the familiar scent of him, could see the flecks of blue in his eyes. She wanted him so badly that it was like a knife turning inside her.

'How dare you come to me like this!' She was angry with herself and even more angry with Joe. 'How dare you rebuke me for upsetting your mistress! Have you no shame left, Joe?'

'My mistress, is that how you see her?' Joe asked.

'That's what she is.' A flicker of hope lit within her; was Joe going to deny that Sho Ka meant anything to him? Was there some good explanation for the way he had been acting?

'Her husband died,' he said flatly. 'She was a widow and I felt responsible for her.' He paused. 'We were betrothed to each other long before I met you.' He shrugged. 'So I brought her back with me to where I could take care of her.'

'So the baby she is carrying is her husband's not yours?' Llinos was shaking with hope now, waiting for Joe to speak, to tell her she was being foolish.

'I didn't say that.' He made a move towards her but Llinos warded him off. 'Don't touch me, Joe!'

'Look,' he said, 'you don't appreciate the Mandan ways, I have responsibilities, I feel obliged to look after Sho Ka, don't you understand that?'

360

Llinos took a deep breath, she needed time to compose herself. 'What I do understand,' she said coldly, 'is that you have made that woman more important than your wife. You have spent time with her when you should have been with me and with our child.'

'We must talk about Lloyd,' he said, 'we have a great many things to discuss, you can't just shut me out of your life.'

She was cold now. 'That is exactly what you have done to me, shut me out of your life. Well if you think you can enjoy your mistress and then come home to Lloyd and me whenever you feel like it you are very much mistaken. We have nothing to say to each other so please leave, this is still my house, remember?'

The door opened and Charlotte peered into the room, her eyes wide. 'Joe! I thought I heard your voice. Please, you two, don't quarrel.' She spoke quietly. 'If Lloyd hears you he will be so upset.'

'It's all right, Charlotte, I'm just leaving.'

Llinos wanted to beg him to stay but the words stuck in her throat. It was too late to heal the rift between them, Joe had taken another woman and there was no trust left between them any more.

'Go then!' she said. 'And don't come back, do you hear me?'

'I hear you, Llinos.' He walked out of the room without looking back and Llinos felt Charlotte's arms around her.

'There there, don't cry, he'll come home when he's good and ready.'

But the house in Pottery Row was no longer Joe's home, he had made that quite clear.

'Come on, Charlotte,' Llinos swallowed hard. 'We might just as well go to bed, there's nothing to wait up for any more.'

As she followed Charlotte up the stairs, Llinos closed her mind to Joe's harsh words. She had sent him away, at least she had kept her pride. But when she closed the bedroom door she knew that pride was a shallow, empty thing.

CHAPTER TWENTY-TWO

'So you're settling in all right then?' Polly was moving around the small sitting room picking up china ornaments, touching the curtain material to test it for quality, almost as if she was making an inventory of the possessions Lily had acquired.

Lily watched her, feeling rather smug about the whole situation. 'I'm settling in just fine,' she said. 'Matthew is not very demanding, he's more interested in his creature comforts than anything else.'

'What do you mean?' Polly looked at her wide-eyed. 'He likes his bed, is that it?'

'In a way.' Lily smiled inscrutably, she knew Polly would be infuriated. She waited for Polly to sit down and give the matter her full attention.

'Go on, you tease! Tell me.' Polly settled herself in the armchair and kicked off her shoes, preparing for a good gossip.

'Well, he likes me to massage him all over with oil.'

'*All* over?' Polly giggled suggestively.

'That's right,' Lily said. 'Then he usually falls asleep.' She laughed at the disappointment on

Polly's face. 'After he's made love to me of course.'

'You devil!' Polly sat forward, her thin shoulders hunched. 'And what's he like, you know?'

'He's kind and considerate,' Lily said. 'And he's quick. That's what I like about him. Afterwards he always gives me gifts as though he's grateful to me.'

'Well he is,' Polly said reasonably. 'A young girl like you in his bed instead of his dried-up old wife, of course he's grateful.' She leaned back in her chair. 'And it doesn't do his reputation as a ram any harm, does it?'

'What do you mean?' Lily asked. Polly could be so worldly-wise that it put her at a disadvantage.

'Well he probably brags about you down at his club.' She laughed. 'I can see it now, him and my Jem talking about the young girls they bed who cry with passion for them and all that sort of non-sense. Men get almost as much of a thrill out of talking about their love lives as they do living them.'

Lily thought it over. Polly was probably right. Somehow the idea of being gossiped about made her feel uneasy. And yet, what did it matter? No-one at the club knew her anyway.

She smoothed down the silky skirt of her gown; the cloth felt fine and rich to her touch. She really owed Polly a debt of gratitude for finding her a man like Matthew Starky who was gentle and did not snatch at her as though she were a piece of fruit on a plate. He thought of her most kindly and she had learned to pretend to be happy in his arms, to love him. In a way she *did* love him but more like a father than a lover.

'I'm glad you brought us together, Matthew and me,' she said and Polly smiled.

'I knew you'd suit each other.' She paused. 'Do you like it now, you know the bed thing, lying with a man? Do you like it a bit better now you're with Matthew?'

'Yes, I think I do.' Lily felt she could answer that honestly. She would never be filled with passion the way Polly was but she was content with her life. Matthew was so generous, so thoughtful.

'Matthew's been so good to me about my work,' she said. 'Come upstairs and see what he's bought me.' She enjoyed the way Polly's eyes opened wide in expectation. Polly could barely contain her excitement as she hurried behind Lily, her hand sliding along the polished banister.

'Don't tell me you're expectin'?' she gasped, the acquired cultured tones deserting her. 'You're not fitting out a nursery, are you? Speak to me, I can hardly wait for an answer!'

The suggestion made Lily shudder, she was not with child and she prayed every night that she would remain that way. She had never fallen pregnant with any of the men she had been with; perhaps she was barren. She certainly hoped so because the thought of a baby mewling and crying in her arms, clinging to her breast, made her feel queasy.

'Don't be daft!' she said flatly. 'What would I want with a baby? I'm not the maternal kind, am I? Anyway, what about you?'

Polly shook her head. 'I think my Jem's too old for that but Matthew is a different kettle of fish, he's a good bit younger than Jem. If you did catch he might marry you, have you thought about that?'

She smiled slyly. 'You got to look out for yourself, Lily, I'm always trying to tell you that. Another thing his old wife won't last long and if you 'ad his kid Matthew might want to make an honest woman of you.'

'Never mind all that. Just see what I've got.' Lily pushed open the door to one of the upstairs rooms and flung it wide with a flourish. Her eyes alighted on the large wooden easel standing near the window. On it was pinned a sheet of paper covered with various designs.

'Is this what you got so excited about?' Polly's disappointment was evident. 'I thought you had some big secret, something juicy to tell me.'

'Trust you!' Lily shook her head. 'The thing is, Polly, I won't be bored out of my mind when Matthew is not with me. He wants me to be happy and I can be happy doing some painting work.'

On an impulse, she pushed Polly into a chair. 'Just sit there and keep your mouth still for a minute, I'm going to draw you.'

She pinned a fresh sheet of paper to the board and stared for a long moment at her friend. Polly was looking flushed, flattered that she was being given such close scrutiny.

Lily began to cover the paper in swift strokes. Portraits were not something Lily was used to drawing; her skills had been limited to patterns for china decoration. Still, she became absorbed, shading areas darkly and leaving others, like Polly's cheekbones, untouched to form highlights. It was only when Polly began to wriggle that she realized that the light was fading.

'Have you finished, love? I'm dying to pee!' Polly stood up and came round the easel to study her portrait. 'Bloody 'ell!' she said. 'It's good, mind, but look at the big nose you've given me! It's like them things in the papers, those pictures that make folks' worst features – well, worse!'

Lily knew exactly what Polly meant; her drawing was more of a caricature than a portrait. Still, it had style and movement and, with a bit of practice, she would probably improve.

'Hey, Lil, why don't you send it to one of the papers? Go on, I dare you.'

'No-one would want it,' Lily said uncertainly. 'It's not all that good, see I could have done a bit more to your hair and . . .'

'Give it to me, then,' Polly said. 'It will amuse my Jem if nothing else. But you must sign it first.' She nudged Lily. 'Please, I never ask you for anything do I?'

She never did and Lily owed her so much. Resolutely, she took down the picture, wrote 'Lily' in a scrawling hand and gave it to her friend. 'Roll it carefully so that it doesn't smudge,' she instructed and Polly smiled impishly.

'I won't harm one bit of it because my Jem will send it to the paper for us, you see if he don't.' She sighed in anticipation. 'Mrs Jeremy Boucher, wife of important figure in the town as drawn by her friend and companion Miss Lily . . . what is your other name, Lily?'

'I never had one, not a proper name, not until I married Tom Wesley. I never had a father, you know that, Polly.' There was still a bitterness at the thought and Lily swallowed hard. She had been born a bastard but even if it took her the rest of her life she would prove she was a person of note.

'I don't like Wesley, it sounds like a man's name,' Polly said. 'Well, we'll just call you Lily.'

She made for the door. 'Look, love, I got to be going now, I told the driver to come fetch me before it got dark. Jem likes me to be there when he comes home.' She rested her hand on Lily's shoulder.

'Look, love, you've fallen in lucky with Matt, don't throw all that away by being too coy with him.'

'He likes me as I am,' Lily said stubbornly. And that was his strength, she realized that now. Matthew did not ask her to be different, to change. He liked Lily just as she was.

When she had waved Polly off and watched the gleaming carriage drive away down the street, Lily returned to the attic. She placed a mirror against the window, conscious of the fading light and attempted a self-portrait. The result was far from pleasing. It was just as Polly said; the drawing emphasized all the worst features of her face. Her nose was too sharp, her lips thin. The only comfort was the light in the eyes, the light of enthusiasm.

Lily put away her drawing materials and then washed her hands. She was more fulfilled than she had been in a long time and it was a wonderful feeling.

'Rosie, fetch me another cushion, there's a good girl,' Alice said. 'And then bring the footstool, my legs are giving me such grief.'

The girl did as she was told; she was docile, never putting up any argument. Not even by a twitch of her eyes did she show any resentment for the way she was treated. That was the way a servant should behave.

'Who came calling last night?' she asked. She was not really interested in her servant's affairs but Alice was bored.

'It was just a friend,' Rosie said. 'I'm sorry, madam, did it disturb you?'

'No, it's all right, if you've got a gentleman caller then good luck to you. Every woman should have a man running after her, it's the natural order of things.'

She was not usually so magnanimous but the girl was useful, more so now that Cook had walked out in a huff. Rosie's cooking was improving and she worked willingly. A man in her life might be just what she needed to cheer her up, give her a bit more sparkle. This man, probably some poor labourer, might prove useful as an extra, unpaid servant.

She heard the sound of the front door and gestured to Rosie. 'Go and let the master in, there's a good girl.' Rosie curtsied and left the room. Shortly after, Edward trailed into the room and flopped into a chair.

'I've managed to put everything in order at the bank,' he said coldly. 'Though I am not happy at the means by which you got the money. I still can't understand why Eynon Morton-Edwards would make us a loan.'

Alice had been careful, she had thought her story out well. She claimed that Eynon knew her

369

father, he was an old friend of the family. He also approved of her efforts to raise money for charity, thought she was deserving of help.

Alice smiled to herself; the charity idea had never served much of a purpose mainly because Alice being married to a bank manager was considered socially inferior to the gentry of the town. Still, she had traded on it with Edward who had waited impatiently for funds to come rolling in. Foolish man!

Edward had become sceptical, over the months he had begun to realize that not everything his wife told him was the truth. There was no money coming in and as far as he was concerned she had made no attempt to see her father.

Ironically, she had visited Father but when she arrived at her old home it was to find he was away on a trip. It had given her a jolt to be reminded of how grand the family seat was and how luxuriously she had lived before she was married.

'Perhaps you had better start telling me the truth, Alice,' Edward said haughtily. 'I am not happy, not happy at all, about the arrangements you have made.'

'I told you!' she said waspishly. 'Eynon thinks the money is for charity. You thought it was a good idea at the time and in any case would you rather face a prison sentence?'

Edward was not easily convinced. 'Look here, you've been sleeping with the man, haven't you? Why else would he give you money?'

'Don't be absurd! And don't go over all that again, Edward, not now,' she said, rubbing at her stomach. 'I am not feeling too well, can't you see that or are you so selfish that you can only think of yourself?'

'Well, I don't like it, a man giving my wife a substantial amount of money for nothing, it doesn't make sense.' He looked at her suspiciously. 'You have been honest with me, haven't you, Alice?'

She sighed. 'I don't know what you mean, Edward.'

'This man, Morton-Edwards, are you sure he wasn't one of your lovers?' He peered at her, as though trying to see inside her skull. Alice was inclined to tell him the truth; she was fast losing patience with him. Who did he think he was? Some potentate who kept his wife behind locked doors? She was about to make a sarcastic remark when his next words made her stop short, her mouth still open.

'Come to think of it, the idea to have a baby came from you.' His lips pressed together in a thin line as he considered the matter. 'It was all rather sudden, wasn't it? If the children don't look like me there will be trouble, Alice, believe me.'

Like most weak men Edward could be quite vicious at times. Alice stared at him, despising him more as each day passed. Why had she helped him out of the mess he was in? Would it not have been better to have taken the money herself and gone back to her father? He would not have been in the least surprised to hear the marriage had failed.

'Shut up, Edward!' she said loudly. 'Don't you dare to talk to me in that way. You know that Eynon is romantically involved with Llinos Mainwaring, so why keep on? I can't help it if my

371

husband is a failure, can I? Apart from which you are the most unattractive man it has ever been my misfortune to meet. If you keep on bullying me, I shall leave you, Edward, and then how will you cope?'

He stared at her for a long time, his eyes burning like coals in their sockets. He clenched his hands into fists and she thought, for a moment, he might hit her, then he subsided and put his hands over his face.

'Alice, what would I do without you?' he wailed. Now he was a little boy crying for his mamma. Alice rose to her feet and swept across the room.

'I will not speak to you again until you apologize for your crass behaviour,' she said in her most haughty voice. 'I find you the help and support you could not get for yourself and what is my thanks? I get accused of the most vile of crimes.'

She made her way slowly upstairs to her bedroom. She felt so weary, she could hardly keep her eyes open. Her body was ungainly, heavy and she hated it. Just wait until the birth was over and done with, there would be no holding her. Edward could go to hell and back for all she cared.

'Are you all right, madam?' Rosie had followed her upstairs and her sweet voice touched a chord, the girl was really concerned about her. Suddenly, Alice felt like weeping.

'No, I'm not feeling well, bring me some tea, Rosie, please.' She paused. 'Rosie, you are a good girl and I'm grateful to you.'

Alice sank onto the bed and lay back feeling the soft pillows behind her head with a sense of relief. She realized quite suddenly that she was lonely;

that the love she had always craved had never been hers. No wonder she had grown a protective shell around her. With no-one to love and care for her she had always been forced to fend for herself.

Tears of self-pity flooded into her eyes and when Rosie entered the room with a tray on her arm Alice looked up at her. 'Rosie, would you say I'm a bad person?' she asked, struggling to sit up.

Rosie put down the tray and helped her to get comfortable, patting the pillows into shape at Alice's back.

''Course not, madam,' she said. 'No-one in the world is all bad.' She smiled her gentle smile. 'We all have a spiteful side to us, I know I have.'

'That's hard to believe, Rosie.' Alice for once was being totally sincere. 'You are a sweet trusting girl, you look out for yourself, watch you don't get hurt.'

'I've been hurt already, madam,' Rosie said. 'I'm not a widow as I led you to believe. I married a man who didn't love me. I couldn't stand that so I left him even though it tore my heart to shreds to do it.'

She handed Alice the cup. 'It was my husband who came calling the other night. He's been over here quite a few times asking me to go back but I never will.'

'Oh?' So the girl was married; it was a bit of a surprise but then Alice was not going to lose any sleep over it. So long as Rosie did her job she suited Alice.

'Sit down by the bedside for a minute, Rosie,' she said. 'Tell me all about yourself.' Talking to Rosie was better than lying in her room alone thinking about the pathetic man she had married.

'Your husband, is he working at a decent job?'

'Oh yes, he's a manager over at the pottery, you know the one Llinos Mainwaring owns?'

That was interesting, this Llinos was one of the victims of Edward's little tricks. He seemed to dislike the woman intensely. No doubt she had not knuckled under to his high-handed manner. Where Edward got his pomposity from Alice would never know. The man was such a mixture, one minute bullying and the next cringing in fear. With hindsight, Alice marvelled that she had ever agreed to marry him.

At first, though, he had seemed presentable enough. A little on the thin side and not cut from the best of cloth. Edward was not one of the élite who formed society but he was a better prospect than the one her father had offered her. If she did not marry soon, she would be cast off without a penny.

She had known right away that Edward was not the material good lovers were made from. He had fumbled at her in bed, eager at first to taste the fruits of the voluptuous woman he had made his wife. But he was inept and their coupling had been swiftly over and had left Alice feeling high and dry. Had Edward proved proficient between the sheets she might have forgiven him everything.

'Did you enjoy his lovemaking, Rosie? That can be enough to make a marriage happy, you know.'

Rosie blushed. 'I might have if I thought he loved me. He was in love before and I don't think he ever got over her.'

'Poor girl,' Alice said. 'Well perhaps you are

better off out of it then. Now tell me, how is Mrs Mainwaring?' Alice realized that Rosie was sitting on the edge of her seat, uncertain if she should stay or go. 'Did I hear that her husband has walked out on her?'

'I don't know, madam. Even when Watt and me were together, he never talked about Llinos – Mrs Mainwaring's – private life.'

'How boring, no wonder you left him. He wouldn't be in love with this Llinos, would he?' She could see by the clouding of Rosie's eyes that she had struck a chord. 'I mean they grew up together and, from what I gather, together saved the pottery from disaster.'

Rosie sighed. 'No, it wasn't Llinos he was in love with. Watt was living with a married woman whose husband had run off.' Rosie's eyes were downcast. 'But Maura died of the whooping cough.'

Alice reached out to catch Rosie's hand. 'And he married you on the rebound, is that it, Rosie?'

'I suppose so, madam.' She looked up, her expression one of sadness. Alice felt an unwelcome pang of guilt.

'I shouldn't be prying into your personal life, Rosie,' she said with a genuine feeling of pity for the girl. 'But you and I have much in common, my husband doesn't love me either.' She sighed heavily. 'He married me for my father's money.'

'Oh, madam, I'm sorry!' Rosie said at once. 'And do you love him?'

She was very naive but so sweet that Alice smiled at her. 'I don't think I do, not now,' she said truthfully. 'If I were to be honest, I never loved him but you never realize what a man is truly like until you live with him, do you, Rosie?'

'No, madam.' She rubbed her wrists. 'At first I was dazzled, I thought Watt loved me but now I see he only married me because he was lonely and because he felt obliged to help the family out.' She hesitated. 'He's a good man and I don't blame him for not loving me but it does hurt.'

'Well look, Rosie dear, ask him to visit you properly, talk things over with him, you could be wrong about him, have you thought of that?'

Rosie shook her head. Alice watched her for a moment, summing up the situation. This man, her husband, he sounded interesting. And he might be able to tell her a great deal about Llinos Mainwaring and her business. He might be close-lipped with Rosie but then she was inexperienced with men. Alice on the other hand used her guile to get the information she wanted.

'I don't think I'm wrong,' Rosie said softly. 'I know Watt likes me and he made me his wife and all that, but I just feel here,' she pressed her hand against her heart, 'that he is still in love with Maura even though she's dead.'

'Ah but you are very much alive,' Alice said. She was not quite clear why she was trying to make the girl feel better, it was out of character and Alice knew it. Still she persisted. 'Love can grow, Rosie, and if Watt is coming to see you, don't you think he must feel something for you?'

'Maybe he does. Can I really ask him to visit, madam?'

'Of course you can,' Alice said and then added, hastily, 'but don't give in to him right away. I

376

mean if he wants you to go back to him hold out for a time. Men don't value what comes to them easily, I've learned that much.'

She did not want to lose Rosie; she was a good maid and was turning out to be a very good cook. However, she was beginning to feel genuine warmth towards the girl and that was a new experience.

'Go on, then, take some time off, go and see your husband, ask him to call on you just as if you were walking out.'

'I don't think I could do that,' Rosie said doubtfully. 'Though I could see Mam, ask her to talk to him.'

'Right then, that's settled.' Alice was suddenly tired of the matter. 'I shall have a sleep now, you may go, Rosie, but draw the curtains first, there's a good girl.'

It was good to lie in the quiet darkness in the softness of the bed, where she could pretend that everything in her life was fine. Where she could pretend that she had a husband like Eynon Morton-Edwards, a man who was skilled at lovemaking, a man who was rich and a powerful force in the town. Slowly, weariness overtook her and Alice fell into a dreamless sleep.

'Gawd! Would you just look at this!' Polly was holding up a newspaper and there, in the centre of the page, was the drawing Lily had done of her. 'Would you believe it, they've got my picture in this week's issue of the *Swansea Telegraph*.'

Lily and Matthew had been invited to the big house to have supper with Jem and Polly.

Matthew, who could scarcely keep his hands and eyes off Lily, chatted to her incessantly over supper. It had been over a week since she had seen him; his old wife had been sick or something and strangely enough she had missed him. Now both men had retired to smoke their cigars.

'Look then!' Polly insisted. 'I've kept this as a surprise for you. Aren't you excited to see your work in the paper?' She shook the page flat and placed it on the table, pushing aside the plates and cutlery with complete disregard for the fine china and silverware. 'See, it says you are my friend and a "friend of the Right Honourable Matthew Starky" Ha!' She laughed. 'Friend, so that's what they call it when a married man sets up home with another woman.'

Lily was pleased; the picture of Polly looked even better in the paper than she imagined it would. She stared at it critically. 'Perhaps next time I draw you I should give it a bit more thought,' she said. 'See, the edge of your gown is not quite right.'

'Stop it!' Polly ordered. 'I have more news for you if only you will listen.' She put down the paper and smiled widely. 'The editor Mr Granger wants you to do a whole series of these.'

'What? Pictures of you?'

'No silly! Not of me but of other people in the town, people like my Jem, Matthew and Eynon Morton-Edwards.' She paused for effect. 'Mr Granger is even willing to pay you!'

Lily began to feel more enthusiastic. This could lead somewhere, she might even become famous. That would be one in the eye for the people who had scorned her, people like Llinos Mainwaring and Watt Bevan.

'Well, what do you feel about it?' Polly was impatient for a reaction and Lily hesitated.

'Well, it sounds all right. I'll do it if Matthew doesn't object.' She had to be careful not to jeopardize her situation with Matthew Starky. It was doubtful she would make enough money from her drawings to live on.

'He's thrilled to his bootstraps!' Polly said. 'He's so proud of you anyone would think you were his wife.'

That hurt. She was as good as his wife and one day Matthew would regularize their position, Lily was sure of it. She concealed her thoughts from Polly, who simply would not understand. Polly had never cared about belonging, about being respectable. And yet, ironically, it was Polly who had found respectability with Jem Boucher.

'I'll talk it over with him all the same,' Lily said obstinately. 'Matthew is a good man and I don't want to upset him.'

'Please yourself.' Polly shrugged. 'Come on, let's go and make nuisances of ourselves to the men. It's about time they finished their brandy or port or whatever and paid us some attention.'

In the drawing room, Matthew took a seat beside Lily. She could see by his eyes that he was happy to be with her again. He put his arm around her waist, his fingers searching upwards to her breast. Lily caught Polly's eye and Polly winked.

'Someone's in for a good time tonight,' she said gleefully. She pinched Jem's cheek. 'Hope you're feeling as randy as I am, my boy!'

Jem shrugged. 'What can I do with her?' he appealed to his friend.

Matthew smiled back at him. 'Go on, Jem, you love every minute of it.'

He was right, Jem was lapping up Polly's attentions, his eyes gleaming at the thought that she wanted him. Perhaps that was the secret to a man, to play on his lust and praise his ability to please in the bedroom. On an impulse, she slipped her hand through Matthew's arm.

'Come on, Matt,' she said softly, shyly, 'I want to be alone with you. Please take me home.' The way his face lit up at her words proved she was right: flatter a man's vanity and you could get anything you wanted from him.

She sighed softly as she sat in the carriage beside Matthew. She snuggled against him and rested her head on his shoulder. It must be wonderful to fall in love. What was wrong with her, that she had never known the feeling? Still, she had her protector and, now, she had a career, however small, as a contributor to a newspaper; and for the time being that was enough.

CHAPTER TWENTY-THREE

It was the worst time of Llinos's life. Not even in the dark days when her mother died, when she was left to run the pottery single-handedly, had Llinos felt as alone as she did now.

There had been no word from Joe since he had come storming into the house a week ago, and Llinos had expected none. He had made his views quite plain; he wanted Sho Ka rather than his wife. It was a bitter thought and Llinos could scarcely bear the pain and humiliation of it.

There was one bright spot in all the gloom: there had been an upturn in trading. Shop owners from Swansea and Carmarthen were taking large quantities of china wares and selling the goods faster than the pottery could provide them.

Watt had sorted out matters at the bank and all the bills were paid up to date. Still, Watt felt she should make a move to another bank and she would, just as soon as she regained control of her emotions. It was ironic, she thought, that while her business life continued to improve, her private life was in chaos.

Llinos was startled out of her reverie by the sound of the large doorbell resounding through the house. She saw that the fire was burning low and knelt near the hearth to place coals on the embers. She really should call the maid but Llinos was used to looking after herself and had no compunction about getting her hands dirty.

She was still kneeling, her dusty hands held out, when the door opened and the maid led a visitor into the room.

'Sho Ka!' Llinos said. 'What are you doing here?' She scrambled to her feet trying to appear composed but her heart was pounding. 'Take a seat.' Her voice was cold, formal. 'I won't be a minute, I need to wash my hands.'

Why had she allowed herself to be caught at a disadvantage by her husband's beautiful mistress? And why was Sho Ka here? Her heart was beating swiftly as she rinsed the coal dust from her fingers.

She hurried back to the drawing room, anxious to know the reason for Sho Ka's visit. The Indian girl was sitting in one of the armchairs, her head high, looking elegant in spite of her pregnancy.

'Is Joe all right?' Llinos asked breathlessly. Sho Ka's dark eyes met hers.

'No I don't think he is,' she said. 'He is missing his family life here with you.'

'Why doesn't he come home then?' Llinos could not keep the asperity from her voice. 'It's his choice that he stays with you, not mine.'

'You don't understand our ways,' Sho Ka said softly. 'We Mandans can accept other women who might be important to our man, it does not mean that Joe loves you any the less because he has me.'

Llinos stared at her for a long moment and it was Sho Ka who looked away first. 'It is *not* our way,' Llinos said. 'Here, we marry one man for life.'

'That is not quite true though, is it?' Sho Ka said softly. 'Where we live in Neath there is a man, a farmer, who has a wife and a mistress. No-one seems to be upset about that.'

'Well I am upset about Joe being unfaithful to me,' Llinos said angrily. 'I never thought Joe capable of such a betrayal. I put him on a pedestal, I worshipped him, can't you understand that?'

'And can't you understand he never meant to hurt you?' Sho Ka said. 'He brought me back here because he was sorry for me.' She looked up, eyes deep dark pools of tears. 'I needed someone to help me through my grief. I had lost my husband, I was so unhappy and I felt Joe was the only one in the whole of the world who cared if I lived or died.'

'And so you invited Joe into your bed and he accepted,' Llinos said flatly. 'Well somehow that does not make me feel any better.'

'Soon, my baby will be born,' Sho Ka said. 'Then I will return to the rivers and the hills and bring my child up as a Mandan. That will fulfil the prophecy made by Mint that the offspring of Wha-he-joe-tass-ee-neen will put new blood into the tribe.'

'How wonderful for you!' Linos said. 'A ready-made excuse for adultery.' She paused to take a calming breath. 'And am I supposed to welcome Joe back with open arms when you leave?'

Sho Ka shrugged. 'I don't know. It's what he wants, I do know that.'

Llinos walked to the window and looked out, not seeing anything of the kilns or the wall at the end of the garden. Her eyes were blinded; jealousy was a hard stone inside her as she thought of Joe making love to Sho Ka.

'I can't forgive him, ever,' she said. 'Now, Sho Ka, if that's all you've come to say then I'll bid you goodnight. I'm very tired.' Suddenly she was, she was weary to the bone. What was her life worth without Joe to share it? She spun on her heel and faced Sho Ka.

'Tell my husband that if I didn't have so many responsibilities I would go into the river and drown myself!' It was a childishly rebellious thing to say but it was what Llinos felt at that moment.

Sho Ka bowed her head. 'I'm sorry.' She got to her feet. 'I shouldn't have come here, I see that now. I wanted to explain things to you but I've only made you angry.'

Llinos sighed. 'It's Joe I'm angry with. How could I blame you for loving a man like him?'

'Please, think about this: Joe loves you very much indeed but he's only a man. What man could resist when another woman offers herself unreservedly? I'll admit I played on his feelings for the Mandan tribe, on his loyalty to his mother. I told him everything would be all right with the Mandan once Joe's heir was born. One day Joe's son will be chief of my people, can't you be generous and forgive him?'

'Just go away home, it's almost an hour's drive to Neath and Joe will be getting worried,' Llinos said bitterly. 'And don't come here again. As far as I'm concerned, you stole Joe from me and he was weak enough to let you. That's an end to it.'

When Sho Ka had left the house Llinos sank into a chair and took a deep breath, what on earth had the Indian girl hoped to achieve by coming here? Did she think Llinos would ever understand and forgive what Joe had done when he walked out of her life and left her to bring up Lloyd alone.

So he was missing his family was he? Well no-one had made him go away. And nothing altered the fact that he had betrayed his marriage vows. Joe could have married Sho Ka long ago and he had chosen Llinos. Now he hoped to have both of them, well it was a false hope.

Llinos ate little of her supper. She was glad to slip into bed and curl up in the darkness. She missed Joe so much that it was like a physical pain but she would not, could not, share him with another woman.

She wanted to cry but the tears would not come. There was a hard knot of anger in her that would not let her rest. She lay wide-eyed, unable to rid herself of the vision of Sho Ka large with child, Joe's child. And then the tears came, scalding along her cheeks and running salt into her mouth.

Rosie walked quickly along the roadway leading towards Swansea. She was meeting her mother at the tea rooms near the Slip and she braced herself for the ticking off that was sure to come. Her mother had lectured her before, telling her that her duty was to be at her husband's side. Well not if her husband did not love her and Watt had practically admitted that love was the last thing on his mind when he married her.

Pearl was waiting for her and she waved a thin hand when she saw her daughter. Rosie hugged her mother, tears of homesickness burning her eyes.

'You're looking better, Mam,' she said. 'See, you've put on a bit of fat now and it suits you.' She sat down on the spindly chair and faced her mother. It was not true, Pearl was looking anything but well.

'I hope you're not going to lecture me again, Mam,' Rosie said. 'I know what I'm doing, I'm a grown woman.'

'Look, love,' Pearl said, 'I don't like to think of you working for that toffee-nosed Alice Sparks and that's a fact.' She frowned. 'Why don't you come home with me now and talk things over with Watt? Surely anything is better than living the way you are, fetching and carrying for that selfish woman.'

'No, Mam, that's where you're wrong. I understand now that Watt married me because he felt responsible for our family.' She shrugged. 'I suppose with Maura gone he had nothing to lose by taking on our problems.'

'He's very fond of you, love,' Pearl said and Rosie shook her head. Fondness was not enough; her mother above all people should know that. She looked up as her mother leaned forward.

'I'm not happy with you working in the Sparks's household. I've heard talk about Mr high-and-mighty Sparks.' Pearl glanced over her shoulder to make sure no-one was in earshot. 'They're in trouble, money trouble.' She nodded as Rosie raised her eyebrows. 'It's true, I heard Watt warning Llinos to be careful with her money and not leave it in the hands of a crook like Edward Sparks.'

Rosie shook her head. 'I can't see it, Mam,' she said. Alice Sparks, far from seeming short of money, spent it as if she had a money tree growing in the garden. As the time for the birth of the twins drew nearer, Alice seemed to become more and more extravagant. She had recently bought two matching carved wooden cribs draped with fine embroidered linen as well as spending a fortune on decorating the nursery with bright colours and the finest quality furniture money could buy.

'It's probably just gossip, Mam,' she said. 'In any case, how would Watt know?' Even speaking his name gave Rosie a sharp pain. It was so hard to be in love with a man who was simply fond of her.

'Look, love,' Pearl was reading her expression, 'just see him, talk to him. Come home with me now and we'll have a bite to eat and—'

'No!' Rosie said, 'I can't do that.'

'Well he's tried to see you and he's turned away all the time,' Pearl was growing impatient. 'Once you see it's him you slam the door in his face. What's a poor man to do?'

'I have left him, Mam,' Rosie said firmly. 'The marriage was a mistake, you know that as well as I do.' She bit her lip trying to hold back the tears. Pearl touched her hand awkwardly.

'Buck up, love, nothing is ever as black and white as it seems, mind.' She patted Rosie's work-roughened hand and sat back in her chair. 'Just try again, that's all I'm saying. Love can grow, see, every woman knows that in her heart.'

Rosie sighed heavily, swallowing the hard lump

in her throat. 'I can't fight a ghost, Mam,' she said. 'Now, let's do a bit of shopping, Mrs Sparks has actually handed over some of the wages she owes me.' She smiled. 'It was like getting blood out of a stone, mind. Mrs Sparks said I would have to wait but when I pointed out that I got less than most servants and did the work of three she gave in.'

'All right,' Pearl said. 'Shopping it is.'

It was about an hour later, when Rosie was laden with parcels and heartily sick of shopping, that she realized her mother was lagging behind. She turned to see Pearl leaning against the wall, her parcels scattered over the road.

'Mam!' Rosie said in panic. 'What's wrong?'

'I feel so queer.' Pearl was white, sweating, and Rosie was suddenly frightened. She looked round for help but the street was empty. Rosie put her arm around her mother's shoulder in an effort to support her but Pearl's eyes were turning up in her head and, slowly, she slipped to the ground in a dead faint.

'Mam!' Rosie was terrified. 'Mam, what's wrong with you?'

'Rosie?' The voice was familiar and Rosie looked up with a sense of relief as Llinos Mainwaring and Mr Morton-Edwards came hurrying towards her. Eynon Morton-Edwards crouched down and lifted Pearl's head, putting his hand against her face.

'She's sick,' he said. 'I'll get my carriage, we'll take her to the infirmary.'

'No, not the infirmary,' Rosie said, 'people die in there. Take us back to Greenhill, please.'

It was strange travelling along the familiar

streets but Rosie scarcely looked out of the window. She realized her mother was seriously ill; her face was gaunt, her hair almost white now. She bit her lip; why had she not been there to help her mother when she needed her?

Watt must have heard the carriage stop outside the door. He stepped out onto the cobbles and sized up the situation at once. 'I'll take her.' He carried Pearl into the parlour and put her down on the old horsehair sofa.

'Fetch some pillows and a blanket, Rosie,' he said. 'And, Llinos, thanks for your help. Can you stay a few minutes more while I go for the doctor?'

'No need,' Llinos replied. 'Eynon has anticipated you, he's sent the coach driver straight down to Broad Street to fetch Dr Stafford.'

Rosie put the pillows behind her mother's head and stared into her pale face. Pearl had not opened her eyes since she had been brought into the house. Rosie felt as if she were in a nightmare world as she waited for the doctor to arrive.

Pearl's eyes flickered and opened. 'Mam, are you all right?' Rosie held her mother's hand, praying that the doctor would be quick. Pearl did not reply; she simply stared sightlessly upwards. Rosie began to cry and Watt put his arm around her.

'Don't, Rosie, it will be all right, you'll see,' he said gently. She shrugged him away, lost in misery. If anything happened to Mam, she would never forgive herself.

When the doctor came, he ushered them all out of the room. Rosie's brothers were standing in the kitchen, eyes downcast. 'Is Mam going to be all right, Rosie?' Dom asked shakily.

'Of course she is!' Rosie spoke with more assurance than she felt. 'Mam's as tough as old boots, you know that as well as I do.' She bustled around the kitchen. 'Come on, all of you, let's get some supper done, shall we? Dom, you go fetch some wood in for the fire, right, boy?'

It was strange to be in the old kitchen, seeing familiar dishes, bringing the bread out of the basket hanging in the pantry. In some ways it was as though she had never left. It almost seemed she was a child again. But she had grown up. She was a married woman, married and separated from her husband in a matter of a few short months. She was servant now to Mrs Alice Sparks, wife of the bank manager.

'*Duw!*' She stopped in horror; Alice would be expecting her back by now. There was tea to cook and cleaning to be finished.

She caught Dom's arm. 'Take a message to Mrs Sparks for me, love,' she said. 'Just explain that our mam is sick and I must stay to look after her.' Rosie began to wash up the dishes that had stood congealed with fat from breakfast time, then she scrubbed the boards of the table until they gleamed white. She could see that no cleaning had been done since she left home.

She lifted her head as she heard the doctor speaking to Watt near the front door. She moved nearer to listen.

'A blood clot on the brain,' the doctor was saying. 'Very little hope, I'm afraid.'

Rosie heard the words but knew they could not be true, Mam was strong as a horse; she worked in the pottery along with the other women, some of them older than she was. Mam was indestructible.

Watt came and took the scrubbing brush from her hands. 'Come in to your mother, Rosie.'

She shook her head, frightened to face the truth. So long as she did not see her mother die, it would not be happening. Watt led her to the parlour and Rosie noticed that Llinos and Eynon Morton-Edwards were still waiting in the doorway.

Her mother was fully conscious now, her eyes focused, frightened. One corner of Pearl's mouth was drawn down and her left hand lay useless, dangling over the edge of the sofa.

'Mam.' Rosie knelt beside her. 'Come on, Mam, you can get better, you have to get better, I need you.'

Pearl tried to speak but the words would not come. She took a ragged breath and tried again. 'The boys, look out for them, promise me.' Her good hand gripped Rosie's. 'Promise!'

'I promise, Mam, but you will be all right, you'll see, you've been working too hard, a bit of a rest and you'll be back to your old self.'

Sadly, Pearl shook her head. 'Tell Willie . . .' Her voice faded, the light went out of her eyes and her hand in Rosie's went limp.

'Mammy!' Rosie wailed. She was a little girl again, wanting her mam. She would never have her mam again. Her mam was dead.

Alice was angry with Rosie; how dare the girl treat her this way? This is what came of spoiling servants, giving them money to spend. With pockets full of money they lost all sense of responsibility.

Her irritation increased when she heard the knock on her door. The knocking was repeated and with a sigh, she heaved herself out of her chair. A young boy stood on the step, his hair tousled over his forehead.

'What do you want?' Alice said crossly. The boy moved from one foot to the other, his eyes wide with misery. 'Speak, boy! If you are begging, forget it! I do not have money to give away, understand?'

'No, miss, I'm not begging, miss, it's my mam, she's sick, see.' He chewed his lip and Alice stared at him wondering what he was babbling on about.

'What's that to me?' Alice said a little more gently. 'I'm sorry if your mother is ill but why have you come here?'

'Rosie, miss, she sent me. She can't come, see because she got to stay and mind my mam.'

It begun to dawn on Alice that he was telling her she had no maid to cook and clean, no-one to make supper for Edward when he came home. Damn Edward, he must be working late again at the bank. She looked past the boy and along the street, there was no sign of Edward's thin figure, why was he not here when she needed him?

She looked down at the boy again, he was pale, his face filled with fear. The children moved in her womb and Alice pressed her hand to her stomach. What if her sons should ever be this miserable?

'What's your name, boy?'

'Dom, miss.'

'Well come in, Dom, I'll give you some things to take up to your mother.' The boy followed her reluctantly, he was probably overawed by his surroundings. Rosie's family lived in a poor district of Greenhill in a two-up, two-down cottage with very little in the way of luxury.

Alice took a basket from the pantry and put a fresh loaf and some butter in it. Perhaps she should send the bit of ham left on the bone, it might come in useful for soup or some such thing. As an afterthought, she added some eggs.

'There, take this carefully and don't spill it.' She suddenly felt the warmth of being charitable to someone less fortunate. 'And tell Rosie I'm sorry about your mother but she must come back tonight to cook the supper, I'm depending on her.'

As the boy hurried away, Alice turned to look up the street again and there, to her relief, was Edward, a newspaper under his arm, his cane in his hand, looking his usual pompous self even from a distance. He would expect a meal when he came indoors but he would just have to wait; there was nothing she could do about it until Rosie came home.

Edward entered the house and threw the paper down on the table. 'Look at this!' His voice was sharp, his nostrils pinched, a sure sign that he was displeased. Alice shook her head.

'I'm not interested in the paper, Edward, I have more pressing problems to think about.'

He shook out the broadsheet and showed her the picture set in the middle of the page. She recognized it at once. 'Good heavens it's me!' True her features had been exaggerated: her nose was sharper, her mouth fuller and her figure, well, she looked like a baby elephant, her pregnancy depicted as an obscene bulge.

'How dare they do this to me?' she asked incredulously.

'Read the caption.' He pointed with a lean finger and Alice took the newspaper from him. She had not been named but the drawing was unmistakably of her. At one side of the picture was a caricature of Edward, true to life in his tight-lipped spareness. And on the other a good likeness of Eynon holding a lead attached to her neck. The printed words accompanying the drawing leapt before her eyes. 'Good wife or a rich man's whore?'

Beneath it, the piece went on to tell of a supposedly fictitious woman who was married but had been seen frequenting the house of a wealthy bachelor from the higher orders.

'How do you explain this?' Edward demanded. He was white to his lips, his eyes mere slits in his face.

'I deny it absolutely!' Alice said. 'I am not invited to visit anyone in the area as well you know.' She stared at him. 'The only visit I paid to Mr Morton-Edwards was to ask him for help. Had I not done so you would have been dismissed from your job, have you forgotten that?'

'Well maybe, but I am still not in the clear. So far nothing has been discovered, I have covered my tracks well, I am very good with figures as you know.'

'And that is about all that can be said in your favour.' Alice wanted to smack his smug face.

'Do you realize I would never have been treated in this scurrilous way if I hadn't married you? As the daughter of Dennis Carrington I was

x

394

considered one of the élite. My father moves among the very best of society while you . . .' She shrugged. 'You must face it, Edward, you are small fry.'

She saw him frown. 'You do realize that I'm not accepted among the successful, wealthy folk of the town because of your lowly position. No-one wants the wife of a bank manager gracing the dinner table. I married beneath me, Edward Sparks and you would do well to remember it.'

'What I am remembering is the money you came into quite suddenly,' he said. 'How much exactly did you get from Morton-Edwards?'

'Don't be absurd!' Alice said. 'You are letting this rubbish upset you unnecessarily. Last week there was a picture in the paper of some other unfortunate woman, I saw it when you left the newspaper on the table.'

'And you know who that was? It was no unfortunate woman, far from it! The picture was of Jem Boucher's wife and no slur was cast on her good name you notice.'

'I can't help that, Edward.' Alice was suddenly weary of the whole thing. 'If you doubt my word go and see Eynon Morton-Edwards and confront him. I should think you'd get short shrift there!'

Edward subsided into a chair, his expression mutinous. 'Anyway, where's my supper? I'm hungry.'

'Rosie's not here, her mother is sick or something.'

'Well then you will have to cook me something yourself, Alice.' He stared at her, disapproval written across his thin face.

'You can forage in the kitchen yourself, Edward,' Alice said. 'I am in far too delicate a condition to work. I have never sunk to the level of a kitchen maid, and shame on you for suggesting such a thing.'

She sank down into a chair and eased her shoes from her feet. 'See,' she said, 'my ankles are swollen, I can't stand any longer.'

Edward stormed out of the room and she heard the sound of china being slammed on the table. After a while, he returned with a plate of bread and a hunk of cheese. He sat opposite her and munched his way solidly through his meal and then helped himself to a large measure of port.

Alice realized that she had eaten nothing since early morning. She sighed and made her way into the kitchen. It was a mess; Edward had left dishes where he'd stacked them and crumbs littered the table.

Alice found some cold soup in a dish in the pantry and scooped it into a saucepan. She stood over the dying fire and did her best to warm the soup until it was edible. Suddenly, she began to cry, it had come to this: Alice, once used to a houseful of servants, had come to eating cold soup in a dowdy little kitchen. How she hated this existence. And it was Edward's fault; he was to blame for everything.

She returned to the drawing room and stood before him hands on her hips. 'I have had enough of you!' she said fiercely. 'You have no thought for your pregnant wife, do you? Well, I want you to get out of my sight and right now!'

He ignored her and shook out the paper,

concealing himself behind it. Alice turned and left the room, tears of anger and frustration burning in her eyes. She would get rid of Edward by fair means or foul, even if she had to kill him to do it.

CHAPTER TWENTY-FOUR

Binnie stared at the letter and for a moment felt a pang of homesickness. 'It's from Llinos,' he said and Hortense looked up from her embroidery and smiled.

'Ah, your lovely little girl from Swansea.' Hortense was beautiful with the sun in her hair and her eyes looking into his with such love that it made his heart skip a beat.

'You are my one and only little girl. Llinos is just a dear friend.' He was so lucky, it was only when he had almost lost everything that he realized just how fortunate he was.

'Poor Llinos!' He looked down at the letter. 'Joe has left her and set up home with the Indian girl.'

'Well, you said it looked that way, didn't you, hon? And these things happen.' Hortense smiled. 'Birds of a feather and all that. And, anyway, the Indian folk have strange ways, strange thoughts, they see things that we don't see, it's in their blood.' She shrugged. 'Perhaps your Llinos should have expected it.'

'She wasn't to know that Joe would take the

woman back home and move in with her,' Binnie said thoughtfully. 'Perhaps I was wrong to tell her and I would like to do something to help but I wouldn't know where to start.' He sank onto the step of the porch, the letter fluttering in the breeze as he tried to read it again.

'You could find out why this Joe took the Indian woman with him,' Hortense suggested. 'Perhaps he was obliged to, honey, as I said, these folks have strange ways.'

Hortense was right; it would only take a day or two to ride to Mandan country and speak with the chief. In a way, the visit would serve a dual purpose. He looked at his wife.

'I didn't want to tell you this but I heard that John Pendennis is hiding out in Indian country. I've been wondering if I should go up there and try to get back some of your father's money.' He looked lovingly at Hortense. 'But I don't want to leave you even for a few days, love.'

'But you'll go anyway?' Hortense said. 'Go on, Binnie, your conscience won't let you rest easy if you don't sort this out. But don't tell Daddy whatever you do or he'll be riding up there with a noose at the ready.'

Binnie sighed. 'You're right as always. I'll get a couple of the men together and we'll ride out at first light tomorrow.'

Hortense put her hand on his shoulder and rubbed gently. 'In the meantime, hon, how do you feel about sharing an afternoon siesta with your wife?'

He could smell her perfume, the sweet scent of her skin and he was immediately aroused. How wonderful it was to have a woman who loved him and excited him at the same time. He would never do anything, ever again, to endanger that love.

It was almost a week later, after days of dusty, bone-wrenching riding, when Binnie caught sight of the River Knife gleaming in the sunshine. He turned in the saddle and waved to the boys he'd hired. Jessie was driving the chuck wagon and, behind him, Karl was riding shotgun.

In his saddlebags, Binnie had some gifts of beads and feathers and in the wagon there were items of pottery that the Mandan tribe might like to copy. Binnie smiled; the tribesmen were skilled potters in their own right, they were a gentle people and usually open to new ideas.

'It's only about four miles to the village,' he said as Jessie caught up with him. 'Should be there before nightfall.'

'Thank the Good Lord for that!' Jessie was a large man with a hearty colour. He was strong and loyal and would watch Binnie's back at all costs. 'It sure hurts me where I sit, I think that wagon hit every stone and every hole in the damn plains!'

'Don't grumble,' Binnie said smiling, 'if you were sitting astride a horse for days, then you would know what pain was.'

They rode the rest of the way in silence and, at last, Binnie caught sight of the walls of the stockade. 'Look,' he said, 'up there on the hill, that's the village of Mih-Tutta-Hang-Kusch, not far now.'

It was good to see the familiar sight of the round earth lodges set neatly close together around a large clearing. The Mandans were meticulous and kept the intersections between the lodges swept clean to make for easy access.

When Binnie approached, the gates of the stockade swung open to allow the small group inside. Binnie was shown the usual hospitality, gifts were exchanged, and Binnie, Jessie and Karl were given sleeping quarters for the night.

As he lay in the soft darkness of the lodge, Binnie thought of his wife and children. Was he mad leaving the comforts of his home to face the dangers of Indian country? The Mandan were a kindly, non-aggressive tribe but that did not speak for the rest of the Indians who populated the plains.

Binnie slept only fitfully and dreamed about Hortense. He woke in the morning reaching for her, and sank back onto his pallet in disappointment. He must make his enquiries as soon as possible and then get back home.

He bathed naked in the river, the sun on his back, and heard laughter as he swam towards the bank. A group of giggling girls was watching him and he smiled. They were beautiful, every one, but not half as beautiful as his wife.

Later he was invited to sit with the chief. The lodge was spacious with a fire burning in the centre and cleaned skins hanging against the earth walls. Binnie sat cross-legged on a pile of mats and accepted a pipe from the official pipe carrier.

He made polite small talk for a time, asking after the health of the chief and his children and tribe. At last, he broached the subject he had come to discuss.

'I am curious about Joe, Wha-he-joe-tass-ee-neen, and the squaw Sho Ka,' he said gently. 'They left the village together, I believe?'

The old chief nodded over his pipe for a long moment and Binnie thought he was not going to reply.

'That is the way it had to be, Binnie Dundee,' the chief said at last. Binnie remained silent; it did not seem polite to ask any other questions. He waited patiently and at last the old chief spoke again.

'It was the dying wish of his mother, Mint, that Wha-he-joe-tass-ee-neen give a child to the tribe.' The chief paused. 'It was also my wish. We need good blood to keep the tribe strong. Too much inbreeding leads to weakness.'

Binnie was intrigued; the ways of the Indian nation were so complex, so rooted in old traditions. He puffed on the pipe, making an effort not to cough.

The chief stared stolidly into the fire. 'Our pots broke, our spearheads were not sharp and our crops failed. So we welcomed the white man John Pendennis into our lodges, offered him his pick of the maidens.' Before Binnie could ask questions the chief held up his hand.

'But he has bad blood, he drinks, sleeps and does no work. We do not want him here any longer. When you leave you shall take the white man away with you.'

Binnie nodded, taking John away suited his purpose very well. There were a great many questions he wanted to ask John Pendennis. The man was bad news; it seemed he was causing as much of a problem among the Mandans as he had among the McCabes.

'I will do as you say.' He drew on the pipe, resisting the urge to cough. 'I will take John Pendennis with me when I leave.'

'As for Sho Ka, she will return,' the chief said slowly. 'Sho Ka is one of us, she will come home when the time is right.

'Soon you will leave our lodges. We want the white man off our lands. He is bad medicine, he fights my warriors and molests their squaws, he is no longer welcome.'

That sounded likely. Binnie sighed. He would never be able to take John Pendennis back home, Dan would kill him if he set eyes on him again. Perhaps the best thing was to go with him to the coast and put him on a ship for England.

'I will leave in two days and I will take Pendennis with me.' He bowed his head and the chief smoothed his pipe between brown fingers before putting it to his lips again. The time for talk was over, it was time to relax, to enjoy the hospitality of the Mandan people.

But already Binnie was homesick, lonely for his wife and his sons and for the rest of the McCabe family. They had become his people, the close relatives he had never known. The sooner he got rid of John Pendennis, the sooner he could get home.

It seemed so long since Llinos had written to Binnie that she despaired of ever hearing from him again. Perhaps he never received her letter. Or maybe he was just too busy to be bothered with her problems.

403

Llinos closed her books; she was not giving them the attention they deserved. Her head ached and from upstairs she could hear Lloyd shouting at Eira. Llinos rubbed her eyes, half inclined to go to her son, but just then Watt entered the room. He looked tired but then he was a worried man. He had funeral arrangements to see to as well as looking after Pearl's sons.

'I should remind you about moving your account, Llinos,' he said. 'I think now that the bills are settled it's a good time. I can do a lot of the work but you need to sign the papers.'

'I know.' Llinos's mind was on other matters. 'I'll see to it when I can,' she said. She could think of nothing except Joe and his betrayal. She kept seeing Sho Ka in her mind's eye, large with Joe's baby and beautiful. Llinos was obsessed by the thought that Joe had slept with another woman.

Ironically, Llinos now felt the way the Indian girl must have felt, as though there was no-one in the world to care if she lived or died. Come to think of it, Watt was the only one to show any concern at all for her these days. Charlotte seemed determined to keep out of her way and even Eynon had not been around for some time. No doubt he was too busy with his own life but then he had professed to love her. Were all men fickle, cheats and liars?

'I'm sorry, I'm not giving much thought to the business.' She tried to smile. 'I'm behaving like a child, hiding my head in the sand. I'll go to the bank tomorrow and sort everything out. Now, what's happening about Pearl's funeral, is everything in hand?'

Watt pushed back his hair. 'I'm managing all right,' he said. 'But I wish Rosie had stayed at home. She only waited until Pearl was laid out and then went back to work for Alice Sparks. She said the woman needed her more than I did.'

'That doesn't sound like Rosie. I thought she'd want to be with her brothers at least until after the funeral.'

'To be fair to Rosie she comes up to Greenhill every day, prepares the food and does the cleaning. But she leaves before I get home. I don't think she can bear to sleep under the same roof as me.' Watt thrust his hands into his pockets. 'She's convinced I married her out of pity.'

'And did you?'

Watt nodded his head miserably. 'I suppose so. It was all too sudden, I should have given myself time to come to terms with losing Maura.' He gave a short laugh. 'I suppose I saw myself as a knight in shining armour coming to the rescue of the family.'

'You did what you thought was best, but a woman needs a man's love like a flower needs water, can't you understand that?'

Watt stood for a long moment without answering and then he shrugged. 'I suppose you're right.' He made for the door. 'I'll get back to work then.'

Llinos shook her head, men would do anything to avoid talking about their feelings and, once again, Llinos was thinking about Joe.

Llinos went to the window and looked out at the front garden of the house. From this room, the kilns were not visible but they seemed to dominate the landscape anyway, their bottle-shaped towers threw out a heat haze that rose above the darkening sky and hung over the area like a halo.

She clenched her hands together, she longed to go to Joe's house, to fall on her knees and beg him to come home. She had no pride left, the pain had become too great for her to think of anything else but her longing for her husband.

It was too late to do anything today but tomorrow, if her courage did not fail, she would go to her husband, tell him how much she needed him, how much his son needed him. She would use any sort of ploy to get him home with her.

'Joe, how could you do this to me?' Her anguished voice resounded in the silence of the room and, even as her mind searched for some answers, she knew there were none.

'I'm heartily sick of your grumbling, so shut your mouth before I shut it for you!' Binnie glowered at John Pendennis. 'As if taking you to the coast wasn't trouble enough, you have to constantly complain about everything.' He held the reins of his horse and, in one easy movement, swung into the saddle.

'Now get on with it or I'll dump you here in Indian country without food and water and let you fend for yourself, do you understand?'

John nodded and as he climbed awkwardly into the saddle the bones of his face seemed sharpened by pain. Binnie knew the signs, for he had seen them before in the lined faces of men in the rooms of the local inns: John Pendennis had become addicted to hard liquor. Well he would get no sympathy from Binnie; John had spent or lost most of Dan's money, he seemed set to wreck his own life and the lives of those around him, and he was best out of the way.

Binnie urged his animal into a trot and John fell in behind him, head hanging low on his chest, the reins of his horse loose in his hands. Good thing the beast was well trained otherwise John would find himself unseated. One sudden movement, one unexpected noise and the horse would bolt. With a bit of luck John would break his neck. Binnie looked up to the heavens. 'May God forgive me for having such thoughts,' he said under his breath.

Jessie and Karl were both riding on the food wagon, Karl having given up his horse to John. Binnie could see that the two boys had no liking for John Pendennis and would not raise a hand to help him if he fell from his horse. Binnie sighed, the sooner John was on board a ship for England the better.

That night, the small party camped under the shelter of an overhanging rock. It was no place to rest if they were attacked but it was beginning to rain and at least the rocks offered some shelter from the elements.

Jessie built a fire against the rock face and the warm blaze did a little to cheer Binnie's spirits. The hot, strong coffee Jessie made was welcome but Binnie shivered as the wind drove the beating rain against his face.

He wished he was home and he would have been if it had not been for John Pendennis. In that moment he could have cheerfully murdered John himself. At last, Binnie rolled himself in his blanket, unaware that it stank of horse and his own sweat. Tomorrow, they would reach the coast and John would be off his hands.

Binnie woke to a bright sunny morning. Jessie was already brewing more coffee and the rich aroma made Binnie feel better. John unrolled himself from his blanket and looked across at Binnie and his eyes, for the first time since the party had left the Mandan village, were clear and bright.

'I've been a damned fool, haven't I?' He rubbed his unshaven chin. 'I've thrown everything away. I left a good wife for cheap women and cheap liquor.'

Even now John was thinking of himself and not of the chaos he had left behind in West Troy.

'You can say that in spades!' Binnie's tone was clipped. 'Not only have you wrecked the lives of the people you should have loved but . . .' He shrugged. What was the point in going on?

'Jo, how is she?' John asked humbly. He looked at Binnie and read his expression well.

'She lost the baby.' There was no point in lying. 'The shock of the row and Melia's death was too much and, well, she lost the baby.'

'Oh, God, what a bastard I've been.' John hunched his knees to his chest and Binnie realized how thin the man had become. He was still young but he looked old and careworn.

'If you don't give up the bottle you are on the road to hell,' he said abruptly. 'You can never put right what you've done to the McCabes but you can try to shape up and make something of yourself back home.'

'I know you're right,' John said. 'I don't

408

understand why I let myself become such a wretch!' He sighed heavily. 'I had a woman who loved me, a good family life and a father-in-law who provided everything I could ever want and I threw it away.' He looked directly at Binnie. 'What am I to do?'

'Go back to Cornwall, find yourself work, honest work. Pull yourself together and make something of your life before it's too late.'

'I can't go back to Cornwall,' John said. 'I promised myself I would only go home when I was rich enough to do to Treharne what he did to me and my father.'

Binnie shrugged. 'Well, go to Swansea then, see if Llinos will give you work.' Binnie brightened suddenly. 'I'll write you a letter, you can deliver it to Llinos for me, that way I'll know it arrived safely.' He looked up at the clear sky. 'We'll make the coast by this afternoon, book into some lodgings and get cleaned up and then tomorrow we'll part company for good, I hope.' He had no intention of hiding his true feelings from John.

'Binnie,' John said slowly, 'I appreciate what you're doing for me, I'll never forget your generosity.'

'Just get wise,' Binnie said. 'Make something of yourself, you speak like an angel and act like a devil, take a good look at yourself before it's too late.'

That night, Binnie luxuriated in the bathtub at the back of the small lodging house and, as the warm water lapped over him, he closed his eyes and thought about his wife and sons and how happy he would be to be home. Once he had seen the ship carrying John away from the shore, he would be free.

The morning dawned bright and clear. Binnie and John walked along the harbour looking for a ship headed for England. When they found one, it was Binnie who paid the captain. 'What the hell have you done with the money you stole from Dan?' he demanded angrily.

John shrugged. 'I don't know what you're talking about, Binnie, I took no money.' He sounded so earnest, so indignant, that Binnie was almost inclined to believe him.

'Well look,' he said, 'here's some money to see you all right when you get to Swansea. Now take my advice and keep off the bottle and everything will work out fine.'

'How can you say that?' John asked. 'I've hurt so many people, I can never forgive myself.'

'You must put the past behind you,' Binnie insisted. 'Pray to God for forgiveness and make the rest of your life count for something.'

On an impulse, he held out his hand to John; he was after all a man from the old country. 'Look after yourself,' he said.

It was some time before the ship sailed but Binnie stuck it out, sitting on the harbour wall, making sure that John left American shores. Only when the ship was out of sight, the sails vanished into the distance, did Binnie feel that he had discharged his debt to the Mandan chief and to the McCabe family.

He walked slowly back to the lodging house and his heart was light. Tomorrow, God willing, he would be able to hold Hortense in his arms.

CHAPTER TWENTY-FIVE

'I'm sorry I've hurt your wife, Joe.' Sho Ka spoke softly. 'I only meant to help, to try to explain how things were between you and me.' She sighed. 'But I didn't realize how angry she would be.'

She was seated in a chair, her shawl wrapped protectively around her ungainly body. She felt sick to her stomach as she remembered Llinos's white face and the tears in her eyes.

'The Mandan ways are not your ways, Joe. You were meant to live as the white man lives, with one woman for life.'

She looked up at him; Joe was not her man but, in the months she had been with him, she had grown to love him. That had not been in the plan. She had been grateful to him for bringing her home with him and for taking care of her. She had quite deliberately enticed him into her bed. Not that he was reluctant, he was a lusty man, but he had betrayed his wife's trust and he felt the guilt keenly.

Perversely enough it was his guilt that built the barrier between Joe and Llinos. He loved his wife deeply and, even though he had been tempted to stray, it was Llinos he wanted.

Still, one day very soon, the parting of the ways would come. Sho Ka would go away from him, away from Swansea, back to America where she belonged. She would be without him and the thought was like a death.

She looked at him now, drinking him in. Joe was staring out of the window, hands thrust into his pockets; he seemed engrossed but she knew he was gazing at nothing. He was missing his home and family.

He did not speak or even turn around and Sho Ka closed her eyes, remembering the sweetness of being with him, holding him, breathing in the scent of him. When he first brought her to Swansea and set her up in a house, he was distant, not wanting to touch her, let alone lie with her.

Sho Ka had put all thoughts of his wife and child out of her mind. She had been determined to have him. She had been shameless in her desire for him. She realized now she had never loved her husband the way she loved Joe.

She drew a ragged breath as she thought about their first night together. She had walked into his room wearing nothing but her beads and feathers. He had looked at her golden skin and she could see the desire in his eyes.

She had slipped into his bed, curled up against him and felt his arousal. He was a man and not made for abstinence. With a groan he had turned to her and her heart soared. He was hers. He had been ashamed in the morning. Unable to face her and afraid to go home to his wife. And yet when

Sho Ka came to him again, he did not turn her away.

It was difficult to explain to a woman not born to Mandan ways the compulsion that drove Joe. He had been Sho Ka's betrothed since childhood; they had grown up together, been inseparable until Joe had been taken away by his white father.

'You have done well to give me a child, Joe. When I go home the tribe will flourish, the crops will grow tall and strong and the Mandan will prosper. Giving me a child was something I wanted so much, so don't blame yourself.' She stared at his straight back, longing to comfort him.

'I wanted you as much as you wanted me, Sho Ka,' he said. 'And I didn't have to take you into my bed but I did, not once but many times.'

'Come here, Joe, please. Let me hold you one last time.'

He knelt beside her, his head resting on her breast. She closed her eyes, thinking again of the early days, of how she had drawn his passion to her with all the wiles she had at her disposal. There was the love potion given her by Grandmother Autumn Leaf, the little pouch wrapped in bison skin that hung even now between Sho Ka's breasts. He had seen it and known at once what it was.

He had stayed with her so long because she was with child and she had no-one else. She knew he ached for his wife, he loved Llinos with all his heart but he was a man with a man's desires.

It was then, when her thoughts were on Joe and their lovemaking, that the pains began. He felt her body tense and looked up into her face.

'The child is coming?'

She nodded; they both knew it would be a boy. Joe's mother was an elder and before she died, she prophesied that the son of Wah-he-joe-tass-ee-neen would one day rule the tribe of the Mandans.

'I'll fetch the midwife.' Joe gently disengaged himself from her arms. He did not have to go far, the midwife was lodging in the house next door.

Sho Ka had never had a child but she knew now that with her husband it had been impossible. She was meant to be the mother of the chief and Joe was the only one who could be the child's father.

The contractions increased but, in spite of the pain, she felt calm and at peace. Her time had come, her son would soon be born.

When the midwife bustled into the room, her sleeves rolled above her elbows, she took Sho Ka into the bedroom. She examined her carefully and at last nodded her head.

'The baby is well on the way,' she said cheerfully. 'This is going to be an easy labour, my love.'

And so it proved to be. Within two hours, the boy lay screaming on the blood-stained sheets, his eyes screwed up, his mouth wide. Sho Ka felt pride run through her; this boy was flesh of her flesh, her son. She looked up at Joe.

'He is going to be a worthy chief and a fine warrior,' she said breathlessly. 'He is handsome just like his father.'

The midwife worked swiftly and soon Sho Ka was sitting up in a clean bed, a cup of tea in her hand. It had puzzled her since she came here why the people of Britain held the drink of tea so highly. It was slightly bitter and dark in colour but she drank it to please the woman who was wrapping the baby in fresh clean linen.

'There, Mother.' She put the child in Sho Ka's arms. 'Here's your boy. I'll come and see you later on today but I don't think you are going to have any problems, that was the easiest birth I've ever attended.'

When she had gone, Sho Ka looked down at the baby: he was golden, his hair, like her own, raven black. He opened his eyes and looked up at her and his eyes were the blue of the river with the sun on it.

'What shall we call him?' Joe touched the petal soft hands and the pride in his face brought a lump to Sho Ka's throat. Her son would grow up on the plains of America far away from his father.

'Blue Rivers,' she said without hesitation. After a moment, Joe nodded. He looked sad, his face bent away from her and she knew his tears were near the surface.

'I will take good care of him,' she said softly. 'All the tribe will love him. He will walk tall like you and be a good fine man. One day he will be chief of the Mandans, what better fate could you want for him?'

'I could want him educated as I was,' Joe said softly. 'I could want him to learn the ways of the white man. I could want a great many things for him.'

Sho Ka shook her head. 'For that you have your first-born son. Blue Rivers is created from Mandan stock, there is only a small part of white man in him.'

'I know.' Joe held out his arms. 'Let me hold

him this once and then I will give him to you for ever.'

Sho Ka watched the love in Joe's eyes and she wanted to weep. Soon she would go home, she would be so alone without Joe. She knew that, back at the village, her suitor waited, the old chief who would take the child as his own. She would live in his lodge, wait on him, lie with him when he wanted it and perhaps she might even grow fond of him, but never would she love him as she loved Joe.

'When I'm strong, I will go home,' she said. 'You must book my passage, Joe.' She hesitated. 'Go now and let me rest, I am very tired.'

When the door closed behind Joe, Sho Ka buried her face in her child's linen wrap and let the hot, bitter tears flood from her eyes.

John Pendennis stepped ashore at the port of Swansea, glad that the long sea journey was over. He had landed at Bristol two days ago and then taken a fishing smack across the channel. On shore, he mingled with the sailors, some with golden skin, some dark as a winter storm. All sorts of people from many nations came and went with the Swansea tides.

He caught sight of a familiar face and stepped behind a pile of boxes. He watched as Joe Mainwaring helped a girl up the gang plank of a ship with sails at half-mast and his eyes narrowed. The girl was dressed in warm clothes, a good gown and a neat coat covered her slender figure. But her hair was as dark as Joe's and he was bending over her in a most solicitous manner. A woman was trotting behind them, she was carrying a baby and, as John watched, Joe turned and spoke to the woman, apparently giving her instructions as he helped her aboard the ship.

Joe and the young foreign woman embraced and then Joe was practically running down the gang plank and leaping onto the dockside as though the devil himself were after him.

It was all very interesting and John felt for the letter that Binnie had entrusted to him. Perhaps he should open it, find out what was going on, it might be something to his own advantage.

First he would find lodgings. He would clean up, make himself presentable, then, when he had sorted out everything in his mind, he would go to Llinos Mainwaring and offer his services.

Llinos stood close to the potter as he threw a large jug, carefully wiping the lip into shape with a damp cloth. She loved the smell of the clay; the sound of the wheel turning was in her blood. She had turned pots herself once when it had been necessary for her to work. She had painted and glazed the china, doing everything that any other potter did. She was still a young woman and should be learning new ways to work and yet she was weary of struggling alone. Without Joe to love and support her she had no enthusiasm for anything.

It hurt that Joe had not even come to Pearl's funeral. It had been a dismal day with clouds racing over the graveyard. Neighbours who had loved Pearl and workers from the pottery crowded around the open grave throwing in flowers, shards of pottery and the dust from the clay. It was their way of sending Pearl to her eternal rest.

Watt touched her shoulder and she looked up, startled out of her thoughts. 'Llinos, John Pendennis is here, he wants to talk to you.'

She nodded. 'I'll see him in a minute, Watt, just show him into the house, will you?'

'Be careful,' Watt said, 'John makes trouble wherever he goes.' He looked down at her, his eyes full of concern. 'He says he has news for you, some story about Joe and the Indian girl.'

'Just bear in mind,' he continued, 'you don't have to believe a word he says. John always thinks of himself first, remember that.' Llinos knew he had seen her face change from indifference to apprehension.

'I'll see him at once.' She hurried up to the house and kicked off her dust-covered shoes at the door. Not waiting for her slippers, she rushed into the drawing room where John Pendennis was standing respectfully near the fireplace.

'Sit down, John,' she said quickly, clenching her hands together to stop them from shaking. 'What do you know about my husband?'

'I'm sorry to be the bearer of bad news, Mrs Mainwaring,' John said gently, 'but I stayed a while in the Mandan village.'

'Yes?'

'I found out that Joe, Mr Mainwaring, had been with this girl Sho Ka when he visited the Mandan tribe. It seems that among the Mandan people Joe and this Sho Ka are considered to be a married couple. They feast openly together, dance those strange Indian dances together, practically fornicating where they stand.'

'Why are you telling me this?' she asked coldly, hating him for rubbing salt into the wound.

'I just thought you would like to know,' John said. 'I saw them on the dock when I landed, your husband and the Indian girl along with her baby were boarding one of the ships.'

Llinos sank into a chair. 'Well, why are you here, John? It isn't simply to tell me this, to hurt me, is that it?'

'No, of course not,' he said. 'I never wanted to hurt you. Though when Binnie Dundee asked me to tell you about Joe, I felt he was right. He knows you better than I do and he thought you would prefer to know the truth.'

'Binnie? What has he got to do with all this?' Llinos rubbed her eyes; she wanted to crawl into bed, to close her eyes and never open them again. She thought of Joe with another child, a baby who would take Lloyd's place in his heart. It made her so angry that she felt physically ill.

John swallowed hard. His shoulders slumped; he was trembling. 'Binnie was good enough to go with me to the coast and see me safely aboard ship,' he said in a low voice. 'He thought you might give me a job. He wanted to help me in any way he could because I'd been through a bad time.'

He paused and rubbed his eyes tiredly. 'My wife, Josephine, she miscarried our baby and it was all too much for her. I lost her too.'

He wiped his eyes impatiently before straightening his shoulders. 'But you have problems of your own, you don't need to hear mine. I'd better go and leave you in peace. In any case, I need to find work and somewhere to stay before nightfall.'

Llinos watched as John walked towards the door. He was very thin, he seemed a shadow of the man he used to be. And if Binnie had wanted to help him it was good enough for her. 'Look, speak to Watt, I'm sure he will find you a job here.' Llinos got to her feet, anxious to be alone.

'I couldn't take advantage of your generosity, not when I've brought you such unwelcome news,' John said. 'I'm sorry for you, really sorry. I know what it's like to lose the one you love.'

John had not been an ideal employee in the past, indeed there was a time when Llinos felt relieved that he had gone to America, but now her heart went out to him. He had aged; his hair was prematurely tinged with grey, his eyes puffy and swollen. Perhaps bad luck followed him around like a curse.

'Haven't you found lodgings for tonight?' she asked more kindly. By the look of the man he had suffered a great deal. He shook his head.

'No but now I have the promise of work I'm sure I will have no difficulty finding somewhere.'

'Look,' Llinos said, 'stay here, at least for tonight. You can sleep in one of the sheds, at least it will be warm and dry.'

'I wouldn't like to impose,' John said. 'It won't take me long to go around Swansea asking for lodgings, don't you worry about me.'

'It's all right,' Llinos said. 'Stay until you find somewhere decent to live, you're welcome.'

'That's very kind of you, Mrs Mainwaring,' he said. 'I've forgotten what it's like to be treated so generously. But, really, I would rather find lodgings in one of the inns nearby. I don't want to impose on your hospitality. Still, I thank you for your kindness from the bottom of my heart.'

'Very well.' Llinos rang the bell for the maid. 'Show Mr Pendennis to the door.' She spoke calmly though it took all her reserves of self-control not to scream and cry and curse her husband's name.

As the door closed behind John, Llinos stared down at her hands, at the ring Joe had placed on her finger, a gold band that she believed tied them together for life. How wrong she had been. It seemed that a few words spoken many years ago over a couple of children living in a Mandan village were more binding than any civilized marriage service conducted in a house of God.

She felt the bitterness of tears burn her eyes. How could Joe say he loved her and then give his love to Sho Ka? Was he simply a good liar? She could picture them on the docks, embracing each other, cooing over the new baby. Joe would be looking down at the Indian girl with the tenderness he had once shown his wife. His hands would touch her hair, her cheek.

'Stop it!' Llinos put her hands to her face. She could not bear to think of them together. She would never forgive Joe for the way he had treated her, never. Nothing on this earth would put right the wrong he had done her. Then why did her body ache for him? Why did her mind and spirit feel so lost without him?

Llinos sighed; she must pull herself together. The only one she was hurting by brooding on Joe's betrayal was herself. In the morning she would speak to Watt, tell him that she had promised John a job. He would not like it one bit; he would frown his disapproval but then that was just too bad. She was the owner of the pottery and the days were long gone when she took directions from any man. From now on, men would have no place in her life, she would have to learn to be independent, to assert herself. She had managed alone before, she would do it again.

Unconsciously she squared her shoulders. She would start with Edward Sparks, she would put the small man in his place, tell him some home truths about his mishandling of her affairs and then she would transfer her account to another bank. If she was destined to live alone then she would make the best of it. One thing she was sure of, she would never trust a man again.

John lay back on the bed in the cosy attic room and stared up at the ceiling. It seemed that once again he had fallen on his feet, he had a roof over his head and he had the promise of a job. He glanced across to where his bag stood on the floor. Inside was most of the money he had taken from Dan McCabe and it was a goodly sum. John supposed he would need to visit a bank as soon as possible, open an account.

He wondered if he would be lucky enough to find a bank manager who would be sympathetic to his needs. Preferably someone not too concerned with the rules. That way, a little money could be made to increase dramatically. Well tomorrow he would go into town, talk to people and see what he could learn. In the meantime, he would enjoy the comfort of a bed that did not move in time to the ocean waves. He closed his eyes and slept.

In the morning, John began to look for proper lodgings. He wanted somewhere cheap and clean where he could impose upon the lady of the house to attend to his laundry. He spent some time in some of the inns on the way into the Stryd Fawr, the High Street where one of the largest banks was situated.

He did not learn a great deal about any of the bank managers and he was coming to the conclusion that they were all as honest as the day was long. It did nothing for his spirits but the beer helped a little. Still, he needed to keep a cool head if he wanted to do business with anyone.

He was leaving the Britannica Inn when he saw a young lady bustling along the pavement towards him, her arms full of packages. She was richly dressed and carried herself like a lady. This impression was confirmed when he saw that she was heading towards a gleaming coach bearing a coat of arms on the door.

The lady dropped one of her packages and John leapt forward to pick it up, doffing his hat politely. 'Thank you, that's so kind of you.' She looked up into his eyes and her expression was that of a harlot not a lady. John read lust there and his pulse quickened. She looked familiar, had he met her before? Or did all whores look the same?

'I couldn't see such a beautiful young woman in distress, could I?' He watched her carefully as she looked towards the carriage, had he misread the warmth in her eyes?

'Could I escort you somewhere?' he asked politely. This would be the test, no respectable woman would agree to trust a man to whom she had not been introduced. She fluttered her eyelashes at him. He had not been mistaken.

'I was just on my way home but I have a raging thirst and could do with a drink of tea,' she said gushingly.

'It would be a delight to accompany you, Mrs . . .?'

'Polly Boucher but you can call me Polly,' she simpered. 'I'll just put my parcels into the carriage and we can go into one of the tea rooms around here if you like.'

'I would like. Very much,' John said easily. He watched as the driver took the parcels from Polly and doffed his cap as she gave him instructions to wait. She came bouncing back to John. Her eyes were gleaming like those of a cat. She was a strange mixture, part lady part whore, and the combination excited him.

He took her into the Castle Hotel and ordered tea. They sat there in silence for a few minutes and then Polly leaned closer to him.

'I must tell you all about Swansea,' she said. 'And the so-called élite of the town.' She had a ready fund of gossip and John listened intrigued. She talked about Eynon Morton-Edwards and his affair with the wife of a bank manager. John smiled at her, encouraging her to go on and she did so, her tongue sharp, her observations even sharper.

'The twins Alice Sparks is carrying, everyone says it's Eynon who is the father.' She dimpled. 'I can well believe it, Mr Sparks looks too effete to produce anything more than a bank draft.'

John leaned across the table allowing his hand to touch hers. Polly did not draw away. 'Ah, you mentioned banks and as it happens I'm looking for somewhere to put my money,' he said. 'I take it you would not recommend I put my trust in Mr Sparks then?'

'Too royal!' Polly said robustly. For a moment she almost sounded as common as a street girl, then she put her head on one side and smiled at him. 'You put your trust in my husband. Jem Boucher is a good businessman and has made a rich living for us both.'

She was once again the lady, well spoken if a little too outspoken. She interested him. 'You are a fascinating lady, you know,' he said softly. 'If you weren't married, I think I could fall for you hook, line and sinker!'

'Oh go away with you, sir.' She looked down, pretending a shyness she clearly did not feel. 'I expect you say that to any lady you chance to take tea with.'

'Well not exactly, I don't know many ladies in Swansea, I have only just returned from the Americas.'

'Oh?' Her eyes were large. 'I hear everyone in America is very wealthy, is that so?'

'It is in my case.' John was exaggerating; he had only the money he had taken from McCabe and, though that was more than John had ever owned in his life, without proper care it would not last him long.

'And you have no wife in America?' Polly asked.

John shook his head. 'I did have but I lost her.' He looked as downcast as he could manage. 'In any case, the marriage was an unhappy one. There were no children, nothing to keep me in America and so I returned to British shores.'

'Ah, marriage, it is not always what we think it to be,' Polly said. 'Though my husband is good to me, he is old and lacks physical prowess, if you know what I mean.' She lowered her lashes but John read her well. If he played his cards right, he would soon have Mrs Polly Boucher between the sheets. Being a paramour to a wealthy woman was a much better prospect than working in the pottery under the surly eye of Watt Bevan.

It was John who brought the interlude to an end. 'I had better return you to your carriage.' He paused and smiled in what he hoped was a rueful manner. 'And, alas, to the arms of your husband.'

Polly seemed taken aback by his decision to leave. She pouted for a moment and then rose to her feet with a flourish.

'You must come to visit us.' She was the haughty lady now. 'We are living in the house once owned by the Morton-Edwards family, do you know it?'

Did he know it? He could scarcely miss what was one of the most elegant houses in the whole town of Swansea. 'I'm sure I could find it.' He leaned forward. 'I have every incentive to do so when there is so much at stake.' She could take that any way she chose. She smiled.

'Are you being naughty, sir?'

'I would love to be naughty with you, Polly.' He kissed her fingers, allowing his mouth to travel to

426

her wrist where a gleaming bracelet hung. He made a quick appraisal. It was made up of at least twelve carats' worth of diamonds, she must be very rich indeed.

'Polly,' his voice took on a sense of urgency, 'please let me see you again, very soon.'

'Tonight?' she said. He looked at her sharply. She rested her free hand against his shirt-front. He congratulated himself on wearing his best linen, bought for him by Josephine.

'Won't your husband object?'

'My dear Jem is away on business and my nights get lonely without him.' She leaned a little closer. 'Just be discreet, that's all I ask. I shall leave the French doors of the drawing room open and you can step inside without anyone being any the wiser.'

'I will count the minutes, dear Polly,' he said earnestly.

As he watched her carriage roll away in a cloud of dust, John smiled to himself. Tonight, if he was any judge, he was in for a good time. Meanwhile, he would spend the rest of the day seeking out Mr Sparks, bank manager. John had the distinct feeling that the two of them would get along very well.

CHAPTER TWENTY-SIX

'Oh for goodness' sake, Edward, be quiet, you're always complaining about something!' This time it was the fact that he might be forced to leave the bank in spite of his efforts to cover up his petty pilfering. Alice was in no mood to listen. She felt her swollen stomach; the twins were overdue, either that or she had got her dates wrong. She would not dwell on that possibility; if she had calculated wrongly, the twins could well be Edward's. The thought left a bitter taste in her mouth. She stared at him now, his thin face lined with misery. 'What do I know about your doings at the bank and more to the point, why should I care?'

She closed her eyes, wishing Edward would go away and leave her in peace. She ached in every bone, her legs and feet were grotesquely swollen and Alice was worried that something was wrong with the twins. Surely it was not normal to go on so long?

Perhaps she would ring for Rosie to bring her some herb tea; the brew was supposed to help a woman through her labour. Alice thought of Rosie with fondness; she had come to depend on her maid more than she had thought possible. She did not even complain when Rosie went up to Greenhill each day to spend a few hours cleaning and cooking in her mother's house.

When Rosie's mother had passed away it was to Alice she came for comfort. To Alice's surprise Rosie's tears had moved her. Perhaps she could ask Rosie her advice about her condition. On the other hand, Rosie was childless; maybe it would be better to have the doctor called in. Oh to hell with it all! She just wanted to sleep.

She closed her eyes but she was restless, unable to relax. 'Edward,' she rubbed her hand across her swollen stomach, 'do you think we should get the doctor? I don't feel well.'

'Who's complaining now?' Edward was triumphant that he had scored a point off her. 'In any case, doctors cost money and, as I keep telling you, that's something we are short of right now.'

Alice was exasperated. 'How can we be short of money after the loan that Eynon Morton-Edwards made us?'

'Don't question me!' Edward rose from his chair. He was thinner than ever, his nose looked longer and was pinched at the nostrils as though he was constantly plagued by a bad smell. He was the meanest man it was ever her misfortune to meet and she was married to him.

'Why shouldn't I question you?' Alice wanted to hit him. 'You haven't been up to your old tricks, have you?'

The look on his face was enough to tell her she had hit the mark. 'Edward! You've been pilfering money again!' She rubbed her eyes. 'You should be looking after me, not worrying me with your troubles at work. What are you doing with all the money, that's what I'd like to know?'

It was not another woman; that much Alice could be sure of. Edward was not one for bed-time games. How she detested him. He was inept at everything he did. He could not even make a decent living for his wife and family.

'Get the maid, Edward,' she said briskly. 'I need something to drink, my throat aches and my head is thumping.'

'It's not my place to fetch the maid.' He was in his pompous mood now, he was such a child. 'I am supposed to be master of the house, you call the maid, the bell is just above you.'

Alice manoeuvred herself to the edge of the chair and, with a great effort, managed to get to her feet. She tugged at the bell cord, feeling breathless even with such a slight exertion. Surely something must be wrong?

'Bring me some tea, Rosie, please,' she said as the maid came into the room. 'And some of that herb stuff for headaches. Hurry, there's a good girl.' She subsided into her chair with a feeling of relief.

The tea was warm and comforting after the bitter taste of the herbal remedy Rosie had prepared for her.

'You shouldn't drink that poison.' Edward pointed at the empty glass. 'It smells foul, you don't know what it's doing to your insides.'

'It cures my aches and pains and that's all I care about,' Alice said defiantly. She leaned back in her chair and closed her eyes. Perhaps she would try again to sleep and then she might feel better. In any case, closing her eyes and pretending to sleep would give her some respite from Edward's constant whining.

Alice relaxed, her mind felt as though it had been wrapped in wool, the pain in her head abated and she slept.

John Pendennis had arranged to see Edward Sparks first thing on Monday morning. He was there bright and early and though he was irritated at being kept waiting he smiled pleasantly and held out his hand.

He could see at once that his manner of speaking and the way he was dressed impressed Sparks; the man managed a smile and gestured towards a chair on the opposite side of the desk.

'What can I do for you, Mr Pendennis?' Sparks spoke in clipped tones as though reluctant to allow the words to pass his lips. John summed him up at once: he was mean spirited and game for anything. He was a crook.

'There is a venture I'm interested in, a real money spinner.' John smiled. 'Within a year I aim to treble my initial investment.'

Sparks sat forward in his chair. 'Might I ask what this investment is?' He was clearly interested. His small eyes gleamed behind his spectacles.

'Ah, now this is where you come in,' John said. 'I'm going to need some help.' He smiled easily, noting the way Sparks sat back in his chair.

'If you are asking me to make an investment along with you then you are out of luck.' He pressed his thin fingers together. 'It is not bank policy to let the managers become embroiled in financial dealings with customers.'

'All I would need from you is some information,' John said.

'What sort of information?' Sparks's tone was guarded. His shoulders were tense and in spite of his attempt to appear casual, the interest was back in his eyes. 'And what would be in it for me?'

John knew he had the man hooked. Greed was an overpowering emotion and Edward Sparks had more than his fair share of it.

'That depends,' John said. He was playing the man along, tempting him and then withdrawing the bait. Sparks was practically drooling at the prospect of getting in on something that would make him rich.

'You could earn yourself as much as a forty per cent share in the profits I make,' John said. 'If the advice you give me is valuable enough.' It was time to get to the point.

'I want to buy the Mainwaring Pottery,' he said. 'I hear the owners went through a shaky period some time ago, unpaid debts, that sort of thing.'

'I am not in a position to disclose personal details,' Sparks said uneasily. John concealed a smile, his information had been correct, it had been well worth him cultivating Polly Boucher; she was a gossip of the first order. She advised John to put his money in safer hands because Sparks was about to be dismissed from his position and lucky not to be prosecuted for misappropriation, if not downright dishonesty.

He smiled; her enthusiastic response in the

bedroom was gratifying, bringing him gifts of fine jewellery as well as generous sums of money. He expected more to come from that quarter and felt that risking his own small resources was no risk at all.

He had only known her a little over a week but already Polly was dependent on him the way women were, clinging to him, begging him to stay with her just a little longer, bribing him with her lithe body as well as with her money.

He met Sparks's eyes. 'Cut the garbage!' he said. 'We both know you were involved in the decline of the Mainwaring Pottery. You did it once, you could do it again and this time with rich pickings.' He smiled.

'Once the property falls low enough in price, I intend to buy it and build it up. Once the creditors know the place is under new management they will supply all that I need to work the place.'

'But have you experience in that line?' Sparks asked uneasily. 'Potting is not such an easy business, you know.'

'I grew up with it, damn you!' John said. 'Do I look the sort of man who would go into something half cocked?'

He rose to his feet. 'If you are not interested then I will find someone who has the intelligence to recognize a good proposition when it comes along.' He paused. 'I have looked at the books, that pottery is a little goldmine, believe me.'

'But Mrs Mainwaring might notice something.' Sparks was weakening. 'I managed to cover the discrepancies up last time, claim there was an unavoidable mistake. Which there was of course,' he added hastily. 'I had no intention of bringing the price of the pottery down, you see it was, as I said, a mistake.'

'But you had a buyer for the place. You were offered a generous sum of cash if you persuaded Mrs Mainwaring to sell, isn't that so?'

Sparks raised thin eyebrows. 'Supposing what you say is correct, what would be in it for me?'

'You would have a nice little sum of money by way of a thank you gesture.' John smiled. 'I understand you might be dismissed from your post any day now.'

Sparks ignored that remark and raised his last objection. 'There's Watt Bevan, he's no idiot, he'd know something was wrong even if Mrs Mainwaring failed to notice.'

John knew the man had picked on the only real flaw in the plan. Watt Bevan was astute and he was in charge of most sections of the potting business. But then, accidents could happen to anyone.

'I'll take care of Watt Bevan,' John said slowly. 'All I want from you is a small diversion of funds from the Mainwaring account to mine.' John took his bag from his belt and threw it on the desk. 'I think you'll find a small sum of money there, just enough to open an account. I expect that account to grow. Do you understand?'

'I'll do what I can.' Sparks's greedy hand reached for the bag. He adjusted his glasses and stared at the contents. The small sum John had mentioned was quite substantial by Sparks's reckoning. 'I think we might be able to do business, Mr Pendennis,' he said.

'Good. Now a receipt if you please. I am a

cautious man when it comes to business.' He smiled and waited while Sparks carefully wrote out a receipt and signed it with a flourish.

John leaned over the desk, his face close to the bank manager's beaky nose. 'Don't double-cross me, I'm not a forgiving man.' He stood up. 'I'll say good-day to you, Mr Sparks, for now.'

As John left the bank he was elated, the first part of his plan had been put into action. He had fooled Sparks into thinking he was very rich and persuaded him to leach funds from the Mainwaring Pottery accounts. Now, his business done, he could have a little fun.

'John!' Polly greeted him with shining eyes and a beaming smile. 'I didn't expect to see you today.'

'My lady employer gave me time off to go to the bank and to find a place to live,' he said, easing himself past Polly's clutching hands. The little trollop could not wait to get him into bed.

'Jem at home?'

'No, silly!' Polly ushered him into the drawing room, issuing a sharp order to the maid that she did not wish to be disturbed. 'He's gone up to London on business, I told you he would be away, didn't I?'

'So you did.' He looked around at the plush room and envied Polly her wealth. 'I can't stay long, I have to look for lodgings. That inn where I'm staying is such a dreadful little place, it smells of beer day and night.'

'No need,' Polly said, a pleased look on her face. 'I've rented a little house down on Broad Street for you.' She began to unbutton his shirt. 'Our own little love nest.'

John was taken aback at the way she was taking charge. Polly was a woman who knew what she wanted and, right now, she wanted John Pendennis. He would be a fool not to be flattered and yet he felt a slight resentment that she was taking him for granted.

'Who says I want to have a love nest with you, Mrs Boucher?' he said and there was a sharp note in his voice that was not lost on Polly.

'Oh dear, have I offended your silly male pride?' She ran her hands over his chest. Her fingers were warm against his skin and, in spite of himself, John was aroused. Polly smiled at him beguilingly.

'I didn't mean to upset you, my lovely, but I have lots of money and I like to give gifts to my friends, please don't be cross with me.'

She had totally misunderstood his mood. John was not averse to taking Polly's handouts; he just did not like the feeling of a woman being in control. Still, he would teach her who was boss when the time was right.

He took her on the rich carpet and was surprised at his own passionate response to Polly's uninhibited lovemaking. It was a long time since he had enjoyed a wanton woman, too long. It was over quickly and he read Polly's disappointment.

'Give me a little time, darling,' he said leaning up on one elbow. 'I will make sure you have your pleasure in just a moment.' He touched her breast with his fingertips. 'And forgive my haste, it's just that you are so skilful a lover and so very beautiful. I just could not contain myself.'

He could see by the glow in her face that his words pleased her. She lay at his side, naked and abandoned, her legs splayed, her arms, pale and beautiful, reaching up for him. She was, he realized, a very lovely girl. She was wealthy and she spoke well and yet, underneath the veneer, John sensed there lurked a street girl, a common hussy who would lie with any man. The thought excited him. He rolled onto her and Polly closed her eyes in ecstasy.

This time, he was more restrained. He teased her and made her beg for release and, when it came, she thrashed beneath him drinking the sensations he was giving her, begging for more.

Later, when they were dressed, Polly saw him to the door. 'Please call again, Mr Pendennis,' she said formally, aware that one of the maids was hovering at her elbow. 'I'm sure my husband will be sorry to have missed you.'

As John walked away, he felt the keys in his pocket and smiled. His relationship with Polly Boucher had begun well and could, if he gave it time, make him a very rich man.

'It's true,' Watt looked miserable, 'the house in Neath is now occupied by a family with five children. There is no sign of Joe, nothing to show that he was ever there.'

'Perhaps he's gone to America to live,' Llinos said, her voice soft, her heart breaking. She harboured a hope that one day Joe would come back to her. But he had chosen Sho Ka, he had probably followed her to America; set up home there among his own people. Perhaps he was more Indian than white man and the tame life married to a small-time businesswoman had never suited him.

'He might come back,' Watt said. 'I can't see him leaving Swansea without saying goodbye, at least to Lloyd, can you?'

Llinos shook her head. 'I don't know anything any more, not about my husband anyway.' She forced herself to smile.

'We'd better get to work on the new designs, the pottery is selling so well that we will soon have to expand the business premises. At least I have no money worries.' Which was just as well because Joe had not thought to see her provided for.

'I don't know about that, Llinos,' Watt spoke slowly. 'For some reason sales have dropped, we are having to cut back on production for the time being.'

'That's strange.' Llinos was puzzled. 'The "Maidens at the Well" design was so popular. What's happened?'

'Jem Boucher,' Watt said glumly. 'He's part of the consortium that owns the pottery next door. He's had his artists copy our patterns almost to the last detail and, what's more, he is undercutting us for price. We will just have to think of something else, I'm afraid.'

Llinos sighed; much as she wanted to put business first and to put Joe out of her mind, it was impossible.

'I have a headache, I promise I'll talk about this tomorrow,' she said. It was as though this last blow was too much for her to cope with. Joe had vanished; he had left the house in Neath without contacting her. Llinos wanted to crawl into bed, draw the sheets over her head and sleep her troubles away.

'That's fine,' Watt said. 'You do look a bit pale. Take care of yourself, Llinos, I'll get off home now, the boys will be waiting for their tea. I'll see you in the morning.'

When she was alone she made her way slowly to her bedroom and locked the door. She wished she could cry but her tears were all dried up and what she was left with was a feeling of despair. She had lost Joe forever. She climbed onto the bed and closed her eyes, praying for sleep. But sleep would not come. She could picture them together, Sho Ka, the baby and Joe, and the thought was like a knife turning in her heart.

CHAPTER TWENTY-SEVEN

'I want you to come back to me,' Watt said. 'Your brothers see you but by the time I come home you've gone.' Rosie looked at him; he was shadowed by darkness, hovering on the back step of Alice Sparks's house. 'I wanted a chance to talk to you. I want you to come home so that we can give our marriage another chance.'

Rosie bit her lip. She tried to read Watt's expression, was there even a hint that he needed her? She waited, perhaps he would plead with her, tell her he loved her, that he realized he could not live without her. He remained silent.

'Why do you want me to come home, Watt? Everything is done for you, the cooking, cleaning and the washing. The only thing I don't do is warm your bed.' There was bitterness in her voice that she had never expected to feel.

He thrust his hands into his pockets, and looked up at the sky. 'That's not fair, Rosie. Can't you see it's not good to be alone all the time?'

'I'm sorry you don't like being alone but that's not my problem,' Rosie said. She was appalled by his selfish attitude; all he worried about was being on his own. 'Well what about the boys?' Watt spoke quickly. 'You can't say they are not your problem. You promised Pearl you would take care of them.'

That was not what she had wanted him to say. 'And I do take care of them! They are well fed and they have clean clothes to wear. And, don't forget, the boys are growing up, they are never indoors during the evenings from what you say about being alone.'

A sense of anger and disappointment filled her. Watt saw her merely as a convenience, a maid of all work at best, someone to keep him company in the long evenings. Well he was out of luck.

'Sorry, Watt, I don't want to come home.' She was energized by her anger. 'I am quite happy here working for an honest living.' She stepped back a pace, shivering as a cold breeze touched her bare arms.

'You married me to help the family, didn't you? And that's what you're doing so don't dare complain to me about it. In any case, I don't want to live my life in the shadow of Maura Dundee forever.'

'Rosie!' Watt sounded desperate. 'You know I care for you, otherwise I wouldn't be here asking you to come back.'

'Caring is one thing, loving is another. You married me out of a sense of duty,' she said stiffly. 'And because you thought I'd make a good housekeeper.' She lifted her chin. 'Well I deserve better than second best. Goodnight, Watt.'

She closed the door firmly in his face and

returned to the kitchen where the new maid was building up the fire. Beatie was a big girl, built like a peasant but her manner was pleasant enough.

Alice claimed that doing all the work was too much for Rosie, she needed her more as a confidante and friend. They had become as close as employer and servant could be. Alice was not the cold-hearted woman she had first appeared.

'Cup of tea, Mrs Bevan?' Beatie was older than Rosie but she was unmarried and showed Rosie the deference her position demanded. 'Mrs Sparks won't notice if we take just a few leaves out of the tin.'

'Yes, why not, Beatie?' Rosie sank into a chair, her head was aching but the ache in her heart was worse than any physical pain. Watt did not love her; he made that clear every time he approached her. Was he too insensitive to realize that all she wanted was to be loved as a woman should be loved?

'Trouble?' Beatie put the cup of tea on the table and sat down. 'I couldn't help hearing the sound of a man's voice at the back door.'

'Nothing I can't handle,' Rosie said quietly. She had no intention of confiding in Beatie. Rosie liked to keep her affairs private. 'Have you prepared the vegetables for tomorrow's dinner?'

'Yes, Mrs Bevan, I've done some carrots and leeks for the stew and soaked the salt fish ready for our own supper.'

'Right then, I think I'll just go up to bed.' Rosie picked up her candle and left Beatie sitting at the table. The hall was large and full of shadows and Rosie longed for the comfort of the small cottage where she had lived with her mother. In spite of her brave words to Watt, she would rather be home than living here in a house that was too large for comfort. Rosie liked the simple life.

She held the candle high as she climbed the stairs. On the landing she stopped abruptly, hearing moaning sounds coming from Alice's bedroom. Rosie hesitated; should she enquire if everything was all right or should she just go to bed?

'Help me!' Alice cried out and startled Rosie almost dropped the candle. The door to Edward Sparks's room remained firmly closed.

'For pity's sake someone help me!'

Rosie opened the door and held the candle high. Alice was crouched on the bed, her eyes wide with fear. 'Get the doctor, Rosie, for pity's sake! My labour's started, I'm in agony!'

Rosie ran back down the stairs and burst into the kitchen. Beatie looked startled as she stepped back quickly from the arms of a strange young man.

'I'm sorry Mrs Bevan!' Beatie sounded panic-stricken. 'My sweetheart called to see if I was all right. I know it's late for callers and it won't happen again.'

'Never mind that!' Rosie said. 'Fetch the nearest doctor, Mrs Sparks is having her twins!'

Beatie took her coat from the back door and flung it around her shoulders. 'I'll be as quick as I can but don't worry, by the sound of her, Mrs Sparks will drop her babies in double-quick time.'

Rosie hoped not. She had enough of babies at home; she did not fancy delivering Alice Sparks's twins. Alice was kind and much more considerate these days but if anything happened to her while Rosie was in charge there would be all hell to pay. Rosie lifted her skirts and ran quickly back up the stairs.

'I've decided to change the patterns again.' Llinos was scribbling over her drawing pad and spoke without looking up at Watt. One glance had been enough to tell her he was not feeling well. His eyes were shadowed and he had become thinner. She did not want to see too clearly. Llinos felt she could only handle her own pain at the moment. She felt she would break under the strain if she took on the troubles of others.

'We shall introduce a more local look to the china. The beach, the rocks of Mumbles Head. Perhaps the ruined castle would make a good design, what do you think?'

'I'm not sure, Llinos.' Watt said doubtfully. 'You know the people of Swansea like the traditional patterns, flowers and things.'

'I have to do something different,' Llinos said. 'You know that our profit is lower than it has been for years.'

'Yes, but something is wrong,' Watt said. 'It's not just that Jem Boucher is undercutting us for price, there's more to this than meets the eye.'

'Well, don't talk about it just now,' Llinos said, not wanting to be drawn too deeply into a discussion about business matters. She was inventing new patterns; she was cutting down on workers, what more could she do?

'I mean that yet again the bills are not being

444

paid.' Watt leaned forward, his hands on the small oval table and forced Llinos to look at him. 'We are in debt with the suppliers for the second time in a few months, something is badly wrong, Llinos.'

Llinos felt as though her head were filled with cotton wool. 'Well, what do you think the mistake is this time then?' Her tone was more than a little sharp.

'This is no mistake!' Watt said. 'We are being swindled!' He thumped his fist on the table. 'Wake up, Llinos, face facts will you? You should have changed banks months ago.'

'I'm just so tired.' Llinos rubbed her eyes wearily. She put down her pencil and leaned back in her chair. 'I can't cope with any extra worry, can't you deal with this for me?'

'No I can't! I can't sign the papers to close the account nor to open a new one somewhere else. I'm sorry, Llinos, but it's time you shook yourself out of your apathy and took charge before everything falls to pieces.'

Llinos held up her hands. 'I know, I know.'

'Look.' His tone was more kindly now he had got her attention. 'I'll come with you to the bank to sort everything out. There should be more than enough money to pay all the bills.'

'Even with the drop in sales we've suffered?'

'Even then,' Watt said firmly. 'Now make up your mind, Llinos, you have to take an interest in the pottery now or our creditors will close you down.'

'All right, we'll go to town tomorrow,' Llinos said quietly. She was tired, so tired. If only Watt

445

understood how disheartened she was, how weary of being alone; of spending long days and even longer nights without Joe. How could she think of business when her heart was breaking?

Watt sighed in resignation. 'All right, Llinos, I'll get down there and make an appointment. We won't see Sparks this time; we'll see the owner of the bank. I understand your father and he were friends? Well, it's about time we started asking serious questions about what's been happening to our funds.'

She scarcely noticed him leaving the room. She looked down at the paper and the patterns merged before her eyes. Watt was right; she had been neglecting everything, the pottery, her sister-in-law and most of all her son. She had been wallowing in self-pity for too long and she should be ashamed of herself. She screwed the paper into a ball and pushed it away. Then she put her head down on her arms and wept.

Watt did not give up easily. The next morning he was there, dressed for a trip to town, obviously expecting her to accompany him. She made an effort to smile. 'All right, I give in, I'll get my coat.'

The sun was shining on the cobbles of Pottery Row as the horse and trap bumped its way out of the pottery gates. Llinos sat beside Watt watching his strong hands holding the reins with ease as he guided the horse out onto the broad road running into town.

'I don't know what we'll achieve,' Llinos said. 'I don't even know if we'll be given an appointment at such short notice.'

'It's done,' Watt said. 'We have an appointment

for nine-thirty.' He glanced at her. 'I'm afraid it has to be Sparks himself, he's been left in charge. Apparently the owner of the bank is not in the best of health. That's the only reason Sparks is still working there at all.'

'I see,' Llinos was uneasy. 'There's something in his manner that gives me the creeps.'

'Then let me deal with him,' Watt said. 'If there is anything to sign, I'll read it over first.' He glanced at her. 'You are doing the right thing, you know, Llinos. I will feel more confident when your money is in another bank.'

'Yes, so will I.' Llinos said. The trap bounced over a stone and Llinos clung to Watt's arm. 'Don't drive so fast, Watt, you'll have us in the road!'

'Don't worry.' Watt smiled. 'I'm used to driving in worse conditions than this. Relax now, we'll soon be there.'

He was right; within a few minutes he was clucking to the animal to stop. He tied the reins of the horse to one of the trees and helped Llinos down.

Mr Sparks kept them waiting for twenty minutes and Llinos was seething with anger by the time they were shown into his office. She stared at him, ready to do battle, but he pushed his glasses more firmly into place, treating Llinos as though he had never seen her before.

'I did not realize you would have company.' Sparks sounded disapproving. 'It is not usual to discuss business matters with a third party present.'

'That's just too bad.' Watt's voice was harsh.

447

'I'm staying and there's nothing you can do about it.' He loomed over the desk and Sparks glanced at him anxiously.

'Please be seated,' he said quickly. 'I'm sure we can clear this matter up very quickly.'

'What matter?' Watt said. Sparks looked at him in surprise. He seemed at a loss for a moment, his Adam's apple bobbing up and down as he swallowed.

'Well, I presume there is a problem otherwise you would not be here.' He recovered his composure and sat up straighter in his chair.

'There is a problem certainly,' Watt said. 'Funds are disappearing from Mrs Mainwaring's account at an alarming rate. We want an explanation.'

'Well, your business, Mrs Mainwaring, it hasn't been doing so well lately, has it?'

It was Watt who replied. 'We know that but, all the same, we were making a more than healthy profit up to a few months ago, the pottery should be able to sustain a bad patch.'

'Well, I don't really know what I can do about your profits.' Sparks adjusted his glasses. 'I am having difficulty working out why you came here.'

'I'll put it bluntly, we came here to close the account,' Watt said sharply. 'And to have a complete audit done on the bank records and I want to know why the last audit was cancelled.'

'The audit was not cancelled, the books were examined and everything was in order,' Sparks said quickly. 'I hope you are not suggesting that anything improper has occurred?'

'We're not suggesting anything,' Watt said.

'We're telling you that we want to withdraw all the money left in the account.'

All at once, Sparks seemed to lose his aplomb. He took a handkerchief out of his pocket and mopped his brow. Llinos could see beads of sweat on his nose and forehead and she frowned. Sparks was afraid, he was hiding something. Was it possible he had been misappropriating funds?

'Mr Bevan is quite right,' she said firmly. 'I want to close my account and I want the papers ready to sign right now.'

'But that's impossible! I can't work miracles you know. You will have to give me at least until the end of the week to sort this matter out.' He paused to take a deep breath. 'I have a life outside the bank, you know, even now my dear Alice is in labour.'

'Your personal life is no concern of ours,' Watt said. 'I repeat we want to close the account and we want to do it today.'

Llinos knew Alice Sparks had been having an affair with Eynon but clearly Sparks had no idea about his wife's infidelity. She suddenly felt sorry for him. He cut a pathetic figure with sweat running down his face and his glasses slipping along his prominent nose but he was a fellow human being. If he ever discovered that his wife had been unfaithful, he would feel as humiliated and betrayed as she did.

'We'll give you until the end of the week,' she said. She held up her hand as Watt made to protest. 'I've made up my mind.' She looked at Watt and saw the protest trembling on his lips but he held his peace.

Once they were outside the bank, he took her arm. 'Llinos, don't you realize what you have done?'

'I've given Mr Sparks some time to put matters right, if, as I suspect, he is responsible for the state of my accounts,' she said. 'Everyone is deserving of a chance to right a wrong, you know.'

'Would you say that to Joe if he should come back to you now?' Watt said and Llinos felt her colour rise.

'That was unkind, Watt.' She spoke unsteadily.

'I know, I'm sorry. Forget I spoke.' Watt helped her up into the trap. 'But I still think you have let your heart rule your head. There is nothing to stop Sparks from clearing off with whatever money he's pilfered from the bank.'

'I know.' Llinos settled her cloak around her knees. Suddenly, she felt cold, as though a chill wind had swept over her. If Joe should come to see her she would fling herself into his arms and forgive him anything. Oh yes, she could forgive him but could she ever trust him again? She looked along the road, it seemed to stretch before her long and empty. It was a reflection of what her life had become. Empty.

'Oh God, Rosie!' Alice clutched the girl's arm, feeling the pain tear through her. 'Am I going to die?'

It was Dr Rogers who replied. 'Stop fussing, Mrs Sparks, this is something women experience every day and you are no different to any other. You are going to be perfectly all right.'

The pain intensified; her bones felt as if they

were being pulled apart. She held her breath and squeezed her eyes shut, scarcely daring to breathe until the pain subsided.

'I don't feel all right, Doctor,' she said. 'Women have children every day and women die in their childbed every day so don't talk to me as though I was an ignorant peasant.'

She could see that the old doctor was taken aback by her tone. He had come into the room with his bag and had patronized her since the moment he first looked at her. Had she been living at home with her father, enjoying the large airy rooms and the huge gardens, the doctor's attitude would have been completely different.

It brought home sharply to Alice that, now, married to Edward, she was considered a lesser person, a woman of little background and even less consequence. She had no doubt that the doctor would not bat an eyelid if she joined the ranks of women whose childbed was also their deathbed.

'If anything happens to me,' she said, 'my father Dennis Carrington will stuff the Hippocratic oath right down your throat, is that clear?'

He looked at her sharply. 'Your father is Dennis Carrington? *The* Dennis Carrington?'

'That's right. So take good care of me, Doctor.' She stopped speaking as the contractions came again, tightening round her body like a ring of fire.

'Are you hoping for a son, Mrs Sparks?' The doctor now had a solicitous tone in his voice. 'A grandson for Mr Carrington?'

Alice glared at him. 'I'm having twins, you fool! Take care that you get this delivery over as soon as possible. Oh Lord! Someone help me!'

She felt the pain swamp her entire body. She was going to die; the twins would never be born. She clung to Rosie's hand and fear was a hard knot inside her chest. She tried to calm herself but the pain was getting worse.

'Oh thank God!' She relaxed as the pain eased again. She appealed to Rosie. 'I am going to be all right, aren't I? Your mother had children and she lived through the birth, didn't she?'

'Bless you, yes! It always hurts a lot but once it's over and you see your babies you forget the pain.' Rosie was trying to sound encouraging but she had little faith in the old doctor, she had heard stories about his incompetence, but this was not the time to say so.

'Will it take much longer now, do you think?' Alice was aware of the pitiful tone of her voice. But she had no pride, no dignity, not with her rear end bare and the doctor fumbling about under her gown.

'Well, Beatie reckons you have the look of a woman who births quickly. It can't be much longer. Just hold onto my hand when the next pain comes and push with all your might.'

Alice heard the doctor grunt; she looked up at him and knew something was wrong.

'I pray to God it'll be over soon,' she said. 'I don't think I could stand much more of this pain. Why didn't someone tell me having children was going to be like this?'

She subsided again as the tearing pain engulfed her. Surely it was more than womankind could bear? She felt the hot flow of blood and cried out in fear. She was going to die; she would never live to see another day, to punish all men for what they had done to her. Damn it! She would not die!

She bore down when the doctor told her to and in between contractions she fell back exhausted against the pillows. At last, the doctor came and stood beside her.

'I'm afraid we have to make a choice, Mrs Sparks,' he said, 'between your life and the life of the infants.'

'Oh my God!' Alice said hoarsely. She looked at Rosie and then back at the doctor. 'What does that mean?'

'All I can say is save yourself,' Dr Rogers said. 'The babies have been through too much to survive.'

Alice began to cry as the doctor returned to the foot of the bed and took a fearsome-looking instrument from his bag. Alice heard her own screams and then she surrendered herself to a merciful darkness where there was no more pain.

When she woke it was to see Edward sitting beside her. A nurse was bustling around the room; of the doctor there was no sign.

'The babies?' she said. Edward shook his head, he seemed grey, his face thinner than ever. 'What's happened?'

'The twins are dead, Alice. They could not survive after what the doctor had to do.'

Alice began to cry; she wanted warm arms around her, she needed comforting words but Edward offered neither. 'Fetch Rosie,' she whispered and Edward, his face alight with relief, disappeared swiftly from the room.

Rosie sat with her, holding her hand. 'It was for the best,' she said but her face was white with shock.

'What did they look like?' Alice asked faintly. Rosie bent her head for a moment.

'The boys would have been a credit to you. But it wasn't meant to be.' She pushed back Alice's hair. 'How would you have managed with sickly children?'

Alice squeezed Rosie's hand. 'Why are you so kind to me?' she asked humbly. 'I'm not a nice person, I'm sharp and thoughtless and I put on you dreadfully and yet you are the only one to show me any compassion.'

'I like you, Mrs Sparks,' Rosie said simply.

'You don't mind when I raise my voice to you and order you around as if you had no feelings?'

'I've seen the other side of you.' Rosie said. 'When Mammy was sick you sent us food, you waited for me to come back to work, you didn't dismiss me. You have a good heart, Mrs Sparks.'

'Thank you for that, Rosie,' Alice said. 'It's the nicest thing anyone has ever said to me. If ever I can do anything for you I will.'

She closed her eyes. 'I will never have another baby, will I, Rosie?'

'I don't know, Mrs Sparks, I just don't know about that.'

'No,' Alice shook her head. 'There will be no more children for me. I'm finished with men for good.' She opened her eyes.

'I'm going to tell you something now, Rosie, that I would never tell anyone else in the whole world.' She sighed heavily. 'The twins were not my husband's, the father was Eynon Morton-Edwards.'

'I know,' Rosie said. 'I've known about you and him for a long time.' She looked solemn. 'In any case the twins were the image of Mr Morton-Edwards.' It was a lie but she told it boldly. 'As I said, you would have been proud of them.'

'I'm glad about that,' Alice said. 'I was so overdue I was beginning to think Edward was the father.' She smiled weakly. 'And I would have hated them to look like him. I'm going to try to sleep now, Rosie, but promise you'll stay with me.'

'I promise,' Rosie said at once, settling herself more comfortably in the chair. Alice sighed wearily; she could sleep now, knowing she was safe with Rosie beside her.

CHAPTER TWENTY-EIGHT

'I am convinced I was not the father of the twins!' Edward was standing over Alice as she lay in bed. The ache in her body was nothing compared to the pain in her heart. She did not care that Edward was glowering at her like one possessed. She had other things to think about. Even ten days after the birth, she was still weak; she had lost a great deal of blood. On the third day her milk had come flowing in and she felt tearful and lost without the babies to hold in her arms.

'I always suspected you were having an affair with Morton-Edwards and this confirms my doubts. Look!' Edward waved the note before her eyes and she turned away. She knew the contents by heart. Eynon had written to her commiserating over the loss of the twins. It was an innocent note, polite and distant, offering help as any neighbour would, but Alice could read between the lines. So apparently could Edward.

'All this talk about you doing good works for charity and claiming that man lent us money because he was a friend of your father, it was all lies, wasn't it?'

'Shut up, Edward,' Alice said flatly. 'And get out of my bedroom, you were never any use in it anyway.'

'So that was your excuse for having an affair with Morton-Edwards, was it?' He was pompous now, even in this moment of anger. His pride meant more to him than the well-being of his wife.

'How many other men have there been, Alice? Tell me that.' His thin face was red, his eyes narrowed, he looked almost dangerous. He was a man on the edge of madness and Alice felt the time had come for a little diplomacy.

'There have been no other men, Edward.' Her tone was conciliatory. 'We are both devastated because we lost our babies but you mustn't take your anger out on me; I did my best.'

He sank into the chair at the side of the bed. 'Alice, I don't know what to believe any more. All I know is that I'm being badgered on all sides. This man, John Pendennis, he promised me the earth if I would leach funds from the Mainwaring account. Then I find that the man is not wealthy at all, he needs other backers to help him buy the pottery and I think he has found them.'

'What do you mean?' Alice asked, struggling to sit up.

'Jem Boucher, the man who bought the pottery from Morton-Edwards, he has a hand in all this. He wants to amalgamate the two potteries.' He walked about the room, his hands thrust in his pocket.

'You see what will happen, Boucher will put up the money to back Pendennis and I'll end up in prison. You must do something to help me, Alice.'

'I'll try,' she said. 'Leave me, Edward. Is the old man still sick?'

'What old man?'

'The old man who owns the bank of course!' Alice was fast losing patience. 'While the old man is not at the helm you must go to the bank and pretend there is nothing wrong. In a few days I should be well enough to take a carriage ride over to my father's house. I'm sure he'll help us.'

Edward's face brightened. 'I need to have money as soon as possible,' he said. 'Otherwise we are ruined. All this', he gestured around the plush bedroom, 'will be taken from us. You will be destitute, Alice.'

She had no intention of being destitute. 'I'll do what I can,' she said. 'Now go, before anyone starts prying into your business at the bank.'

'It's all that woman's fault,' he said moodily. 'What sort of woman marries a half-breed? And then she couldn't keep him. He ran off and what else could you expect from an ignorant foreigner?'

Alice closed her eyes. 'Go away, Edward,' she said. 'I need to rest if I'm to do battle with Father.'

Mercifully he went then, closing the door firmly behind him. She had helped Edward out of his last escapade; she would not help him again. She could hear him banging about in the hallway, raising his voice, berating Rosie for something that was not her fault. Poor girl, it was a wonder she put up with it. The front door slammed; Edward had left for work.

Alice rang the bell and Rosie came at once, her face flushed, her lips tightly closed.

'Take no notice of Edward.' Alice pushed aside

the bedclothes. 'He's a fool.' She slipped out of bed. 'Fetch my travelling clothes, Rosie,' she said. 'And pack up a few things for both of us.' Alice smiled. 'You and I are leaving at once. To all intents and purposes I shall be convalescing at my father's house but if I have any say in the matter we will never set foot in this place again.'

She saw Rosie hesitate and knew at once what was bothering her.

'Daddy does not live very far, Rosie, it's just a carriage ride away. You can visit your brothers as often as you like, I promise.'

Rosie nodded. 'Thank you, Mrs Sparks.' She pulled the travelling bag out of the wardrobe and neatly packed into it the clothes that she knew would be needed. That was one thing about Rosie, she could think for herself, she did not have to be told every little thing. And she did not ask questions. She was prepared to go with Alice, to trust her, and that made Alice warm towards Rosie as she had never warmed to anyone before.

'I'm very fond of you, Rosie,' she said. 'I wouldn't have managed without you these past weeks.'

Rosie smiled. 'Well, I could say the same.' She straightened. 'I had nowhere to go, I couldn't live with Watt once I knew he didn't love me.'

'There, then, the arrangements I've made to go home to my father should suit the both of us.'

'What about Mr Sparks?' Rosie said tentatively. Alice smiled widely and put her hand on Rosie's shoulder.

'Mr Sparks is not worth a moment's consideration.' She allowed Rosie to help her dress.

'He has made a mess of his life and now it's up to him to sort it all out.' She shrugged her bodice over her still full breasts. 'He can rot in jail for all I care, I've helped the man as much as any wife could and he still can't manage his affairs.'

When she left the house Alice did not even look back. That part of her life was over for good. Her father would take her back; he would have to or she would threaten to expose him to all his friends as a man who would turn a sick daughter away from his door.

'Come on, Rosie,' Alice said. 'There's a better life waiting for us and you and I are going to enjoy it to the full.'

'The week you allowed Sparks is almost up, Llinos.' Watt was looking worried; he approached the table where she was busy writing. His eyes were heavy as though he had not slept. 'I think we should go down to the bank again, find out exactly what's happening.'

'I'll leave you two alone.' Charlotte put down her sewing and got slowly to her feet. Llinos tried to smile cheerfully. 'No, don't go, Charlotte.'

'I need my afternoon sleep,' Charlotte said. 'I'll speak to you later.'

When the door closed behind Charlotte, Llinos sighed. 'Look, Watt, wait until tomorrow. If Sparks can put matters right then he will. I'm sure he has no intention of going to prison.'

'Did you know that his wife has left him?' Watt persisted. 'I went over there to see Rosie but she wasn't there, neither was Mrs Sparks. The maid, Beatie, couldn't say where they'd gone. Perhaps

Mr Sparks intends to join his wife once he's milked the account dry.'

'And perhaps not,' Llinos said. 'I don't think he will run away, I have a feeling that even now Sparks has something up his sleeve, some way of replacing the money he's pilfered.'

'And in the meantime our creditors are banging on the door wanting to be paid. This isn't doing your reputation any good, Llinos.'

She looked at him, her eyebrows arched. 'And when have I ever worried about my reputation, Watt?'

'This is your livelihood we're talking about, Llinos,' he said. 'I remember the days when we ran the pottery on a shoestring; we don't want to go back to that, do we?'

'What are you going to do about Rosie?' Llinos deliberately changed the subject.

'What can I do? She's gone off without even letting me know where she'll be staying.'

'I'm sorry,' Llinos said. 'But then you shouldn't have married her, you've never really loved her.'

Watt thrust his hands into his pockets; his face was turned away from her and Llinos was ashamed of her spiteful remarks.

'You think that makes the situation any better?' he said in a low voice.

Llinos tried to think of a reply but was saved by a sudden rapping on the door.

'Someone to see you, Mrs Mainwaring,' the maid said. 'John Pendennis is asking can he speak with you?'

'All right, let him come in.' Llinos looked at Watt. 'I'm sorry,' she said, 'I should mind my own

461

business, your private life has nothing to do with me.' She paused. 'I wonder what John wants.'

'Want me to stay while you talk to him?' Watt asked. 'I think I should especially if it concerns the pottery.'

John came into the room just then and glanced at Watt and it was plain he was not pleased to see him. Watt stood his ground and John ignored him and spoke directly to Llinos.

'May I speak privately with you?' he asked, his voice genial. 'I won't keep you long.'

'All right.' Llinos smiled. 'I'll see you later, Watt, thanks for your concern and please don't worry, we'll sort it out.'

John was not dressed for work. He was wearing a fresh linen shirt and good breeches. His boots were of rich polished leather. Llinos wondered where his sudden wealth had sprung from. When he first came to her, he had nothing, so he claimed.

'I understand the business is in bad shape,' John said easily. He seated himself close to her and Llinos stared at him.

'I don't know where you have got your information from but my business is no concern of yours.'

'I think it might be,' John said. He took a piece of paper out of his pocket and looked down at it for a long moment. 'I came across this, I thought you would want to see it.'

He pushed it across the desk and Llinos felt a prickle of apprehension. There was something in John's tone she did not like.

She looked down and gasped in shock as she

saw the cartoon pencilled boldly across the paper.

'Where did you get this?' she asked. She bit her lip in anger as John shook his head.

'That's not important,' he said. 'What matters is that tomorrow, unless you and I can come to some arrangement, this will be in the newspapers.'

She looked at the drawing again, studying the caricature more closely. Her features had been exaggerated. She was depicted with a fierce mop of hair and huge, woeful eyes. Her clothing was in rags and she had a sign with the words 'Debtors' Prison' around her neck.

'What is the meaning of it all?' Llinos asked.

'I want to take over your business,' John said. 'I know that your account is in trouble, your creditors not paid. I will bail you out and buy the pottery at a fair price.'

Llinos rose to her feet. 'You can go to hell!' She tore the paper into shreds and John laughed.

'That is only a rough copy,' he said evenly. 'I think you would be advised to think things over carefully before you come to any decision.'

'So you and Sparks are in this together,' Llinos said sharply. 'He is stealing money from me and your role is to step in and buy the property at rock-bottom price. Who are you working for?'

'I have backers, of course,' John said, 'but I am the one in charge. You have no money to operate the pottery, your competitors are too big to fight, so why not give in gracefully?'

She shook her head. 'So Jem Boucher is behind all this? He's always wanted to get my pottery for the consortium.' She stared at John defiantly. 'Well your blackmailing tactics won't work. I intend to report the matter to the owner of the bank who happens to be a friend of the family. He will see that everything is straightened out.'

'So, what will happen then?' John said. 'Sparks will languish in jail for filching money from your account and you will still be penniless.' He smiled. 'I could suppress this.' He tapped the pieces of torn paper. 'Save you the humiliation of being pilloried in public.'

'I don't care about the drawing, hasn't that sunk in yet?' Llinos demanded. 'Whoever did this cartoon will be the one to suffer.' She walked to the door and opened it. 'Haven't you heard, John? Everyone sympathizes with the underdog. Your spiteful little cartoon will bring me nothing but offers of help.'

She forced a smile. 'Oh, a few people might chuckle over the cartoon but I am a deserted wife, remember? Most of the other wives out there will be angry for me, imagining themselves in my place. You are not a very good judge of human nature, are you?'

'I'll give you until tonight to change your mind,' John said. 'I'm offering a fair price for the pottery, you must see it would be a good option for you. Face it, you are no longer interested in running the place otherwise you wouldn't be in such a mess, would you? You would have sorted a pipsqueak like Sparks out long ago if your heart was in it.'

'Just leave,' Llinos said. 'If I see you near my property again I'll have you horsewhipped. Do you understand?'

He left the room and strode across the hall. At the door he turned. 'I would think about it, Mrs

Mainwaring, if you turn down my offer, you have everything to lose.'

'Not everything,' she said. 'I will still have my integrity. Goodbye, Mr Pendennis.' Llinos felt her courage desert her; now she was alone, she could see again the drawing of herself being led to a debtors' prison. How her father would have hated the disgrace of it. She swallowed hard. She had come to the lowest point in her life and she had no where to turn for comfort.

Rosie looked around the room: it was a large, elegant hall with high windows facing the sea. Alice's father must be a very rich man indeed to own such an impressive house.

He had not met his daughter with open arms and he looked askance at Rosie as she stepped into the house carrying the bags. After a moment, he beckoned his daughter into the privacy of the library. Alice had been shut in there for over an hour now while Rosie sat staring around her, the bags at her side, wondering what was going to become of her.

Perhaps Alice's father would throw his daughter out into the street. He looked just the sort of man who would do such a thing without a qualm. It was no wonder Alice had grown up to be selfish, impatient with the failings of others.

At last, Alice emerged looking triumphant. 'We are to have the east wing to ourselves, Rosie,' she said briskly. 'My father doesn't want to be troubled with our presence, so we'll keep out of his way.'

Rosie carried the bags upstairs, walking slowly

behind Alice. Alice paused for breath on the huge landing. 'I'll be glad to get into bed, I feel so damned weak.' She pointed. 'Go along there, you can choose any room you fancy. Father's servants can make up the beds for us with fresh linen.'

An hour later, Rosie sat beside the newly built fire in the large bedroom and stared down at her hands. Alice had fallen asleep in the next room, giving Rosie time to take stock.

Did she really want to live in an enormous mansion miles away from Swansea? She could not lower her pride and live with Watt but she would miss her brothers and she would not be able to visit them so easily now. But she had made her choice and that was to stay with Alice. Well now she must live with it. She kicked off her shoes and climbed onto the silk counterpane. She was tired; she would follow Alice's example and sleep.

John Pendennis left the noisy atmosphere of the Castle Inn, his hands swinging at his sides, his head high. Filled with good meat and even better wine, he was confident, pleased with the direction in which his life was moving. He would win the day, he was sure of it. Once Llinos Mainwaring thought it over and accepted the fact that he meant to make the drawing public, she would capitulate, sell him the pottery at any price he chose to mention.

Polly was waiting for him in the bedroom of the house she had rented for him. He had not expected her and for a moment he was angry at her intrusion. She smiled up at him and leaned forward, exposing her breasts to full view. She wanted him. She was insatiable. He smiled. He might as well give her what she had come for.

When at last Polly lay gasping at his side, a glow of bliss bringing colour into her face, he stretched out beside her.

'What surprise have you got for me this time, Polly?' he said, his hand trailing across her breasts. She rolled away from him and walked casually towards the dressing room, unashamed of her nakedness.

John heard the sound of water running into the bowl and smiled; Polly was fastidious about her cleanliness. Or was she worried her doting husband might suspect her of allowing another man to taste her delights?

She returned to the bedroom and pushed back her tangled hair. She was not a beautiful woman, her nose was slightly too large and her mouth wide. But she had a sensuality that was hard to resist.

She dressed quickly and he guessed she was needed at home. Normally, Polly would dally around the house in a silk robe, padding about the rooms on bare feet. He watched as she delved into her bag and brought out a leather pouch.

'Here!' She smiled. 'See if you like it.'

The gold watch slipped into his hand, rich and satisfyingly heavy. The ornate scrolling and the elegant face added to the charm of the piece. It reminded him of his father's gold watch, the one he had sold because he needed the money. Well he would make sure he was never in need again.

'If you are good, I might just buy you a good chain to go with it,' Polly said, moving to the door.

'Busy tonight?' John asked, mellowed by the gift. 'What a shame, I could have earned myself that chain right now.'

'Patience, John, darling,' she said. 'I have to save something for poor old Jem, don't I?' She left the bedroom and John scrambled off the bed and pulled on his breeches.

'What's the hurry?' he asked. She shook her head without answering and pulled open the front door. Outside the carriage waited, the driver asleep at the reins. Polly hesitated.

'What is it, what's wrong?' John asked.

'Bad news.' She shrugged. 'The paper will not use Lily's drawing of Llinos Mainwaring. The editor thinks it could have legal implications.'

'Hell and damnation!' John felt frustration well up within him. The euphoric effects of the alcohol and Polly's eager response to his lovemaking were wearing off. Now all he felt was tired and disheartened.

'All is not lost, my darling,' Polly said. 'Just tell Mrs Mainwaring that the editor is holding back for a day or two. Use the brains God gave you, John Pendennis.'

She was right. Polly was not as flighty as some might think. Behind those eyes that flirted outrageously with any man she met, Polly had a good mind. Perhaps when Jem Boucher gave up the ghost, Polly would move John into her house on a more permanent basis.

He might even marry her. The fact that he was married to Josephine McCabe did not come into the matter. Jo was in America; a mighty ocean separated them. No-one in the whole of Britain knew that she was even alive. In any case, if Binnie Dundee could get away with bigamy surely John Pendennis could do the same?

'What are you thinking about, John?' Polly said curiously. John smiled.

'Wouldn't you like to know?'

'Come on, tell me!' Polly clung to his arm and John took her face in his hands.

'I was thinking that you and I make a good team, my love,' he said. 'One day, I might even do you the honour of marrying you.'

'Oh really?' Polly pushed him away. 'Don't count your chickens, my boy. Even if I was free, I wouldn't marry you.' She flounced off towards the carriage. 'I like a stallion in my bed but not at my dining table,' she said, turning to look over her shoulder.

'The next man I marry will be rich and young then I won't need anyone else to keep me happy.'

'Don't fool yourself, Polly!' John called. 'You are the sort of woman who will always need more than one man.'

She waved her hand as the carriage jerked into motion and John returned indoors. He sat looking at the watch for a long time. So Polly wanted a rich man, did she? Well he would be rich one day. He smiled. And the first step towards his goal was to get control of the Mainwaring Pottery. And get it he would, by whatever means he could.

CHAPTER TWENTY-NINE

Lily was upset. 'Why didn't the paper take my picture of that stuck-up Llinos Mainwaring?' she said acidly.

Polly stared at her, eyebrows raised. 'You know why,' she said gently. 'It was too controversial!' She laughed. 'But it was an excellent likeness, Lily, you are clever!'

Lily was not mollified by Polly's praise. She had hoped for a good sum of money and a chance to get back at Llinos at the same time. Llinos thought she was a cut above the people she employed to run the pottery but Lily remembered the days when Llinos had no money. When the few people remaining at the pottery had worked their fingers to the bone to help the business survive. Lily herself had worked for just her bed and board, using her painting skills on crass earthenware products.

She realized now that she had been wasting her talents all along. Now that she had seen her work in print, had received money for her drawings, she knew she could have done better than stay in a smelly paint shed.

'There's nothing stopping you sending your picture to another paper, though,' Polly said.

'What do you mean?'

Polly sighed. 'You'll never make a business-woman. Good thing you've got me to look after you.' She bent over the drawing.

'Look, why not take out the sign that says "Debtors' Prison" and just show the old castle? We all know people who can't pay their way get put in jail there, don't we?'

'But I liked the sign, it made the point so clearly that Llinos Mainwaring is in trouble,' Lily said.

'I know it's all very clever but it's too daring as it is, love. Do as I say and I bet you will get some rich pickings for it from a big Cardiff paper without them worrying about being sued. At least it's worth a try and you'd get more money that way and your fame would spread.'

'Do you think so?' Lily was quite flattered. Polly usually knew what she was talking about. Sometimes it irked her that Polly, who made her living by stealing from casual lovers, had risen high enough to be accepted in polite society. Polly certainly had the brains to make the most of herself.

'Nothing to lose, is there?' Polly looked around the room. 'Nice place this. Matt takes good care of you, mind.' She rose to study a richly coloured painting on the wall. 'This is really good,' she said. 'I bet it's worth a fortune.'

'No, I think it's a copy of one of the old masters,' Lily said. 'Matthew brought it from his house, he said it would please me.' And it did. It was a painting of a woodland scene with the trees

471

disappearing ghost-like into the distance. It always gave Lily a sense of freedom, of the open air.

'It's not a copy, you idiot!' Polly said. 'It's the real thing, you ask Matthew. Gawd! If ever you was ditched you could sell the painting and live on the profits for the rest of your natural.'

Polly reverted to her street language, something she always did when she was excited. 'Look, Lily, why don't you do a copy of this and put it in the frame, Matthew would never know the difference. You could get yourself a nice little nest-egg with the proceeds.'

Lily looked at her open-mouthed. 'I couldn't do that!' she said.

'Why not? You're clever enough.'

'No, I don't think I am.' Lily stared at the painting; she had stared at it for long hours on the nights Matthew did not come to see her. She almost knew the contours of the land, the feathery leaves of the trees off by heart.

'Just have a go in a small way at first,' Polly said. 'Draw a bit of it, a tree or a hill or something, you know better than me, you are the artist.'

It was an idea worth considering. Lily put her head on one side and studied the painting. She might just try her hand at copying the scene. She was not at all convinced she was up to the task but at least it would be something to do when the evenings stretched endlessly before her.

Lily hated to be alone; she even preferred to put up with Matthew's advances rather than sleep in the big house all by herself. Though, to be fair to him, Matthew managed to see her most days. She realized quite suddenly that she liked Matthew more than a little. She had come to depend on him, to want him to hold her. She would never like the intimacy between a man and a woman but at least with Matthew it was gentle and he treated her as though he really cared for her.

'How's Jem?' Lily said, aware that Polly was watching her. Polly had a nasty habit of reading Lily's mind.

'He's well enough for an old codger!' Polly laughed. 'Up to his usual bedtime tricks. It's a wonder the man don't wear himself out.' She twisted the gold band on her finger. 'I'll miss him when he goes, mind.'

'Goes?' Lily said.

'Pops his clogs, silly! He's not a young stripling any more, is he?'

Lily thought about it. Jem was even older than Matthew who was in his fiftieth year. 'How old is he? Jem I mean?'

'I dunno, about sixty, I can't really tell.' She smiled broadly. 'To him I'm a young spring chicken fit enough for bedroom capers, that's all he cares about.'

She sighed. 'Talking of Jem, I'd better go. We've got some boring people coming to supper tonight.' She minced across the room. 'The Honourable Mr Tassle Jones-Price and his grumpy old wife.' Polly smirked. 'If only the old cow knew that The Honourable isn't so honourable, she'd have a fit!'

Polly was incorrigible. 'You've not played up to him, have you? Not with Jem in the house.'

'Jem laughs about it,' Polly said. 'He thinks it great fun that the old buffer tries it on with me.'

Lily shook her head; she would never

473

understand why Polly and Jem stayed together. Perhaps it was because they both behaved like children at times. Jem was a good businessman and Polly had a wise head on her shoulders but over matters of the bedchamber they could both be so silly.

'Heard the gossip about Alice Sparks?' Polly said casually. Lily was irritated.

'You know I never hear any gossip,' she said. 'The only scandal I get to know about is what you tell me.' Trust Polly to drop something juicy into the conversation just as she was leaving.

'The twins she had were not her old man's kids at all.' She chuckled. 'There's talk that Eynon Morton-Edwards was the father, the two were having an affair after all.' She leaned forward confidentially. 'Not that those babies were even in one piece when that butcher Dr Rogers got 'em out. Poor little mites!' She sighed. 'But their hair was like spun gold so I heard.'

'Who told you?' Lily asked, her eyes wide.

'I talked to the nurse who came in after the delivery. Terrible time the Sparks woman had. I don't like her nor that fool of a husband of hers but I wouldn't wish that on my worst enemy.'

Lily shuddered; she would never long for a baby, never. It was all too sordid for words.

'Does her husband suspect anything?'

'You bet!' Polly laughed. 'Alice's up and gone, supposedly to holiday with that rich father of hers but I reckon her old man chucked her out. Scream, innit?'

'I don't suppose Alice Sparks thinks it's funny. Still, she deserves it, she was never nice to me.'

Lily saw Polly to the door, reluctant for her to go. 'Can't you stay for a bit longer?' she asked but Polly was already climbing into her carriage.

Now she would be alone for hours. Matthew was attending a business meeting tonight, something to do with the bank in town. Lily had heard a whisper that something was going on.

It seemed that the local auditors were not happy about the bank's affairs and that London auditors were being called in to investigate matters. She had not listened very hard when Matthew had talked to her about it; it was not that interesting.

She watched as Polly's carriage rolled away, envying her. Polly had everything, a good husband, respectability and wealth. But then since Matthew had come into her life Lily had not done badly herself. The fact that she was sometimes lonely was nothing to worry about. She had her work, her painting and Polly was right, she might just as well do her best to capitalize on it. Slowly, she closed the door and went inside to light a few more candles.

'You don't know where Alice Sparks is then?' Llinos was seated opposite Eynon in the plush tea rooms of the Neath Hotel. Outside, she could see the waves washing over the beach, rushing forwards and retreating, sucking shells back with the pull of the tide. 'Won't you try to find out?'

'I'm not really interested. Well, would you be?' Eynon said. He sighed heavily. 'She's made her choice, gone away without letting me know where. I feel I've done my best for her, I've helped her financially and,' he paused, 'well, all that's water under the bridge now.' He smiled. 'I'm free to find someone else, aren't I?'

Llinos smiled wanly. 'You would like me to think you are hard but I know different. You are upset that Alice lost the twins, aren't you?'

Eynon shook his head without answering and Llinos did not pursue the point.

'I had a letter from Mr Sparks asking to postpone our meeting,' she said. 'He hinted there was trouble of a domestic kind. I knew exactly what he meant of course and I couldn't help feeling sorry for him.'

'I wouldn't trust that man further than I could throw him,' Eynon said. 'Why you still bank with him I just don't know. We've all warned you, Llinos, and you've been too apathetic to do anything about it.'

Llinos was silent; these words were harsh ones coming from her best friend. She had rowed with Watt over what he saw as yet another delaying tactic by Edward Sparks and she did not want to argue with Eynon as well.

The trouble was she knew they were both giving her good advice, advice she should have heeded long ago. She had a bundle of bills in her desk that she should be attending to right away. But she felt tired and too dispirited to care about anything.

'I know, Watt keeps on at me about it.' Llinos bit her lip. 'I meant to close the account but, well, things happened and I put it off.'

'Look, don't worry,' Eynon said. 'When the London auditors have done their work I'll step in and guide you through everything, how's that?'

'Yes, thank you, Eynon but I'm tired of the

whole business. Let's talk about something else, shall we?'

'Like what?' He reached out and took her hand. 'I'm concerned about you, Llinos. I want to take care of you. More so now that Joe seems to have gone and abandoned you.'

She knew he was talking sense but hearing him put Joe's betrayal into words was painful. She felt tears well up in her eyes and she stared unseeingly at the brown china teapot. She would not cry. She would not let Eynon know how distressed she was. She still had some shred of pride left.

'He's happy with his Indian girl.' She had to force herself to speak. 'He's probably followed her to America by now. He's left me for good, I know that.'

'Llinos, I hate to see you like this, so pale and thin. Why not let me take care of you?'

'How can you?' she asked. 'There would be such a scandal if I lived with you, you know that as well as I do.'

'Who cares about scandal? Look, your well-being is more important than any gossip. You could live with me and we could find a chaperone so that everything appeared to be above board.'

'I will always be married to Joe,' she said. 'I think the world of you, Eynon, you know that, but if I can't have Joe I won't have any man.'

'I know you don't love me,' he said. 'But I have enough love for the both of us. Think about it, Llinos, why should you spend the rest of your life alone? You don't deserve that, you are still a young woman after all.'

Llinos smiled. 'No I'm not. I'm getting older, Eynon, I've even got some grey hairs!'

477

'Rubbish! You are as lovely to me as the day I first met you. You will always be young and beautiful in my eyes, Llinos.'

She stared at him, at his dear face, his fall of pale hair, his eyes bright with admiration and it was a soothing balm to her damaged pride. She loved his company, she could enjoy being with him, laughing with him, but to share his bed would be unthinkable. She was Joe's woman and whatever he had done she would always remain his in body, heart and soul.

'We could never have children together,' she said and they both knew she was making excuses, putting up obstacles, trying to rationalize her feelings.

'I have my daughter and you have your son,' Eynon said reasonably. 'What more could any of us want?'

She could want a great deal. She could want Joe's arms around her, to breathe in the scent of his skin and to feel the silk of his hair against her cheek. She did not say so; she had no intention of hurting Eynon more than she had to.

'We'd better get back,' she said softly. 'I will have to think seriously about my business. I will *have* to make arrangements to meet with Mr Sparks. You are right, I've been silly and apathetic letting things slide the way I have.' She looked at Eynon. 'But any woman who has been left by the husband she loves would behave in exactly the same way.'

'I'll drop you off home,' Eynon said, drawing back her chair. 'But if you need any help, I'll come to the bank with you. I can't see Sparks lasting very long now. So far he's covered his tracks but it won't help him when the books have been examined by experts.'

'I'll deal with it, don't you worry.' As Llinos walked out into the sea-fresh air, the tang of salt drifted in from the shore. The sound of the waves was carried on the inward breeze and Llinos sighed. It was so wonderful here, so peaceful, if only she could stay here, forget her business, just leave everything to fate.

Eynon helped her into his carriage. The seats were comfortable, the leather covered with a warm shawl. Eynon sat next to her and took her hands in his. Llinos was taking advantage of his love for her and she wondered if the day would come when her friendship would not be enough for him.

When she arrived home Watt was waiting for her, a newspaper in his hand, his face white with anger. Llinos knew he was going to tell her something she did not want to hear.

She allowed the maid to take her coat and bonnet and beckoned Watt to follow her into the drawing room.

'What is it?' She braced herself as he spread the newspaper wide and pointed to a drawing on the centre page.

'It's a paper published in the Vale of Neath,' he said. 'I'm not surprised that no Swansea paper would print it, it's an outrage!' He paced around the room. 'It will make our creditors very nervous.'

She looked at the drawing for a long time. She had seen it before, in the hands of John Pendennis. It had been modified but the message it sent was clear enough.

She crumpled the paper into a ball and threw it across the room. Why did people have to rub salt into the wound?

'John Pendennis has carried out his threat,' she said. She sank into a chair and looked up at Watt. 'When he came here the other day,' – she pointed to the newspaper – 'it was to blackmail me with that. He demanded I sell him the pottery.'

'The bastard!' Watt's face was white with anger. 'I always said he was a bad lot didn't I?'

'He's just an added irritation, Watt,' Llinos said. 'I'm getting weary of all the problems that running a pottery involves. Perhaps I should sell, just get out of here for good.'

Watt picked up the paper and put it on the table; he was shaking his head in exasperation. 'Don't let this piece of spite influence you, Llinos!'

'I know it's only spiteful gossip.' Llinos sank into a chair, her eyes closing wearily. 'But I just can't cope with things any more, I think you know that.'

She wished Watt would go away, stop bothering her. She longed to curl up beside the fire and think about Joe and the happiness they had shared before Sho Ka came on the scene.

'Can't you see it?' Watt asked. 'You are letting these scoundrels beat you.'

Llinos sighed. 'I don't care, Watt, I don't care about anything any more.'

Watt stood shaking his head in silence for a moment and then, abruptly, he left the room. Llinos knew he was angry with her. He had a right to be; she was ignoring her problems, hoping they would go away. She was well aware that the day of reckoning must come tomorrow or the day after; the pottery workers would grow tired of waiting for their wages.

She tried to imagine the pottery in the hands of strangers, the pottery her father had loved and cherished. If she did not act promptly everything she had worked for would fall apart before her eyes, is that what she really wanted? She closed her eyes, she would rest a little and then, when her mind was clear, she would take control once more.

It was a fresh day and for the first time for months, Llinos felt grateful to be alive. She looked up at the clouds, light and fluffy overhead, and breathed in the scent of the wild flowers growing in the hedgerows.

'Thank the Lord you've come to your senses,' Watt said. 'This is a big meeting with all of the top men present. It's vital that we be there.' He extended his hand and helped Llinos to seat herself beside him in the trap. She glanced at his hands, strong as they held the reins, and she felt a rush of warmth for him.

Watt was like a brother to her. He cared about her. All his nagging was in her best interest. She had preferred Watt's company rather than Eynon's. Watt after all was part of her business.

He flicked the reins and the horse began to trot away from Pottery Row and downhill towards the town. It was a fine day though the air was a little chilly for the time of the year. Llinos wished she had wrapped a woollen shawl around her shoulders; she felt the cold acutely these days.

Watt looked down at her as she folded her arms across her body.

'Cold?' he said. 'It's no wonder, you haven't got an ounce of fat to cover yourself with. I wish you would look after yourself, Llinos, for Lloyd's sake if not for your own.'

She nodded. 'I know. I promise I'll try to eat more. I am beginning to feel better now, can't you see it in my face? I think at last I'm getting over my upset with Joe.'

'No, you look just as pale and peaky as always. Look, I'm upset, my wife's left me, I've been abandoned too but you don't see me doing without my food, do you?'

Llinos did not answer. It was pointless trying to explain that 'upset' was too mild a word for what she was feeling. She had been devastated by Joe's betrayal. He had cut the very root of her life away when he had gone to live with Sho Ka. Joe was the husband she had worshipped. She would have given her life for him and he had thrown her love back in her face. But life goes on; at least that was what everyone was trying to tell her.

Llinos gave a sigh of relief as Watt guided the horse into the roadside. He tied the reins to a tree and then helped Llinos down from the trap. Llinos lifted her skirt away from the dusty roadside and began to walk towards the bank. Suddenly, she came face to face with Lily and for a moment their eyes met.

'Day to you, Mrs Mainwaring.' Lily seemed to be making an effort to be polite. 'I hope you are managing all right now that you have no husband?'

The barb was there and it hurt. Llinos looked carefully at Lily, not showing by so much as a flicker of her eyelashes how the words had struck home.

'I am fine, Lily,' she found herself saying. 'I am still a respectable married woman while you, well, the gossips are having a field day, they say you have been set up by a rich gentleman.' She paused. 'In return for giving him your favours of course. I hope you are managing all right now you are a mistress.'

She regretted the words as soon as they were uttered, ashamed she had sunk to the same spiteful level as Lily.

Lily flushed and swept past her and Watt took Llinos by the arm. 'Well done, Llinos, that put the little viper in her place good and proper.'

'I have enough enemies,' Llinos said. 'I shouldn't be trying to add to them.' She walked into the dimness of the bank and the smell of beeswax polish permeated the air.

After a wait of a few minutes, she and Watt were ushered into a back room. Mr Sparks was clearing his desk.

'How can I help you, Mrs Mainwaring?' he asked. It was Watt who replied.

'We have not come to see you, we are attending the meeting of the directors of the bank.'

'You are too late, the meeting is over.' He continued to put papers and files into a box. Watt looked at Llinos in bewilderment.

'How can the meeting be over?' Watt's voice was harsh. 'We were informed it was to take place at eleven-thirty.'

'The time was changed unbeknown to me. I had no say in the matter.'

'Well what's happening now?'

'I have no idea except that your account, along with several others, has been frozen.' He glanced up, his eyes narrowed. 'I told you a long time ago that you should let your husband handle your affairs, well now it seems he has.'

'What do you mean?' Watt demanded. Sparks did not look at him.

'I think, Mrs Mainwaring, that your husband took out what little was left in the account. At least that's what I assume he was doing here at the bank.'

Llinos did not hear the rest of the argument between Watt and Sparks. All she wanted was to get out of the bank, away from the malicious smile on Sparks's face. So Joe had been into Swansea, had called at the bank and apparently left his wife and his son without any means of support.

'I want to go home.' She walked through the bank without seeing anything of her surroundings. How could Joe have treated her this way? Even if he no longer loved her, what right had he to take her livelihood away from her?

Watt followed her and caught her elbow. 'Wait, Llinos, you can't just accept that man's word for it, we must speak to someone else in the bank.'

'I don't want to speak to anyone else!' Her tone was clipped. 'I hate Joe, do you know that, I hate him!'

She stood in the sunshine and took a deep breath to steady herself. This was the end of the road for her and Joe; as far as she was concerned he had gone forever. The worst had happened and now she must dig deep within herself and find the courage to rebuild her life without him.

CHAPTER THIRTY

The public rooms of the Castle Inn were filled with people, some of them travellers taking a meal and a rest from their journey. Most were local folk enjoying a drink of beer after a long day's work. The smoke from the fire belched forth from the grate driven by the wind howling outside. In a corner, slightly apart from the crowd, John Pendennis sat, elbows on the table, staring at Edward Sparks.

'Foul night.' John drank from his tankard. 'I hope you've got good news for me.'

'Good news! Don't you realize I'm ruined? I'm out of a job, I need that money you promised me and I need it now.'

'Tell me about Mrs Mainwaring,' John ignored the man's remark. 'Is she going to sell the pottery?'

'She'll have to sell, the foolish woman, I've left her account empty. What I've done is bound to be discovered in time which is why I need money to get away from Swansea altogether.'

'But she will sell,' John insisted.

'I suppose so. I told her that her husband had

cleared out her account. The lie will at least give me breathing space.' He glanced at John and his face lightened. 'You should have seen her, she swallowed the story hook, line and sinker.'

John despised the man. He had disliked him on sight and right now Sparks was revelling in another human being's pain. But for all that he might still prove useful.

'As a matter of interest, what have you got against Mrs Mainwaring?' he asked.

'I had a buyer for her pottery some time ago, the offer was a good one and the stupid woman would not sell. I lost a great deal of money because of her stubbornness. Women have no place in business, you know that as well as I do.' He leaned forward. 'You are going to pay me, John?'

John rubbed his chin and answered Sparks's question with a question of his own. 'You *are* coming in with me on the venture I take it, so why don't you hand over the money you owe?'

'I can't go into any business deal now, surely you can see that? Look, John, have you got the money or haven't you? There's a lot at stake here.' He paused. 'I did my part, I pushed Mrs Mainwaring into a position where she would have to sell and risked my own neck doing it. It's your fault I'm in a mess now.'

'You've got it wrong,' John said, shaking his head. 'I didn't ask you to risk losing your job, I thought you were cleverer than that. I just wanted to buy some property around here and make us both rich men into the bargain.'

He lifted the tankard; the pewter lip was cold against his mouth but the beer was good, made from strong hops. Not half as good as Cornish ale but good enough. For now. One day, he would return home with a fortune behind him. Then he would be able to take his revenge on Treharne. The sour taste of bitterness was in his mouth as he remembered how his sick father was turned out into the night. Banished from the home that had been in his family for a hundred years or more.

John had not been close to his father but he was angry that he had died in a run-down lodging house. He had been buried in a paupers' grave and all because of Treharne. But the day of vengeance would come and sooner than Treharne imagined.

He focused his attention on Sparks. The man was spiteful and weak. He bore Llinos Mainwaring a grudge because she would not fall in with his plans and sell the pottery when he asked her to. He wanted her ruined just because he had lost a few sovereigns on the deal. He would need watching.

'I'll go and see her tomorrow,' John said. 'This money you embezzled, I take it you can have it ready within a day or two?'

Edward Sparks hesitated and John leaned closer to him. 'You *will* have it ready?' he said insistently. 'You do have it, don't you?'

Sparks sat back in his seat as though disturbed by John's closeness. John frowned in anger; he had learned to be hard on those who thwarted him. He had been soft once, young and untried, and a ruthless man had taken everything away from him. That would not happen again.

'If you've kept that money for yourself you are a dead man,' John said. He had expected Sparks to bring the cash with him; all the money he had taken from various accounts must add up to a large sum by now.

'It's all right, you go ahead,' Edward said, 'speak to Mrs Mainwaring, make her an offer and I'll do the rest.'

'Good enough.' John relaxed. 'Now, let's forget business and have a little fun, shall we?'

Edward Sparks looked owl-like behind his glasses. 'What sort of fun?'

'We'll find some women, take them back to my house.' It was Polly's house and she would not take kindly to women from the streets enjoying the comforts she had provided for John but then Polly would never know.

'I don't know about that,' Edward said. He took a deep drink from his tankard as John lifted his hand to the landlord for another jug of beer.

The jug was brought and John spoke quietly to the landlord. The man nodded and money changed hands.

'There, all done.' John poured beer into Edward Sparks's tankard. 'Drink up, this is a night you are going to remember, this is a night to celebrate our rise to the ranks of men of property.'

John noticed that the more Sparks drank, the more his face streamed with sweat. He presented a far from attractive prospect for any woman. But, then, these would be women of the streets; they would not be too particular so long as the money was there at the end of the night.

The landlord made a sign to John and he nodded. 'Come on, Sparks,' he said, 'the girls are ready for us.'

Sparks still hesitated and John nudged him

489

impatiently. 'Here take these few sovereigns and pay me back later. Come on, man, you've no wife to go home to and a man needs to sow his wild oats.'

Outside the inn, a carriage was standing at the ready. Two eager faces peered out at John. A girl with abundant dark hair dimpled at him. At her side was a small, pale-faced woman and John decided she looked a little too delicate for his tastes.

He pushed Sparks into the seat beside the pale one and slipped his arm around the other girl. She responded immediately by putting her hand on his breeches and pushing her full breasts towards him.

'I'm Bella, I think I'm going to like you,' she said.

'No rush to find out,' John replied. 'We've a nice warm bed to lie in and all night to lie in it.'

The drive did not take long. John opened the door and led the party inside. 'Wait, I'll light the candles.'

In the brighter light, John saw that Bella was older than he had first thought but she was still a beauty with curving hips and shapely breasts. 'I think I'm going to enjoy you, Bella.'

'Which is the best bedroom?' she asked looking up the stairs. 'Come on, sir, let's get to it, I can't wait to take your clothes off you.'

John directed Sparks to the smaller bedroom and the man appeared more as though he was going to his doom than having a dalliance with a lovely, willing woman.

John took Bella into the bedroom and closed the door. She smiled at him, her eyes flirting with him, her hands on the waist of his breeches. John felt aroused, it was several days since he had seen Polly and, eager for him and generous though she was, John found her constant chatter irritating. Apart from which, variety appealed to him, it always had. He had never been faithful even when he was living with Josephine McCabe and beholden to her damned family.

'Come to bed, darling,' Bella urged. 'Let's have fun!' She flung off her gown and he saw she was wearing nothing beneath it. He stared at her white skin and rounded body and knew this was going to be a night he would never forget.

Edward was elated he had managed to make love to the pale, slender Sarah twice in as many hours. He had even enjoyed it. He wondered why he was so good with her when he could not perform for his wife. But then Alice was domineering, always bossing him about, and Sarah, well, she was delicate, pliant, accepting rather than demanding. He was excited by her passiveness and somehow comforted by the knowledge that he was paying for her favours. It released him from any responsibility.

From next door came the sounds of violent lovemaking, it seemed John had more stamina than he had. Sarah sat up and looked at him, her eyes large.

'Do you want to do it again?' she asked and he shook his head. Enough was enough, he doubted he could perform a third time.

She sighed in relief. 'Well then,' she said, 'will you take me home? Your friend told the driver to wait outside.'

Edward was happy about that; it would get the girl off his hands. Then he would go home to his own bed. Sarah held out her hand and Edward felt the bile rise in his throat; all he had with him was the small amount of money John had given him. He handed the girl one of the coins and she seemed satisfied.

Edward began to worry, all he was doing was getting himself deeper into debt. If only he had not listened to Alice, had not agreed to her high-flown ideas. Damn Alice! She had run up bills, landing him in dreadful debt. And now Edward needed to find a way out of the mess, to keep himself from the bankruptcy court or even prison. It was either that or run away from Swansea and stay away.

Sarah was dressed by now and she looked quite respectable with her little jacket and matching bonnet. He put his finger to his lips as he opened the door, no need to let John know how soon he had left the house.

As the carriage jolted away from the doorway, Edward glanced back hoping that John would be too involved with the vivacious Bella to notice he was leaving. Bella was dark and lovely but she reminded him too much of Alice. He had been quite happy with little Sarah. What a great pity he had not found a respectable woman of the same type, a woman who would acquiesce, would make no demands. A woman who would not ruin him financially.

'We're nearly there.' Sarah was peering out of the window. 'See, it's that cottage there, the third one along in the row.'

The carriage pulled in to the side of the road

and, as Edward climbed out to help Sarah down, the door behind him opened. Edward spun round, suddenly frightened. What if he should be face to face with an irate father?

'Lovely night for it!' The voice boomed out and a large hand clamped on Edward's shoulder. 'Enjoyed my little girlie, did you?'

Edward looked at Sarah and she dipped into her bag, handing the man the money she had collected. 'Here you are, Bull.'

'Ah, a generous man, I see.' He clapped Edward on the shoulder. 'Come in, good sir, we've got a card game going, might as well make a real night of it now, eh?'

Edward was pushed into a smoke-filled kitchen with a large table in the centre of the room. Around it were seated men of various ages and occupations. Some were clearly labourers; one or two dressed like gentlemen. He was obviously in a house of ill repute and Edward was uncomfortable.

'Make room.' Bull pushed a battered stool into the small gap between two of the men. On one side of Edward sat a beefy man with the blue scars of the collier. Occupying what seemed to be the only decent chair in the room was a portly man with a gold watch hanging from a thick chain around his belly.

'Evening to you!' The man nodded, not taking his eyes from the cards in his hand. 'Good player are you?'

Edward was not sure. He had played a little at cards but was no expert. Still, most of it was down to luck so he had as good a chance as anyone else.

'You'll be in the next hand,' Bull said. 'Come on, boys, shove your money onto the table, let's see the colour of it.'

Gold sovereigns poured onto the rough boards and Edward felt his stomach lurch; he had not anticipated such high stakes. Still, if only luck was with him he might win enough to solve all his problems. He looked around him and decided it would be foolish to try to leave now.

He was dealt into the next hand and the cards he held were good ones. He felt a new excitement rising within him. He had never been a gambler but that had been from lack of opportunity rather than choice. He soon found he was good at the game and by the end of the hand he had a heap of money on the table before him.

With confidence now, he gambled, knowing that the money he might lose would not come out of his own pocket.

Bull looked at him with narrowed eyes and pushed a cup of porter towards him. Edward drank; his mouth was dry with excitement. He felt elated, a real man in bed and out of it. That was something Alice had never done for him, given him confidence in himself.

He was unaware of something being slipped into his drink. He played as though possessed, winning hand after hand. Perhaps he should leave now while he was ahead.

Bull would not hear of it. He pressed Edward back into his chair, standing behind him as he refilled his cup. 'Come on, man!' he bellowed. 'Enjoy yourself, have a good time, that's what we're here for.'

Edward lost the next hand and a good deal of his money was swept away across the table. He was not too worried; he would make it up next time, he was sure. The hand was dealt and as he looked at his cards, Edward's heart sank. All he could hope for now was to bluff his way through the game. After all, he was playing for high stakes.

He put out a great deal of his winnings in an effort to convince the others that he was holding a good hand. But as the game came to an end, he realized he had lost again.

'We'll take a note, old man,' the portly gentleman at his side said encouragingly. 'We can all see that you are well positioned, in short a gentleman of honour.' He looked round him. 'We all trust each other here, right?'

Edward signed a note, his mind was fuddled, he had not drunk too much but his vision was clouded. He tried his best to concentrate on the game. He scribbled more notes, laughing a lot as he threw in his hand. Nothing seemed to matter any more. At last, he felt his head slip onto the table and then he slept.

When Edward woke, his mouth tasted as if it was full of sawdust. He was lying on the floor and beside him, snoring like a thunderstorm, was the big figure of Bull.

Edward sat up abruptly and felt a violent pain in his head. He rubbed his hand against the sharpness of his untrimmed beard. Beside him, Bull stirred and opened one eye; he was like a dog ready to wake at any sound.

'I'd better get home.' Edward scrambled to his feet; he ached in every joint. A feeling of dread swamped him as he thought of the notes he had written. He had signed away more money than he could ever hope to repay.

Daylight was trickling in through the kitchen window. Stumps of candles littered the floor. 'I'd better get off and clean myself up ready for work,' he said. He knew instinctively that he must act as though everything in his life was under control.

'Aye, better had, young sir.' Bull scratched his fat belly and broke wind loudly. Edward turned away, appalled at the crudeness of the man. How could he have spent the night in such company?

He lurched towards the door and leaned on the latch for a moment, trying to control the jerking in his limbs. 'I must clean up before I go to work.' Why was he repeating himself? He sounded like a halfwit. He looked down at his clothes, they were crumpled and a red stain ran down the front of his shirt. He was a mess.

'Don't forget you have your notes to repay, mind,' Bull said. 'Our Sarah 'as written out on a piece of paper what you owe to various gentlemen that sat in on the game.'

Edward took the paper and tried to read Sarah's writing. It was neat enough but his eyes would not focus properly. He realized he had lost his glasses.

'Looking for these?' Bull held them out to him and Edward rubbed them against his coat. When he could see clearly he was shocked at the amount written at the bottom of the page.

'Jest bring the money round and me and Sarah will sort it out with the others,' Bull said genially.

Edward walked home in a daze. If he sold

everything he owned, he would never raise enough to pay his gambling debts.

He took the back streets, praying he would not meet anyone he knew. He was ashamed of his behaviour. He had slept with a whore and then he had sat in on a gambling ring and thrown away everything he had worked for.

And where was Alice? She was just fine; she was at her father's house, living like a queen. It was she who had caused all the trouble in his life. Alice had ruined him, had made him a thief. She had brought him to the pit of hell. If he could get hold of her now, he would put his hands around her white throat and squeeze until there was no breath left in her.

He reached the safety of the house and threw off his soiled clothes in disgust. He found water still in the jug in his bedroom and scrubbed himself until his flesh was red. It was as though by purging his body he could purge his soul of all his sins.

He dressed in fresh clothes, noticing that the shirt was the last clean one in the cupboard. He sat on the bed thinking of his debts, his head bent in despair. He would have to pay them off however he did it. The sort of men he had kept company with would not stop at harsh words.

Edward shuddered; Bull would have no compunction about torturing him by way of entertainment before beating him to death. Everything looked hopeless. He put his hands over his face and wept like a baby. He had lost everything – his good name, his reputation as a respectable businessman – and now he might even lose his life.

At last, he pulled himself together. There was nothing else for it, he would have to pay off his gambling debts with John Pendennis's money. Just how he would explain it all to John he would have to figure out later.

'So what do you say, Mrs Mainwaring, will you sell the pottery to me?' John was standing near the door of the drawing room and Llinos looked up at him, her mind in turmoil. If only Joe were here, he could save the pottery. But even if Sparks had lied about Joe clearing out the account, which on reflection seemed likely, Joe was no longer interested in the pottery or in his wife and family.

'I don't know.' She rubbed her eyes tiredly. 'I suppose I will have to sell. I know you are a villain but what choice do I have?' She walked to the window and stared out, seeing the tall chimneys of the bottle kilns and the haze of heat that hung like an aura around them. The pottery was her family, her life. She did not know how she would survive without her work. The potting had become part of the fabric of her being.

Llinos would never be without a roof over her head. Eynon would take her into his own home and no questions asked. But she had always been independent, had always made her own way however tough the going got.

'Look,' John said, 'we can compromise, you could still live here, I am quite happy in the little house I've rented in town.'

Llinos felt a glimmer of hope; at least John was offering her the chance of staying in the home she had grown up in. But how would she live? How would she pay for the basic necessities of life, food and clothing? She had to face the fact that she was destitute.

The spectre of the workhouse loomed. She had taken in orphans and given them employment at the pottery and she could end up behind the grim, grey walls herself.

'Give me a day or two,' she said at last. 'I will have to think seriously about your offer, I know that.'

'Of course, Mrs Mainwaring.' John's harsh tone had softened. 'I can see the position you are in but I am offering you a way out. You could stay in the house and live on the money I'd pay you for the pottery.'

Llinos shook her head, she knew and he knew that as things stood the pottery was worth very little. There were too many outstanding debts to be paid off. It would be an uphill struggle for anyone who took over from her. Perhaps John Pendennis did not realize that. 'It will be difficult for anyone to make the business profitable again,' she said truthfully.

'I do understand that,' John replied. 'And I understand how you must be feeling. I am not a total waster, you know, I have lived through bad times myself.' He paused.

'Look, when I was eighteen I was cheated out of my inheritance.' John's expression was sombre. 'My father fell sick, he was on his deathbed when we were thrown out of our house.'

Llinos looked at him warily. He had her at his mercy; why was he seeking her sympathy?

'It was the middle of the night,' John continued.

'This man, an enemy of father's, sent his bailiffs to throw us out into the cold night air. My father could barely stand. I begged Treharne to let us stay at least until morning but the man was ruthless.' John sighed as if the memory was still painful.

'I took my father to a lodging house, I managed to scrape together enough money for one night. But my father died anyway.'

He looked directly at her and his eyes were shadowed. 'I was frightened. I ran away and left him there in that mean house for strangers to find.'

'I'm sorry,' Llinos said. She turned to look at him. 'I can't think straight, just give me a little time, will you?'

'Of course.' John nodded. 'And I would like to apologize for trying to force you into selling the pottery, that was wrong of me. I would like you to know it was none of my doing that the dreadful caricature of you appeared in the paper.'

Llinos walked towards the window and stared out. John might not be the villain she imagined him to be. He had suffered as she had suffered.

'All right, John. I'll sell,' she said. 'There's no point in putting it off. I'll get someone to draw up the documents as soon as I can. If you are sure I can still live here, that is.'

'I'm sure,' John said. 'And you won't regret your decision.' He forced a smile. 'At least you will know that I will do my best to make the pottery viable again.' He shook her hand and made for the door.

Llinos followed him. 'I'll be in touch,' she said. 'Just as soon as I can make arrangements.'

She watched as he strode away towards the road. He was walking with his usual confident air, head high, shoulders straight. Appearances were deceptive; underneath his assured manner was a man who was vulnerable, who blamed himself for the way his father had died.

As she closed the door, Llinos bit her lip in an effort to stop the tears. What good was crying? She was a woman alone and she needed to survive in the best way she knew how.

CHAPTER THIRTY-ONE

'But, Polly, you can't be thinking of leaving Jem!' Lily stared at her friend aghast. 'You'd be giving up all this, the fine house, the servants, everything.'

'At the moment I am just *thinking* about it.' Polly smiled. 'Just in case, I've salted away quite a bit of money. And I've got some lovely jewels as well.' She smiled. 'Now let's change the subject.'

'Yes?' Lily spoke warily knowing that Polly was about to say something outrageous.

'Lovely painting this.' Polly stood before the picture of woodland and landscape that Lily had always admired. 'I've got a buyer for it.'

'Hey!' Lily said indignantly. 'You can't do that, the painting isn't yours to sell.' She watched as Polly lifted the picture from the wall.

'It's not yours either and that Matthew don't know the value of it, do he?' She laughed, staring at the canvas. 'Aye, this is going to give us a little bit of security, Lily, and you need it as much as me.'

'What do you mean?' Lily asked. 'I don't need

anything. Matthew looks after me perfectly well.'

'Aye, he does now,' Polly said. 'But what about when his old gel passes on, what then?'

'Well, as you said, he might marry me when he's free.'

Polly shook her head. 'No he won't love. I've found out he's very friendly with the father of that awful Alice Sparks. They get on well, two rich old men together. They visit each other at least once a week, I'm surprised you didn't know that about Matt, you don't talk to him much, do you?' She did not wait for a reply. 'Anyway, now it seems old Matt's taken a shine to Alice.' She shrugged. 'No accounting for taste, mind.'

'But that's not possible, how would Matthew get to know her? Alice Sparks is a married woman.'

'Don't you know anything!' Polly was exasperated. 'Alice Sparks has gone home to her father, supposed to be for a rest after losing those babies but I reckon she's got wind of the trouble at the bank and has left the old bugger Sparks in the lurch.'

'I don't know anything about that,' Lily said sulkily. 'In any case, what good is Alice Sparks to Matthew? He can hardly marry her and I don't see her agreeing to be his mistress, not if her father is as rich as you say.'

'You always was a bit on the dull side when it came to life as it is.' Polly smiled. 'Rich people, well they have ways of making someone like Edward Sparks disappear.'

The thought of Edward Sparks disappearing was not such a bad idea. Lily remembered Mr Sparks and his whining voice well. He had treated her like dirt when she was his maid. He had a maddening way of looking down his long nose at people. 'How do you mean he could disappear?'

'Gawd!' Polly sighed. 'I knew you was daft but I didn't think you were that soft in the head. Sparks could have an accident, you know.' She drew her hand across her throat in a cutting gesture.

'No, Matthew would never be involved in anything like that.' Lily shook her head, Polly was talking a lot of rubbish. The thought of Matthew doing anything underhand was absurd.

'We'll see.' Polly left the room, clattering upstairs to the studio singing tunelessly as she went. She returned a few minutes later with the picture Lily had painted.

'See, perfect.' Polly hung the painting on the wall and Lily had to agree that it was a pretty good copy. As yet though it was far from perfect, there were glaring mistakes in the brushwork. Still, her painting was improving every day. The thought cheered her, if Matthew did ever cast her aside, she could always find work.

'Thank you for the compliment,' Lily said dryly, 'but I still can't let you sell Matthew's property, it would be far too risky.'

'Don't try to boss me around, my girl.' Polly sounded determined. 'I'm going to sell the painting whatever you say so you'll just have to put up with it.'

'Don't go acting so hoity toity, now, we got to look out for ourselves in this life. Don't you realize you could be discarded like an old shoe any day?'

'Do you really think Matthew is tired of me then?'

504

'You never know what's round the corner, love, specially if you don't have a gold ring on your finger.' Polly twisted her own wedding band thoughtfully.

'I suppose you're right,' Lily said. 'But you wouldn't think seriously of leaving Jem, would you? Especially for a waster like John Pendennis?' Lily felt uneasy, worried by Polly's hints that Matthew might be getting tired of her. It seemed safer to change the subject.

'That John Pendennis is nothing but an adventurer who is after all the money he can lay his hands on. You must be out of your mind to trust him.'

'Well, put it like this, I trust him so long as I'm holding the purse strings. But I am getting tired of Jem, I'm young yet and I don't want to end up nursing a sick old man.'

'Why not?'

''Cos I can't abide anyone being sick. And John, well, he's handsome and talks nice and he's so good in the sheets.' She laughed wickedly. 'He can make my body sing like no other man ever could.'

Lily sighed; there was no arguing with Polly when she was in this mood. 'Well it's your life and you'll do what you want whatever I say.'

Still, she would not mind changing places with Polly. Lily would never leave a secure marriage for a Johnny-come-lately like Pendennis. Jem might be old but he was generous and he really loved Polly. For her friend to throw away all that would be madness. She tried one more time to make Polly see sense.

'Why not stick it out with Jem? You said yourself

he's very old. Look at all the money you'd have and that lovely house. If you must have John keep him as a lover.'

Polly nodded. 'Aye, you could be right, girl.' She sank down into a chair still staring up at the fake painting on the wall.

'But there's more to John than meets the eye. He lost his wife and his baby when he was in America. That's why he came home, he couldn't bear to live with his sad memories.'

That did not sound like the John Pendennis Lily had met. John was a man of iron. Anyone without money or influence was beneath contempt in his eyes. He had a burning ambition to make himself rich but Polly, usually so hard-headed, could not see that. Everyone said that love was blind but she never thought it would happen to Polly.

'You're used to living in luxury, Polly, I hope John has got plenty of money,' she said innocently. Of course she knew he had nothing. If John was rich why was Polly paying out for a house for him, buying him clothes, a good horse, setting him up like a gentleman?

'Yes of course he's rich, he came back from America with fistfuls of gold but his money is tied up.' She winked at Lily. 'John's got plans, big plans, he's going to buy the Mainwaring Pottery.'

'Oh?' That was an interesting piece of news. 'What's he going to use for money?'

'Don't be more stupid than you can help!' Polly said angrily. 'I've told you he's got money.'

'And are you putting money into this scheme?'

Polly smiled slowly and tapped her head. 'I might be in love but I haven't gone completely off my rocker. No, I'm not putting any money into the scheme, it's all down to John.'

'Are you sure?' Lily was sceptical. 'I bet you anything you like that he'll ask you for money to "tide him over" or something.'

'Well, if he does then I'll believe you that he's after my money.' Polly was suddenly serious. 'I am in love for the first time in my life, Lily, but I'm not so gullible that I can't see the signs.'

'Signs?'

'Yes, bloody signs!' Polly leaned back against the chair, her eyes closed. 'I know I'm paying for everything right now, John's clothes, his keep, everything but I'm giving him the chance to prove to me he's telling the truth, that he's got money. If he can't do that then it's curtains for him.'

'What about leaving Jem?' Lily asked reasonably. 'Once you've done that, the die is cast.'

'You underestimate me, love,' Polly said, opening her eyes and sitting up straight. 'John is to get his money today, or tomorrow at the latest. If he does, I'll think about leaving my husband. Until then, I'm staying put.' She laughed but without humour. 'As I said, I may be in love but I'm not ready for bedlam just yet.'

Lily shook her head she would never understand the workings of her friend's mind. Polly was clever, and hard-headed when it came to money, but she had a softness about her now that worried Lily.

'Have you ever been in love, Lily?' Polly said lazily. 'I mean so much in love that you melt when a man kisses you and you feel as though all the rainbows in the world are gathering in your belly when he makes love to you?'

Lily shook her head. 'No, thank the good Lord!' She would never let her heart rule her head. Look at Polly: for all her bravado she was not the strong woman she appeared to be. Lily hoped in her heart that John Pendennis would fail to live up to expectations. She had no wish to lose Polly's friendship, and lose it she would, as sure as the sun rose in the morning, if Polly left Jem.

Lily could see the scene now, Jem distraught, Matthew comforting him, telling him that Polly was no good, that her list of lovers was numbered in dozens. Then Matthew would tell Lily that she was not to see Polly again or even to speak about her. Lily would be forced to obey Matthew or lose everything.

She was startled out of her thoughts by a sudden rapping on the drawing room door. The maid peered into the room with large eyes. 'A gentleman to see you, Mrs Lily,' the girl said.

Lily was puzzled; no-one ever called on her, certainly no gentleman. Matthew saw to that.

Polly was on her feet at once, her eyes wide with anticipation. 'Show him in, girl!' she said sharply.

'Polly, what's going on?'

Polly put her finger to her lips and composed her face into a smile of welcome as a tall, elegantly dressed man was shown into the room.

'Ah, Mr Robinson, how good of you to call,' Polly said sweetly, her cultured accent back in place. 'Come to see the painting, have you?'

The man bent over Polly's hand and kissed it. He scarcely glanced at Lily. 'I have indeed, dear lady,' he said smoothly.

'And here it is.' Polly waved her hand towards

the genuine painting standing now against the wall. 'Please examine it, take your time, these things can't be hurried, we all know that, don't we, Lily?'

Lily closed her mouth tightly; she could have killed Polly. How dare she take control? How dare she offer Matthew's property without so much as a by your leave?

'Take it to the window, Mr Robinson, see for yourself the exquisite detail, the brushstrokes, the fine texture of the oil.'

She was talking like an experienced collector. Polly must have been doing her homework well. She had read anything she could find on the subject of art and on the particular artist whose work she was planning to sell. Her next words confirmed what Lily had been thinking.

'This is one of the artist's finest paintings, I'm sure you, Mr Robinson, as a discerning collector, will see that for yourself.'

Mr Robinson studied the painting for what seemed an eternity. He held it to the light and peered through a silver-handled glass that enlarged the minute detail. At last he nodded, satisfied.

'I will take it and at the agreed price,' he said smiling. 'And here, as you requested, is the money in cash.'

He drew a heavy bag out of an inner pocket of his coat and Lily could hear the coins jingling inside.

Polly thanked him graciously, putting the bag on the table as though careless of its contents. 'Might we offer you refreshments, Mr Robinson?' she asked solicitously. 'You must be thirsty after your long coach ride.'

'No, thank you, Mrs Boucher,' he said. 'I want to make it home before nightfall. I don't want anything to happen to my prize.' He tapped the gilt frame of the painting.

'Ah, I see you have a copy here.' He stood before Lily's painting and studied it carefully. 'Not badly executed but done by an amateur.' He smiled. 'Though a gifted amateur of course. Is this your work, Mrs Boucher?'

'No, no.' Polly shook her head. 'My friend Lily, here, she is the artist. You might have seen her drawings in some of our local journals?'

'Ah indeed. Pleased to meet you, madam,' he said. 'If ever you need work, don't hesitate to come to me. Mrs Boucher here has my address.' He looked back at the copy. 'With practice you could become extremely good. A little studying, a little more finesse and your paintings could well be saleable.'

He bowed and left the house carrying his purchase as though it was the most precious thing in the world to him. Lily was suddenly triumphant, Polly had been right to sell the painting. If Matthew was cultivating Alice Sparks, Lily would need to look out for herself; the more money and assets she could amass, the better she would be prepared for the future.

Rosie stood at the fresh grave and raised her bowed head to look at Alice. Mrs Sparks had claimed to hate her father but now she was actually crying.

'He never loved me.' Alice stared at the grave adorned with a white marble headstone and threw a flower onto the newly turned earth. 'I wish he could have cared about me, Rosie, I wanted him to love me but he never did. I tried every trick I could think of to make him notice me. All I succeeded in doing was to turn him more against me.'

It had been a shock, the sudden death of the old man. Alice's father had seemed in robust health, had eaten a hearty supper before he went to bed but in the morning the maid found him dead.

'I'm sorry, Mrs Sparks,' Rosie said gently. 'It's hard for you to come home to try to make amends, only to lose your father like that.'

Alice sighed heavily. 'At the end Daddy must have cared about me because he made sure I would inherit his wealth.'

This was the third time they had visited the grave in as many days. It was as though, even now, Alice was seeking her father's approval. Rosie felt sorry for her; Alice had never been loved for herself. Even Mr Eynon Morton-Edwards had cast her aside when he no longer wanted her.

'Come on,' Rosie said, 'let's go home, it's getting cold here.'

'Poor father.' Alice allowed Rosie to draw her towards the gates of the cemetery. Outside, on the dusty lane, the elegant coach was waiting to take them back to the house.

'Your father reached a good age, remember,' Rosie said. 'I know it's not much comfort but he went when he was in good health and enjoying life.' She touched Alice's arm. 'And you had come home to him, what more could anyone ask?' Rosie bit her lip. 'My mam died too young,' she said softly.

'I know,' Alice touched her hand. 'We're both alone now, we'll just have to look after each other, won't we?' She was forgetting that Rosie had a husband. Even if Watt was now a husband in name only, Rosie was still married to him.

The short carriage drive was soon over and Rosie climbed down from the steps the driver had provided. Alice lifted her skirt and, still with tears in her eyes, put her arm through Rosie's.

'I know I've always been selfish, Rosie, but I mean it when I say that I really value your friendship.' She wiped her eyes with her fingers. 'You don't ask for anything, you don't even get an honest wage, but you're so kind. I don't know what I would do without you, promise you won't leave me.'

'I won't leave you,' Rosie said and she meant it. She had seen a different side of Alice in the past weeks, the soft, vulnerable side of a woman who had been badly hurt.

'I have to tell you something,' Alice said slowly. 'I hope you won't be too angry with me.'

'I won't be angry with you,' Rosie smiled. 'I'm hardly ever angry with anyone. Except Watt Bevan that is.'

'It's about him,' Alice said. 'He called yesterday when you were fetching butter from the farm. He wanted to see you but I sent him away. I did do right, didn't I?'

Rosie had mixed feelings about Watt; the thought that he had come looking for her was somehow comforting and yet nothing had changed;

he did not love her, had never loved her. 'Yes,' she said, 'you did the right thing.'

'He might come back today,' Alice said. 'If he does, you'll stand firm, won't you?'

'I'll stand firm,' Rosie said but her heart was leaping in her chest and somehow the day seemed to be brighter. Perhaps Watt had realized that he did love her after all. But no, she was as sad as Alice, clutching at straws like a child. Well she was a grown woman now and she had her own life to make. Sadly it did not include Watt Bevan.

Watt lay across the bed in the small house in Greenhill, staring up at the cracked ceiling. He had spent a sleepless night examining his feelings. He had married in haste, that much was true. He had married Rosie for all the wrong reasons so how could he blame her for running off, for being unwilling to accept second best?

He had found out where Rosie was staying and, yesterday, he had ridden from Swansea to see her. Alice Sparks had sent him away; she had told him in no uncertain terms that he did not deserve a gem like Rosie.

'That girl needs to be loved,' she said. 'You took her dreams of romance and stamped them into the ground. Did you really expect a girl of Rosie's quality to put up with that?'

He had been angry but, now, after thinking about it all night, he realized she was right. Rosie was beautiful and intelligent. She had pride and spirit. Any woman who had the courage to leave a loveless marriage deserved the best life had to offer.

Did he love her? He was not sure. But he definitely wanted the chance to find out. He pushed himself up from the bed. The dawn light was breaking over the land, and the world seemed fresh and lovely.

Later, when he was dressed, he walked across the bellying hills towards the large house where Rosie worked. His heart beat swiftly at the thought of seeing her. He could only hope that she would agree to seeing him this time.

He was not turned away as he expected, instead he was invited into the kitchen. The fire roared in the grate and servants worked busily, ignoring his presence. After a time, Rosie appeared in the doorway and beckoned to him. He followed her eagerly into one of the back rooms and stood staring at her.

The morning sun lit her hair and touched her cheeks with gold. She had matured; she was no longer the innocent girl he had married; she had become a beautiful unobtainable woman.

'Rosie,' he began, 'I've been a thoughtless fool and I want a chance to make it up to you.'

'Don't you think it's a bit late for that, Watt?' She spoke calmly, her brow unruffled. She was not angry with him and that worried him.

'I was wrong to marry you, I see that now. Pearl and I were old friends and I felt responsible for her. I knew that her family meant a great deal to her and I suppose I wanted to comfort her when she fell sick. The only way to take care of you all was to marry into the family.'

She nodded as though the answer was what she

expected. She looked down at her hands and he felt his heart melt within him. She was slender as a reed, the fly-away hair secured by pins. His wife was so lovely he felt his heart melt.

'Rosie,' he said softly, not touching her, 'can I come courting you?' She did not look up; she was silent for so long that he wondered if she had heard him.

'Please, Rosie, I want us to get to know each other, to start all over again. Will you think about it?'

She met his eyes. 'I will think about it. But I am not moving back home with you, Watt, not now, perhaps not ever.' She smiled wryly. 'I've promised not to leave Alice and I intend to keep that promise.'

'Rosie, can't we just spend some time together?'

'Come to see me Sunday, it's my day off. We'll go out, we'll walk and talk. As you say, we need to get to know each other. I think you'd better go now, Watt, I've got work to do. I'll see you on Sunday.'

He left the house, his heart light with hope. Rosie was a lovely woman; she was good and kind as well as beautiful. If only she would give him the chance he would show her how much she meant to him.

He realized quite suddenly that he did love her with all his heart. He had been a blind fool not to have realized it before.

At least Rosie had not rejected him outright. She was willing to see him again. He thrust his hands into his pockets and whistled as he walked. One day, one day not too distant, he would take

Rosie in his arms and repeat his marriage vows to her. And he would love her as no man had ever loved his wife before.

CHAPTER THIRTY-TWO

John strolled along the road breathing in the fine evening air. It was a good day for a man to become a landowner, to find his rightful place in society again. John could not forget his roots. He had been born to luxury; he was not one of the lower orders, he was a gentleman.

Life as a working man had never been easy for him. But soon he would be the owner of the Mainwaring Pottery and it was a good thought. He would have to rename the place of course and the Pendennis China Company would do nicely. All that remained was for him to collect his money from Sparks.

He smiled to himself. Everyone thought he was mad buying a failing business. But he knew why it was failing and so did Edward Sparks, the cunning bastard! Just give him a few months and John Pendennis would be the owner of a fine business.

The house looked deserted and John frowned. Edward had been conspicuous by his absence lately and, suddenly, John felt uneasy.

John hammered on the door more loudly and at

last heard footsteps coming across the hall. Edward himself answered the door. The man was unshaven; he looked as if he had been drinking. His bleary eyes focused on John and he stepped back a pace. 'Oh, John, it's you.'

'Yes, it's me.' John pushed past him, it was clear that Sparks had no intention of asking him in. 'I've come for my money, I do hope you have it ready for me.' He strolled into the drawing room, looking round him appraisingly. Elegantly furnished though it was, the place smelled of stale smoke and there was a port stain on the side table.

'It's not convenient right now,' Sparks said, his speech was slurred; he seemed like a man in a daze. 'Can you come back in the morning?'

'What is this?' John spun on his heel and looked closely at Sparks. 'You know I needed that money today. Just go and get it, if you know what's good for you.'

'I'm in serious trouble.' Edward Sparks sank into a chair and put his hands over his eyes. 'The auditors have found my alterations to the books.' He looked up suddenly, his eyes were bloodshot and he was sweating.

'I still want my money.' John was becoming angry. 'Your problems are no concern of mine. Come on, where is my share of the money you've embezzled?'

Sparks spread his hands wide. 'It's gone, just gone.'

John felt a pain in the pit of his stomach. 'All of it?'

Sparks nodded. 'All gone.'

'What about the sum of money I gave you at the

start of our deal?' John said desperately. 'I want it back right now!'

Sparks shook his head. 'It's no good,' he said. 'I meant to invest your money but I never got round to it.' He glanced at John, a frightened expression on his face. 'Everything has gone wrong, can't you understand? I've been dismissed from my job. I might go to prison.'

John grabbed him by the throat. 'My money, where is it?'

'I had debts, gambling debts and it's all your fault.' Sparks was nearly in tears. 'I'm sorry, I'm so sorry, everything is crashing down around me and I can't stand it!'

'Sorry!' John felt the blood pounding in his head. The man had ruined the best deal John would ever be offered in life and he said he was sorry.

John's fist shot out and connected with the side of Sparks's head. The man fell to the ground, cringing like the coward he was. His glasses went spinning across the room and cracked.

'I can't help it, John!' Sparks blubbered. 'I'm in deeper trouble than you know, so please don't hit me again.' He lay against the carpet, his eyes closed. 'I gambled, like a fool I wrote promissory notes. If I don't pay the rest of my debts I'll be killed for sure.'

John kicked out at Sparks's booted foot. 'Then the job will be done for me!' He left the man lying on the floor and began to search the house.

He dragged open drawers and threw the contents on the floor. He searched the rooms one by one, coming up with only a few cheap trinkets.

When John returned to the drawing room he found Sparks crouching in a chair, his eyes wide with fear.

'Is there a safe in the house or anything of value?' John demanded. Sparks shook his head; he seemed to be in some sort of dream, as though his mind had deserted his feeble body. John slapped him hard.

'Please,' Sparks said, 'please don't hit me, there's nothing here. If there was anything to sell don't you think I would have sold it by now?'

John pulled the gold watch from Sparks's pocket. It would not fetch a great deal of money but it was something. 'Have you a safe?' He hit Sparks again and the man began to cry. John hit him again and, finally, Sparks nodded.

'It's in the cupboard under the stairs,' he said. 'But it needs two keys to open it and I don't know where they are.'

'You'd better think about it then if you don't want me to flay the skin off your back,' John said angrily.

'But there's nothing in the safe.' Sparks protested. 'Alice took everything when she left.'

John punched Sparks in the face and left him sprawling against the chair, blood pouring from his nose. The man was trash; he did not have the wit of a new-born child. 'I know that's a lie! Tell me where the keys are.'

'I don't know, I tell you, I don't know.' The man was blubbering and John pushed him away scornfully.

'I'll just have to look for myself, won't I?' The safe was a solid one made of heavy cast iron. It looked impenetrable. John felt on the floor behind the safe, a favourite hiding place for keys. His fingers found only cobwebs.

Crouching on his heels, he looked around him and saw the plant pot in the hallway sporting a large leafy succulent. He dug his fingers in the dirt and grunted in satisfaction as they closed on something cold and metallic. Both keys were there and John wiped the earth away from them carefully.

The safe swung open with ease but all that was inside was a bundle of papers. He drew them out and took them to the hall table. The deeds of the house crackled crisply between his fingers. John searched through all the documents and found, to his surprise, that the house was fully paid for. At least that was something. He thrust the papers into his pocket.

He looked around; the house was a good solid building, he would have no trouble selling it. But first he must get Sparks to sign it all over to him.

Sparks had not moved from the chair. He was holding a kerchief to his nose and his eyes were beginning to turn black.

'If you do as I say, we'll be able to salvage something out of this mess,' John said.

Sparks looked up at him hopelessly. 'How?'

'The house,' John said, 'it's yours, free and clear.'

Sparks shook his head. 'Alice paid for it with money from her lover. It's not my property, it's hers.'

'You must sign it over to me. What's your wife's is yours, you know that as well as I do.'

521

'That would take time, we'd need a notary or someone to witness it all.' He sat up straighter in his chair. 'Anyway, how could I trust you to give me any of the money for the house even if you do have time to sell it?' He seemed to have recovered some of his spirit.

'That's your problem.' John was congratulating himself for his good luck. He could find a lawyer within the hour and, even if the house could not be sold immediately, it provided enough collateral to impress even the most careful bank manager.

'All right.' Sparks seemed resigned now, willing to do whatever John suggested. He had nothing better to offer.

'I'll be back within the hour,' John said. 'Don't leave the house under any circumstances, do you hear me?'

'I won't leave the house, you can depend on that,' Sparks said quietly. 'I haven't left the house in days. I told you, I have gambling debts and I have no intention of getting my throat cut or something equally brutal.'

John let himself out of the house and stared up at the evening sky. Clouds were racing in from the east and a chill wind had sprung up. Under normal circumstances no-one would find a lawyer willing to work at such a time of day but these were not normal circumstances. In any case, John knew a man of law who owed him a favour. John smiled to himself; he had learned a long time ago that it was a wise move to make anyone of influence beholden to him.

'You've agreed to sell! What are you thinking of,

Llinos?' Watt said incredulously. She shook her head at him.

'There's nothing else I can do, you must see that.' She sighed heavily. 'You know the debt we're in, the problems we face. At least by selling to John Pendennis I can keep a roof over my son's head.'

'I never trusted John Pendennis, you know that.' Watt paced across the room. 'This is just madness, we have made a handsome profit over the last year, where's all the money?'

'What if Joe has taken it as Sparks claimed?' Llinos asked.

'Never in this life! Joe wouldn't leave you penniless, it's not in his nature. In any case, we all know that Sparks is under suspicion, he's been suspended from the bank and he might well be facing criminal charges.'

Llinos's mind was on Joe; even his name had the power to thrill her. She remembered his bright blue eyes smiling into hers, his silky black hair brushing her skin. She tasted again his mouth on hers, thought of the warmth between them as they lay entwined in each other's arms, and the pain in her heart was almost too much to bear.

'I know you're right but, whatever's happened, even if Sparks has been stealing from my account, the end result is the same, I have no money to pay my bills.'

'But you have to fight for your rights!' Watt said desperately. 'You can't just go under like this.'

'Perhaps, but I'm tired. I've racked my brains to think of another way out but I can't.' Llinos felt like weeping. 'The debts have piled up and there's no money to pay for stock. I don't want to fight any more. I've got that right, haven't I, Watt?'

'Maybe, but Joe is your husband, if I contacted him he would fight for you, can't you give him credit for that at least?'

'How long would it take to find Joe, Watt?' Llinos said. 'We don't know where he is, probably in America with Sho Ka. Anyway, it's too late to hope for help from that quarter.'

She saw a strange look on Watt's face and stared at him closely. 'Have you been in touch with Joe? Come on, Watt, tell me the truth.'

He nodded. 'Don't be angry, I sent Joe a letter some time ago. He did not follow that girl back to America; he's been living on the border, on his own estate, for some time now.' Watt brushed back his hair.

'No wonder Charlotte has been talking about going back home lately.' Llinos took a deep breath. 'Am I the last one to know where my husband is living?'

Watt did not reply and Llinos felt anger growing inside her. 'So I'm not to know where my husband is until you see fit, is that it? How dare you, Watt!'

'I'm sorry, Llinos, I didn't know what to do.'

She felt close to tears. 'You are a man, Watt, explain to me why Joe was unfaithful to me?'

'Men are not like women.' Watt was clearly uncomfortable. 'A man can be *with* a woman and she can mean little or nothing to him.'

'I can't believe Sho Ka meant nothing to Joe. In any case, did you sleep with another woman when you lived with Maura?' She stared at him, daring him to lie to her. He looked away.

'No, I didn't. But that doesn't mean I wasn't tempted.' He ran his hand through his hair. 'If I saw a lovely girl I lusted after her, I admit it.'

'But you didn't do anything but think about it, did you? That's the difference between you and Joe. You stayed faithful to Maura while she was alive.'

Watt sighed. 'Look, don't ask me to be wise! I've made a right mess of my love life, haven't I? People have faults, Llinos.' He smiled ruefully. 'And men can be coerced into anything given the right set of circumstances.'

'Were you forced into a marriage you didn't want, then?' Llinos stared at Watt, he was trying to excuse what Joe had done by claiming men were weak. Well it would not wash. Joe had betrayed his wife and his child. He had left them destitute and all for another woman.

'In a way, I was,' Watt said. 'More by my own conscience than anything else. I felt obliged to help Pearl.' He smiled then, like a wicked boy. 'And I admit I fancied Rosie like crazy.'

'But you didn't love her?'

Watt sighed heavily. 'Not then. I do now and love might have come too late for me. Think carefully before you write your marriage off, Llinos, give Joe a chance.'

Before Llinos could reply, the door opened and the maid peered in.

'A visitor, madam.' She bobbed a curtsey. 'It's Mr Eynon Morton-Edwards, shall I show him in?'

Llinos nodded and gave Watt a warning glance. 'Don't say anything about my troubles to Eynon, right?'

Eynon was flushed from the fresh morning air. He swept Llinos into his arms and kissed her on both cheeks.

'Llinos, you're looking lovelier than ever.' He turned to Watt and shook hands with him. Watt might be below Eynon in station but Eynon had never been a snob.

'You looking after my lovely friend properly, Watt?' Eynon felt at ease in Llinos's company.

Watt forced a smile. 'I'm doing my best but Llinos is a strong-minded woman, you know that as well as I do.'

Eynon nodded. 'I do indeed.' He paused. 'Enough of the pleasantries, I want to know what's going on.'

Watt moved rapidly to the door. 'I'd better get back to work, there's a lot to be done, kilns to check, pots to be glazed, you know.'

When Watt left the room Eynon seated himself in one of the armchairs, his fair hair falling over his brow. He was looking at her questioningly and she forced a smile.

'I'm just fine, Eynon, how about you?'

He sighed heavily. 'Did you really think I wouldn't find out about the trouble you're in?'

'I don't want to talk about it, Eynon.'

'Well you're going to have to talk about it. Look, Llinos, I only want to help you.'

'How?'

'I'll pay off the creditors for a start and then I'll tear that man Sparks from limb to limb!'

Llinos thought of the little bank manager with his long nose and his sweating brow and shuddered. Surely he was too weak, too pitiful, to have stolen money from her account?

'Sparks has been caught embezzling.' Eynon must have read her thoughts. 'No wonder your bills weren't paid, the money was finding its way into Sparks's own pockets.' He shook his head. 'The man wasn't even clever in the way he went about it. His bookkeeping was crude to say the least. He's bound to end up in prison.'

He leaned forward and stared earnestly at Llinos. 'Give me all your bills and let me see to them for you.'

'No, I'm all right, there's nothing going on that I can't handle.' Llinos looked away; she had no intention of letting Eynon take over her life. She knew that he would give her any amount of money she asked for but she would not be beholden to any man ever again.

'But I want to help.'

'Don't!' Llinos felt she could take no more. She rose to her feet and walked to the door. 'I have to rest, Eynon, forgive me,' she said and, quietly, she left the room.

Edward stared at himself in the mirror above the mantelpiece. He looked a sight; his glasses were cracked and his nose would not stop bleeding. But the few smacks John Pendennis had given him would be nothing to the treatment he would receive if Bull did not get his money.

He tried to think clearly, to find a way out of the mess. Surely there must be a way to keep himself alive if not out of prison? Soon John would be back, coercing him into signing away his house but why should John Pendennis get away with anything? Edward was in the mire and it would give him some satisfaction if John ended up in the mire with him.

Why not offer Bull the deeds of the house as payment of the debt? Perhaps he should clean himself up and see Bull right away. Galvanized now, he hurried towards the safe. It was empty. John had taken the deeds with him.

Edward sank onto the floor and put his head in his hands, it was the end of the road, he was ruined, he would rot in jail until he died. Or worse, he would die a violent death.

How he hated everyone: Alice and her spend-thrift ways, Llinos Mainwaring and now John Pendennis. They were all out to get him, to see him brought down like a hunted animal. Well he would not give them the satisfaction, not any of them.

There was a sudden thunderous knocking on the door and Edward jerked backwards, fear turning his belly to water. He knew who it was, Bull come to get his money. A rough voice called to him from outside and his worst fears were confirmed.

'Open the door, you lily-livered bastard! You've hidden away long enough! Come on, open up, I want my money and I want it now.'

Edward clambered to his feet and picked up the bottle of brandy that Alice had kept for her more elegant visitors. Not that there had been any. Just as well; he needed another drink right now.

He took off the stopper and held the decanter to his lips, allowing the tawny liquid to slip down his throat. It stung like fire and Edward gasped for breath. But the drink warmed his belly, made him feel in charge of his destiny. He tipped the bottle up again and again until it was almost empty.

'Fire water!' He staggered across the room. 'Hell fire and damnation! Damnation to you, Alice!' He belched loudly. 'And to you, Mrs high-and-mighty Mainwaring! Damnation to all gamblers, most of all damnation to John Pendennis. I'll cheat the lot of you yet.'

He lit a taper from the fire and set light to the edge of the curtains. The flame took hold and roared upwards with a sound like a great gale. Edward laughed. 'Hell fire!' He drained the bottle and flung it into the grate. The flame leapt from behind the bars, picking up the dregs of brandy, and raced towards the carpet.

'Burn, you bastards! Burn, the whole damned lot of you!' He staggered from the room and, clinging to the banister, staggered up the stairs. He left the door of the bedroom open and flung himself onto the bed, seeing, with fascination, the flickering glow of fire from the hallway dance on the ceiling and walls.

The large quantity of brandy he had consumed was making his head spin. Spirals of smoke were weaving across the room towards him like hissing snakes. He held up his arms as if to welcome them. If he had to die then it would be by his own hand. Edward Sparks would show them all just what he was made of. He would never rot in a stinking jail. He would not allow himself to be humiliated by men no better than himself. This house was his and it was fitting it should burn to the ground rather than belong to someone else.

He began to cough as the smoke became thicker. He breathed it in and felt it sear his lungs. A great darkness was coming to close him in and he welcomed it.

CHAPTER THIRTY-THREE

The doctor had just left and Alice was lying against her pillows, her hair dishevelled, her face pale, but then the doctor had bled Alice quite copiously, a practice that Rosie would have declined had she been the patient. She had remained in the room throughout the examination; she had heard the doctor tell Alice that she had an inflamed stomach. Privately, she thought the doctor was making light of Alice's condition.

'I'm sure it's worse than he's telling me.' Alice's words reflected Rosie's own thoughts. She propped herself up on the pillows and Rosie hastened to help her. 'I feel so ill.'

'Try not to worry,' Rosie said. 'It's only a little over a week since you buried your father remember, you are bound to be unsettled.'

Alice looked up at her a little sheepishly. 'I know, I suppose I'm already putting father out of my mind. I'm so selfish, aren't I?'

'Of course not!' Rosie protested. 'You just are at a low ebb right now.'

Rosie was adjusting the bedcovers when one of

the maids knocked on the door and peered inside. 'Please, madam, there's a message for you.'

Alice looked up at her. 'All right then, come in, girl, and give it to me.'

The maid handed her a letter and stepped back as though frightened of Alice's reaction.

'Oh my God!' Alice looked up at Rosie. 'He's dead, Edward is dead.'

'He can't be!' It was a stupid thing to say. Rosie took the letter and read it herself and she shook her head.

'How awful, to die in a fire like that!'

'There's a big spread about it in the newspaper, madam,' the maid ventured and Rosie waved her away impatiently. 'Not now, Sadie!'

'Bring it.' Alice's tone was curt. 'I want to see what they say about him.'

Rosie led the maid to the door and closed it firmly behind her. This was the last thing Alice needed right now.

'I'm sorry, Mrs ... er ... Alice.' She would never get used to calling Mrs Sparks by her given name, Rosie thought. 'I would have tried to stop Sadie telling you had I known. You've had one awful shock after another, no wonder you feel ill.'

'Don't be sorry,' Alice said heavily. 'Edward dying might be the one decent thing he's ever done in his life. He was a crook and a liar and a mean-spirited man into the bargain.'

'It's a shock all the same,' Rosie said firmly. 'Shall I cancel your visitors for this afternoon?'

'No!' Alice shook her head. 'I'm not too ill to receive guests for afternoon tea, Rosie. You heard what the doctor said, I've got an inflamed stomach not a sore tongue.'

The maid returned with the newspaper and handed it to Alice. 'Cook says it's good riddance to him, madam.'

'Don't be impertinent!' Alice flapped her hand impatiently and the girl almost ran to the door. Alice smoothed out the creases of the paper and began to read.

'Says here he drank himself to death and set fire to the house accidentally.' Alice's slim finger pointed to the page. 'Oh dear, I knew Edward was in trouble with the bank but it seems my husband mounted up heavy gambling debts into the bargain. Doesn't sound at all like the Edward I knew.'

'They do exaggerate things though, don't they?' Rosie plumped up the pillows. 'Rest now and you'll be nice and fresh in time for tea.'

Alice flung down the paper. 'It's all so much rubbish!' She rubbed her face wearily. 'Stay for a while, talk to me, you are the only one who cares about me at all. You won't leave me, will you, Rosie?'

'No of course I won't,' Rosie said stoutly. 'But please, try to sleep a little. I'm sure you'll feel better after a rest.'

It was as if Alice had not heard her. 'Edward would have been heir to my father's money by law, you know,' Alice said. 'My father tied it all up as best he could but, eventually, the entire estate would have gone to my husband. Good thing he didn't find that out before he . . . well.' She smiled wryly. 'If he'd known he was rich, he would never have died, I'm convinced of that.'

Rosie did not comment; she was not familiar with the law regarding such things. She would never possess wealth to any great degree so had never been interested in women's rights.

Women had a place in the home, bringing up children, while the man went out to work. The right to rule over her own house was all a woman should want. Still, on reflection, perhaps it was wrong that the law gave a man the right to take his wife's inheritance.

Alice sighed. 'Had I given birth to a healthy son things might have been different. Father might have been able to leave his estate to his only male heir.' She shrugged. 'Anyway, it's my money now and I can do as I like with it.'

Rosie could see that the thought gave Alice a great deal of satisfaction. She need never be dependent on any man for as long as she lived.

Rosie knew her own position in life was vastly different to Alice's. Rosie would always have to work or else be kept by a man. Life could be so unfair sometimes.

It was as if Alice had read her thoughts. 'I am going to put some money in trust for you, Rosie,' she said. 'I want to repay you for all the kindness you showed me when I had nothing but debts hanging around my neck.'

'But . . .' Rosie was about to protest and Alice held up her hand for silence. She smiled; her spirits seemed to have revived. 'Don't argue, it's something I want to do. I know you and Watt haven't exactly seen eye to eye and I don't want you to be dependent on him.'

She hesitated. 'I haven't been a very nice person

to live with, I know that, Rosie. I've been selfish and high-handed. My father reared me to despise the lower orders but knowing you changed all that.'

She shook her head sadly. 'And being Edward's wife has made me realize what it's like to live a joyless, friendless life. Now stop going on at me to rest. Get me out of this bed and help me dress. I'm expecting an admirer to come calling, remember?'

Later, when Alice was satisfied with her appearance, Rosie helped her down the curving staircase and settled her in front of the fire in the drawing room.

'Just in time, Rosie.' Alice smiled as the front doorbell clanged, the sound echoing through the house. Rosie instinctively got to her feet. Alice waved her back into her chair.

'You are not a servant now, Rosie, you are my companion, my chaperone.' She giggled. 'That's rich, isn't it, me who enjoyed all the sins of the flesh, having a chaperone. I'd say it's just a little too late for that. But stay when my visitors arrive, won't you? I like to appear to be a lady even if I'm a whore at heart.'

'You must not be too hard on yourself,' Rosie protested. 'You make yourself out to be a bad person but really, deep down, you are just like the rest of us, looking for love.'

'You understand me so well.' Alice sighed. For a moment her face fell into lines of sadness. It was at such times that Rosie saw the real woman behind the laughing, flirtatious façade Alice presented to the world.

The door opened and suddenly the room

seemed full of people. Rosie felt uncomfortable as the two gentlemen and their ladies seated themselves around the room, all of them ignoring Rosie in her drab calico gown and worn shawl.

Rosie recognized Lily though she was wearing fine clothes. She was the painter who had worked at the pottery with Rosie's mother. Now she was clinging to the arm of an old man who was making every effort to untangle himself.

'Matthew, how nice to see you!' Alice was graciousness itself. No-one would suspect she had just risen from her sick bed. 'And Jem Boucher too! You are most welcome.' She paused. The pause lengthened. Rosie hid a smile; Alice could insult without opening her mouth. She was deliberately sizing up the two women, making it obvious she felt their social superior.

'And your,' she paused again, 'your ladies are welcome too. I will ring for some refreshments, you will take tea with me and my companion here?'

It seemed to Rosie that hundreds of pairs of eyes stared at her, seeing her in a new light. Lily's face was hostile; she had never liked Rosie's mother and no doubt Lily was uncomfortable in Rosie's presence, Rosie knew far too much about her past.

Alice was quite aware of the situation and not prepared to let matters rest. 'Ah, Lily, you used to work at the pottery, didn't you?' she said. 'And then for a time you came to me as a maid. Not a very good maid at that.' She giggled. 'Perhaps being mistress to a rich man suits you better?'

Lily stiffened. Her thoughts were written plain on her face: she had realized she was foolish to come here, to put herself in such a vulnerable position. Her friend leapt to her defence.

'Lily is a fine painter,' Polly said. 'She's even had drawings in some of the better papers.'

'I know,' Alice said. 'I believe I was the subject of one such drawing. Do you enjoy ruining reputations, Lily?'

Rosie concealed a smile; Alice was at her best when she was fencing spiteful words with an adversary she did not like.

'At least I am not tied to a man who should be in prison,' Lily said huffily.

'Neither am I.' Alice's tone was touched with ice. 'It might have escaped your notice but my husband is dead, consumed by flames, hell's flames in your opinion I take it? I thought the British judiciary deemed a man innocent until proven guilty.'

Lily had the grace to blush. Her remark had been tasteless in the extreme. It was Matthew Starky who filled the sudden silence.

'I'm so sorry about your sad loss. Your husband's death so soon after the demise of your dear father must have hit you hard.' He took Alice's hand. 'I'm sure we are all here to offer our deepest sympathy.' He glared at Lily and she looked quickly away. Even Rosie could see that Lily's days as a rich man's darling were almost over.

Tea was served and Rosie settled herself in a corner seat, prepared to watch and listen. She had no intention of becoming part of the conversation; she was out of her depth with such people and knew it.

Rosie observed that the attention Matthew was

paying to Alice was more than just friendly. He seemed genuinely interested in her but then, as Alice caustically put it, her inheritance would excite any man.

Alice flirted outrageously with Matthew, enjoying Lily's dark glances. Alice had rouged her cheeks to give herself some colour and, animated as she was now, she was very beautiful.

Lily fidgeted; the girl was edgy, clearly aware that her hold on Matthew was wearing very thin. He had his sights set on a fresh conquest and she did not like it one bit.

It was growing dark by the time the visitors left. Alice sighed with relief and kicked her shoes off her feet, stretching her toes towards the cheerful fire.

'Thank the good Lord for that!' she said. 'Did you see how that old goat Matthew was making eyes at me? He's got more chance of winning you over than me and that's saying something!'

'You don't like him then?' Rosie asked. 'I thought he was rather nice.'

'He is nice.' Alice chuckled. 'But I don't intend to marry him or anyone else. Why should I give my father's fortune to any man? No, I'll content myself with a lover or two, there will be no marriage for me. Would you marry again if you had your time over?'

'Not to Watt, not as soon as I did, anyway. It was all a terrible mistake. I do love Watt but I'm not happy to always walk in the shadow of his first love.'

'I've got something to confess.' Alice looked across at Rosie. 'I should have told you before, a letter came for you, from your husband.'

'From Watt?'

'Yes, from Watt. I read it.'

Rosie did not know if she felt amused or angry at Alice's interference. 'Did you answer it as well?'

'I didn't go that far.' Alice pointed to the small table near the window. 'It's over there. You must answer it as you see fit.'

Rosie picked up the letter, her hands shaking. 'Will you excuse me, Alice?' she said quietly. Alice nodded.

'If I must.'

Rosie took the letter up to her room and sank onto the bed as she smoothed the crackling page flat. Watt's writing seemed to spring up at her; his signature was a bold flourish. Watt was an educated man, he had been brought up with Llinos Mainwaring and had probably learned a great deal from her.

Rosie's education had been sketchy but she could read well enough to know that Watt wanted her back. He asked for another chance to talk to her. He even signed the word 'love' on the bottom of the page.

Rosie felt her heartbeat quicken. Did Watt love her or was it just a word he used to sign off his message? In any case, she must see him, give him the chance he asked for. She took a sheet of paper from her drawer and began to write. Her letter was brief and to the point. She had agreed to see Watt and talk to him but he must take nothing for granted.

She folded the note and let her lips rest for a moment on the cool paper. She wanted Watt to love her more than she had ever wanted anything in the whole of her life. But for now, at least, Rosie would stay where she was really needed, at Alice's side.

'You were making sheep's eyes at her all the time we were there.' Lily was sitting on the edge of her chair in Polly's luxurious sitting room. 'I have never been so humiliated in all my life!'

'I was the one to be humiliated!' Matthew was standing before the fireplace, a glass of port in his hand. His colour was high; he did not appreciate his mistress's attempt to belittle him before Jem and Polly. 'You contributed nothing to the conversation, all you did was make a tasteless remark to our hostess. I suppose the lack of breeding was bound to show one day.'

'How dare you!' Lily stood up abruptly, her face as red as Matthew's. 'I'm not a whore or a serving wench, I am a respectable woman.'

'So it's respectable to live like a parasite on a foolish old man, is it?' Matthew demanded. 'Well, I've had enough of you, Lily, you are free to go and be respectable at someone else's expense.'

Polly tried to intervene; she raised her hands and looked to Jem for help. 'Don't let's argue,' she said, 'we will all feel better when we calm down.'

Lily ignored her. 'Very well, I'll go then.' She walked to the door. 'If you no longer want me, Matthew, I won't stay around. I have my pride you know and I am not the fool you take me for, Matthew.'

He refused to answer, keeping his face turned away from her; his shoulders were hunched. He was really angry; he wanted her out of his life. A great sense of bitterness filled her. Matthew was the one man with whom she had felt safe. He had been protective and kind, but now he wanted another woman and Lily was to be cast away like a worn coat.

'She'll never have you,' she said bitterly. 'Alice Sparks is too wise for that. Do you really think she would tie herself to an old goat like you when she has pots of money of her own?'

Matthew turned and glared at her, his eyes were bright with anger. 'Leave now, madam.' He ground out the words. 'Leave before I lose my temper and raise my hand to you.'

Lily saw that he meant every word. She left the room and hurried across the hall to the front door. Her vision was blurred; she had burnt her boats. Matthew would never forgive her now.

Polly followed her and caught her arm. 'You silly little fool!' she hissed. 'You handled that the wrong way. Matthew would have pensioned you off, made sure you kept the house, all sorts of things. You know what men are like when they feel guilty; they'll give you the earth. Now you'll have nothing.'

'Go back to your husband, Polly,' Lily said wearily. 'I've learned a lot from you, remember? I have stored away gifts of money and jewellery as well as my share of the money for the painting you sold that art dealer. You see, I can thieve and cheat and lie, you taught me well.'

She climbed into Matthew's carriage; she was damned if she was going to walk back to her house. She smiled at Matthew's driver. 'I've got a headache, Johnson,' she said softly, 'the master wants you to take me back to his house at once.'

The man obeyed without question and Lily sank back in the seat. She turned to look back once, watching the small figure of Polly disappear from view, and then she began to make plans for her future.

She would go to Matthew's house, take everything of value she could carry. Then, when she was ready, Lily would shake the dust of Swansea from her feet for ever.

CHAPTER THIRTY-FOUR

Llinos stared into the fire; the house seemed even emptier without Charlotte's cheerful presence. Was it only a week ago that she had seen her sister-in-law safely on the coach to Joe's estate on the borders of England and Wales?

Dear, sweet Charlotte had held Llinos in her arms and apologized for not being able to do more for her.

Llinos had been reassuring, telling her to enjoy her holiday and to come back refreshed.

A gentle tapping on the drawing-room door startled her out of her thoughts. 'Llinos, it's me, am I disturbing you? I'm sorry to call so late.'

'Come in, Watt, I'll be glad of the company,' Llinos said quietly.

Watt sat down. 'Terrible about Mr Sparks dying in the fire. I knew he was a crook but no-one deserves such a fate. Anyway, I was wondering what would happen down at the bank now he's gone.'

'Everything will be sorted out, it will just take time. But that's not what you want to talk about is it? What's really bothering you?' Llinos asked.

'I always knew you could see right through me.' He handed her Rosie's note. 'See? She wants to stay with Alice Sparks at least until the woman is well again.' He sighed. 'Oh, I suppose she'll come up to Greenhill every week to see the boys. She'll do the washing and spend a few hours baking but she won't stay. It looks to me as if Rosie has got a taste for high living these days.'

Llinos read the brief letter. 'I'm sorry, Watt,' she said returning the note. 'I can't blame her for not leaving Alice Sparks right now. The poor woman sounds quite ill and she *has* just lost her husband. Look on the bright side, at least Rosie's willing for you to call and talk to her, that's hopeful isn't it?'

Watt threw the letter into the fire. 'I'm a fool,' he said. 'I didn't treasure Rosie when I had her. Well, the shoe's on the other foot now.'

'She'll come round, just give her time.' Llinos bit her lip; who was she to advise when her own life was far from perfect? But then no-one's life was ever perfect. Folks had to make the best of what they had.

'Watt, do you mind if we talk about business?' Llinos asked. He nodded and she took a deep breath. 'I haven't heard anything from John Pendennis, it looks like he's backed out of the deal he made me.' She stood up and paced across the carpet.

'I've been so weak, I've let everything slide because my husband deserted me. But that's all in the past now I've decided not to sell. I'm going to fight tooth and nail for the pottery so at least I can say my career was a success.'

'I'm so glad!' Watt said quickly. 'That's more like the Llinos I knew.' He leaned forward, his expression earnest. 'Remember when your mother died? You were little more than a child, I was even younger, yet we muddled through somehow, didn't we? You were so brave then, I admired you so much.'

'Well, I'm going to be brave again, Watt.' Llinos rubbed her hands against her skirts. 'I'm going to see Alice Sparks, ask her to make amends for what her husband has done. She can well afford it from what I've heard.'

'You heard right! Mrs Sparks inherited her father's estate; she has more money than she will ever use. But whether she will hand any of it over to you is another matter.'

'I'm sure I can persuade her,' Llinos said. 'Rosie is so loyal to her Alice Sparks can't be all bad.' She suddenly felt alive again, inspired. She was like a sleepwalker waking from a long dream. 'She might be obliged by law to repay the bank for the money her husband embezzled but, even if that is the case, it would all take far too long. I'd be bankrupt by the time the matter was settled.'

She smiled at Watt. 'So I mean to approach Mrs Sparks woman to woman, it's by far the best way. In the meantime, I will send letters to my creditors, tell them about the trouble at the bank. Surely the whole country must have heard of the fire that burnt the manager's house to the ground and him with it?'

'I'm sure you're right,' Watt said, 'repercussions will be felt outside the Swansea bank. And I do feel that Mrs Sparks will be held morally responsible if not legally responsible for her husband's debts.'

'That's the way forward then. You see, Watt, I'm beginning to find my courage again.'

'I can see that the light of battle is back in your eyes, Llinos, and it warms my heart. Look, I've got some money put away, you can have that to start with.'

'But you were saving to buy a little house, I can't take your savings,' Llinos said.

'Call it a loan,' Watt replied firmly. 'I'm quite happy in the little house in Greenhill, keeping an eye on Pearl's boys.' He grimaced. 'Not that they need me very much these days, they are out working or courting most of the time.'

'Well then, if you're sure about the money why don't we become partners?' Llinos said. 'If we can pull ourselves up by our bootstraps we might even make a profit again one day.'

'That sounds like an excellent idea. Let's get started right away. You write the letters to the creditors and I'll deliver them in the morning for you.'

'Oh Watt, we'll make it work, won't we?' She rubbed the tears away from her lashes.

'Hey!' Watt said. 'Don't go all weepy on me now! And yes we'll make it work, I promise you.' He walked towards the door. 'Now I'm going to bed but, first thing in the morning, I'll want those letters ready, all right?'

Llinos walked across the hallway with him. 'I'll have to dig out my old aprons,' she said.

Watt glanced at her, his eyebrows raised. 'Why, taking up cooking are you?'

'No I am not taking up cooking, but I'll need to work just as hard as you in the pottery, I've done it before and I can do it again.' She shivered in the cold night air.

'Good night, Watt, and thank you, for everything.' She watched as Watt walked across the yard then she returned to the drawing room and, taking some sheets of paper from her desk, she began to write.

John had packed his few belongings in a shabby bag and now he was waiting near the fire at the Mackworth Arms Inn for the coach that would take him round the borders of Gloucester, through Bristol and back to Cornwall.

He frowned; he was going home as penniless as when he had left. The watch he had taken from Edward Sparks had made him enough for the trip but with very little left over.

There was nothing in Swansea for him now that Polly had dismissed him from her life with a few well-chosen words. She had learned about his trips to the bawdy houses of Swansea and, worse, that he had brought whores into the house she had bought as a love nest. Curse Polly!

He felt a blast of cold air as the door swung open; a woman stepped inside, her eyes darting anxiously around the room. John stared at her. She was well dressed, her bag was new and shiny, everything about her appearance spoke of affluence.

She felt John's gaze and looked directly at him. He recognized her then, she was Polly Boucher's friend and Matthew Starky's mistress.

'Good evening.' He crossed the room towards her. 'We've met before, I'm sure you remember.'

She clearly did remember because she smiled and held out a gloved hand to him. 'Of course, Mr Pendennis, how good to see a familiar face.'

'I see you are going on a journey, would you like to sit with me while you wait for your transport?'

She smiled up at him in relief. 'Thank you so much. I'd been uncomfortable with the idea of travelling alone.'

'Where are you heading?' He led her to the corner seat he had secured for himself. 'And why are you leaving Swansea?' He wondered if his abrupt questions were too impertinent but she looked up at him, her eyes bright with anger.

'It seems I have served my purpose, I no longer have a place in Matthew Starky's life.'

He heard the bitterness in her voice and recognized it as an echo of his own.

'As for where I'm going,' she continued, 'I have no idea. I booked on the first coach travelling to the West Country. And you?'

'Like you I have no reason to stay in Swansea now,' he said. 'When that fool of a bank manager burnt down his house, he ruined me.' He looked at her carefully. Lily was wearing good jewellery and her boots were made of the finest leather, she was, obviously, still quite affluent.

It was possible that Matthew Starky had given her a good pension, which was the usual way a man disposed of a troublesome mistress. In any case it looked as if Lily had been wise enough to feather her own nest. It might be to his advantage to throw in his lot with her if only for a little while.

He cursed his honesty in telling her how he was placed. Still, he might be able to salvage something from the situation with a few well-chosen lies.

'Come with me to Cornwall,' he said. 'I have an estate there, you know.' He was at his most charming. 'I wanted to make my own fortune instead of living on my father's money but, there,' he shrugged, 'I didn't account for a crooked bank manager.'

'I never liked the Sparks man,' Lily said, 'but all the same it was dreadful that he burnt to death.'

'I agree, of course,' John said hurriedly. 'Well now that we've established that we know each other, what do you think? Are you coming with me to Cornwall? I can offer you protection until you find your feet, as it were.'

'I have only booked the coach as far as Bristol.' She looked up at him from under her lashes, her flirtatious expression encouragement enough.

'That can soon be remedied.'

'Well, let me think about it on the journey.' Lily was being cautious. 'We have plenty of time to get to know each other, haven't we?'

'Of course, you're right,' John said, making an effort to smile. He must be patient, the journey would involve several days of travelling, he had time enough to charm her. They would be obliged to make overnight stops at coaching inns and John had no money for such luxuries but with Lily so well placed that would be no problem.

They ate a meal of freshly baked bread and fine cheese and John insisted on paying the landlord. He was well aware that his meagre supply of money would not last very long but it was important to make a good impression right away. Lily would be repaying him a thousandfold, John would make sure of it.

It was almost dark by the time the coach was finally equipped with fresh horses and all the baggage loaded. John glanced at Lily. By the time the coach made its first stop he would be well in with her.

'Polly grown tired of you, I understand?' Her bluntness was a shock. Lily was not as easily fooled as he had first believed. 'She quickly forgot her whim to run off with you into the sunset.'

He decided to stick as close to the truth as he dared. 'Once Polly heard I had no prospects she no longer found me interesting,' he said tersely.

'Oh dear.' She allowed him to pull a rug over her legs. He was playing for time, thinking of some way to get round her. He need not have bothered.

'Look,' Lily said, 'I'm not a fool, I know you have nothing, why else was Polly paying all the bills for you?'

'It was an arrangement that suited us both,' John said. 'We were never in love but she needed a strong young man and I was happy to play the part.'

'I'll make you a deal,' Lily said, lowering her voice as other passengers came on board. 'I long for the respectability I had with my husband, I've had enough of being a mistress. You marry me, make me Mrs John Pendennis, and I'll look after you until you sort yourself out.'

He thought about it for a moment. What harm would there be in going through a ceremony with

Lily? It would not be valid, he was still a married man, but Lily did not know that.

'Lily,' he said, 'I would be honoured to have you as my wife.' He put his arm protectively around her shoulder and whispered in her ear.

'Let's start acting the part now, shall we? I'll be happy to take care of you until we make our vows in church.'

She smiled up at him. 'That's a lovely idea, husband.'

She was quick-witted, John realized with a dart of pleasure, together they might well make a good team. In any case he would at least get food and shelter out of her for the duration of the journey.

The driver shouted a command to the horses and the coach jerked into motion. 'We're on our way,' John said and, taking Lily's hand, he covered it with his own, congratulating himself that once again he had fallen on his feet.

'The creditors have agreed to my request.' Llinos sat at her desk and looked up into Watt's smiling face. 'See, I have the letters here. Now we've got a real chance to make the business prosper again.' She got to her feet and, on an impulse, hugged him. 'Thank you, Watt. For everything.'

'Don't thank me, your letters did the trick.' Watt hugged her back. 'I was just the delivery boy.'

'No I won't have that, your money certainly helped; nothing talks as loudly as money.'

'Well, I'll be paid back a thousandfold so don't worry about it. Listen, I have to go into town again today,' Watt said. 'Shall I take Lloyd with me? We could go across the river on the ferry boat, he'd like that.'

'That would be lovely for him,' Llinos said. 'I've hired a carriage to take me down to Alice Sparks's home so I'll be out most of the day.' She looked up at Watt. 'Have you got a message for Rosie?'

'Just tell her I love her.' Watt looked away in embarrassment. 'I'll go and get Lloyd.'

Llinos was putting on her coat in the hall when Lloyd came galloping downstairs, his scarf flying, his hat crooked. 'Mamma, I'm going across the Tawe on the boat!' He hugged her waist. 'Can we come back on the boat too?' He moved impatiently from one foot to the other as Llinos buttoned his coat around his chest.

'Well I should think so,' Llinos said. 'Otherwise you'd have to swim and it's a bit cold for that, isn't it? Here, put your hat on straight.' She kissed him and, as he twisted away, she smiled to herself. Lloyd believed he was too manly for kisses now. 'Behave yourself, do you hear me?'

She watched as Lloyd walked sturdily beside Watt and love flowed through her. Her son was everything to her now, the only one in the whole world who really needed her.

It was early afternoon by the time the carriage drew up outside the mansion where Alice Sparks lived. For a moment Llinos was intimidated by the sheer size of the building but, at last, she took a deep breath and rung the bell.

Alice was in the drawing room and Rosie was sitting with her, working a sampler in coloured silks.

'Rosie, you keeping well?' Llinos said quickly. 'Watt sends his love.'

'Mrs Mainwaring,' Alice intervened, 'I've been expecting you. Please take a seat, make yourself at home, we will have tea shortly.'

'It is very kind of you to see me, Mrs Sparks,' Llinos said awkwardly, 'though I'm sure you know my visit is not strictly a social one.'

'I do know and I'm happy to talk business but let me just say first how warmly Rosie has been singing your praises. She tells me you are a fine woman and a woman alone at that.'

Alice shook her head. 'Men! They can be such a disappointment. My husband had no time for women in business but then he was an ignorant spiteful little man.'

Llinos felt uncomfortable; everyone knew that Mr Sparks had died a terrible death. It seemed wrong to talk disparagingly about him.

There was silence for a moment and Llinos decided to get to the point of her visit before she lost her nerve. 'I explained my request in my letter to you,' Llinos said. 'I need a swift injection of money to build my pottery trade up again or it will be finished.'

Alice smiled. 'I know you won't say it, you are far too polite, but the decline in the business was my husband's doing.'

The maid brought the tea in and Rosie took the tray from her. Rosie seemed quite at home in the opulent surroundings of Alice's mansion.

'I have decided to reimburse you at once,' Alice said as she took a cup of tea. 'I know that the legalities of such a complex matter could go on endlessly by which time the pottery, as you say, would be finished.'

553

'That is very generous of you.' Llinos had not expected her request to be granted so easily.

'Put it down to Rosie's high regard for you,' Alice said smiling. 'And, I have the desire to see your little pottery succeed again.'

'Why should you care about the pottery?' Llinos asked.

'It will keep Rosie's husband busy.' Alice laughed out loud. 'I know the man wants her back and I want her to stay, at least for a while.'

'I see. Well thank you anyway.'

'Now with the business done let us just gossip like women, shall we?' Alice asked. 'What's happening in Swansea? I hear my friend Matthew has rid himself of his mistress.'

Llinos smiled. Alice, for all her wealth, was just an ordinary gossipy woman.

It was almost dark when Llinos returned to Swansea. As the carriage carried her past the river she could see the bobbing of lanterns on the bank and frowned in bewilderment.

'What's happening? What is it, driver, can you see?'

'Seems to be some sort of trouble with the ferry boat, Mrs Mainwaring.'

Llinos felt her heart begin to pound. 'I must go and see for myself.' She scrambled down from the seat, her feet slipped on the damp earth. She lifted her skirts and took the path leading down to the river.

Llinos caught the arm of one of the men holding a lantern. 'What is it, who was on board?'

'Full boat, Mrs Mainwaring. Seems your boy

along with Watt Bevan boarded the ferry at Foxhole. But don't worry too much, the rescuers are working as swiftly as they can. They'll have all the survivors ashore before long.'

The word 'survivors' sent chills through her. 'Please God,' Llinos whispered, 'don't take my son away from me!'

The rain pounded against her face, the cold wind whipped her dress around her legs as she strained to see the river through the darkness. The waters could be cruel on a night like this.

A crowd of onlookers surged onto the bank and Llinos fought to keep her place at the edge of the water. She could see figures bobbing like corks on the swell. It seemed impossible that anyone could be rescued in the cold and the darkness.

The clouds sped swiftly above her head and parted, a shaft of moonlight illuminated the river and Llinos gasped as she saw the full scale of the catastrophe. The hull of the boat jutted up like a rock from the water; bits of timber littered the river, washing seaward with the tide.

'All on board must be lost.' She heard the voice behind her and waved her hand as though to push the words away from her. 'Lloyd, my lovely boy, where are you?'

A body was dragged out of the river, a man with his face pallid and his hair plastered to his skull. A woman began to scream. It was a nightmare, this could not be happening. Any moment Llinos would wake up and all would be well.

Slowly, almost majestically, the rest of the hull disappeared under the water and waves eddied shoreward. Llinos put her hands over her eyes; she could not bear to watch as the water dragged strong men down in the undertow.

All at once a warm glow encompassed her. 'Joe?' She knew that he was close by, she could feel him, almost touch him, though she could not see him.

'Look! Someone is coming out of the river!' A man's voice carried above the noise of the waves. The cry was taken up by the crowd and Llinos was pressed even closer to the muddy edge of the water. She felt as though a warm blanket of love was being wrapped around her and, even though the river water lapped coldly at her feet, she knew that Joe was near, that everything was going to be all right.

'It's the big Indian!' The cry echoed in her ears and Llinos staggered as the crowd pressed closer.

Like a Phoenix from the ashes, a man was rising from the river. His hair streamed water and mud smeared his face but Llinos knew at once that it was Joe. Watt was with him, clinging to Joe's sleeve as he was hauled from the grip of the river.

Llinos could think of nothing, see nothing, but the small body in Joe's arms. 'Lloyd?' she whispered. She watched, her heart in her mouth, as willing hands dragged the two men and the boy onto the bank.

'Lloyd! My lovely boy!' As Joe put their son on his feet, Llinos took Lloyd in her arms and held him close. He clung to her for a moment, his wet head against her breast.

'I'm all right, Mamma,' he said. 'I'm not hurt so don't worry.'

'Let's get you home,' Llinos said shakily. She was almost afraid to look at Joe, wondering if he would disappear into the night as quickly as he had come.

Llinos held Lloyd's hand and led him up the bank and onto the roadway. A carriage was waiting there with Charlotte sitting beside the driver, her face pale in the moonlight.

'Thank God!' she said. 'Come here, Lloyd, let me wrap you in my shawl.' Llinos just stood there, her senses blunted by shock and fear. It was Joe who took charge.

'Watt, go with Charlotte, I'll take Llinos home.'

'There's a carriage, the one I hired, it's waiting just there, look.' Llinos felt her mouth tremble as she tried to speak. She felt chilled to the bone. She wanted to cry but the tears would not come.

Joe helped her into the seat and climbed in beside her and, as the carriage jolted into motion, Llinos fell against Joe's shoulder. She felt his wet hair touch her cheek and was filled with indescribable longing for the way things once were between them.

'How did you get here? How did you know our son was in danger?' Her teeth were chattering. She still could not look at Joe even though he was sitting close beside her.

'There was no magic to it,' Joe said. 'I came home earlier today. I brought Charlotte with me.' She could hear the smile in his voice. 'Or perhaps I should say she brought me.'

She felt her heart lurch; so he had not come back because he wanted her, he came back because Charlotte asked him to. The moon disappeared, the crowds had dispersed, the silence of the night folded around her and Llinos felt she was alone in the world with the stranger who was her husband.

The lanterns were lit to welcome them when the carriage drove into the pottery yard. Joe helped Llinos to alight and spoke a few words to the driver. The carriage wheels rang hollowly on the cobbles and, then, Llinos and Joe were alone.

She forced herself to look up at him, this man who was her husband. He stood there, his tallness a surprise to her. She had forgotten how big Joe was. His hair gleamed black in the slant of light from the lanterns. He smiled and Llinos felt as though the breath had been snatched from her body.

He held out his hand and she stared at him as though she could not believe he was really there. She hesitated for only a moment and then she put her hand in his.

She could not speak; her legs trembled. She felt that if she stood there any longer looking into her husband's eyes she would fall into a faint. He drew her closer and she could smell the scent of him, the scent of sun and wind and the salt of the river.

She thought briefly about Sho Ka, about the child, Joe's child, but his nearness was blotting out all the pain. His mouth was only inches away from hers; she felt his love reach out to her. She swayed towards him and his arms folded around her.

'I love you, Llinos,' he said tenderly. 'I've never stopped loving you, however it looked, whatever you thought.'

She believed him. The questions could come later but for now it was enough that he was here in her arms. His lips touched hers and it was the sweetest kiss Llinos had ever known. Happiness flooded through her. The river that had almost taken her child roared past in the distance, the water churning angrily towards the sea, but all she could hear was the sound of two hearts, hers and Joe's, beating as one.

THE END

A SELECTED LIST OF FINE NOVELS
AVAILABLE FROM CORGI BOOKS

14058 9	MIST OVER THE MERSEY	Lyn Andrews	£5.99
12637 3	PROUD MARY	Iris Gower	£5.99
13631 X	THE LOVES OF CATRIN	Iris Gower	£5.99
13686 7	THE SHOEMAKER'S DAUGHTER	Iris Gower	£5.99
13688 3	THE OYSTER CATCHERS	Iris Gower	£5.99
13687 5	HONEY'S FARM	Iris Gower	£5.99
14095 3	ARIAN	Iris Gower	£4.99
14097 X	SEA MISTRESS	Iris Gower	£5.99
14096 1	THE WILD SEED	Iris Gower	£5.99
14447 9	FIREBIRD	Iris Gower	£5.99
14448 7	DREAM CATCHER	Iris Gower	£5.99
13915 7	WHEN NIGHT CLOSES IN	Iris Gower	£5.99
14537 8	APPLE BLOSSOM TIME	Kathryn Haig	£5.99
14538 6	A TIME TO DANCE	Kathryn Haig	£5.99
14566 1	THE DREAM SELLERS	Ruth Hamilton	£5.99
14567 X	THE CORNER HOUSE	Ruth Hamilton	£5.99
14686 2	CITY OF GEMS	Caroline Harvey	£5.99
14535 1	THE HELMINGHAM ROSE	Joan Hessayon	£5.99
14692 7	THE PARADISE GARDEN	Joan Hessayon	£5.99
14603 X	THE SHADOW CHILD	Judith Lennox	£5.99
14492 4	THE CREW	Margaret Mayhew	£5.99
14693 5	THE LITTLE SHIP	Margaret Mayhew	£5.99
14658 7	THE MEN IN HER LIFE	Imogen Parker	£5.99
14752 4	WITHOUT CHARITY	Michelle Paver	£5.99
10375 6	CSARDAS	Diane Pearson	£5.99
14655 2	SPRING MUSIC	Elvi Rhodes	£5.99
14636 6	COME RAIN OR SHINE	Susan Sallis	£5.99
14708 7	BRIGHT DAY, DARK NIGHT	Mary Jane Staples	£5.99
14118 6	THE HUNGRY TIDE	Valerie Wood	£5.99
14640 4	THE ROMANY GIRL	Valerie Wood	£5.99